Vapormage
Zoe Landon

Book Cover by Ryan Mulford

ISBN: 9780997222531

For the lost

MEMORANDUM FOR CHIEF OF DEFENSE

FROM: Captain Thomas Vaughan, 7th Knight Infantry

SUBJECT: Discovery of Military Summon At Rijest Outpost

- Last night at 21:38, Specialist [REDACTED] identified the presence of an "unnaturally large and aggressive" strix-model vapor summon. The summon approached through the mountains along the Farolian border.

- Summon was described by Specialist as behaving in a confused and dangerous manner. Its approach tracked towards defensive postings with apparent malicious intent. Detailed description of behavior included in attachment (CLASSIFIED).

- The summon was successfully deterred by six members of 7th infantry. It retreated into the mountains towards Farolé. No farther sightings have been reported by standing Knights.

- During the following morning inspections, Private First Class [REDACTED] indicated that civilians were present in the area the previous evening. PFC indicated civilians may have witnessed the summon's appearance.

RECOMMENDATION: Issue investigative force to the Farolian border; deliver diplomatic missive to Her Majesty's Speakers (missive template A-13).

— Cymona Security Office Memo #8390,
Dated 03/10

CHAPTER ONE

Clearly, the mountains wanted Kell dead. It was only a matter of how.

The lingering remains of the road running along the ridges of the Tharsis Mountains, now only two or three shoulders wide at best, kept disintegrating beneath Kell's feet as they traversed it. Rocks and dirt gave way down the steep gorse-covered slope with each step. Stretches that looked stable at first glance, dark soil piled flat and firm against a clean wall of rock uphill, began to betray them the moment they approached.

Kell tried to pull their weight along by clinging to the thick evergreens that towered over the trail, but the mossy bark sabotaged their grip. They walked low for balance, their dark cloak dragging in the dirt. A patch of land giving way nearly threw their small, lanky frame onto all fours. They staggered with a groan. *For Owain's sake, Kell. Just walk.*

The display on Kell's visor blipped. Their helmet, a large and glossy thing they always wore on duty, was laden with sensors and other vapor-fueled technology, much like the mobiles everyone else carried in their pockets. It was also acting up. Again. The air was a little colder and thicker with vapor than usual, but nothing worth blipping about.

Kell felt more land slip from under their feet. They took an anxious jump as the trail gave way behind them. They landed with a damp, annoyed thud.

"You alright back there?" Rocko had the mountain's favor. He casually walked the trail several paces ahead, sword and shield bouncing on his back, stopping only when he heard Kell's landing. "We gotta keep moving."

"I know, I know," Kell said, venting their frustration. "I'm trying."

Rocko finally noticed the decaying trail behind Kell. "I can start setting up rope lines if--"

"I'm fine, Rocko," Kell insisted, brushing dirt off their glove.

"You sure?" He leaned on a hefty, slanted evergreen and peered down the trail ahead. "Path's not getting much better."

"So why go this way?"

Rocko shrugged. "Landslide or something closed the tunnel. Boat would take too long. And it's not like we can march straight into Farolé. They'd know what we're up to. This is what the briefing said to go with."

"You got a briefing?" The yellow eyes on Kell's visor bent, as if they were raising their brow.

Rocko's gait slowed. "You didn't?"

"Not really," Kell grumbled. "Fontaine shoved that memo about what happened in Rijest in my face and said to follow you. You're in charge."

Rocko chuckled at the idea. Rightly. It was a bit absurd, for the two to work together and let the knight be in charge. That wasn't how things were done. Sure, knights in Cymona had some prestige and respect among the people, even more so when vapor-poisoned beasts breached a town's walls, or when rowdy sahagins or troublemakers cropped up and demanded their attention. But whatever power the position represented carried little responsibility. Command told them where to go, command told the knights when to attack, command took credit for their successes and absolved them of their sins.

Kell, on the other hand, was a vapormage. The exceptional. The otherworldly. Cymona's greatest weapon. That was the marketing, anyway. It made the unit celebrities of a sort. Vapormages were rarely seen in public at all, and never seen without the cloaks and helmets and dark green uniforms that encased their entire bodies. When one did appear, people took notice. Civilians would even stop them on the streets of Candhall, asking for spellcraft demonstrations. And autographs.

Not that the marketing was entirely wrong. Their command of vapor meant they carried great power in combat, greater than the knights. Even Kell, who would readily admit they were the worst in the unit at conjuring up a devastating attack, could do more with vapor than any knight had ever achieved. That power brought responsibility to match. Whatever happened when a vapormage appeared--success, failure, life, death--was on their head. A vapormage was expected to do whatever necessary to get the job done, laws and permissions be damned. Commander Fontaine, who oversaw Kell and all the other vapormages, probably expected them to go over Rocko's head and take charge.

Instead, as another chunk of land fell away under Kell's feet, they caught themself clinging to the side of a tree like an enrobed, frustrated sloth.

Rocko waited for them to disembark and gave them a friendly knock on their helmet. "Well. I was told to grab a partner and get to Bellum. Someone there will give us more details. Then we go and make sure another war doesn't start." He unspooled a bundle of ropes that had been hanging from his hip. The trail had given out entirely a few meters ahead; they would need a rope line after all. "Seemed pissed that I picked you."

Kell wiped some collected mist off their visor. "I'm not exactly subtle."

"We're scouting," Rocko said. "We'll keep off the roads. We're fine." He tied some ropes to a nearby tree trunk, then threw a separate rope over a branch hanging from it. "And I'm not about to grab one of the other knights."

"They still don't like you, huh?" Kell said.

"Never have."

"Sounds like knights, alright," Kell muttered.

"Man, you don't know the half of it." Rocko gathered the ropes in his hand and tugged them to check that the setup would hold. "Besides, if we're looking for some kind of super-summon, it just makes more sense to have a mage."

"You just wanted to work together," Kell said knowingly.

With a chuckle, Rocko positioned himself at the edge of the landslide and knocked on the shield on his back. Kell gathered ambient vapor around their rod's focus and forged it into a wind aspect. They knocked it squarely into the abstracted dragon's claw, the mark of the Guardian Owain, pressed on Rocko's shield. He swung over the crevasse, landing on the other side with an enthusiastic yelp.

"Of course I did!" he called out. "We make a great team, Kell!"

As Rocko secured the ropes, Kell returned their rod to the holder on their back and examined the gap in the trail. *What even happened here? This is too fresh. Hasn't been raining much lately, so the fog wouldn't have anything to do with it. Haven't seen wildlife. Man, I don't know. Not like I'm an expert on dirt.*

Rocko pulled on the ropes, knotting them taut to a tree on the opposite side, and gave them an almost playful pluck to test the tension. "They teach you much about summons?"

"Nope." Kell found their balance on the ropes and started sliding across. "Never even made one. Wouldn't know if something's a military weapon or a kid's pet. Unless it was obvious."

Rocko beckoned Kell along the line. "You don't think it'll be obvious?"

Kell's feet landed on the far side of the crevasse. The rope, still in Kell's hand, rippled. The mountain vibrated-- a small shake, but enough for Kell to notice it. "I think we need to get to better ground," they said.

Better ground was scarce. The road through the Tharsis Mountains had been in regular use in its heyday, but its heyday was centuries ago, back when Bessetrae and Cymona were consumed by the same empire. Even then, walking it had required vigilance. When the tunnel was excavated, the road was almost immediately abandoned. Its width shrunk steadily from erosion as rocks and trees fell across it, adding to the impediment. Only ruins of the infrastructure remained, offering scarce and scattered hints of the road's forgotten story.

Earthquakes were never part of the road's story of decay. They never happened. So when another tremor shook the mountain, Kell tensed up with physical alarm. They spotted an outcropping on the north face of the mountain, facing into Bessetrae. They rushed towards it. Damn the route's condition. The wider ground would surely be safer.

Rocko followed and peered past the cliff, towards the woods below. The day was foggy, blocking the view of anything farther than a kilometer. Without the fog, the view would be magnificent: expansive forests, shining cities, possibly even the mighty Purro River. The varied, natural beauty of the northern half of the continent, Linnute. A true sight to behold.

Instead, Kell looked out at the grey before them. "At least we're making good time." They tapped the side of their helmet, bringing a map and several diagnostic readings into their view. "Couple hundred meters and we start descending properly."

Another shake. Then another, this one paired with a strange slamming noise. Rocko and Kell, almost in unison, turned their heads up the trail towards the source of the noise. Among Kell's diagnostic displays was now a warning about vapor density increasing. Rocko scrambled away from the ledge, ready to draw his sword.

"A summon! It's gotta be!" Kell shouted as a massive orange beast emerged from the fog ahead.

"A strix? Really?" Rocko said, more confused than surprised. The summon resembled a giant, bulky owl, with a tall crest of feathers that shimmered orange and red as best as the surrounding fog would allow. Aside from being twice as tall as Kell or Rocko, it didn't look all that different from the summons seen doing chores around town. Its talons slammed the ground with each hefty step, a puff of vapor quaking the earth away from it. Its head tilted and turned, as if it too was confused by the situation.

Gradually, the strix found its focus, its wide blue eyes gazing at Rocko. It let out a ghastly, uncanny roar and swung a wing wildly, putting Kell and Rocko both on the back foot as they dodged away.

They both watched the creature's movements. It swayed and swung with a regular rhythm, its wings jutting suddenly and legs stamping as though it were dancing. It seemed almost oblivious to Rocko's feints and shuffling around it.

"I think I see the pattern," he called out after a moment of observation. That was the weakness of summons: They were little more than vapor fused into physical form and given a specific purpose. They were programmed. Like all things programmed, they could only handle errors so well, which was fine for those kept as pets or in controlled business settings. But it also meant that, if Rocko and Kell could throw the creature into a situation its programming wasn't ready for, it would seize up.

As the summon swung another wing at Rocko, he made his move, diving between its legs with his sword swinging wildly. Kell, meanwhile, drew their rod and tried the spell meant to disperse a summon. The clear waves of vapor crackled against the strix's false feathers, petering out into nothing. The spell failed. Of course it would.

A pair of pops rang from below the beast, followed by a plume of flame from the spellbombs Rocko had dropped mid-dive. The sudden use of the weapons, and the fact that both bombs even worked as intended, caught Kell off guard and interrupted their own spells.

The two soldiers tried to move unpredictably, acting more like children pretending to be Masks of Owain than any sort of trained professionals. Yet the strix matched even their most erratic movements, evading sword swings and anticipating trick attacks. The confusion in its motions had vanished the moment it had something to actually fight. After a few volleys, Rocko muttered a swear and righted his stance. Deflecting another wing swipe, he lunged forward, thrusting his sword squarely into the beast's middle. It was a clean, strong, professional strike. And a predictable one.

The summon reacted immediately. Reeling, with thick purple-green smoke seeping from its center, it slammed a leg into the ground. The earth shook violently. It stomped again and the side of the mountain began to give way, the trail disintegrating, rocks rushing down the face.

Kell dove, grabbing a tree nearby and praying breathlessly to the bark. Their grip held, but barely, as rocks pinged loudly off their helmet. By the time the noise subsided and they turned around, they could see no trail. No strix. No Rocko.

B

A few meters of patient, frightened clambering brought Kell to flat ground. A line of flat rocks, the bedrock of the old road, gave them somewhere safe to land. They sprawled out on the first rock their feet could find. They hated swinging among trees.

Kell's visor was angry. Their helmet had taken a beating, breaking the communicator embedded within. The sigil complained with the occasional glitchy, sharp chirp. Kell would have to take care of that at some point, some day.

"You alright?" they shouted into the sky, hoping Rocko was anywhere close enough to hear.

After a moment, a reply. "Kell? You're not answering comms." The voice was distant, far down the mountain.

Kell scanned the trees below, looking for Rocko. "It's busted."

"Well that's great." Even sarcastic, Rocko never truly sounded frustrated. "Where are you?"

Kell finally saw motion. Barely visible below, between leaves and mist, was a glint of brass and an ashen-haired figure. "I caught a tree," they yelled to Rocko. "Helmet's beat up, but no injuries. What about you?"

"Just my shield," Rocko yelled, the glint flickering in demonstration.

Kell sighed in relief. "Any sign of that summon thing?"

"Negative. Kell, we gotta go back," Rocko shouted, gesturing south. "We've got no route."

From what Kell could see between wisps of fog, he was right. He was standing in a small pool of water, surrounded by sheer rock faces in most directions. Unless there was a passage to the west--and Kell hadn't seen any on the map--Rocko could only head back to Lehia, where the two had set off from earlier.

But Kell was still on the trail. Technically. They had to hope more of it hadn't been lost in the landslide, but they could proceed.

"I'm still good," they yelled. "I have a route! I'm going!"

"Are you joking?" Rocko shouted.

"You know how bad I am at jokes!"

"Kell, c'mon!" Rocko pleaded. "We can drop the mission! It's not safe!"

"I know, I know. I'll just--" Kell caught their hesitant breath. "I can do this, Rocko. I'll keep the mission going. Have them find me in Bellum."

Kell continued down the trail, hearing no more argument from Rocko. They kept hoping for some. After minutes of walking in silence, they leaned against the sheer rock beside the trail. They gave it a quick, aggravated knock.

What am I doing?

The two were playing their roles too well. But then, Kell thought, of course Rocko would want to fall back. For as much as he could goof around, he had always taken his job seriously. And as a knight, he had been trained to take danger conservatively. Knights were meant to be tactical, to understand the situation as well as it would allow before rushing in. The unknown was a dangerous thing, it was said, and there was little shame in retreating if it allowed for returning wiser and stronger. It fit well with the overarching national identity of Cymona. Humble. Thoughtful. Meek.

Vapormages were to be none of those things. They were trained to rush in, full of bravado and power. Kell had worked through so many training exercises meant to build up that instinct, days of drills designed to make them indifferent to the concept of death. It was supposed to be part of their signature, part of what made the force so threatening to Cymona's enemies, just as much as the mages' command of fire or lightning.

Such bravado never came naturally for Kell. It rarely came naturally for any of the vapormages. Most of them put on a show of it when challenged by Commander Fontaine; the less serious among their ranks turned it into a full melodramatic performance worthy of *Trouble in Paradise*. Kell was among the quieter mages, but even they would play along when the commander left, quoting the latest cheesy Bryn Achterberg role they had seen in the theater. Rocko knew about all of that. There was no pretense between them.

Why am I acting like I have anything to prove here? Kell thought as they followed the slowly improving trail. *Not like this is gonna impress anybody. Oh, the runt finally did a mission, big deal. Gah. Come on, Kell. Focus. Just do the job, don't cause trouble.*

The trail began to descend. Kell repeatedly checked the map in their visor, anxious that they would wander off in the wrong direction and be lost with no way of being found. The communicator and all the other technology in their helmet meant there was no real point in carrying a mobile, but now, not carrying a mobile meant nobody had any way to find them.

The old trail markers slowly eased their nerves, each small obelisk on the side of the path offering a worn reassurance. What gaps existed in the trail were now known gaps, chasms from hundreds of years ago, with bridges built to cross them.

Kell came to one gap, where the remnants of a collapsed stone bridge served as supports for one made of rope and wood. They approached, testing the first plank before committing. The wood groaned and the rope shuddered, but the bridge held.

Okay. It's fine. Just go.

They picked up their pace, taking long strides two planks at a time as they reached the middle of the bridge. But the planks did not like being skipped, and so they creaked louder, and louder, until one gave way, plunging Kell's weight suddenly onto the neighboring wood, shattering it as well, until the bridge was no longer a bridge, only tattered rope and wood, and it tumbled, and Kell tumbled, and a tangled mess of mage and bridge smacked into the scree below, and the whole mess slid farther to the forest at the base of the mountain, rock beating on wood beating on mage beating on rock, until it all came to a stop in a clamorous, exhausted heap on the ground.

C

Kell knew they had been lying on the pile of wood and rock for some time. An hour, perhaps, if not longer. It felt that way. They remained motionless, their visor blank, slowly breathing and collecting themself.

Eventually, they opened their eyes. The morning sun fought the remaining fog, eager to shine behind the spruces towering in the background. In the foreground, Kell's eyes focused on the large sword pointed squarely at their throat.

They closed their eyes again. "Hello."

The woman holding the sword said nothing. She stood tall, her face wearing a scowl strong enough to be seen even when silhouetted by the murky daylight and obscured by her light, hanging hair. The tears in her worn and tattered jacket formed spikes like teeth, all fangs and canines.

Kell exhaled. "I take it I fell north."

The woman scoffed. "The fuck do you think you are?"

Like any soldier, Kell had been trained on how to respond should they be captured by enemy forces. Bessetrae and Cymona weren't at war, not these days, but a claymore to the throat was close enough. "Private first class Kell Rusalka, they of the Cymonian vapormages. We're training in Lehia, and--"

"Shut it." Her voice had the subtle grate of authority. These were her woods. "I didn't ask for your story."

"I'm just saying what happened," Kell said. They tried to keep their voice neutral, and where they failed, leaned towards pleading. "I got turned around after the quake."

"Bullshit." The woman adjusted her grip on her sword.

"It's what happened," Kell insisted, trying to stay calm. "I just got turned around. That's all."

"You're telling me a soldier doesn't know where north is?" She scoffed. "Knew you were idiots."

Kell wanted to argue, but they also wanted to get out of the situation alive. "It is a pretty foggy day."

"Should've tried invading at night, then. Maybe you would've escaped."

"Sheila!" a mature voice shouted from behind the woman. Her posture loosened at the sound. "What's going on?"

Sheila's sword dragged against the loose rocks that surrounded Kell, cutting a slash in the dirt as she pulled it away from their neck. "Just doing my job," she said flatly. "Come 'ere, look at this fish I caught."

Kell used the moment of safety to sit up. They could see the owner of the voice: a stocky vian man, his beak tapping slowly in thought, the downy brown feathers around his head held down flat by the humid air. At a glance, he was perhaps old enough to be a town elder. His stoic demeanor, hands staying in the pockets of his tight overcoat as he inspected the situation, lent weight to the assumption.

"And what do you plan to do with it?" he said to Sheila. His voice was breathy, almost flat, which was common for vians, but his was particularly so.

"Gut it."

Kell's stomach tumbled. She was far too casual about the idea.

The vian scoffed knowingly. "That so?"

"Why shouldn't I?"

"Well . . ." Kell stopped themself. For as much as they wanted to explain things, talking probably wouldn't do them much good.

The vian looked at Kell. Kell stared back, the yellow eyes on their visor lit in a pleading shape.

The man slowly shook his head. "We're not at war anymore, Sheila." He extended a feathered hand to Kell. "And fish don't talk. You hurt?"

Kell accepted the hand and stood. "Not too badly. Somehow." They brushed rocks and dirt off their uniform and nodded to the vian in thanks, then to Sheila out of politeness. "Private first class Kell Rusalka. I guess I'm in Bessetrae, then."

"You guess?" Sheila said.

The vian chuckled. "Afraid you are, kid. Name's Cory. I look after things 'round here. Now I'm guessing you got a good story 'bout how you got here. C'mon into town and tell us."

He walked off, down the faint trail into the foggy woods, leaving Kell no opportunity to argue. They followed, with Sheila close behind, sword still in her hands. Kell wanted to check the rod on their back, to see if it had been damaged in the holster, if it was still there at all, but this was not the time to check their weapon. They walked through the woods assuming they were unarmed, and that they would remain that way until they weren't being followed by a rather angry woman with a rather large sword.

After a few wordless minutes, the three arrived at a small ramshackle gate straddling the trail. The arch was flanked by rotting, aged fences on either side. They could easily have walked around it, but Cory nonetheless opened the gate and held it open for Kell and Sheila. "Right then," he said, "welcome to Milend. Our humble little home."

"Humble" was apt. The town was more like a campground: a few cabins spread amongst the trees, dirt paths leading from their fronts in meandering routes before combining at the fire pits and outhouses that made for town squares. Some paths branched off to wooden platforms that once held cabins but now bore drab tents. Some paths went nowhere. Ropes criss-crossed higher in the trees, some holding laundry that the fog was keeping too damp to take down.

"Quiet out today," Kell said off hand. Maybe some friendly chatting would smooth out tensions.

"They're all hiding," Sheila growled from behind them. "From you."

Kell kept quiet. Their mind was racing, trying to assess the situation, yet they knew they were trapped for the time being. Playing innocent was their best option. They took idle looks around at the settlement as they walked, hoping to see small moments of rustic daily life in the background.

There was nobody. Even when Cory knocked on a cabin door and seemingly spoke to a person inside, Kell couldn't see them at all. The conversation was too quiet, and Cory had stood to block the view. Either Sheila was telling the truth--and they had little reason to doubt her--or Milend was a complete ghost town.

After the door shut, Cory finally turned to Kell and gestured towards a nearby bench. "Right then, kid," he said, "gimme your story."

Kell obeyed, sitting on the bench and staring at the fire pit before them. They exhaled deeply and lit their visor with the most sympathetic eyes they could manage. *The story will hold. Trust the story.* "We were training. In Lehia. Couple of us were sent towards the mountains. Y'know, adverse terrain? Mountains are usually pretty rough ground. I took point, got . . . I thought not even close to the border. Then the quakes happened. You felt them down here too, right?"

Cory nodded. Kell looked at Sheila, who had refused to sit. After a moment, she nodded as well. Kell kept their relief private.

Trust the story. "That caused a bunch of landslides," they continued. "Lost my bearings, fell a ways. Helmet's damaged, mobile's gone. I was yelling for my team, nothing. No reply."

"What were you doing to cause the quakes?" Sheila asked.

Kell looked quickly at the vian sitting next to them. Cory wasn't about to interject. "We weren't doing anything," they said. "I mean, nothing that would cause that. This was terrain readiness. Besides, I mainly do fire and wind myself."

Cory stayed silent, nodding with an inquisitive look.

The silence hung a moment too long. *They're waiting for me to slip. Fuck it, this should work.* "And I'm pretty sure I saw something," Kell continued. "Think it was the source. A summon."

Sheila scoffed. "A summon? Really?"

"What makes you think that had anything to do with it?" Cory asked, his voice kind, leaving Kell even more unsure if they were facing genuine interest or a skilled interrogator.

"Well, it kinda looked like a strix, but not really. For one, it was way too big. Like twice my height, easily. The color was off, it was weirdly bulky. Like its wings were too small. And it was just kinda dancing around. I could feel it when I was close, maybe it's heavy enough, I don't know."

"Doesn't sound like any summon I've seen," Cory said.

"I know." Kell glanced at Cory and Sheila. *Play dumb.* "That's not Vakonivak, is it?"

"Absolutely not!" Sheila shouted. "That does *not* sound like her, and she would *not* be roaming the mountains!"

Kell recoiled. They knew it wasn't Bessetrae's Guardian they had encountered, but they hadn't expected such a visceral reaction to the idea.

"Well then," they said after a pause, "it was something else. I gotta assume it was a summon. What else could it be? And Farolé is using them for combat now, it was in the news. That thing could've been one of theirs. Hell, it could've been meant for you, for all I know." *Make it about them. Not me. Please.*

"So you came here to warn us?" Cory asked.

Kell shook their head. "No, I just got lost. Helmet's all busted up, the nav is useless."

Cory stood up with a shrug. "I've scribed a few sigils in my day. Pop it off, I'll give it a look."

Shit. Kell froze. The yellow eyes of their visor turned downcast. "I can't."

"Oh?"

Sheila reached for her sword. "You heard him."

"I can't!" Kell insisted. "I would if I could, believe me, I'd appreciate the help. But . . ." They sighed and hesitated, choosing their words. "If this helmet came off, I would die. And, most likely, so would the people around me when it did."

"That a threat?" Sheila had decided it was.

"No!" Kell shouted, panicked. "Do I sound like I want to hurt you? I just want to get home."

Cory stood between the two. "I can understand that, kid. Everyone wants to be home. So, you better be off then. Main road's to the east. East is that way," he added, pointing over his shoulder and chuckling.

"It's also closed off," Sheila said. "Remember? Tunnel's blocked, it's why your brother's not back."

"I've heard the same thing," Kell said. "Is Bellum nearby? That place has an embassy, right? I'll go talk to them. They can sort me out."

A slight smirk came onto Sheila's face. "That dinky little town? Naw. We're going to Cuesta. Cutting through the woods."

"We?" Kell said.

"Bessetrae's a tough place. You're not going anywhere without an escort. Keep an eye on 'em, Cory, I'll be right back." Before another word could be said, Sheila rushed to a cluster of cabins the group had passed earlier.

Kell stayed on the bench, sitting quietly, cursing the shift in destination. They couldn't continue the mission in Cuesta. They'd be a failure. Still, a safe extraction was better than the alternatives.

They started stretching, both to ease some of their tension in their body and to mask that they were checking for the rod on their back. It had snapped. The upper half was still there--not ideal, but Kell was already deep in less-than-ideal circumstances. They'd accept it.

After uneasy minutes, Sheila emerged from around a bend, her hair tied back, a satchel draped tight against her chest. Her pants, which already looked durable, were now covered by mismatched plates of armor. Her right shoulder had a dark leather pauldron draped over it. She was geared out for a fight.

"Good," she said, "you're still here. Let's go. We'll be there around nightfall."

Kell stood, equally eager to leave and resigned to their fate. Cory stuck an arm out in front of them.

"Sheila. A word?" he said kindly.

The two stepped away from the fire pit. Kell, as surreptitiously as they could, slid a finger along the side of their helmet, amplifying the sound around them. The birds above let out deafening chirps and calls. The fire in front of them crackled violently. Unless Cory's whispers were particularly muted, they'd be able to hear what he had to say. If there was a plot being hatched, their life might depend on it.

They watched Cory drape a fatherly arm over Sheila's shoulder. He leaned in close and clicked his beak sharply. "Listen." The air of his voice filled with a bitter smoke. "We talked about this. You're not that clever. And I know you ain't gonna listen to a threat. But . . ." His voice dipped, indistinct. " . . .do anything to that kid, it's gonna come back to you . . . No. Sheila. Don't start. You know it will." Some crosstalk, as Sheila tried to get a word in, kept Kell from understanding Cory. Eventually, she relented, and he continued. " . . .what those bastards can do. You are *not* bringing it here. That kid dies 'cause of you, you better hope you die with 'em. We square?"

He gave Sheila a firm pat on the back. Kell slid a finger along their helmet, re-adjusting their audio as Cory walked back to the fire pit. Clearly, his instructions to Sheila were not up for debate.

ABSTRACT

Extant pre-Alvacin anthropological sources are known to describe humans using details that fit into the four known species of human: the "pig-skinned" hunn, the "feather-holder" vian, the "dog-head" gnoll, and the "fish-belly" sahagin. Recent determinations in linguistic drift have raised questions in certain translations, particularly in these pre-Alvacin sources. These findings raise the possibility of the existence of other human species at the time. This study of pre- and post-Alvacin sources aims to align current translations with previously examined works, demonstrating that these fifth and sixth human species are intended as statements of cultural myth rather than descriptions of verifiable fact.

— excerpt, *Language and the Species of Man*, deRoche et al.,
University at Port Mab press

CHAPTER TWO

For as rough of a settlement as Milend seemed to be, it still followed a core principle that any successful city anywhere in the world would follow. It was built along water. Its northern gate, as much a worn-down formality as the southern one, stood near the banks of the small Eraka River. Small fishing traps and gathering buckets sat along the shore. The river's source was up in the mountains, and as Sheila explained, it flowed all the way north into the Purro. So many smaller rivers in this part of Linnute did the same. The Purro was one of the grand rivers of the continent, driving through both Bessetrae and Farolé, its control the source of many conflicts between the two nations. Control the river and you control trade, farming, and dozens of other aspects of keeping a country running. Both countries had plenty of coastline as well, but on the northern edge of Linnute, that only offered so much.

The Purro River would be Kell and Sheila's destination, and the Eraka River their route. Cuesta was the country's largest city, beyond its capital, and it sprawled along the Purro's edge. For as much as Kell didn't like the idea of visiting it instead of Bellum, it was at least a reasonable destination. There was a good chance Sheila was telling the truth and that it did have a Cymonian embassy.

More importantly, there was a good chance the embassy would be staffed. The Winters' War had ended six years earlier, with the Bessetran president Bathroy and Cymonian prime minister Lyon making grand proclamations about mutual understanding and peace and the like. To the Cymonian citizens Kell knew and overheard, the proclamations were just words, but officially, the countries were at peace. The thin border between them was open. The nations traded, when people didn't just get things from Banner Goods instead. Despite the resentment that lingered, someone should be able and willing to help. Kell just needed to find them.

The route to the city followed the Eraka River tightly, mimicking its bends along the way. What few trail markers existed mirrored those Kell found in the mountains: the same style of obelisk, pairs spaced at seemingly the same rate. The trail was likely an extension of the road through the Tharsis Mountains that they and Rocko had been following and was likely built to go to the Purro River, if not all the way north to the coast. Milend, then, was built on top of the remnants of that trail.

Kell's throat tightened slightly as they considered the implications. Had things gone according to plan, Rocko and Kell would have stumbled upon that town, a settlement they didn't know existed. The two had been pointed directly at it. Between the two of them, Kell was the better improviser. A knight without a plan was a knight without a shield, but a vapormage without a plan was par for the course. They barely had a viable story for their own circumstances. *Two* foreign soldiers marching on a town . . .

"Trail breaks to the right, over the river." Sheila snapped Kell out of their wandering train of thought. The two were approaching a leftward bend in the river, where it pivoted and sprawled out over a pile of rocks worn smooth by flowing water. Sheila was leading from behind, giving Kell directions as they marched along the faintly trodden trail. It would've been easier for her to lead from the front, but as she put it, she wasn't letting Kell out of her sight.

"Here?"

"Yep. No bridge. Hope you don't mind water."

Kell didn't. They shrugged and slid into the cold, murky, waist-high water. The river flowed slowly, calmly, letting them keep their footing as they trudged across. The current barely tried. They reached the opposite bank and climbed up to land, kicking river water off their legs, and looked around among the trees and foliage. "I don't see the trail over here," they yelled. "All overgrown."

Sheila chuckled, having stayed put and dry. "Well, darn. Guess I misremembered. C'mon back."

The eyes on Kell's visor narrowed. *Now you're just messing with me. Very funny.* "Fine. Coming." They exaggerated their motion as they crossed the river again, taking some swimming strokes, soaking even more of their uniform. "See? Don't mind water. Totally fine with it. Happy?"

"You keep howling like that, you'll draw some aellos," Sheila taunted. "They start peckin', that's on you."

"What, you can't handle a bird?" Kell immediately regretted getting snippy, but the words were out. They started shaking themself dry and wringing out their cloak until they were only slightly sodden, then instinctively grabbed the remnants of their rod to help dry and warm their clothes.

Sheila glared at their drawn weapon. "I can handle plenty," she growled.

Fine. Kell put away their rod and sloshed along in their still-wet uniform. "Is that why they put you in charge of defending the town, then?"

"I put myself in charge." Sheila couldn't mask the pride in her voice.

Kell grumbled to themself and continued on the actual trail, wet and insulted, followed by the snidely pleased Sheila. They'd had worse traveling companions before, but the fact would do little for their annoyance. The mission was supposed to be simple. Long, but simple. An easy enough way to prove they could do their job. And taking the mission with Rocko would've been far more tolerable than some of the other vapormages. Certainly less tense than with Sheila. Even the most disagreeable vapormage was unlikely to threaten their life.

It was not long after crossing the river at its actual, bridge-bearing junction that Sheila's earlier taunt became a prediction. A large, goose-like bird glowing with a faint green-purple aura stood in the middle of the trail, its wings folded forward across its body. Its long neck pivoted repeatedly, its head changing position as it kept its eyes homed on Kell and Sheila. A cocky, ghostly caw echoed out of its beak. The aello was sizing them up.

An aello was just any sizable bird that had suffered vapor poisoning. Swan, hawk, didn't matter. Southeast Bessetrae was somewhat higher in ambient vapor--though not nearly as high as somewhere like Candhall--so an old enough animal that had eaten too much vapor-rich food was at risk of vapor poisoning. Such was the way of nature.

When that happened, if it didn't kill the animal outright, they would change. Their demeanor would become vicious. Their corrupted muscles would bulge, rendering them flightless but tenacious. A timid hedgehog, or anything else that would normally flee from the rustling of humans, would become bold and confrontational. The aello standing in the road, beak still red from nipping at the rat beneath it, was bold enough to confront travelers.

Unfortunately for it, those travelers were heavily armed. As it spread its distorted wings, Sheila wordlessly drew her claymore. Kell pulled what remained of their rod from beneath their cloak. The bird's first lunge was met with a sideways swing of Sheila's sword, knocking it away as blood and vapor smoke dripped out of the wide wound. It staggered back up, but its boldness was not paired with strength, and a blast of lightning from Kell stopped it for good.

With the aello dead, Sheila let her sword dip to the ground. She glared at Kell, who still had their rod in their hand. "I didn't need help." She kept her stern, dark hazel eyes on Kell until they sheepishly returned their rod to its holder.

They hung their head, their visor apologizing silently. *Stay out of trouble, Kell.*

Sheila breathed deeply before approaching the corpse and examining it from a slight distance. She held her head back, turning the aello with the tip of her sword.

"It's no good for food," Kell said.

"I know," Sheila said, testy. "But the feathers sell for a bit. If you didn't singe too many." She tightened her gloves and started manipulating the corpse, turning it over carefully, holding her head away as if it had already started to rot.

"Do they, now?"

"Of course. Clean bits, stuff from a normal goose or whatever, takes a shitload to be worth anything. But stuff that's got poisoned? Hard to get. Banner pays a lot for it." She pulled a few candidates from the bird's wing. "It's worth it."

Kell stood by and watched. They weren't about to judge. It was clear to them that people in Milend had little to their names. Kell had little to their name at the moment as well; they carried no local currency and only a mission's worth of food and water.

Shame we can't eat that thing, they thought as they watched Sheila prune the aello corpse for more feathers. They knew what would happen to a person poisoned by vapor, though. How their body and mind would betray them in increasing degrees, twitching and steering their muscles like a marionette, rendering them a tragedy at best or a monster at worst until death ultimately took them. No amount of food was worth the risk.

B

As the trail progressed, winding past glens and small lakes, the faint outline of buildings began to emerge from behind trees. The fog had largely dissipated, but with little idea about Bessetrae's geography, Kell felt compelled to ask. "Up ahead. That Cuesta?"

Sheila paused. Kell noticed and turned around to see her staring at them with a scowl. "What do you think?" she said, sternly.

"I think you're the local." Kell took another glance down the trail. "But now I think I'm wrong."

"Very."

The buildings came into clearer view with each bend of the trail. Eventually, the outer walls of the city emerged, cracked and jagged stone that seemed poised to fall on invaders. The guard towers, or what remained of them, loomed overhead. Even the surrounding trees sagged, their bark scarred, an air of defeat dripping from them like sap.

"Stay close," Sheila said. "This is Windglade."

Kell did as they were told, slowing down to walk alongside Sheila. "Dangerous?"

Sheila stopped. "Forget that easily?"

That was all she needed to say. Kell knew how the war left scarred towns in both Bessetrae and Cymona. They had spent the night in one of those towns, on the Cymonian side, before heading off to the mountains. Kell quickly realized that Windglade was another one of those scarred towns. It wasn't a capital or other particularly notable city. It was probably, like Lehia, chosen arbitrarily for destruction.

Kell didn't know many details about the Winters' War, but then, it often seemed like few people did. Even as it was going on, the whole campaign was marred by chaos. Cymona had little idea how to apply its brand-new vapormage unit and even less idea how to lead them. Where confusion didn't reign, incompetence did instead. Bessetrae had no way to counter a squadron of mages, but Cymona lacked a sound tactical approach. When Bessetrae pushed into Cymonian territory, their own unpredictable leadership sabotaged the effort. The damage done was erratic and meaningless, the losses monumental, the gains nonexistent.

What Kell did know, in an instant of looking around, was that the damage surrounding them was the work of vapormages. There was no other explanation for the twisting of stone and mutilation of trees. The lingering effects of nature turned into a weapon were everywhere. Lehia had been cleaned up and rebuilt, but it seemed Windglade was never given the courtesy.

"I know what you're capable of," Sheila sneered. "You . . . mages. Whatever you are. I've seen what you can do, what you're willing to do. Throwing vapor at whatever you want, whatever's in your way, who cares if it's another person. You just don't care, do you? You don't care if they boil from the inside, screaming in pain, trying to cry as they wish their last seconds would just end already. Do you? You don't even look them in the eye, you fucking cowards! You don't care! They rip that bit of your soul out or something? Huh? Or are they not even human to you? Were we just bugs to you?"

Sheila was shouting, looming over Kell, her face red. Kell tasted bitterness rising in their throat but kept quiet. Sheila desperately needed to let it all out, and the worst thing they could do in the moment was interfere.

"You know how many people used to live here?" she continued, gesturing at the town's decrepit gate. "Thousands. Tens of thousands. You know how many are still here? Do you?"

Kell stayed silent.

"Nobody. Nobody! They're all ghosts because of you!"

Kell stood as still as they could, their muscles tingling with anger. Letting that anger out at Sheila was not an option. She wanted justification. She was fishing for a reaction, and they were not going to give it.

"You gonna say anything for yourself, mage?" She was growling at them like a drill sergeant.

Kell exhaled and glared at Sheila. "I wasn't involved."

"You expect me to believe that?"

"Honestly?" Kell said. "No. But it's the truth. I get that you're pissed, and for what it's worth, I'm sorry. But I'm too young. I was still in training during the whole Winters' War. Okay? I have *never* been here before. Be as mad as you want at Cymona, fine, you're right to. But you're not laying it on me."

Sheila reached for her sword. "Problem is, you're here. They're not." She rested her blade on her pauldron and stood ready to swing.

The bile churned in Kell's stomach. They wanted to throw Cory's words at her, but those were words they weren't meant to know. "So what, you want to fight me? Even if I didn't have anything to do with this? Even if I've made it as clear as I possibly can that I don't want to hurt anyone?"

"You're one of them. I don't care."

"Then how are you better than us?"

Sheila stared them down. "Excuse me?"

"I don't know if this is supposed to be justice or revenge or what," Kell said. "But whatever it is, you've got the wrong mage."

"So? You're still a threat."

Then maybe I should act like one, huh? Kell fumbled for any of the bravado they would put on for Fontaine. It hardly ever convinced him. It probably wouldn't convince Sheila. But it was their only idea.

"I've been a threat from the moment you found me, Sheila." They stood a little stiffer, pretending they were proud. "I'm a goddamn vapormage. If I wanted you dead, you would be dead. But I don't. I want to get home and watch stupid detective shows. Now are you gonna help with that or not?"

Kell thanked the helmet they wore. If Sheila could see their face, she'd easily know how afraid they really were.

Sheila stared. Her claymore slid off her shoulder and pointed at the ground. "You're pathetic."

"Yeah," Kell said sarcastically, equal parts frustrated and earnest. "I am. So are you gonna help me?"

The two stared each other down. A pained howl sounded in the distance. Wind gushed by. After several more silent moments, Sheila relaxed her pose and sheathed her weapon. "Watch for zombies."

Windglade was a simple, utilitarian town in its day. It was built along the highest point of the Eraka River that could safely take boat traffic, which allowed for some imports but kept away the larger ships with more exotic options. Its soil produced enough hardy plants, offering an array of tubers and root vegetables, but seemed to reject anything more fragile and interesting. The result was a community built upon stability without flair, function without fashion. Boring, in other words.

This attitude was reflected in the buildings that still stood around Kell and Sheila as they walked past. The marketplace was lined with simple, square buildings, their frontage indistinct whether the shop had been a butcher's or a carpenter's. Some windows still had posters and displays in them, worn down by the passing of years. Those hollowed-out shells of shops were the lucky few, the survivors standing among piles of rubble as tall as a person.

For most of the fallen buildings, only a quick glance was necessary to work out what happened. The vapormages had flattened the town with reckless abandon. Charred wood stuck out of one pile; metal whipped into jagged sheets topped another like glistening baklava. Every invocation Kell knew that wove vapor into some natural element had an equivalent victim among the ruins.

Sheila kept close to Kell, looking repeatedly at them as she looked at everything else around her. She was on alert, and rightly so. Since the town fell, it had been overrun by corpses animated by vapor. They were slow and meandering foes, easy for any competent fighter to handle, but they were still hostile.

The eerie, anxious silence that saturated the market was broken by a sharp howl coming from nearby. Sheila's head snapped to face the source, one hand instinctively moving towards her sword. Her body radiated the tactical alertness of a skilled soldier.

"You heard that too?" Kell asked.

Sheila nodded. "Wolf. Yote. Or just a dog. But if it's here, it's dangerous. Stay close."

That was Kell's plan. Sheila was the leader, they were the follower. Even if they didn't think Sheila intended to be leading them through Windglade, even if they weren't sure Cuesta was actually where they were headed. They would have to trust her.

Past the fallen chemist's shop near the town's northern gate, the fresh corpse of a looter swayed on the gravel, the motion catching Sheila and Kell's attention. Some manner of canine, bloated and stretched to the size of a bear, was working to tear a bony leg from the rest of the body. Its fur was matted and orange-brown, streaks of blood and dust running along the sides of its body. Kell could see bare tendons on the canine's hind legs and sagging hunks of flesh around its jaw, the unnerving amalgamation of decaying zombie and vapor-soaked beast. It lacked the faint glow of an animal fully lost to vapor, but it was close enough. Its hazy eyes slowly turned to Sheila and Kell, staring at them as it ripped the leg from the corpse.

The standoff dragged on as a small pack of canines, standing nearer the scale of still-living dogs, approached. Sheila grabbed Kell's arm and sidestepped with them towards the gate. Their escape was desperate and futile. The smaller canines penned them in until the leader could make its move. When it did--the bone in its jaws dropping to the ground, a sharp howl whistling from its rotting lungs--Sheila grabbed her sword and assumed her stance.

"I got this," she said, pushing Kell behind her.

Kell grabbed their rod. "Sheila."

They started gathering vapor around the rod's focus, twisting it until it glowed orange. They aimed the ball of flame at Sheila's blade and released, bathing it in a smoky red glow. The infusion wasn't going to last very long, but it wasn't meant to. Of anything they could offer, it was the best chance to end things quickly. No sense dragging out the fight.

Rather than say her thanks, Sheila swung the blade squarely at the attacking canine, knocking it away with a pair of smoldering swipes. It rose to its feet and leapt, landing a strong bite on Sheila's right arm and drawing blood. Sheila nearly fell to the ground under the beast's rotting weight. With a heave, she shook the canine loose, and with a following, full-bodied swing, struck it down for good. The watching pack scattered as the canine smoldered on the ground.

Sheila set her sword on the gravel. She shook her wounded arm loosely, muttering and grumbling. "Damn," she said. "You trying to melt the blade or something? That thing is *hot*."

"It won't melt the blade," Kell said. They focused on Sheila's sword and dispelled the fire engulfing it. "You got gloves on. Figured it would help."

Sheila shook her head. "I guess. It still got me though." She reached for the bag draped across her chest.

"Here." Kell reached for the wound on her arm.

Sheila recoiled. "No."

"I can treat it."

"It's just a scratch. I have bandages."

"I have vapor." To end the argument, Kell held a hand over the bite. The spell worked quickly and colorlessly.

Sheila winced as the wound closed up. She glared at Kell as she sharply wiped the blood off her arm. "At least you can do that right. They teach you that in vapormage academy?"

Kell grabbed Sheila's sword from the ground, finding it to be heavier than they expected. "They didn't focus on healing. Wound up learning it myself." With a heave, they handed the sword to Sheila. "You learn how to use this yourself?"

"A lot of people taught me." She tested the blade; it wasn't too hot, so she sheathed the sword with a scoff. "I'll teach you if you can ever hold the thing up."

Kell rolled their eyes and shrugged off the offer, figuring it was just another taunt. Not that it mattered to them. They had no interest in swinging a sword.

C

The overgrown road leading out of Windglade turned clear and unassuming the moment a crossing road intersected it. It rolled its way along the hilly countryside, signs of normal life rapidly returning, as if the fallen city was a world away and not a kilometer away. The sun began its retreat behind the tall trees that separated the western side of the path from the farmland beyond.

Not far from where the road regained its structure, a Banner Goods shipping van sat idly off to the side. Its back was wide open, the packages inside rummaged through and thrown about. The driver, too, had been thrown about; a small flock of crows flew away from a mostly intact body as Kell and Sheila approached. Kell took a moment to examine it. The driver was a relatively young vian woman, not long into adulthood. Her body seemed emaciated. There were lesions that likely came from scavengers, but no other evidence of injury, nor of vapor poisoning. There was no apparent damage to her vehicle, ruling out a crash. It was probably still drivable, even, but Kell had never learned how.

Sheila, meanwhile, gave the boxes in the van one more good rummaging. "Find anything?"

"Not really," Kell said. "Nothing obvious about how she died."

Sheila shrugged. "Yeah, who knows. Sucks for her." She carried on down the road. "C'mon. Nothing in there worth looking at."

Kell jogged to catch up, leaving behind the break in the road's monotony. Sheila idly rubbed the wound on her arm as the pair walked, side by side. She wasn't calling attention to it, but Kell noticed every time her gait shifted.

Hours down the road, the two dipped over to the nearby Eraka River to refill their canteens. Sheila had stopped rubbing the wound on her arm and started scratching it.

"Your arm feeling okay?" Kell asked casually.

Sheila stopped. "It was just a scratch."

"I mean, did it heal alright? When I've done it for myself, it kinda burns for a while."

Sheila rotated and stretched her arm. "It's fine." She started off on the road again. "How'd you do it?"

"Mend. It's a pretty normal nursing spell," Kell said. "Pretty useful to know, I figured. It's just a bit tricky."

"Well, yeah," Sheila said, "people go to school for years to learn that stuff. Figured, if one of you guys were doing it, had to be some different technique."

Kell shook their head. "They're just spells. I mean, if I do this . . ." Kell stopped, their visor going dark, as they held their right arm up in a defensive pose. Their posture pulsed, their right arm jutting forward. Their fist was quickly enveloped in fire-aspected vapor. Their visor lit yellow eyes again. "It's the same idea as someone making a flick flame." They shook their hand out loosely, away from Sheila, spraying flame into the road that swiftly dissipated on contact. "You can do that, I assume?"

Sheila looked at them with a classic, practiced, "are you serious?" look.

"Right? You can do a flick?" Kell had decided they were going to get their point across, one way or another.

"Yeah, of course." Sheila flicked a weak flame from her right thumb before quickly extinguishing it. "You learn that in primary."

"Exactly," Kell said. "It's like . . . one of my instructors had a really good way of putting it. Using vapor's like using a tool you can't see on a material that doesn't exist. So really, all we'd do is just keep making the tool bigger, or . . . use the tool harder, I guess?"

Sheila laughed. "Use the tool harder?"

Kell laughed a self-aware laugh. "Okay, it's not the best comparison, but it usually works."

Sheila wasn't buying it. "I always look at it like, vapor's just this clay in the air you can mold."

Kell considered for a second before the eyes on their visor lit a little brighter. "Okay, that works better."

"So of course you can't just be working the same clay as the rest of us," Sheila said.

"We are, though," Kell said. "That's the whole point of *Trouble in Paradise*, honestly. You know that show?"

Sheila shook her head.

"Well . . ." Kell huffed out a quiet laugh. "Good, it's not realistic at all. But that's the whole point of Hitchens, the Bryn Achterberg character. He just does spells in weird ways that solve the case, and everyone's like 'oh detective, you made a new spell!' and he just does that stupid smile. It's great."

"Oh, that show." Sheila definitely wasn't a fan.

Kell immediately felt embarrassed by their enthusiasm. "So, yeah, that's basically how it is. The spells I've got, they're nothing different from what anyone else does."

Sheila shrugged. "Just hard to believe that. All that cheering and yelling about you guys, there's gotta be a trick."

"There really isn't," Kell insisted. "It's just really intense. Four years of training, at the least. Took me a lot longer. They had all sorts of experts and scientists coming in to teach us stuff that . . . hell, sometimes *they* didn't know how to do it."

Sheila was incredulous. "You went to university!" she said.

"Kinda!" Kell had certainly thought of it that way plenty of times. "I don't think real universities are that intense, though. They definitely don't have the capsule."

Sheila looked askew at Kell. "You're gonna have to explain that one."

"Was one of the techniques they tried. I think it's been made public?" Kell shrugged off their own question. "The idea was to try and get us in this really focused state. Really intense vapor, really . . . sensory focused? Dark, cramped, you know."

Sheila looked skeptical. "How cramped?"

"You lie down in a little bit of . . ." Kell thought for a second. "I think it was vaporized water, might've just been plain. They closed the lid and you just kinda float there, totally still. After a while, you don't feel anything. Even gravity. It's kinda like you stop existing, I guess. Definitely puts you in a different state of mind. You can really taste the vapor in there. It's like copper and dragonfruit mixed together, kinda weird."

Sheila's gait dragged for a moment. "They shoved you in a coffin? What the fuck?"

Kell laughed her off. "It's not a coffin, Sheila. You're making it sound worse than it is."

"You're not making it sound good!"

"Being a soldier isn't easy. And, all due respect--"

"Don't," Sheila barked, cutting them off.

Kell's arms went up quickly to defuse. They clearly still needed to watch their mouth. "I'm just saying. I know you have good reasons, but you're assuming the worst from Cymona. But there are good people there."

"Good people don't lock someone in a box," Sheila said.

"I'm not saying we're all good," Kell said. "But some of us are."

"Maybe."

Kell bit their tongue. They had gotten themself on good terms with Sheila. Good, but fragile. It wasn't worth rocking the boat.

As the farmland dissipated into coppices and dense clusters of towering trees, and the paving of the road slowly improved from rough cobbles to stretches of macadam, Cuesta gradually came into view in the far distance. They still had kilometers to go, but the tallest of its steel-clad towers peeked like lighthouses over the horizon.

"Better not be in a rush," Sheila said. "Sun'll be setting by the time we get there."

"I'm fine. Do you need to go back?"

"Cory said he could hold down the fort. If he can't, well . . ."

Kell realized the thought would remain unfinished. "By the way, I appreciate the help."

Sheila gave them a quiet, confused look.

"The escort. Just glad to have a local's help, with being in a rough spot and all."

Sheila furrowed her brow. "You already forget about this morning?"

"No, but I can't exactly blame you. It had to look bad."

Sheila looked like she had won an argument. "You must have a lot of people wanting to kill you, with how calm you are about it."

"I'm a soldier," Kell said without any sign of pride. "It's the job."

"I know the job," Sheila said. "It ain't like that here. Besides, you're supposed to be indestructible. Isn't that the whole point?"

"Not really," Kell said, kicking loose rocks as they walked. "Gutsy, sure, but honestly? Half the time one of us goes out, we don't come back. That's how it feels, anyway."

"So you're reckless."

Kell shrugged. "Some of us. I think it's more that we get all the dangerous assignments."

"Like invading Bessetrae?"

The eyes on Kell's visor narrowed to paper-thin lines as they faced Sheila. "I appreciate the escort, Sheila, but I don't *need* it. You can go home if you want."

"Nice try."

Kell grumbled under their breath.

Sheila took a glance over her shoulder, back towards Windglade and Milend. "I get it, though. When you're the only one willing to do the dangerous stuff, stick your neck out or whatever. That's what gets you killed sooner or later."

"I know what you mean," Kell said. "You never see an old mage, after all."

"Not like you've been around all that long, right? There weren't vapormages before the war."

"Right, but there were the Masks."

Sheila laughed to herself. "Honestly, I forget they aren't just a movie thing."

"Nope," Kell said, "they're a big deal back home. The big heroes of Cymona. Folks love 'em, more than they love us. I've had a bunch of people say they're related to some old

Mask of Owain, generations back, or maybe their kid was a Mask but they didn't survive a battle or something. None of 'em are around anymore. Heard the last few died in . . . what did they call it, a 'maritime accident'?"

"Sounds like you don't believe it."

"I mean, I wasn't around," Kell said, shrugging it off. "And they were anonymous. And then the whole 'hand-picked by Owain' thing? That always sounded ridiculous. Like, sure, Owain's a Guardian, but he doesn't really *do* anything."

"Good," Sheila snapped.

Kell rolled their eyes. Clearly, Sheila cared far more about the behavior of Guardians than they did. "Look, I understand wanting the secrecy, there's reasons to do things that way. But it means we never knew anything about 'em. Barely know their tactics, let alone their names, what they looked like, any of that stuff. You could be an old Mask of Owain, Sheila, nobody would have any idea. We don't even know they're really gone."

Sheila laughed, amused by the suggestion. "I'd never fight for Cymona."

"You know what I mean. It's what I hate about the place, everything there's so damn secretive. Y'know? All coded language and hidden agendas and shit. Like nobody in Cymona wants to trust anyone. Just means nobody can trust them, too. It's frustrating."

"It's the way to live, though."

"Seriously?" Kell hadn't expected her to commiserate, but they also didn't expect her to disagree.

Sheila shrugged. "There's no guarantee anyone's ever got your back, kid. Never is. So if I don't trust someone, and it turns out I could've? Who cares. Changes nothing. But if I do trust someone, and I shouldn't?" She gestured across her throat. "It's my head. Easy choice."

"You really go on like that?"

"That's life for ya. Always be vigilant."

"Sounds exhausting," Kell said.

"If I'm tired, I'm not dead," Sheila said with a dismissive dryness.

Kell stepped past a tall tree's long shadow, letting the setting sun--and the day's exertion--wash over them. By Sheila's measurement, then, they were very much alive.

                    HITCHENS
               Still calling, then?

                    YOSHIDA
     Plenty. Says he's concerned. Thinks there's summons
     glitching out, doing whatever they want. Says he heard a
        couple going off at the docks, making a ruckus.

     HITCHENS shakes his head and stands. He's tired. He
     starts towards the door.

                    HITCHENS
              Then I hear a wolf barking.

                    YOSHIDA
                   Think so?

                    HITCHENS
     He said he couldn't have heard the murder for the constant
     noise in the area. Now he's bothering us that there's
     noise at all. Either he's distracting us or his whole
        testimony is suspect. I'm going with that one.

                    YOSHIDA
          Bit early to be ruling out testimony.

                    HITCHENS
     I was ruling it out from the moment I heard it. His whole
     story requires sahagins to be smart. I know better. _You_
                 know better, Detective.

                    YOSHIDA
     I know better than to avoid due diligence. Getting thrown
        in Ness's office again? Not worth the price.

HITCHENS gives YOSHIDA a reassuring pat on the shoulder. He walks for the door.

> HITCHENS
>
> Don't worry, I'm buying.

4A EXT. PARADISE MARKET SQUARE -- DUSK
Establishing.

5 INT. BANDERAS CHEMISTRY -- DUSK
The store is quiet, but not empty. HITCHENS walks in, behaving like a regular customer. YOSHIDA follows.

> HITCHENS
>
> Evening, Loren. Keeping the fish out?

> LOREN
>
> Better than you guys have. Glen told me one of 'em killed
> a dockhand last week.

> HITCHENS
>
> Told us the same thing. Then he told us a bunch of things
> that don't make sense.

> YOSHIDA
>
> Your summons behaving lately?

> LOREN
>
> Haven't seen anything unusual, why?

— *Trouble in Paradise* s6e8,
"Man Behind the Glass", excerpt

CHAPTER THREE

The sun set the sky on fire as Sheila and Kell stopped at an intersection outside Cuesta. A trio of Banner Goods vans rolled rapidly by, kicking up dirt and disregarding their surroundings. Kell started moving again the moment the vans passed, but Sheila grabbed their arm to pull them back.

"Just gonna go waltz into town?" she said.

Kell shrugged. "Yeah? The embassy's there, right?"

"Put your hood up. It's not like you're a sahagin or anything, but the guards are still gonna have questions about that bowl on your head. And you won't take it off."

"Can't," Kell firmly corrected, pulling up the hood of their cloak.

Sheila sighed. "Just don't cause trouble."

She took charge, addressing one of the dozen summons posted in a line in front of the city gate. The tanukis functioned as gate guards, doling out a standardized interrogation of mechanical yes-or-no questions that travelers of all stripes put up with, sometimes calmly. Inexperienced travelers and those with complex itineraries would confuse the summons, forcing whatever human was overseeing the lot to pick up the slack.

Sheila was not inexperienced. The guard ultimately let her and Kell through with nary a glance. Not that he would have the time; Cuesta was too busy, with too many merchants and travelers and couriers coming and going. It may as well have been unguarded.

Kell was barely more than a block into the city before they were surrounded by the familiar crowding of city life. At that hour, laborers and clerks alike would be headed home, or to the tavern, or wherever they spent what little time they had to themselves. Each street's intersection was an intersection of lives, people with little in common sharing a space for a brief moment before forgetting each other once again. Anyone who happened to share the space with Kell would forget them just as quickly, too. So they hoped.

As they stood, waiting for a streetcar to clear an intersection, Sheila gave them a nudge in the shoulder. "Not freaking out being around all these people, are you?" she asked.

Kell gave her a sideways glance. "I'll be fine. We drop into town every so often. I'm not totally isolated over at base."

"They just let you walk around?"

Kell laughed sharply to themself. "They *love* it when we walk around. They ask for autographs. Last time I went out, Jeng and I had just gone to a show. Jeng's one of the other mages. Couple folks came up to us, asked us for autographs. And they asked me to sign it 'Novak'!"

Sheila looked at them, confused. "What, like Francis Novak?"

"Like Francis--" Kell grumbled, cutting themself off. "I'm not a fucking movie character, y'know? I'm a person. The Novak movies aren't even good. But that's what people know, so, I kinda just have to play along. I don't like to cause trouble."

"Well good luck with that," Sheila said. "Trouble does what it wants."

Sheila wove through the crowd and flagged down a patrolman. After a few curt questions about the sword she carried, she got directions to the Cymonian embassy. It was nearby, nestled among several other government buildings, each of them nearly identical: a functional, rectangular geometry with few windows and stonework that bore enough detail to exude authority and importance. Only the signs outside and the uniforms on the guards gave away which building was connected to which country.

"Sorry, miss." Sheila had approached the embassy only to be met by a guard's outstretched hand. "Closed for the evening."

"You're Cymonian, right?"

"This is Cymona's embassy, yes." The guard's voice was as sharp as his hair.

Sheila shrugged and turned to Kell. "Guess we come back tomorrow."

"If you need an inn," the guard continued, "there's a place two blocks from here, in the Wall Hill district--"

"Do we look like we can afford that?" Sheila scoffed.

Kell, who had kept their head hung to better hide their helmet, looked up at the guard. "Do they take marks?"

The guard looked at Kell and coughed. "I'm sorry, there's an inn at the pan alley--"

"Oh piss off," Sheila said dismissively, walking away.

There was a small park nearby. It was surrounded by offices and the like, so when the people of Cuesta went home for the night, the trees and grasses sat quiet. A nice, secluded place for a simple camp. Kell dropped to the ground beside a tree and fell asleep easily.

They awoke to a screech in their head. As it dissipated, they tapped the side of their helmet. Diagnostics popped up before their eyes. Everything they expected to be working was working; everything they expected to be broken was broken.

Comms again. Dammit. They sat up and looked around, eyes adjusting to the morning. Sheila was sitting against a nearby tree, facing them, looking like a propped-up corpse.

"Hey." Kell spoke quietly. "Sheila. You awake?"

Silence. Then a violent jolt. "Oh good. You're up."

Kell stared. "Did you sleep at all?"

"No." The rocks in her voice backed her up. "Let's go."

With the embassy finally open, the two walked inside to the smell of bureaucracy. They were greeted by a spartan, anonymous hall of crisp limestone and dark wood with an array of low-walled offices filling the space beyond the front desk. The statue near the door of the dragon Owain, Guardian of Cymona, was the only sign of whose domain they had walked into.

Kell approached the clerk at the front desk, letting down their hood to show their helmet. "Hi there. Private first class Kell Rusalka, they of the vapormages. I'm separated from my unit, my communicator is broken. I need safe passage home."

The clerk stared from behind thick glasses as though she had never seen a vapormage before. "I see. Kell was it? Who's she?"

"A local. She escorted me here."

"Right." The clerk tapped the screen of a tablet sitting on her desk. "You couldn't call anyone?"

"Took a bad fall during an exercise. Helmet's banged up, lot of damage." They weren't about to go off their story while Sheila was around.

"Just go to a Banner shop."

The eyes on Kell's visor blinked. "Seriously?"

The clerk nodded towards the door. "There's one a few blocks away. Go on."

Kell took the cue and walked away, reluctantly stepping outside with Sheila close behind.

"*That's* the great plan, huh?" Sheila said. "Just have Banner fix it?"

Kell donned their hood and dragged their feet down the road. "Might as well. She's obviously not going to help unless I do."

Like most people of Linnute, Kell relied on Banner Goods to get them nearly everything. The company was simply too convenient: a few taps on the screen of a mobile, and a courier would be on the way with whatever convenience or necessity you requested. Their delivery vehicles clogged every transportation artery. Virtually everyone who didn't live a military life--and even some who did--spent some part of their years under Banner's umbrella, whether working a warehouse or venturing out to make deliveries. It wasn't the best work, often tiring and dangerous on a good day, but it was work. For many who took it up, it was their only option at the time. It could often be the only option a person's life ever had.

Their all-encompassing scale was the only thing that could rival a military's ability to move resources and people around. Small surprise, then, that soldiers like Kell would rely on them for anything their quartermasters didn't provide. They wouldn't get a replacement helmet from Banner, but a replacement satchel or mobile? Their account had the credit for it.

They would only find mobiles in the store, though. Those were the gateways to Banner Goods, so a shop like the bright and clean one Kell walked into had little reason to stock anything else. The store was mostly for people in their situation, people with no way to start buying. That morning, it seemed the only other person in that situation was a small businessman in a purple-lined suit.

"Ahoy!" the young clerk--a gnoll, to Kell's flicker of surprise--called out. "What can I help you folks with?" A small tanuki-model summon scurried around busily behind them.

Kell paused, unsure how much to reveal. "Hi. I'm in a bit of a situation. Can you help with military procurement?"

"Sure. What's your name?"

"Kell. Rusalka."

The clerk gave them a curious look.

"What?"

A shrug as the clerk started typing. "Just haven't heard that name before. Kell."

Kell could think of a dozen people they shared a name with, from primary school teachers to old actors. It was a common enough name to them, but also nothing worth causing a scene about.

Instead, they glanced idly around the shop, avoiding eye contact with Sheila. Kell spotted the businessman doing much the same, looking around as if he was waiting for something rather than shopping. His eyes lingered a little too long on Kell, in the way that someone who never expected to meet a celebrity would when they finally got the opportunity. Kell knew the look. The businessman quickly left, though, sparing Kell a conversation.

The clerk, brow raised, turned their tablet's screen to Kell. "Am I spelling it right?"

Kell nodded to confirm, their visor's eyes turning equally confused.

"That's really strange, then. You don't seem to have an account."

Kell sighed. Of *course* military accounts would be set up differently. The whole errand was never going to work; the embassy clerk just wanted to be rid of them.

"Give 'em your real name, then," Sheila said.

"What? That *is* my real name."

"Same one you've always had?" the clerk asked.

"I've never been anything other than this." Kell tapped the side of their helmet in thought. They could just walk away, but without any other ideas for what to do next, it was worth exhausting their options. "Can I check if someone else has an account?"

"That's technically supposed to be private info."

"Oh," Kell said. They were starting to feel defeated. "That's kind of . . ."

"Pointless, I know," the clerk said with a chuckle.

"What?" Kell glanced at the wall behind the clerk, at advertisements and rows of mobiles, looking for either explanation or inspiration. "Oh, wait." Explanation had struck. "You guys have gifting services. I could just try to send a bunch of gifts, couldn't I? Can't send a gift to someone who doesn't have an account."

The clerk smiled at the small conspiracy. "That is how it works, yeah."

Kell huffed in relief. "Could we try sending a gift to Rocko Larson, then?"

The clerk tapped their tablet. "Yep. Candhall?"

That wasn't what Kell wanted to hear. If Rocko wasn't in the system, then it would have been a military account problem. It would make sense. Instead, it was as if Kell themself simply didn't exist. "Well, okay, but then what happened to me? I bought stuff four days ago." Kell started pacing.

Sheila leaned on the counter, her eyes barely refusing to close. "Sheila Takeda. It's me."

"Sure." More taps of the tablet. "Hmm. Junior? No? Weird. There's two accounts with that name, one marked Type 7." The clerk laughed to themself. "You do look dead on your feet, miss, but you're not dead. I'll fix that up."

"Don't touch it," she growled as she stood up straighter and walked to the door. "Get me a mobile. Give it to them. Use my credits."

"I have marks," Kell said.

"Your money's no good here, mage," Sheila said. "I'm getting you out of my hair. You owe me." She tumbled through the door before the argument could continue.

Resigned, Kell accepted the arrangement. They took the cheapest mobile in the store. They already felt indebted to Sheila, and now that debt had a dollar amount to it. Or a store credit amount, though even beyond Banner's stores, one was often as good as the other.

With the errand finished, Kell exited to find Sheila slumped against the building's facade.

"Now what?" Sheila said.

The eyes of Kell's visor lifted in sympathy. "Now we find somewhere for you to get some rest."

"I'm fine."

Kell didn't believe her. "Be honest. Do you really think I'd do anything to you? In the middle of town, crowded city, broad daylight? I'm too busy worrying about even being here. You don't have to worry about me."

Sheila tried to push back. "You don't have to worry about *me.*"

"I owe you, Sheila. Least I can do is make sure you're okay before you go back to Milend."

Sheila stared, glassy-eyed, at Kell.

"You were up all night last night," Kell continued.

"So? I do it all the time." Her voice was growing groggier.

"All the time? That can't be good for you."

"I sleep eventually."

"Sheila." Kell tried to sound more sympathetic than judgmental. "When was the last time you slept?"

No response.

"Sheila?"

"Fine, Cory," she mumbled.

B

Sheila tossed a messenger bag on a nearby bench. The moment her head touched it, she was asleep. Kell sat on the ground in front of her and tried to stay small. The clerk didn't seem to care that they were a vapormage, but that didn't mean everyone who passed by would feel the same.

Kell called Commander Fontaine. The line was dead. They shrugged it off; the mobile was new, with nothing set up, so of course it wouldn't connect directly to military command. With the due diligence out of the way, they found the line for the embassy they had visited earlier.

The same clerk responded, though she now sounded distracted and stressed. A clamor could occasionally be heard in the background. In the midst of arranging Kell's extraction back to Cymona, she suddenly asked if Kell had read that day's newspaper.

"There's something weird going on at the monument garden, on the east side of town," the clerk continued. She sounded as if she was reading from the newspaper as she talked. "Some statue just started . . . dancing around, I guess. They were trying to get a good vapor engineer to take a look at it, but a mage could handle it, right? And I'm sure the folks of Cuesta would be really happy about it. There's a lot of historical stuff over there."

Kell sighed. The clerk wasn't making small talk, she was giving them a mission. "Well, if I've got a few hours," they complied, "I'll see what I can do."

They started putting together a plan. The order seemed sudden, almost arbitrary, but it was better than idling around. And the clerk was right: It would be a small way to pay back the Bessetran hospitality they'd received. It might even show that their skills could be useful for something beyond waging war. Sheila probably wouldn't care, but they could pay her back later.

With map and strategy in hand, Kell stood up to get their bearings, bumping into the bench they had been leaning against. The nudge jolted Sheila awake.

"Shit, sorry," Kell said.

Sheila shook herself awake. "Whatever. I'm up. What's going on?"

"They'll be picking me up tonight. In the meantime, I'm going to the monument garden. Apparently, there's a situation I can help with."

"Not alone, you're not," Sheila said.

Kell sighed at the stubbornness. "Do you know a lot about self-animating statues? Just let me handle it."

Cuesta was something of a winding city. Intersections landed wherever they felt like, creating the occasional convoluted block where two or three t-junctions fell in an alternating row, one after another. Buildings took whatever shape they could, or they barreled through a road, introducing dead ends to an otherwise pristine avenue. If people were lucky, they were offered a lobby to walk through. Even the materials in the architecture were inconsistent, a stubby tower of pure limestone sitting beside a rowhouse wrapped in steel and wood. The city had no consistency, no unified voice. It did what it wanted.

If there was a straight path to the monument garden, Kell would be surprised. It certainly wasn't on the map they had projected on their visor. Sheila, still half asleep, dragged behind, offering no assistance in navigating. Perhaps she had no energy to do so, perhaps she enjoyed watching Kell get lost. Or perhaps she didn't know Cuesta nearly as well as Kell had assumed. Whatever the reason, she was eerily silent, like she had all but disappeared.

It made her suddenly speaking up all the more startling. "So where are we even going?"

"The monument garden," Kell said hesitantly. "Already told you."

"Oh. Right." Sheila was not awake. "Who put you folks up to that?"

"I dunno where the clerk got the idea," Kell said. "But it came off pretty official. Whoever they arranged the extract with probably brought it up."

Sheila scoffed. "What did you guys do to the thing?"

"Not everything is Cymona's fault, Sheila." Kell's defense was half-hearted; it was less about Sheila accusing Cymona and more about her being so stubborn.

"Then why drag you into it?" Sheila said. "The Secretaries can't handle it?"

It was Kell's turn to scoff. "What, is the president too busy?"

"Bathroy doesn't do shit," Sheila said. "I swear."

That was about what Kell expected. They knew some of the politics of Linnute, the bits that they could pick up by osmosis while focusing on life as a vapormage. The information mostly focused on Cymona and its parliament--a parliament in name only, with how Prime Minister Lyon would run roughshod over it whenever he pleased. But Kell had also picked up bits about Zeimatia's priests, while the controversy around Farolian Queen Eileen II's continued lack of a succession plan was inescapable in news broadcasts.

Kell didn't know anything about President Bathroy. Until Sheila spoke up, they weren't even sure she still was the Bessetran president. The last they saw of her was the truce agreement after the Winters' War. Since then, any stories that involved Bessetrae would involve one of the many Secretaries instead. At least, that was true as far as Kell could remember. If it wasn't news that threatened to disturb the international peace, Kell didn't pay too much attention to it.

The walk east was long and meandering enough to get Sheila's blood flowing. Eventually, she had her own ideas for how to handle *Apollo Tracing the Sun*. That was assuming the sculpture even was causing a problem. Most of those ideas involved striking the statue very hard with her claymore.

Kell, however, insisted that they could handle things themself. They figured it would be no different than forcibly dispelling a summon, and that spell was easy. Not always effective, but easy.

As expected, the monument garden was closed. The surrounding streets were placid. Perhaps everyone was too busy to gawk at the sight. The patrolman posted at the entry had no problem with Kell and Sheila entering once they explained why they were there.

"So you're aware," he said casually as he led the way, "they've already commissioned a replacement. Do whatever you need to."

"Really?" Sheila said. "Don't wanna keep it bouncing around?"

The patrolman chuckled. "Yeah, get it to put on a show. What I'm told, the Parks Secretary is with ya, but Safety says no, and prez went with Safety."

"Just ask her again," Sheila said, "she'll change her mind."

"Would if I could."

"Well, I appreciate the information," Kell said. "We'll try not to be any trouble."

They walked into a small wooded glen, surrounded by busts on plinths and sculptures depicting Bessetrae's history. Several more esoteric and artistic works were kept in the northwest corner, where the living statue also stood. True to the article, a marble figure of a half-naked hunn man took stiff aimless hops around a clearing. The statue moved in circles, almost as if it were dancing. It was too much like the strix.

"Bizarre," Sheila said to herself as she watched.

Kell silently agreed. *Maybe it's a summon.*

They quickly ruled out the idea when they noticed a small yellow streak along the chisel of the statue's chest. It looked like a sword wound that had long since scarred over. After adjusting the filters on their visor, they could make out a faint glow in the streak each time the statue moved.

They watched patiently, working through the information. A stone couldn't be poisoned by vapor, so that possibility was out. The statue could have simply been enchanted to some unknown end and it was only now that the spell was showing its effects. It would explain what they were seeing, though it would raise a whole host of other questions.

But Kell's eye kept going back to the yellow streak and its unusual glow and gloss. That, they figured, could be a piece of solidified vapor. They had only ever seen one piece like it before. Some government scientist had brought a tiny turquoise shard to the base several years back, one claimed to be from a meteorite that fell decades ago. If they remembered the demonstration correctly, it couldn't be made without the pressures of the cosmos. Certainly not a piece this big.

Kell held their arm out in front of Sheila and stood. They had a new plan. They carefully started to approach the statue, broken rod in hand. Tremors started to form around the statue as it noticed Kell. They held their footing as an orb of aquatic vapor coalesced around their rod and shot out in a thin missile. The shot drilled through the human-shaped statue, piercing where its heart would be.

Kell had missed their target, but the impact had weakened and angered the stone. The statue jumped towards Kell, kicking up dirt and soil and rocks, throwing the earth at the mage, rocks clanking against their armor and trying to crack their visor, until Kell struck with a concussive blast of vapor, and the statue's torso separated from its limbs. Each piece of *Apollo Tracing the Sun* dissolved into a pile of rocks on the ground with a clamorous crumble.

Sheila didn't have a chance to touch her sword.

Kell snapped their rod back into its holder and inspected the rubble. The yellow streak was intact, buried under dusty marble, glowing only to the calibrated eye. The yellow seemed to permeate the sharp object, giving it the feeling of uncut heliodor even if its texture was more metallic than anything else. It was just not quite like anything Kell had seen before. Their visor offered no warnings about its presence, nor any advice.

"That what was causing it?" Sheila asked, having approached to loom over the mage.

"No clue. Maybe." Kell tossed it into a satchel. "Can hopefully find someone who knows."

"Just gonna keep it?"

"Do you want it?" Kell retorted.

"I just don't want you to have it. Who knows what you'll do with it."

Kell's eyes narrowed on their visor. "I'm going to leave it at the embassy. Don't believe me? Tag along."

Sheila tagged along.

C

Kell called the embassy on their way back and told the clerk--a different one than before--of their success. The clerk sounded happy to hear from them, but seemed less interested in the monument garden mission. It made little difference to Kell; the work was for Bessetrae's sake, not Cymona's. Even if the only Bessetran they had spent any time around obviously couldn't care less.

The embassy was unguarded and suspiciously dark when the pair arrived. It looked like the place had closed for the day, even though the front door was open. Kell and Sheila stepped inside to an echoing quiet, the silence of a court anticipating a verdict. Once the clerk at the front spotted Kell, the silence was broken by the squeak of boots against polished stone. Wide, rushing strides approached from the depths of the building. A Cymonian knight appeared. Kell hoped he was the guard on duty, running late.

"Kell Rusalka!" the knight shouted. He drew his sword. "Hands up!"

Kell started to comply with one hand, while the other started to reach for the shard taken from the statue, as if it were the source of some misunderstanding.

Sheila reached for her claymore. "The hell's going on here?"

The knight swung abruptly. It was a clumsy swing, an opportunistic one, a swing that tried to take Kell's head but only took air.

"The fuck?" Their visor blinked in confusion as they dodged, falling backwards. They quickly stood back up, keeping their footing loose and ready to move, even if they had no idea where to move to.

The knight started to swing again. Sheila intercepted the blade with her own, pushing the steel away.

"Out of the way!" the knight barked. "The mage has to die!"

Sheila kicked at the knight's leg, knocking him off balance. "Kell, run!"

They were frozen in confusion. Why was a knight trying to kill them? Was he a knight? He couldn't be. Why did Cymona want them dead? Did they? Why was Sheila protecting them?

Before another thought could enter their mind, a glint of light bounced off the knight's sword and across their visor. The sword was moving again.

The flash of steel snapped Kell out of their bewilderment. They ran, slamming open the embassy's front door with an explosive bang. Sheila knocked the knight down with another kick and bolted into the street behind them.

They shared panicked breaths over the stones of the road. "What the hell did you do?" Sheila yelled.

"I don't know! I don't know what's going on!" Kell gasped for air, glancing at the embassy, expecting the knight to appear. "What do we do?"

"The docks!" Sheila shouted in epiphany.

"What?"

"The river!" She started rushing down the street. "We grab a boat. This way!"

The two ran north, weaving among the city crowds. They swerved through knotted intersections and down serpentine roads. They pushed past pedestrians, slicing across and through whatever clusters were in the way. They no longer cared about being inconspicuous. Kell's legs burned. Adrenaline coursed through Sheila. They made it to the docks in record time.

Sheila ran towards an anonymous wooden shed, situated on the edge of the main yard and overhanging the water on one edge. It was one of the few buildings around that wasn't a massive Banner Goods warehouse. A dock hand yelled for the two to stop as they careened around a metal fence and reached the shed's locked door. Sheila jostled the handle.

"You own a boat?" Kell asked between breaths.

With an aggressive slam of her armored shoulder, the door shattered opened. "I do now."

Sheila ran inside to assess the situation. The shed had a few small metal skiffs. One of them, fitted with a motor on its stern, was already in the water, tied to a post, ready to use. Sheila found a jerry can that sounded like it had fuel and tossed it in, followed by whatever other useful supplies were in arm's reach.

As she untied the boat from its mooring, Kell looked frantically for the mechanism that would lift the gate. They found it tucked behind the open door. They pulled the lever. A clattering sound came from the ceiling. A second clattering sound came from outside.

"There!" The knight had kept pace well enough to catch up. He pushed his way past a pile of crates and advanced.

"Come on!" Sheila yelled. The gate slowly climbed up the wall, groaning in mechanical protest. Kell dropped their left foot into the unmoored boat, pausing as their weight shifted over the water. They stuck their arms out for balance. The knight, sliding through the open door, took a desperate swing.

Kell screamed in pain.

Sheila saw Kell tumble into the boat. She saw blood hanging in the air. She saw the world around her convulse and shake. She saw the knight, his sword dripping, panic on his face. She saw red.

Kell saw a barrage of warnings on their visor. They saw Sheila raging. They saw the ghostly shape of a lion surround her as she swung at the knight in retaliation. They saw blood, their blood, blood spilling from their arm, mixing and splashing with river water. They saw black closing in. They breathed deeply, slowly, stubbornly, anything to stay conscious, to stay alive.

The skiff's engine roared. It bounced across the waves as it launched Kell and Sheila to the middle of the broad Purro River. Kell focused on the rumbling noise, their eyes closed, their right arm grasped tightly. The pain gave way to the sting of trauma. They fought to keep control of their breathing.

Sheila was breathing rapidly, losing that same fight. "Holy shit. Holy shit. Kell, are you with me?"

The mage nodded slowly. A bright green tarp sat crumpled in the boat, bogged down by water and blood. They slowly reached with their left arm and dragged a corner of it up to them, shuddering in pain with every movement. They draped it over their wound, blood and water slipping off. The bright fabric was the only thing they could see. The rest of the world all bled together into black.

"Sheila," they said with a panic that fought to appear calm, "I need you to kill the engine."

Sheila was muttering to herself. "Shit, that's a lot--"

"Please, Sheila," Kell pleaded. "Hold my arm. Exactly like this. Do not move it. Not even a fraction. I need to be perfectly still. Can you do that? Please?"

"I--" Sheila's arms were shaking. She clenched her fists, her eyes closed tightly, as though she was willing herself back to reality. When they opened, she reached over Kell's head and stopped the engine. "Yeah." She grasped Kell's right arm, her gloves quickly sodden with bloody water. Following Kell's guidance, she held their wounded arm in the position they wanted it in. Kell struggled to hold back shouts of pain with each movement.

Their visor went blank. They focused on their breathing, on the pain, on the steady rise and fall of the waters. They put their left hand over their upper right arm, over the spot where it had been cut, nearly severed, slashed to exposed bone. The waters rolled. Kell winced, groaned, muttering as vapor gelled and coalesced onto their arm. It pulled muscle back together beneath the tarp, glued together flesh with the slick and foamy texture of a vapor-saturated liquid.

Minutes as long as lifetimes burned in Kell's body. When the work was done, the entire length and depth of the wound covered by the residue of the spell, their shoulders relaxed. They sat motionless, breathing slowly. Color returned to the world around them. They weren't bleeding out. They were alive.

Beneath the tarp, they cautiously, painfully, curled a finger on their right hand. Then another. Then another. Satisfied, they gradually lifted their arm under its own power. They pried Sheila's iron grip off of it. "There."

Sheila sat down, the blood and water splashing against the armor on her legs. "Did you . . . did you just reattach your arm?"

Kell nodded slowly. They had also used a lot of vapor and lost a lot of blood. They were weak, cold, out of energy.

Sheila stared at their blank visor, mouth hanging slightly open, as the sun set behind them. "What are you?"

Objective

Each player aims to navigate their six pieces across the Twenty Squares board, while surviving the strategies and schemes of their opponent!

Equipment

Two four-sided dice, numbered 0-1-1-2, are provided. In lieu of rolling these, four coins can be flipped; a "heads" flip is treated as a 1, while a "tails" flip is treated as a 0.

Play occurs on the provided board. Each square is marked with one of four symbols, used in various rule sets described later in this manual: The Lined Circle, The Hollow Square, The Lesser Arrow, and The Diamond.

Setup

Distribute play pieces to each player, such that each player has all of the pieces of a given color. Each player rolls the dice to determine who moves first. The higher roll goes first. Ties are re-rolled. If both players roll a sum of 2, a player that has rolled a 0 and 2 goes first over a player that has rolled 1 and 1.

Before play begins, players should agree on any rule variants they wish to use, as well as which set of circuits (the "green line" or the "yellow line") they will follow in the game. For fairness, both players should follow the same circuit.

Your Turn

Roll both dice and sum up the number displayed on their bases. You may move one piece this many spaces, following the decided-upon circuit line.

Two pieces may not occupy the same space at the same time. Attempts to move a piece onto a square occupied by your own piece, or onto any occupied square considered Safe for that player, are invalid. Moving a piece onto a non-Safe square occupied by an opposing piece will return the opposing piece to that player's base.

If you are capable of moving any piece along the circuit based on your roll, you must do so, even should it place you in an undesired position.

A player may have as many pieces on the board at the same time as they wish, provided their rolls allow.

Standard Rules

The squares bearing a lined circle are Safe. When a player lands on a Safe square, they are granted an extra turn. In addition, pieces on Safe tiles cannot be removed. No other special squares are used in Standard rules.

A piece may be removed ("cycled") from the board after completing a circuit only on an exact roll. For example, a piece on the final square may only be removed via a roll of 1.

A game is won when all of a player's pieces have been "cycled".

Regional Variants

- Owain Variant

This variant treats both the lined circle and diamond squares as Safe. Safe squares in this variant do not grant an extra turn. In addition, multiple pieces owned by a player may occupy a single space.

- Goldstone Variant

Popular in Bessetrae. This variant has no pre-defined safe squares. Before the match, each player may select one symbol on the board to use as a Safe square (following Standard Rules definitions). During play, the selected symbol is Safe only for the player who chose it. For example, if Player 1 chooses the Diamond and Player 2 chooses the Lesser Arrow, then Player 1's pieces cannot be removed when they are on a Diamond, but they can be removed if they are on a Lesser Arrow. The opposite would apply for Player 2.

- The Gauvencian Trade

Compatible with other variants. This common "house rule" states that, when attempting to remove a piece from the board, a player may elect to use a larger-than-allowed roll. In doing so, however, the player forfeits their next turn. This rule cannot be invoked for removing a player's final piece.

— Rules for Twenties,
as printed in Sauvie Games editions

CHAPTER FOUR

The Purro River was at peace. Large cargo ships, piled high with boxes of Banner-branded goods, flowed like fire ants up and down the waters. They made up the bulk of the traffic on the river; pilots of smaller, personal boats knew to get out of their way. Banner stops for nobody.

The boat Sheila had commandeered struggled to keep pace. It wasn't meant to. The skiff was a practical military vehicle, familiar from her time in the army, with enough room for a handful of people and their supplies and little else. It made for a great escape vehicle, nimble and simple to use, but it was never going to hold up for a lengthy voyage out in the open sea. It wouldn't even have the fuel to make it to Granberg. So she pointed it east instead, upriver, towards the border with Farolé. That route had its own problems, but fuel was unlikely to be one.

Night fell. The forests along the river's banks housed the occasional fishing settlement nestled among the trees, their lamps easily visible in the twilight. Sheila found herself repeatedly turning to the back of the boat, looking for the lamps of Kell's eyes. Cory was right; if the mage died, it was on her head. Didn't matter if she made the killing blow or not. She'd be accused, and nobody would believe her. She cursed out the helmet that Kell wore, keeping her from any confidence about their state. Their visor would look the same, she figured, whether they were asleep or dead.

She steered the skiff down a branch in the river where an enterprising fisherman had set up a supply depot. After bartering for a bit of cured tilapia, she returned to the boat to see the yellow lights of Kell's visor, dim and barely open, leaning against the engine. She tried not to express relief.

"You're alive," Sheila said.

"Yeah," Kell said quietly.

"Want some food?"

Kell rolled their head slowly. "I'm fine. Still got enough Pemmash for a week, at least."

Sheila's face turned, as if the fish she was gnawing on had gone bitter. "That powder stuff? You live off that crap?"

"Just in the field." A faint slurp came from Kell's helmet. They were probably "eating" the stuff right that moment.

Sheila started the engine and steered the boat back into the flow of traffic. "What about back at base? Got a favorite food?"

"Why do you ask?"

A cargo ship trudged past, the lights on its deck illuminating the river around them. "Just curious. And I guess I want to make sure you're still alive and all that."

Kell sat up slowly, watching the waters pass. "Well, I am."

Cagey little . . . "Alright," Sheila said, "better question. How did you do that?"

"Do what?"

"With your arm. That was *not* a normal nursing spell. You can't *do* that."

"Well, I did," Kell sighed.

"*How*?" she said. "What else can you do? Can you just patch up anyone like that? What are you doing out here, not working in a hospital?"

Kell rolled their head to stare at Sheila. "Now you want me out there healing people? Yesterday you wanted me dead."

"I still do." She spoke honestly, without thinking. "Especially if you've got all that power and you won't use it. But when that knight showed up, I just . . . It was instinct. That's all." She grumbled and turned back to the boat's controls. "So I guess I'm your bodyguard now. Or your commander. Whatever, you owe me a ton, and you're gonna act like it."

"You evoked."

Sheila was hit with a chill separate from the river water misting around her. "Excuse me?"

"After he hit me," Kell said. "I saw your glow. Looked like a lion, I think."

Sheila stared out ahead. "That's shock, Kell," she said, shaking her head. "You were imagining things."

"You don't think evoking happens?"

"Doesn't matter. That's not what happened."

"So what did?"

Sheila couldn't answer. The moment was a complete blur.

Kell chuckled quietly. "So, yeah. Thank you."

Sheila sighed and navigated in the dark. Kell was making quite the claim. Evoking--a sort of stress-induced summoning, for lack of a better description--was so rare that there was earnest debate whether or not it ever occurred. Every story about it involved some deep emotional strain, which always made her write the idea off. If that was what made people evoke, then she would've seen it on the battlefield a dozen times. There was nothing more viscerally stressful, more taxing on the body and soul, than the sprawling fields of war. And even if she had evoked . . . a *lion*? If she were to evoke, surely it would come out resembling Vakonivak.

Ah, Vakonivak. Blessed Wings, Mother of Skies, Guardian of Bessetrae. She was the good one. She didn't poke her beak into Bessetrae's affairs like Owain obviously did in Cymona, but her serene influence was there if you knew where to look. And the one time she left Mt. Grann during the Winters' War ended with the Cymonians being thoroughly routed. She was something Sheila could respect, something to look up to, something that made her proud to be Bessetran.

"Also." Kell broke the silence. "Thanks for the boat."

"It's not my boat," Sheila muttered.

Kell let out a weak laugh. "Troublemaker."

"Don't give me shit."

"Takes one to know one," Kell said coyly. "I was a punk of a kid back home."

"Well if you haven't noticed," she snipped, "you're not home. You're up shit creek and you're only alive because of me." A frustrated pause. "I could've ripped your arm off," she said abruptly.

"Huh?"

She turned to face Kell, still crumpled against the back of the skiff. "Right? When you were attaching it. I could've just . . . rip. Tear it right off." She mimed tugging sharply with both arms and throwing the phantom limb overboard. "Done. Just let you bleed to death. *That* would be some trouble for you, now wouldn't it?"

Kell shook their head. "You're not the type. There's not a world where you do that."

"You don't know that."

Kell rubbed the wound on their right arm. "Sure I do. You're just like one of the other mages. Rey. Always talks tough but he's such a sweetheart."

"Well, I'm not him."

"Obviously. But you wouldn't be here if you didn't care."

"Never said I do."

"Well, I've got your back," Kell said. "You've already got mine. Right, bodyguard?"

Sheila looked overboard at the inky water. The sight of Vakonivak swooping in to protect her people returned to her mind. A bold, inspiring, heroic sight. Sheila could never be that kind of guardian, but maybe she could come close.

"Yeah. Sure."

Kell's visor strobed gently as they drifted in and out of sleep. Sheila stood stiff at the bow, kicking her legs periodically for some degree of movement. As blurry as her exhaustion made the world around her, she wasn't about to rest until they made it into Farolé.

The border came into view, and with it the checkpoint that straddled the river. The invisible line was too illuminated for Sheila to sneak the skiff past. She gently shook Kell awake.

"Hey," she said, "do you think you can swim?"

"What?" they replied, groggy. "Maybe, why?"

Sheila gestured ahead. "The border. We have to ditch the boat."

Kell sighed. "My arm's trash. It'd be risky." They ducked as the light from a passing cargo ship beamed into their eyes. "Hold on. I have an idea." They took control of the boat and steered it close to the passing ship.

"What do you think you're doing?"

The mooring rope was piled in the middle of the boat. Kell kicked it gently. "Think you can throw that? Loop us to that boat?"

"Are you serious?"

"Look at the lifeboats. They're the same as this thing."

Sheila looked up. Kell was right, or at least right enough for the time of night. One davit hung close to the water, though it looked too rusty to hold anything. It was a dumb idea and probably wouldn't work, but she didn't actually want to swim.

"What about us, though?"

"How much of the tarp is left? We can hide."

Sheila grabbed the tarp she had cut free from Kell's reattached arm. She held it up, assessing the size. "You're lucky you're scrawny."

With Kell gunning the engine to keep up, Sheila put the plan into motion. After a few attempts at lassoing, the rope found its target on the cargo ship. Sheila carefully fastened the boat as Kell cut the engine. The two hid in the bloody humidity under the tarp, the skiff silently dragging behind Banner's vessel.

The border inspectors were meticulous. Their assessments of personal craft were thorough, covering an exhaustive checklist, taking however long they needed. The policies went into place ages ago, when the tensions that would become the Winters' War had only begun to flare, but even years after, the regulations and policies hadn't been touched. If the laundry list of security requirements wasn't enough to keep people from crossing on a whim, the constant backlogs and delays would do the work. There was no way a stolen military boat, holding a wayward mage whose homeland wants them dead, would pass such a detailed inspection.

But that was for personal craft. For Banner's fleet of cargo ships, they simply looked at the manifest, looked at the ship number, and stamped the captain through. Banner Goods deliveries required a freely flowing fleet able to move across Linnute without delay. Otherwise, the trademarked uncannily fast service people across the continent expected could never happen. At the end of the day, border inspectors were people too. The particulars of the silent agreement were never really questioned. If Banner was bribing inspectors, then the company was "bribing" everyone.

As a result, neither inspector nor captain noticed the extra "lifeboat" dragging along the stern of the *Jomon*. The skiff remained unnoticed for the entire night, its passengers hiding long after the border crossing faded into the distance. The ship worked its way up the river and ultimately drove into port at an industrial town.

As the summons and crew aboard the ship unloaded cargo, Sheila and Kell found a ladder up to the dockyard and abandoned their bloodied boat. Kell's climb was slow as they groaned with each rung, their bandaged arm unable to bear much weight. The two ducked between the massive containers that lined the dockyard, dodging the occasional summon, and made their way to a quiet portion of the fence. They found a seam and slid through, stepping into the dimly lit street with a shared sigh of relief.

The gambit had put Kell and Sheila in the town of Vaaland. Idle factories peaked around them in the twilight. They could find no trees to sleep under and no benches to sleep upon. A narrow alley close by stank of industrial waste and was littered with metal refuse, but a quick sweep made a space good enough to sleep in.

B

The slam of a door woke Kell with a start. They sat up, leaning against a box of metal scraps, and felt the morning sun through their uniform. Their corner of the alley was safe, with only rats for company. Kell kept watch and let Sheila continue to get her much-needed rest. They rubbed their arm occasionally, reminding themself it was still there. They considered loosening the bandages over the tarp and letting the wound breathe, but, no. Sheila was sitting right there. Not worth the risk.

The time alone let Kell think. From what they had been told, they were now lost behind enemy lines. But that was before the knight started swinging. That incident could be a sign of something worse going on, or it could be part of a ruse. They didn't know if that knight was even Cymonian to begin with.

But even if they were still on their assignment, they had no information on how to proceed. It made a certain kind of sense for further details to be waiting for Kell and Rocko when they got to Bellum. That would reduce the chance of spies eavesdropping. But now, spies would be the only ones who could have the information.

They pulled out the mobile Sheila had bought them and tried to call Rocko. No answer. Kell's weary stomach sank; if Cymona was after them, they'd be after him, too. That, or he was in on it. Sheila was paranoid, Kell figured, but not entirely wrong. If Kell had been trusting Rocko when they shouldn't have been, it could have been what nearly killed them. They sat anxiously with the thought for longer than they wanted.

The sun was high when a factory worker spotted the two tucked in the alley, Sheila still asleep. He shooed them away, waking up Sheila as he did. He seemed upset with their presence but indifferent to who they were. The two left without an argument and wandered down the street.

"Well, mage, any idea what to do now?" Sheila said.

"I don't know," Kell said. "Can't reach anyone back home. Probably shouldn't go back anyway. Much as I want to."

"Absolutely not."

"Could try to get back to Milend."

Sheila sighed impatiently. "We stole an army boat, Kell. That's not an option either."

"Well, we can't stay here."

"Why not?"

"The summons!" Kell said. "They attacked Cymona."

"And Cymona attacked you," Sheila said. "Enemy of my enemy."

Kell shook their head. "They are not going to see it that way."

"Well, how about this way?"

Sheila grabbed Kell's hood and turned their head towards a nearby factory. A steady trickle of smoke emerged from its chimney. A conveyor belt sticking out of a window dropped the occasional pile of wood into a lower chute. The factory was clearly working, but far from its limits.

"If this place was going to war," Sheila said, "those buildings would be running full steam, nonstop. Even if they somehow had summons fighting, even if they were that stupid, they'd still need to make supplies."

"Unless they get those from Banner, too," Kell said.

"There's no way they get everything." Sheila craned her neck, looking a few blocks down the road. "Let's find a pub. If there is a war coming, people will know, and they'll be talking about it."

A tavern should have been easy to find. Surely, a town built on the backs of industrial labor would be littered with watering holes for people to drown their stresses in. Sheila claimed, between exasperated groans, that that was how Windglade had always felt. No reason for Vaaland to be any different. Never mind Farolé's seeming bias towards pomp and spectacle that, beyond its borders, morphed into a stereotype of drunken reverie. They passed by dozens of buildings with no luck, though in Kell's mind, any of them could've been pubs that simply didn't advertise their presence.

The most obvious shop they passed was one of Banner's. Sheila ducked inside to sell off the aello feathers and other vapor-soaked beast parts she had been gathering. Since Banner Goods sold nearly everything, they had need of nearly everything, and would offer good credit for hard-to-find materials. The scraps Sheila offloaded would be enough to cover the first round when the pair finally found a place.

The inside of the Fogbank Tavern was sedate, the bare bricks given little chance to bounce conversation around the room. Sheila and Kell took a corner quietly and did their best to eavesdrop on the few chats that did occur. Kell tuned their helmet to hear the room around them a little better, though not too far. Sheila's voice had a way of booming, the tone of an army major barking orders even when she was trying to sound softer.

Conversations in the tavern were banal: local marketplace trends, clerks complaining about rule changes, excited gossip about Crystal Greene and other celebrities. Apparently, Crystal's latest chart-topping single, *Romance in Blue*, was finally about to fall to Cigarette Wife's *Improvise*. This was a big deal, according to the tone the news was being delivered with. Kell didn't care. They didn't even know how either song went.

They finally perked up when a nearby woman, decked out for traveling, started complaining about a bag of her supplies having been stolen along the road. Kell paid attention, as inconspicuously as they could. Until they could finally get home, they were a traveler too, and could use any insights about bandits or other hazards.

"A couple sahagins" were behind the theft, "obviously," though the woman would concede to her weary companion that the whole incident happened while she was fast asleep. The bag could easily have been stolen by any manner of passersby, or even a particularly enterprising shrew. Or, there was the explanation her companion's tone indicated was the most likely: She forgot it, and wanted someone else to blame.

The tavern had little business for the afternoon, so the tavern keeper had no complaints with Sheila and Kell taking up a booth. Sheila kept her orders frugal and sparse--some basic stew for food and some light ale--while Kell largely kept to themself. They only relented when they found their canteen was empty. The ale was light enough that it may as well have been water.

The keeper, having a lull in her tasks, took to supervising her staff from near where Kell and Sheila sat. "Don't get many travelers like you folks," she said.

Kell wasn't about to respond.

Sheila took a moment before she finally spoke up. "Get many travelers at all?"

"Naw, you're right, there. Scarlet's gang sweeps through sometimes," she said as she gestured to where the griping traveler had been sitting earlier, "but that's about it. Not a lotta folks care 'bout old Vancius--they'd rather be up north. Not me, can't stand how cold it gets."

Kell suppressed a groan. *She's just gonna keep talking, isn't she.*

"Loaves not crumbs! Loaves not crumbs!" The rallying chants interjected from outside, bleeding into the tavern. A man in the corner of the tavern, deep in his cups, chanted along weakly.

Sheila let the chants fade off. "Bit of trouble in town?"

The tavern keeper chuckled. "It's always something. Lately, folks are acting upset 'cause they're saying Dolya Bay doesn't have enough food. Like, honey, you're on the coast!

You've got food." She tutted to herself. "Some folks just want the Queen to solve their problems for them."

"She doesn't solve problems?" Sheila asked.

"You two are from Cymona, aren't you?"

Sheila gave Kell a glance. Their head was hung, their hood drawn. They wanted nothing to do with the conversation. But they were still a vapormage, clear as day.

"It's a bit different here," the tavern keeper continued. "Don't have that Lyon guy in everyone's business, tellin' folks what to do. Got a lot more wiggle room up here. Folks can do their own thing."

"Almost sound like you're from Bessetrae," Sheila said with a frustrated familiarity.

"Wouldn't say we go that far." The tavern keeper wordlessly directed a nearby server to bus some now-vacant tables. "This place ain't chaos, we got rules. Those stupid Grounders don't follow the rules, look what it gets 'em. Wouldn't last a week in the old Vancius days, I tell you."

Sheila quietly scoffed as the keeper walked away to tend to her business. Whatever Sheila was thinking as she quietly rolled her eyes, Kell probably agreed.

C

The day dragged on. Sheila and Kell were content to simply rest for a bit. They both had little desire to talk, and little to talk about, interacting only over the occasional game of Twenties. The tavern keeper, meanwhile, seemed eager to continue filling the few quiet moments she had by chatting with the pair of unfamiliar faces. Sheila's repeated attempts to cut off the conversation were much less effective at the task than the waves of regulars that were piling in as the factory whistles began to blow.

The tavern was getting crowded. Too crowded. The two settled the tab and stepped outside into the twilight to debate their next course of action.

Before they could start, a hunn man in a clean suit tapped Kell on the shoulder. The right shoulder, specifically. Needles of pain shot down Kell's arm. They recoiled and groaned.

"Oh, terribly sorry," the man said. He was shorter than Kell, but only barely, with his chaotic dark hair more than making up the difference. "But, are you Kell Rusalka?"

Kell stepped backwards, wary. A stranger shouldn't know their name.

Sheila stepped between the two and used her own height to intimidate. "Who's asking?"

"Oh, my apologies. Alejandro Quintana, he of Her Majesty's Speakers. We're the diplomatic agency for the Four Kingdoms of Farolé." His tone was professional, the words measured and creaking with authority, an air of maturity far beyond his apparent age.

"So what does the Queen want?" Sheila said.

"She wants the last vapormage," Alejandro said calmly. "Dead, I'm afraid."

"Excuse me?" Sheila reached for her sword.

"Last?" Kell asked, surprised and angry.

"Miss, this doesn't concern you. If you would?" He gestured towards the tavern.

She drew her sword. "The hell it doesn't."

"What do you mean, 'last'?" Kell demanded.

Alejandro straightened his suit jacket and reached for a pocket on its inside. "Miss, I am perfectly capable of handling both of you, if I must."

A glint of steel shot out from his pocket. Sheila barely had her sword in position to deflect the dagger. Alejandro took a lower, agile pose, a knife in each hand. He lunged at her. Sheila dodged, stumbling off balance.

Kell awkwardly grabbed their rod with their left hand. They sent desperate concussive blasts of vapor towards Alejandro. Their aim was off, but they made space. With a few practiced gestures, Alejandro put a thin shield of vapor around himself.

"What do you mean, 'last'?" Kell shouted again, dodging around swipes.

"Exactly what it sounds like," Alejandro said.

Sheila's claymore interjected, slamming into the ground between the two, kicking up loose cobblestone. "You kill the rest?" she yelled.

Kell released a line of flame. "That what this war's about?"

Alejandro's shield of vapor was hit. He shook off the heat. "What war?"

"Shut it!" Sheila swung in a wide arc, hoping to strike the diplomat down.

Alejandro dodged. The claymore was too slow, his small frame too nimble. "Hold on!" He held an empty palm out to Kell.

Sheila growled. "You don't get to run!"

"Sheila!" Kell barked.

The three stood, sizing each other up.

"What war?" Alejandro repeated.

"Don't play dumb," Kell said. "You sent summons over the border. Attacked our outpost. That's war."

"We did no such thing."

"You expect us to believe that?" Sheila growled.

"It's the truth, miss," Alejandro said sharply. "Farolé isn't foolish enough to use summons. And if there was a war already happening, I would know about it. It's my job to." He turned his head to Kell. "Why are you surprised?"

"That you're trying to kill me? I'm not."

"That you're the last vapormage."

Kell's visor blinked. "Since when?"

Alejandro's eyes darted back and forth between Kell and Sheila, confusion growing on his face. "What are you doing in Farolé?"

"You're not asking questions here!" Sheila yelled.

"Sheila, calm down."

"Something is very wrong here," Alejandro said. "Kell. Why are you here?"

Kell swallowed. Their cover story was already wearing thin, and the diplomat seemed to know more than he was letting on. Best to come clean. "Summons from Farolé attacked

Rijest. I was ordered to cross the border via Bessetrae. Find out what I could, stop things if it was possible."

Sheila turned to face Kell. "You *were* invading."

"I was passing through."

"When was this?" Alejandro said.

Kell shook their head and pointed their rod at Alejandro. A reminder more than a threat. "I told you enough. Tell me what happened to the other mages."

"I don't know. I was told that you fled with critical intelligence and equipment. And that you were coming here to start a war."

"I came here to *stop* a war."

Alejandro scanned the surroundings. "We need to speak somewhere more private."

"The hell do you think you are, making demands?" Sheila yelled.

Alejandro stood stiff and composed. "I make no demands." He held his knives by the blades and extended the handles towards Sheila. "I don't expect you to trust me, given how I've introduced myself. But I do think we should talk further. Something is very wrong here."

Sheila stared him down, rejecting the offer.

Kell took him up on it. They grabbed the knives and followed Alejandro to the inn attached to the tavern, Sheila still on alert as she followed.

Alejandro made a point of emptying his pockets. He piled his possessions atop the bare dresser in the inn room he had rented. Sheila buried them with her bags and stood in front of them, arms crossed. His weapons were hers now, her stance declared.

"Right then," Alejandro started, "Kell. When did your mission start?"

"You're answering the questions here," Sheila said.

"I'd like to establish the timeline," he said. "My orders came three days ago."

"And they said there were no other vapormages?" Kell asked.

"Indeed. Yesterday, en route, I happened to spot you two in the Banner store."

"Dammit, that was you," Sheila realized.

Alejandro nodded. "I didn't realize you were together. And it didn't add up, supposedly you were already in Farolé. I left to confirm. By the time I did, you were gone."

"By the time you did," Kell said, "we got attacked by a Cymonian knight."

Alejandro held his chin in thought. "Who gave that order?"

"No clue."

Alejandro closed his eyes and swung his free hand around, drawing the timeline as if conducting an orchestra.

"My orders came six days ago," Kell said. "That was the last time I saw the other mages. We started going through the mountains three days ago."

"We?" Sheila said before suddenly recalling. "Oh, your team. You mentioned them."

"It was just two of us. Me and Rocko. He didn't make it."

"Perished?" Alejandro asked.

"No, we split when a summon attacked."

Alejandro paused to think. "Kell." His voice had the earnest tone of a therapist. "If the summon was Farolian, why would it be on the Bessetran border?"

Kell found no answer.

"Unless it was hunting you," Sheila offered.

"That doesn't align with my information," Alejandro said.

"Your information is garbage," Sheila sneered.

"What *is* your information?" Kell asked, trying to steer the conversation.

"I told you. You were a fugitive with important and dangerous resources, looking to use those resources to cause an international incident, with the goal of goading either Her Majesty or your Prime Minister or both into open conflict. You were a danger to Farolé. My job is to handle those dangers."

"If you killed me, and every other mage was also gone . . ." Kell had to pause and close their eyes tightly. They didn't like what they were considering. "What kind of 'gone' are we even talking about here?"

"From what I've been told, the unit is certainly disbanded," Alejandro said.

"But they're still alive?" Kell said. "They've got to be, right?"

Alejandro tapped his chin. "I think I see how this story is supposed to come together. Your unit has disbanded. That would be the fact of the matter. The story goes, you were upset about that. Enough to turn traitor. But Farolé wouldn't know that, so they would have me . . . kill you. To your people, we had just killed a beloved vapormage for no reason. To my people, Cymona had invaded. I would *think* I had the truth of it all, and perhaps do something with that, but . . . well, I'd say we've put lie to all that."

"And you trying to justify it would only cause more chaos," Kell said.

Alejandro nodded sagaciously. "That it would."

"But that doesn't explain the summons," Kell said.

"Did you see the one that attacked Rijest?" Alejandro asked.

"Of course not." The eyes on Kell's visor lit brighter. "Wait. Could that have been fake?"

Alejandro contemplated the idea. "That would require Her Majesty and your Prime Minister to be in cooperation, would it not?"

Sheila scoffed. "Guys, forget all this conspiracy bullshit. Doesn't matter. You kill a diplomat, or a diplomat kills a foreigner, it's gonna cause trouble no matter what."

Alejandro looked at her flatly. "Do you remember Secretary Reeve, Sheila?"

Sheila thought for a second. "What about her?"

"She was quite the opposition to Bathroy's calls for peace after the Winters' War. No surprise for the War Ministry. She was positive Cymona would strike again, happy to strike in self-defense, and eager to spill that over any border in the way. And then," Alejandro said with a casual snap of his fingers, "she died. Food poisoning. Was a whole scandal."

"Because it wasn't food poisoning," Sheila grumbled, "and they wouldn't hunt down the Cymonian bastard who did it."

"You're talking to that bastard." Alejandro leaned back, smirking. "The Speakers don't typically cross borders to operate, but she wanted to bring war. So I made sure she didn't."

"Then help me stop this one," Kell said.

"Do you see me trying to kill you?" Alejandro said. "The Speakers are going to be your foe here. After this, I'm not wont to be one anymore."

"So we're not safe here either."

"Says you," Sheila said. "Think we'll take our chances."

"No, we won't," Kell said.

"You seriously trust this guy?" Sheila's voice rose. "He just tried to kill you!"

"And I hear a wolf barking. I mean," Kell caught themself, "...you know what I mean."

"Achterberg fan, are you?" Alejandro said with a chuckle.

Kell sighed at themself for the distraction. "So where do we go, then? Do you have some route into Zeimatia?"

"No. And regardless, I know where I stand here. I wouldn't expect you two to go along with anything I propose."

Kell, truthfully, would consider anything Alejandro proposed. He seemed aggressively competent.

"Could try Rinculo." They immediately disliked their idea. "No, are there even boats this time of year?"

"I don't see why not," Alejandro said. "It's not too cold yet. Trains can get us to a port rather easily."

"Who said you were coming along?" Sheila said. "We got your info. Get out of here."

"I thought you didn't trust me. Wouldn't you want to keep an eye on me, then?"

Kell stood between the two. Alejandro didn't sound like he was trying to rile Sheila up, but they knew he would anyway. "Look. I'm willing to have you tag along, Alejandro, but we don't trust you yet. If you want that, you've gotta earn it."

Alejandro nodded. "Fair enough."

"And Sheila?" Kell said. "At least give him a chance to earn it. Alright?"

Sheila grumbled under her breath. "It's your head."

"I know." They turned back to Alejandro. "Be in the tavern at sunup. We'll move from there."

D

Sheila was the first in the tavern the next morning, largely because it was where she had spent the night. While the locals commiserated about labor woes and the occasional lonesome gentleman tried in vain to flirt with her, she studied maps of the surrounding area and the transit routes that spanned Farolé. Whatever plan Alejandro was about to suggest, she didn't trust it. She needed to have her own plan at the ready. It was how she had protected Milend for years, and aside from a vapormage stumbling in, no trouble ever came to that town.

Alejandro sauntered down the steps connecting the inn and the tavern. He looked as though he had just rolled out of bed. He seemed relaxed, almost happy.

Sheila was immediately suspicious. "Where's Kell?"

Alejandro shrugged. "Still in their let, wherever it was. I would assume."

"Sun's been up for a bit. If you did anything, I swear to Vakonivak--"

"Everything alright, you two?" the manager called from behind the counter.

"We're quite fine, thank you," Alejandro said.

"Good to hear," he said with a laugh. "My wife had an eye on her all night, after that little scuffle. Didn't want to see her running off somewhere before her man could make amends."

"My man?" Sheila said, confused.

Alejandro couldn't stifle his laughter.

She glared at him. "You're in good spirits for someone on such a short leash."

"You haven't met the Queen, then," Alejandro said. "This is the longest leash I've ever been on."

"Well, don't get comfortable."

"Understood." Alejandro reclined in his chair. "I'm curious, Sheila. You've been traveling with Kell for a few days now, yes? Are they always wearing that uniform? Sleeping, eating, all of it?"

Sheila said nothing. It wasn't a difficult or uncomfortable question--she just didn't want to give him the satisfaction of an answer.

A dark green shadow stepped sluggishly and noisily through the tavern door. Kell sat down with a heave as they joined the group.

"You didn't sleep well," Sheila said.

Kell's visor stayed blank. "Someone called." They pulled out the mobile Sheila bought for them and tossed it on the table. "Nobody has this line. I've called . . . three people, total."

"Probably some Banner sales call," Sheila said.

"There was nobody there. It buzzed, I picked up, said hello a few times. Nothing. Just a roar. Then it went dead."

Sheila stared at the mobile on the table. "Weird."

"Recognize the line?" Alejandro said.

Kell shook their head. "That summon I mentioned, though? In the mountains? I'd swear on my life, it was the same roar."

"Seriously?" Sheila asked, skeptical.

"I know, it doesn't make sense."

Alejandro tapped the small device on the table. "You should leave this behind, then."

Kell turned to Alejandro, then Sheila, their visor still dim. "You two have mobiles, though. Right? You going to leave yours too?"

Sheila almost considered it. "I need to make sure Cory's holding down the fort."

"And mine has too much valuable information. Can't leave it lying around."

Kell nodded, grabbing their mobile and tossing it in a satchel. "Then there's no point, is there? If someone wants to find us, one way or another, they'll find us."

NOTICE OF VENDOR POLICY UPDATE

To our sales partners,

   We thank you for your continued participation and support in the Materials Acquisition Program. This letter is to inform you of changes to the MAP that may affect you.

- Class C (raw wild) materials will be subject to a minimum delivery load of 250 Credit per material, increasing from the present 120 Credit.

- Class E (vapor wild) materials can no longer be delivered via courier and must be brought to a Banner Goods storefront for examination prior to sale. On-site staff may reject materials submitted at their discretion.

   These changes will go into effect 01/05. We trust this will be ample time to adjust to the new needs and specifications.

   We know these changes may be difficult for you and your business, but they are necessary for the continued success of the Banner family of companies.

   Banner Goods thanks you for your continued loyalty.

— Issued by Banner Goods,
Dated 28/04

CHAPTER FIVE

A lejandro had no interest in being found. Speakers were to be clandestine, out of the way of the general public. Not secretive, necessarily, simply not drawing attention. It was a job that claimed every moment of a diplomat's life, demanding competence and control.

And it was not a job one simply left. There was no formal process for leaving Her Majesty's Speakers; either a Speaker claimed a position of power within the Royal House, or--to be Cymonian about it--the fieldwork took its toll on them. Declaring to your handlers that you intended to quit was a quick way of ensuring the fieldwork took its toll, and violently so.

The plan, then, was to sneak north. The Southern Line from Vaaland would probably encounter a Speaker or two. If headquarters had figured out why he hadn't been answering his mobile, then Alejandro wasn't making a trip in that direction without a confrontation. He could handle it, he was sure of it, but it wouldn't buy him any favor with Kell and Sheila. Favor was a currency worth carrying, given what it buys.

Sheila had spent all night reading the maps and had a plan of her own. A day's walk through the Felmata Forest would get the three near a station on the Central Line, which passed through Gauvencia just as well as any other. Her justification for the route was to avoid the traps Alejandro had surely left along the close-by Southern Line. He responded with practiced, diplomatic indignation. It was exactly the route he had intended to suggest, but if Sheila thought she had gotten clever and caught him out, perfect.

The road they took out of Vaaland was once a rail line of its own, though evidence of the fact was thin. The Felmata Forest had been slowly reclaiming the land, young trees encroaching upon the flattened stone trail. It spilled over the border into Bessetrae and had grown to cover much of Farolé. Alejandro could have confidently told headquarters that he was in the forest, if he was so inclined. It would barely narrow things down.

The sun was reaching its highest as the three began spotting makeshift buildings along the route. They had seen and passed stone remnants of buildings that were clearly part of the road's rail history, but these structures were too new. Too complete. Alejandro regarded them with concern, veering towards the opposite side of the trail when he spotted one. People who lost Farolé's zero-sum game tended to find themselves in places like these. Alejandro was obviously a Speaker; he still wore the suit he donned for the role. So if the people here had issues with the government and could identify him from his wardrobe, it might cause a spot of mess.

The structures were passed without incident. Kell and Sheila treated them as the unremarkable landmarks they proved to be. The two talked like enemies and walked like friends. Sheila's pace regulated itself to match Kell's, rather than pushing the mage to move faster. They were the leader then, clearly, and Sheila was the bodyguard. Anyone who wanted to get to Kell would have to go through her first.

All the observations and conjecture, the marathon of thoughts that a Speaker had to undergo, buzzed through Alejandro. It was tiring, but he could neither mind it nor stop it. It was part of his job. It kept his mind busy. Kept him on his game.

The sun set over the nearly abandoned Nohlgara station. The planks of the wooden platform were warped and rotting. Low foliage encroached on the tracks.

Alejandro wiped down a slab of metal that made for a bench and took a seat. "Lovely timing. We won't be waiting too long."

Sheila's pacing around the platform stopped abruptly. She glanced around for a schedule board but spotted nothing. "What makes you so sure?"

"This is Farolé, after all. Plenty of things we could do better, but we're quite good about our transit." He smirked at Sheila when she turned to face him. "I do know the trains quite well, I'd say."

Sheila stared. A hand moved, almost instinctively, towards her sword. "Oh fuck you."

Kell's visor blinked. "Sheila, what the hell?"

"This was all his plan!" she yelled.

"This was *your* plan!" Kell yelled back.

"You're both right." Alejandro stayed calm. "I was going to suggest Nohlgara as well, but Sheila did first. Who am I to disagree?"

"You smarmy little--"

"Sheila!" Kell stepped between the two. "Are you really gonna give him shit for having the same idea as you?"

The light of an approaching train appeared in the distance.

"Just calm down, alright?" they continued. "The train's coming. Do we have enough credit to get on?"

"I have us covered." Alejandro patted a pocket of his suit jacket. "Enough for my original assignment, but it will cover us here."

As the train pulled in, Alejandro revealed the overtly large wad of kroner that would secure passage for the three. He handed it to the train attendant with a decisive whisper.

"Fortunately," Alejandro said as they entered the empty sleeper car, "we won't arrive in Gauvencia until tomorrow. Though it will be early."

The three huddled into the first cabin of the line. They had laid claim to a fairly upscale sleeper, paneled in dark wood and trimmed with still-lustrous metal, with only four cabins along its length. Each cabin would spaciously fit the three travelers, and since they weren't yet using the beds as beds, there was more than enough room to sit and stretch legs.

"Fortunately?" Sheila said.

"We have a chance to rest," Alejandro said. "That can be a bit of a luxury."

"Seems like you know all about luxuries, being the Queen's lapdog."

Alejandro passively flicked his wrist. "I suppose. Though, regrettably, I've only experienced them around people who want the influence she can dole out. Nothing ruins luxury quite like the people who seek it out, in my opinion."

"Not a fan of your handlers?" Sheila said snidely. She was looking for a way under his skin.

Alejandro knew better. "I'll refrain from saying more."

"Like that here too, huh?" Kell said.

"I don't know what you mean," Alejandro said.

"Of course you do." They rubbed their arm idly. "If I start going around, saying Lyon's gotta step down or whatever, I'll be lucky if all I lose is my uniform. Probably just get killed."

"I'd like to think we're not that harsh," Alejandro said. "I know there's a cluster that's been trying to oppose Her Majesty. They've been around a while."

"Really?" Kell said. "You haven't had to do anything about them?"

"Not directly. In part, because we don't know what we're looking for. Not like you. You were easy to spot. I've had theories, of course, but . . ." He stared out the window and applied melancholy to his voice. "Hardly matters right now."

"You sound awfully . . ." Sheila paused. "What's the word? Like you regret quitting."

"Not the case," Alejandro said. "Truthfully, I should have a long time ago. After that business with the farm."

"Do tell." She was desperate to wear him down.

Alejandro brushed her off. "It was a very complicated and political sequence of events. Just know there's a plot of land out in the forest that's abandoned because of the Speakers, and I'm not too proud of it. In another world, that would've been the end of it. I would've just walked away. But, being a Speaker isn't a job you just leave."

"Isn't that what you just did?" Sheila said.

"I finally had a plan." He turned to Kell, who had already unlatched and claimed a bunk. "Once I pieced together your story, Kell, I knew you'd have to keep running. And if I quit, I'd have to run. There's strength in numbers. So, we run together. Two of us. Three of us, perhaps, though I doubt that somewhat. Still, we're birds of a feather, as it were."

Kell rolled over to look at Alejandro, their visor showing their displeasure. "We're not."

"Pardon?"

"I'm not running. I'm going home."

"The home that tried to kill you?" Sheila said.

"Maybe that wasn't a Cymonian," Kell said. "That whole part still doesn't add up to me."

"Did the knight look Cymonian?" Alejandro asked.

"What do you mean?" Kell said. "Maybe I just don't get out, but I can never tell where anyone's from."

"They had a uniform on," Sheila said. "That's good enough for me."

"A uniform doesn't mean much," Kell said. "There's been stories about fake vapormages running around, 'cause someone got their hands on a uniform."

"Doesn't help that you won't take the helmet off," Sheila said.

"Can't." Kell's voice rose.

"Sure."

"You can't?" Alejandro inquired.

"I don't wanna have this argument again," Kell said. "I'm sorting this mess out, then I'm finding a way home. That's it. Sorry."

That's the way of it, then. Alejandro stared out the window as the train picked up speed. "I take it I'll need a cabin of my own this evening."

Sheila nodded, sternly and silently.

"Thanks for getting us on here, at least," Kell said. "That looked like a lot of money."

Alejandro shrugged. "Wasn't mine," he said as he walked to the back of the train car, leaving the others to their bunks. The money had been one part payment and one part bribe. Their accommodations were more than covered, but the band used to hold the kroner together would clue in a knowing Farolian that the money was courtesy of the Queen herself. When one of Her Majesty's Speakers overpays, they don't expect change. They expect cooperation. Alejandro claimed his own room on the train, confident that the message had been heard.

B

The three slept easily. Their cabins were separate enough from the rest of the train that there were no worries about interlopers. It helped that the individual cabins were impossible to break into from within the train. The doors were too secure, their locks unexposed. Alejandro knew at a glance. The windows were a weak point, perhaps, but nothing came of it.

Morning brought the train to the edge of Gauvencia, offering a wide view of the city as it sloped down towards the Vesper Sea. The orderly grid of streets, the sterling metal buildings, the refined royal palace: all were easily visible from the station platform, as if the rail's path was specifically chosen to show off.

Alejandro pointed the group to the docks but quickly let Sheila take the lead. He kept pace beside Kell, following tightly behind, and scanned the surroundings. Kell had their hood drawn for safety, regardless of how necessary it was. Days ago, they were told this was the capital of a hostile nation, and they still acted like it. Alejandro could understand the behavior. The dense foot traffic in the heart of the city let the three blend in. It would do the same for attackers. Enemies could be anywhere.

On such a breezy autumn afternoon, the docks to the north should be similarly busy: Banner cargo ships lined up past the horizon, travelers on business scurrying about like desperate mice, researchers from the nearby university insisting on their importance. The street outside the docks should be filled with circles of laborers taking a smoke break, travelers from farther up north stuffing extra layers into bags, and summons shuffling mechanically from one duty to the next.

But there was nothing. The docks were quiet. The line of cargo ships sat idle in the water. A few locals milled about. Those who didn't seem local seemed stranded. An academic-looking vian holding a harpoon, his once-red feathers almost all greyed with age, was deep in a one-sided debate with a guard who had been listening far too long to the man's arguments.

Alejandro let them be and casually approached a different guard. "Morning, Mandy. Awfully quiet today, isn't it?"

"Sure is," she said. "Border's closed."

"Entirely?" Alejandro said. "As of when?"

"Got word earlier today. No boats in or out."

"Even the fishing tour? That doesn't leave our waters."

Mandy shrugged. "We're just being safe. Tours will resume when the border's open."

Sheila threw her arms in the air. "So how are we getting to Rinculo?" she cried in frustration.

You don't just… Alejandro paused to sustain his composure. Mandy was a good source. He needed to keep things smooth around her. "Do you have any thoughts when the border might reopen?"

Mandy chuckled. "You know that stuff better than I do, Al. Didn't even tell us why it's closed. Sounded like something weird is going on."

A buzz. The mobile in Kell's satchel was going off. They waved Sheila and Alejandro to a nook between two buildings to take the call.

"Hello?"

Silence.

"Hello?"

Alejandro watched, curious, wondering if the roar would emerge again and prove that there was indeed something on Kell's tail that they needed to run from. Sheila, disinterested, watched some stranded travelers.

A gruff, masculine voice abruptly broke the silence. "21:48 tonight. Dock 6C. Get there."

The line went dead before Kell could respond. It remained dead when they tried to call it back.

Kell looked at Alejandro, their visor's eyes plainly baffled.

"Who . . .?" Alejandro asked.

"No clue." Kell almost sounded shaken.

"You don't recognize the voice?" Alejandro said. Kell shook their head.

Sheila, having finally realized the brief call was over, turned her attention back to Kell and Alejandro. "So what was that all about?" she asked glibly.

"No idea," Kell said. "Some guy told us to be at the docks tonight."

Sheila's head slowly turned to Alejandro. "This some Speaker bullshit?"

"I'd be quite surprised," he said, fully honest. "This isn't at all how we'd operate. I take it you don't get calls like that often."

"Of course not," Kell said. They looked up, glancing at the docks. "Does somebody want us on a boat? How're we gonna get on it?"

"Wait, you're taking directions from some random call?" Sheila asked.

Instead of an answer, she received a tap on the shoulder. She jumped, reaching for her sword. Her grip loosened when she saw the older vian man with a harpoon standing in front of her, visibly concerned about the startle he gave her.

"Terribly, terribly sorry," he said, "were you in the middle of something?"

"I'm afraid we were," Alejandro said, gently gesturing for him to leave.

"Oh, well, I see. But you said something about getting to Rinculo?"

Kell glanced at Sheila. She had indeed said something while Alejandro was trying to get information--and said it quite loudly. "Why do you ask?" they said. "Do you know a route or something?"

"No, no, I was hoping you did. I teach a course up there, and classes start tomorrow. Need to get up there quite urgently. Bit of a pickle I'm in, you see."

"Wait," Sheila said. "You're a professor? In Rinculo. A day's boat ride away. Your class starts tomorrow. And you're out here? Today? *Fishing*?"

The vian furrowed his feathery brow. "It's the best season. Impeccable waters this time of year."

Sheila sighed and started walking away. "Whatever. Good luck with your problems."

Kell, shrugging, walked off with her, leaving Alejandro behind. He gave the vian a more apologetic shrug of his own. "Sorry," he said. "She can be a bit judgmental at times. I suppose, if we manage to get there before you, we could let them know about your predicament."

The professor chuckled, waving Alejandro off. "Oh, they know. Gave 'em a ring about it. Besides, the kids know what they're signing up for! Fulton Time is a famous phenomenon around campus, you know."

The boast, curious as it was, clicked something in Alejandro's mind. "Excuse me? You're Dr. Fulton? Dr. Tobias Fulton?"

"The one and only!"

Oh, he could be useful. A sly smile sat on Alejandro's face. "Well, if you've nowhere to be, perhaps we could talk for a moment."

C

Sheila roamed Gauvencia's smooth brick roads with forceful purpose, as if late for something, but soon started doubling back as arbitrary turns became circles. Clearly, she had no destination in mind. Kell, despite this, could barely keep up.

"I'm pretty sure you lost him," Kell said as Sheila slowed, bogged down by the foot traffic of a posh commercial district.

Sheila stopped entirely. "I wasn't trying to shake him."

"Then what are you trying to do?" Kell strained to keep the question from being too much of an accusation.

"Don't know," Sheila said, frustrated. "But I sense a trap. I don't trust that guy."

"You don't trust anyone."

"And you do?"

Kell shrugged and glanced down the road. Alejandro was approaching, still a ways away. "Not like I have a choice. Just, stay close, alright?"

Sheila and Alejandro exchanged distant waves. "Gonna be hard to kill him," she said quietly.

"Is it ever easy?"

"Sorry about that," Alejandro said as he came within earshot. "He's a talkative one. So then," he turned his focus to Kell, "what's our plan?"

Kell hesitated. "We don't have a plan, do we? We don't have any other way out of Farolé. We're gonna have to follow that call." They were unhappy with the idea.

"We're seriously taking some random directions?" Sheila complained quietly, as though the call was supposed to be some closely-guarded secret. "We don't even know who made that call."

"Do you have anything better?"

Alejandro stepped in. "I may be able to help, then."

"Oh, is this how you Speakers operate?"

"*Former* Speaker, Sheila. And no, this is quite unusual." He pulled a keychain, stuffed with a variety of keys, from his suit pocket. "Fortunately, I do have this. A perk of my old job. I can get us into any building run by Farolé, or by Gauvencia itself, for that matter. This has been my home, after all."

"How perfectly convenient," Sheila said, dripping with sarcasm.

Alejandro rolled his eyes. "Sheila."

"So you can get us on the docks, no problem?" Kell said.

"The port authority is frustratingly independent," Alejandro said, composing himself, "but the waterways aren't. They empty right at the shore. Follow them along, loop back, we're at the docks."

"And you expect us to play along?" Sheila said.

"Sheila." Alejandro spoke as if addressing a child. "Unlike the two of us, you're perfectly safe here. The Speakers would have no interest in you, and if they did happen to investigate . . . well, it's painfully obvious how much you despise me. You'd talk. You might even make a friend. If you want to stay in Gauvencia and just go about your life, you're welcome to do so. Encouraged, even."

"I'm not leaving Kell behind," she replied sternly.

"Then we should make sure our supplies are in order," Alejandro said with a flippant wave of his hand. "And perhaps be quick about it. Our fourth is waiting."

"Our fourth?" Kell asked, fearing they had missed some conversation.

"Yes. Dr. Fulton." A sly smile grew on Alejandro's face.

Sheila grumbled. "This isn't some social call, you idiot, this is dangerous."

"Agreed," Alejandro said. "Which is why I recruited him. We're quite likely walking into a trap."

"Of course we are," Sheila shouted, "it's your trap!"

"Good thing I'm known to be so disarming." Alejandro took his turn with sarcasm. "Especially when we're the disposable ones."

"Excuse me?" Sheila said with a glower.

With a flick of his shoulders, Alejandro's suit jacket straightened out. "Dr. Fulton is a bargaining chip." Alejandro's voice had shifted to a more upright and professional tone. "If there's any sort of trap, it's clearly meant to ensnare Kell. You and I, Sheila, we're nothing to worry about. Disposable collateral. We live or die, nobody cares. We have no celebrity, no status, nothing that would rally people. We are nobody. But if an internationally recognized expert on summons from the University at Port Mab is injured or abducted, well. That would change our adversary's calculus, would it not?"

"Wait." Sheila pieced together what he was suggesting. "Dr. Fulton is the fisher guy? Really? *Him*?"

Kell put their good hand on their helmet's forehead. "Alejandro." They spoke slowly, frustration creeping into their voice. "I thought you wanted to earn our trust. But you're not. I'm with you on the waterway idea, sure. It'll suck, but, fine. I've gone through worse. But we don't know that Fulton guy. We don't know how much of a risk he is. To just bring him on out of nowhere is . . ." Kell's grumble barely left their helmet. "We're straining as a team already. We can't have someone else in the group."

"He won't be in the group," Alejandro said coolly. "If there is no trap, then we've simply escorted him to the university. A good deed done. But if"--he gave Sheila a stern glance--"*if* this is a trap, then he's not 'in the group.' He's a tool."

"And if Fulton is the trap?"

"We kill him." Alejandro showed no hesitation.

Kell conceded with a wave and a sigh. Alejandro was simply more adept at putting together a plan and making his case. While he went off to a chemist's shop for supplies, they joined Sheila in sulking outside.

Sheila's right, they thought. *Shoulda got rid of the asshole. The nerve. Going over my head like that. Well, our head? Sheila's the leader, she should be pissed about it.* They glanced at their grumpy traveling companion. *Well, more pissed than usual.*

D

Dr. Fulton could not be more conspicuous if he tried. The traffic around the unmarked stone building he was standing in front of consisted of couriers, laborers, and merchants. Everyone around him was dressed simply and practically, their coats and slacks dirtied by their work, while he stood idly in a clean tweed vest, a dark overcoat, trousers that could only be described as "loud," and sleek, professional goggles protecting dark brown eyes. He idly bounced his harpoon from one feathered hand to the other, stopping only when he noticed Alejandro approaching, Sheila and Kell reluctantly in tow.

"Dr. Fulton." Alejandro returned to his professional tone.

"Oh, please, Tobias is fine," he responded. "You've wrangled up everything you need, then?"

"Indeed, we have," Alejandro said as he unlocked the building's front door. "I will warn you; this is the city's waterways. If nothing else, we're likely to get wet."

"Well, you'll hear no complaining from me!" Tobias said.

"Will we hear anything else from you?" Sheila snapped.

Tobias chuckled, either oblivious or indifferent to her anger. "Depends on what questions you ask, my dear. I have plenty of answers."

"And we have plenty of ground to cover," Kell said. They didn't feel comfortable taking on Alejandro's business-like approach, but the acrid smell of the waterway was already making itself known. It had to be unbearable for those not wearing a helmet. They just wanted to get it over with and get on that boat.

Inside the service building, Alejandro opened a second door that sat down a flight of stairs. The crashing roar of water joined the lingering odor of mold and feces. For as bad as it was, the smell could have been much worse. It had rained upstream the day before, swelling the river, pushing away waste and debris, sloshing water into the overflow channels that ran perpendicular to the current. The footpaths and wooden bridges meant for maintenance workers were slick with water and slime, an occasional pile of trash and bone coagulating in a corner. The beams of wood and stone that held Gauvencia above its waste were equally poor hand grips, coated with smooth and brittle fungus.

Alejandro flicked his fingers and formed a flame of vapor. It would easily offer enough illumination to make out a path, but Kell knew they could offer something better. They grabbed their shattered rod and lit the focus with a ball of burning vapor, holding it ahead as a potent torch, rendering nearly an entire city block's underside visible at once.

They led the group through the winding channels. The paths mirrored the streets above, aside from the sluice gates and debris that blocked off channels with little obvious rhyme or reason. The surface of the city was orderly, as it had dumped all of its chaos below.

As Kell rounded a corner, Sheila grabbed their cloak. She gestured for Kell to extinguish their light. Hesitantly, they did, and almost immediately a muffled shout came from the distance.

" . . .light . . .check?" Though most of it was drowned out by the flowing water, it was clear enough to Kell that they had been spotted. They gave a quick glance to their allies, barely visible even as their visor augmented their sight in the dark.

"What's going on?" Tobias said at a normal volume, only to be immediately shushed.

A dim light emerged from a distant channel. It passed by, moving towards the sea. Kell hoped it was just someone doing some kind of maintenance work, as wishful and naive a hope they knew it would be.

"We gotta move," Kell whispered. They lit their rod again, a much dimmer flame this time. It might give away their location, but that was better than being ambushed in total darkness.

The group routed around a closed sluice gate that, judging by Alejandro's complicated gesturing, seemed to be near the docks. The tunnels had begun to show signs of twilight breaking in. Faintly illuminated, in the middle of a slick channel free of flowing water, was a lone wrought-iron chair. It sat plainly, openly, intentionally. There was no way it had washed up in such a perfect position.

"Well, you came to us, then!" The voice of a confident young man, undercut with a playful taunt, echoed from nearby. "Might as well get comfortable."

"For what?" Alejandro shouted, looking around for the source.

The sloppy footfalls of sodden boots approached from the shadows. A gaunt figure casually juggled a knife as he emerged, dressed in dark, damaged clothing. His orange eyes and flat, scale-covered teal face glistened in the twilight as he cracked a toothy grin.

"Oh, I wasn't expecting a party." The sahagin sized up the group from a distance. "And what a party. Scar! Nina! Get over here, we got visitors."

"What are sahagins doing here?" Alejandro muttered to himself.

"What does it look like?" the leader sneered.

"Hey, we don't want trouble," Sheila said. Her voice was confrontational, the end of the sentence leaving itself unsaid. *So get out of our way.*

"Tough shit!" the sahagin shouted. He glanced at Kell and smirked. "You *are* trouble!"

The sahagin took a quick lunge at Kell. They dove to the side, leaving the sahagin's blade to only rip into the edge of their cloak. Sheila swung her sword to force the sahagin to back up.

"Kell, fire!" she shouted as they got back to their feet. Kell was already preparing to imbue her blade with flame. Not that they thought she'd call out for it, or that she'd do it so readily.

Sheila stepped towards the attackers, her blade held low and defensively, poised to parry into a strike. Tobias kept near Kell, standing with a slight squat, ready to move. Alejandro, knives drawn, took glances behind the group. They were at a clear tactical disadvantage. The sahagin's reinforcements could come from any angle.

"Nice tricks, mage," the sahagin spat with bitter contempt. He sent jets of watery vapor at Sheila's sword, pushing it back towards her body. The flames held. "Got anything new?"

Kell didn't reply. They didn't want a fight, but they also didn't want a conversation. A movement from their left caught their eye. Tobias was getting fidgety. *He didn't sign up for this.* Kell held their staff out in front of him, subtly gesturing him back. Tobias didn't seem to react, so Kell sidestepped in front of him.

They glared at the attacking sahagin, watching his movements, as a larger sahagin emerged behind him, carrying a sword on par with Sheila's and bearing a nickname's worth of scars on his face and arms. A third sahagin with darker scales followed, appearing more hesitant. She held out a wooden rod with a metal branch that swirled around the grip and up to the focus, where it joined in a double-headed point. It was a dead ringer for the first rod Kell was issued as a vapormage. Those rods were all retired years ago, but clearly, some had escaped destruction.

"Havoc, look out!" the large sahagin shouted. Alejandro had sensed an opening and threw a dagger at the sahagin leader, but his move was spotted and deftly dodged.

"Appreciate it, Scar," Havoc said.

Sheila tried to take advantage of Havoc's position, swinging her sword in the widest arc the waterway would allow, but Scar's blade met hers, stopping the strike with a piercing metallic clang. Alejandro and Havoc sized each other up, dueling in close, taking opportunistic kicks and swings of their knives. Kell kept an eye on Nina. She was doing little in comparison, as if she had no pretense about being a fighter like the others. Yet she was defensive, not passive; any effort Kell made to turn the tide in the two conflicts was immediately interrupted by Nina's own vapor.

Alejandro held his own but seemed to be losing the duel with Havoc. The sahagin, comfortable in the cramped and wet setting, managed enough of a feint to get the upper hand, knocking the hunn off balance before delivering a strong slash to his abdomen. A bright red tear appeared on Alejandro's shirt. As quickly as the bleeding appeared, it subsided. Tobias had been watching, waiting for the right moment, and had healed the wound. Kell flushed with relief, having been spared the need to change their focus from offensive spells. *World expert on summons*, they thought. *Of course he knows a spell or two.*

Tobias used his harpoon as a rod, focusing durable shields of vapor onto the group. Scar, seeming to realize the tide was turning, swung more aggressively at Sheila. The aggression made an opening. Sheila parried, controlling the weight of the swords, and connected a grazing, burning blow on the sahagin, adding another mark to his body.

"Scar's hurt!" Nina yelled, terror seeping into her voice.

"Then Mend him!" Havoc shouted, his grin staying wide. "Sahagins fight to the death!"

Kell did not want to hear those words, even if they knew that was the only way the fight would go. The sahagins weren't reasonable--at least, their leader wasn't. There could be no negotiating. Kell could only fall onto their duty as a soldier. Soldiers fight. Soldiers kill. Soldiers die or live with their orders. Never mind if they were reluctant or eager. And for a Cymonian soldier, killing some sahagins was always expected to be an easy order to live with.

Kell fired a Bind spell at Scar. Sharply warped air moved too fast for Nina to intercept it. She retaliated by knocking Kell to the ground with a concussive blast, but they had done enough. Scar's limbs seized up. Sheila took advantage and struck squarely in his chest with a deep, fatal slash. Nina screamed. Sheila swung at her next, felling her with a glancing blow. Havoc barely realized his comrades had fallen before Alejandro pushed him over and sliced his throat with practiced precision.

The group collected themselves, breathing heavily and checking for additional wounds. Kell staggered over to where Nina fell, the wound across her chest still smoldering. Something was amiss. When they got close, they heard a faint groan. They knelt down over her, gently setting their splintered rod on the ground. The air around Nina was thick with the residue of spellcasting, a vague metallic smell that tried to fight against the sting of waste and water. Twilight bled in, highlighting a look of acceptance and defeat that consumed Nina's flat, scaly face.

"May your ghost become the wind, Nina," Kell gently whispered.

Nina strained to see an expressionless visor above her. She exhaled faintly. Her blood-shot eyes closed. With a jolt of electrified vapor, her heart stopped.

"Was that the trap, then?" Sheila said loudly, between strenuous breaths.

Kell flinched. The lights of their visor's eyes lit again.

"Certainly came off as one," Tobias said.

"We're not even at the docks," Alejandro said with a sore groan. "We don't have much time. Let's go." Leaning against the slick walls, he righted himself and started running towards the sea. Tobias followed closely behind.

Kell remained where they were, kneeling over Nina's corpse.

"Kell! Move!" Sheila ordered.

Kell grabbed the rod Nina had used and pried it from her lifeless hand. "I'm coming, I'm coming," they said as they stood, snapping the rod to the holder on their back.

E

An open sluice gate emptied onto a firm beach. The group was close to the docks but still had a short run and a fence to scale before they could reach their destination. And they would need to run. The time was 21:44. They were late.

Only one ship was docked, a massive cargo freighter lined with Banner Goods livery. If it wasn't docked at 6C, then the four had definitely been led far astray. "That's our ride!" Alejandro shouted, confident, before grabbing the top of the fence with a single leap and pulling himself over. Sheila and Tobias followed in kind, each with a little less grace than the one before them. Kell opted to put their borrowed rod to use and catapulted themselves with a gust of wind, clearing the fence without touching it.

Alejandro quickly assessed the docks, still well-lit despite the closure. There were several levels of pier across the complex's width, to more easily support multiple sizes and shapes of vessel. The tiers were subdivided further with fences and gates, to keep commercial traffic flowing seamlessly while also allowing individuals to safely access ferries and the like. It was a surprisingly efficient setup that, to most people, made perfect sense when going to or from their boat. It was also awful for anyone trying to storm through the breadth of the system, full of twisting turns and blind corners.

By the time the group saw specific signs pointing to 6C, the clock nearby claimed the time was 21:47. The group was exhausted, but close. A few more turns through winding corridors and they should be at the dock at the exact time they were told.

What then? Kell could barely form the thought, focused and tired as they were, but they couldn't ignore the uncertainty fizzling in their chest. They had no idea who actually made that call, if it came from the ship's crew or someone pulling an absurd prank. And Banner's operations were famously refined, down to the weight of ships. There was no way the group would go unnoticed. And yet, they had managed to sneak across the border by tying their boat to one of Banner's, and that stunt had seemingly gone unnoticed.

The four rounded a corner and slid to an abrupt halt. An oversized strix was standing in their path. It took one look at the group and roared.

"Oh, bloody hell." Alejandro grabbed his knives, still slick with sahagin blood.

"This was it!" Kell said. "In the mountains."

"I thought you killed it?" Sheila said.

"Must be another." Kell could see the boat in port 6C, the Banner-branded freedom meters away. The creature was not going to let them near it. "It's just a summon. Act erratic, throw it off."

"No." Tobias stared at the strix. His voice was suddenly stern. "This one will adapt."

"I know how to handle these," Kell said.

"I know more," Tobias said. He looked up at the strix's light blue eyes as they darted mindlessly around. "Who are you?" he muttered.

The strix roared again, cutting off the inquiry. Kell stuck to their original plan, peppering the summon with random elemental spells. Even if Tobias was right, they didn't want to do anything that they'd seen set off its programming. The docks were more stable than the mountainside, so they shouldn't collapse if this strix also started shaking the ground. But the possibility gnawed at Kell's mind. And the boat was *right there*.

Sheila, a bit less reserved with her options, swung her sword madly against the summon's legs. It stamped and kicked in retaliation, knocking her across the dock. Tobias leapt, barely slicing the strix's shoulder with his harpoon. The summon sagged and staggered as he gracelessly pulled it out. Alejandro used his knives like ice axes to climb along the strix's side, pulling out streams of vapor smoke before it shook him down to the ground.

As the massive summon started to succumb, Kell looked over to the cargo ship. It was moving. They shouted and started running for the next pier, hoping to catch the ship as it passed by. The boat's stern approached as Kell reached the end of the pier. Without hesitation, they leapt for the boat's deck. The rest followed closely behind, Tobias barely making it in time.

Kell squirmed and rolled, grasping their right arm in pain. It had taken more of the landing than they'd intended. They groaned steadily, suppressing the desire to scream it out. Alejandro groaned from a similarly rough landing and the impact of breaking Tobias's awkward fall onto deck.

Sheila, meanwhile, had tumbled smoothly aboard and was already back on her feet, getting her bearings. She lightly kicked Kell's boot to get their attention. "You okay? How's the arm?"

Kell breathed deeply, looking out at the sharp lights of Gauvencia as the boat took to open sea. "Been better," they groaned. "Been better."

COMING THIS FALL

The Langley family's new summon is helpful, kind, diligent, and . . . a total troublemaker! Kid-friendly antics all over in this brand new sitcom about a summon with a mind of her own.

Florence Salo and Maxwell Devos star in:

RIKKI THE STRIX

Available exclusively on BV1, after *The New Adventures of Raurack*

CHAPTER SIX

C aptain Joyce Flannery, Banner Cargo Ship DE-728, designation *Tane Mahuta*, knew nothing about the call Kell received earlier that day. She knew nothing of their mission into Bessetrae or their slip into Farolé off the back of Ship BA-019. She had been told nothing of the massive, violent strixes or of the war they supposedly indicated.

All she was told upon receiving clearance to resume her route was that, should the boat have stowaways, they must be brought to the bridge and crew support must be called. When a jaculus-style summon monitoring the deck approached her, flailing its tiny scaly wings in an alarm loop, she sighed and followed upper management's instructions. Whatever it was that brought the annoyance into her world, she knew better than to question it.

She called out reassurances that the group was expected, and eventually found them damp with sweat and sea mist near where they had landed. The jaculus, its programmed alarm process complete, returned to its standard patrol in front of the group. It immediately detected their presence and shrieked again. Joyce had to escort the jaculus as well as the stowaways back to the ship's towering bridge.

The bridge was empty, save for a pair of ordinary tanuki-style summons that stood at different points of the broad control panel, chittering back and forth, handling the rote aspects of navigating the ship. Joyce dropped herself into her seat and started following her instructions, leaving the four to lean against the back wall. The bridge was fairly narrow and lacked any seats besides Joyce's. Kell opted to sit on the floor. Tobias slumped onto the ground next to them. Sheila and Alejandro stayed on their feet with differing levels of stubbornness in their stances. Sheila was beyond exhausted, but there was no world where she sat down before Alejandro did.

Joyce spun around in her chair. "Alright, you four," she said, "get up. This is yours." She pushed a button on the panel in front of her, lighting up a small green light. "*Tane Mahuta*, Captain Flannery speaking."

"At ease, Captain." A calm, masculine voice emerged from the control panel. "Video, please?"

"Aye." She pressed another button and the wall behind the group began to glow. An image soon appeared: an older hunn man, grey hair flecked with black, alert brown eyes behind his sleek rimless spectacles. The slowly focusing image made him look artificial, like clay.

"There we are," he said. "Thank you, Captain. You must be Kell's brigade. Jakob Banner, pleasure to meet you."

The four nodded politely towards the wall. None of them knew the face, but they knew the name. Jakob Banner was impossible not to know, though he rarely appeared to represent Banner Goods in person, leaving his contact with the outside world to statements and press releases appearing in newspapers. He rarely gave interviews, and even more rarely to anyone who would dare ask why he was so hard to see, but his attitude was clear. He had a very, very large business to run, the largest in Linnute. He was busy.

For most people, that explanation was plenty. Sheila certainly never gave much thought to the man behind the company. Jakob was much more interested in seeing the four than the other way around.

"Pleasure, Mr. Banner." Alejandro stepped forward and put on his diplomatic voice. "We thank you for the assistance. It sounds like this rescue was coordinated, and the captain did well to execute."

"Banner Goods is known for quality execution," Jakob said. He leaned forward, as if examining the video. "I can't help but notice, there's a fourth with you?"

"You expected otherwise?" Alejandro said.

"I did. Is that . . . Dr. Fulton? Of Port Mab?"

The fatigue in Tobias's body vanished in an instant, his face beaming. "You're darn right it is!"

Jakob laughed heartily. "Well, everybody is lucky today. Dr. Fulton, your research work is remarkable. We wouldn't have the world of strixes and tanukis that we do without it."

"Oh," Tobias chuckled, "we just proved what you could do! It's your people who keep doing it so impressively. If you'd like to talk shop with the source, I'm more than happy to!"

"Wonderful! We will want to sit down at some point, but I am a bit pressed for time this evening. Kell, I suppose I should quickly explain why I've offered my ship to you and your folks.

"Running such a large company means I have to be quite particular with my time. Prioritize, you see. So I've prioritized our international connections. After all, leaders of nations need to work with leaders of industry. And while things have been just fine as of late with President Bathroy, and Her Majesty, and everyone else, really . . . Mister Lyon's gone silent."

"Can't say I've ever spoken with him," Kell said.

"Of course, of course," Jakob continued. "But then I heard this talk of the vapormages going away, which has some implications for our contracts. But I've been able to verify the rumors, even though it's not public knowledge. If the Prime Minister is hiding something from the public, and not honoring his agreements . . . As they say, Kell, something is rotten in the state. But truly, you could not have wandered into my store at a better time. Thank you for the business, by the way, as always."

"Sure, sure. What happened to the other vapormages?" Kell asked.

"I haven't a clue," Jakob said. "That's a matter for your commanders, I would assume. I only hope your leaders haven't run afoul of our contracts."

"So what exactly are you asking of us?" Sheila said, finding the "quick" explanation was starting to ramble on.

"The ship that you're on is headed to Rinculo. Port Mab, as it happens, funny enough. It'll dock at 7:17 tomorrow morning. Take some time there to rest. You four look like you've been through a lot. My people will be in touch to ferry you all safely to Cymona. Find out what's going on with Lyon and report to me."

"All of us?" Tobias said, sounding more intrigued than concerned.

"Don't see why not," Jakob said. "You seem like a bunch of go-getters. Problem solvers. I'd imagine you work well together."

"And what if we say no?" Sheila said.

Jakob chuckled. "Well, I can't imagine you would."

"We won't," Alejandro said. "It seems a reasonable enough arrangement. But it's also wise to acknowledge where everyone stands in a negotiation, is it not?"

"Ah, boy," Jakob said with his voice dipping, "never show your full hand when negotiating. Gives you no chance to adapt."

"Fair enough," Alejandro politely disagreed.

"Well then," Jakob perked up. "I take it we have a deal? Good to hear. As I said, my people will get you into Cymona. I trust you four will get in front of Lyon and figure out what's going on. Looking forward to working with you."

With a bowing nod, Jakob Banner disappeared from the wall. The bridge of the *Tane Mahuta* went dim.

As the call finished, Captain Joyce let in the jaculus that had been walking the deck looking for stowaways. She opened a reference manual and flicked through its pages repeatedly, a hand out to shift the summon's programming.

After a moment, she pushed the manual aside. "Alright," she said, "follow the jack. We've got a spare cabin you can crash in."

"Just the one?" Sheila asked.

Joyce rolled her tired eyes. "You could sleep in the hall."

Sheila, also too tired for an argument, followed the group as the summon led them below deck.

B

Tobias was the first to step into the narrow, wood-paneled quarters with sparse bunks on either wall. He tossed his possessions on a top bunk and knelt down to pet the jaculus. "Thanks, little guy!" he said, rubbing its scaly head playfully.

The jaculus, having not been programmed to respond to affection, stood completely still before abruptly waddling off.

Alejandro sat on the bunk beneath Tobias's and unbuttoned his shirt, getting a better view of his wound. The slash was gone, barely scarred, with only a few bruises against his regular tanned complexion.

"You work well, professor," he said. "Kudos."

"Oh, it's no matter," Tobias said. "Glad for a bit of excitement, at my age."

"You sound like you enjoyed it," Sheila said.

Tobias shrugged. "Not in so strong a word, but perhaps. Though politics aren't exactly my specialist subject. Won't be much help there."

"I've seen my fair share of convoluted politics," Alejandro said, buttoning up his bloodied shirt. "This seems like much more than another one of those stories. I've heard too many contradictions in the past few days. Hardly any of this adds up. Something is rotten, indeed."

Sheila sighed, leaning against a locker near the door. "Nobody believes this guy, right?"

Alejandro cocked an eyebrow. "Me?"

"Banner. He doesn't add up because he's bullshitting. Has to be. The guy's got a giant corporation under his thumb, he's got all the resources in the world, why would he want us?"

"He doesn't want us," Kell said. "He wants *me*."

"And why would he want you?" Tobias said. "No offense meant, of course."

"No, you're right," Kell said. "I was trying to piece it together while he went on, but I've got nothing. I mean, I'm a vapormage, sure, but I'm nothing compared to other folks in the unit."

"Assuming there is a unit," Alejandro said.

"You glued your own arm back on," Sheila said, "don't tell me that's not impressive."

Tobias perked up. "Come again? You reattached it?"

Kell rubbed their right arm as they moved it, opening and closing their hand slowly. They let out a soft, involuntary groan of pain. "Yeah. Bind to hold it in place, Mend to keep the blood flowing. Kept me from dying."

Tobias looked skeptical. "An amputation wouldn't be fatal."

Kell's head twitched, as if they heard something sharp and sudden. "Would be if I bled out or went septic. Besides, it's Mend. Not going to hold forever."

"Don't sell yourself short, Kell. I was preparing that Mend for Al since your blades were drawn. To heal yourself under such stress is remarkable mastery! You kids, I swear. May I see the arm? I'd love to see your work."

"Sorry." Kell sounded pained. "Suit stays on, helmet stays on."

"Might I ask why?"

"Long story. Excuse me." They got up and walked out of the cabin, their left hand supporting their head.

Tobias watched indifferently as they left. "Mystery for another time, then." He shrugged.

"I should at least go check on them," Alejandro said.

"No, you shouldn't," Sheila commanded. "I know Kell. They'll be back."

"Fair enough," Alejandro muttered. "Something's certainly wrong with that helmet, though. I'd be curious to know exactly what. And what's under their helmet, for that matter. They've *never* removed it?"

"They get pissy about it," Sheila said. "I've asked, they acted like it'd kill me to see."

"Don't see how that would happen," Alejandro said.

"'Cause it wouldn't. Been trying to figure out what they're hiding. I'm this close to just trying to rip that helmet off myself."

Alejandro rolled onto his bunk and stared up, a pensive look on his face as the ship rolled with the waves. "Hmm. Could they be poisoned, perhaps?"

Sheila considered the idea. "Maybe. Don't know."

"No, no," Tobias said, "couldn't be. I've worked with victims of vapor poisoning in my day. Even in mild cases, when there's little physical effect and all the cognitive functions are fine and dandy, speech is still the first thing to go."

"Every time?" Sheila said.

"Every time. However you ingest the vapor, it gets to the throat and seems to just shred it. Larynx, esophagus, everything. It's why the victims usually die of starvation. They can't get anything solid down anymore."

Sheila reflexively swallowed. "Grim."

Alejandro nodded. "And very unlikely, given that. Could be they're . . . disfigured in some way," he offered. "They're just ashamed of how they look."

"You would just say that," Sheila said.

"Shame is a powerful force," Alejandro mused.

"For normal people," Sheila sighed.

Tobias's face grew concerned. "They could be a summon."

Sheila sputtered out a dismissive laugh. "Come on, doc, they don't act like a summon."

"They don't act like a *familiar*," Tobias said. "Though I'm happy to see them flourish, it's long annoyed me that Banner took our work and marketed them as summons. They're merely refined familiars. That strix on the docks that we were forced to confront? That was a summon. A true summon. There was definitely something flawed about it, to make it attack us, but it was far smarter than a familiar." Tobias took a glance at the cabin door. "And producing a summon like Kell would be possible if--"

"Doc, I saw them bleed. Okay? I saw their arm *sliced open*. Summons, familiars, whatever, they don't bleed like that."

"So you did see their arm!" Tobias said. "What did you see?"

"What do you mean? I saw their arm cut open, I saw blood, and . . . bone, and muscle, and . . ."

Sheila sat on a bunk to let her stomach settle. Kell's bloody arm flashed in her mind, the sanguine red and bone white so bright it turned the rest of the boat into a blurry, dusty black, like charcoal. The image suddenly shifted to the deep gash she had inflicted on Scar earlier, the cauterized sahagin skin framing the muscles and organs she had exposed; it shifted again to a wild fox, gutted and skinned, that she had to kill to eat; it shifted again to the Winters' War, to a Cymonian knight she had pummeled, ripped the armor from, cut open and bleeding out so he wouldn't do the same to her, cursing her past his dying breath.

The cabin went silent. Sheila blinked and breathed until her muscles returned to her. "Good night," she said, rolling on her bunk to face the wall.

C

SCREEEEEEEEEEECH

The piercing pitch in Kell's head bubbled and faded with rhythmic persistence. Their communicator was loudly failing. They wandered the decks, the engines' vibrations pushing a discord through their body. Every door they passed was closed, though they doubted all of the cabins could be occupied. The ship hardly had any crew. A pair of unfamiliar voices having a loud argument over cards in a common room proved that there were at least some hands, but Kell refused to believe there were many.

One room had been left open. A supply room, from first glance, the walls lined with shelves dotted with nondescript boxes of myriad sizes. "PROPERTY OF BANNER GOODS -- NOT FOR RESALE" was stamped on each one. Kell had no idea what could be in them, nor did they particularly care. Their attention was, instead, on the door. They stepped into the storage room and examined the door carefully to determine how securely it would lock. They turned the heavy deadbolt a few times, receiving a loud thunk of confirmation with each twist. Once satisfied, they shut the door tightly and locked themself in.

They sat on the cold metal floor, unwilling to disrupt any boxes around them, and exhaled deeply. They reached up with both arms to the sides of their helmet. Their thumbs found the hidden clasps on either side, situated just above their neck, and with a single loud snap released them. Their helmet came loose. They took it off, dropping it in their lap, and deeply inhaled, breathing out the ocean air like a drag on a cigarette. The air was musty and heavy, the hint of seawater mingling with the miasma of engine fuel, but it was still the closest thing to fresh air they had tasted in a week.

Kell sat still for several moments, their eyes adjusting to the true light of the cargo ship. They could have easily fallen asleep in such a position. The steady footsteps of somebody walking past pulled them back into alertness, while the chirp echoing out of their helmet reminded them of their task. They pulled a small multitool from their satchel and flipped open a blade from it. They knew their helmet. It was a part of them, like a blacksmith's hammer or anvil. They knew where everything was. They cut a slit in the lining and exposed the technology within. With a bit of force and a bit of leverage, the screaming communicator, no larger than their thumb, popped out of their helmet and fell to the ground. They rose, looming over the sigil, before crushing it under their foot like a cockroach.

D

The *Tane Mahuta* docked in Port Mab at 7:16 the next morning. Kell and Alejandro were both awake and ready to disembark; Sheila and Tobias, each for their own reasons, took more persuading to come above deck. Still, all four were off the boat before the familiars scurrying on the deck could offload any cargo.

They left the docks and made their way to a clearing on the edge of the nearby university's campus. A handful of gazebos with small braziers in their centers dotted the field. Kell lit one and the group huddled around. The isle of Rinculo was north of the mainland, and the cold was steadily descending.

"Well then, professor," Alejandro said, "I take it you have some business to address."

"Hmm?" Tobias was still half asleep. "Oh, yes, yes. Of course. The dean will be quite surprised."

"Didn't you say your classes start today?" Kell said.

"Indeed. 7:30, sharp."

"You *really* ought to get going, then," they said.

"Bah!" Tobias waved them off with a dismissive chuckle. "It'll work itself out. Besides, my time is now spoken for. Though, since we have the day free, wouldn't hurt to show you kids around the campus, would it? Come along! The place will be absolutely buzzing today." He got up, abruptly full of vigor, and started rushing towards the campus center.

Sheila jabbed Alejandro with her elbow. "Not part of the group, huh?" she said. Alejandro glared back with equal displeasure. Rather than argue, the three gradually got up and followed the vian professor to his home university.

The campus had a way of defining the town. Port Mab radiated out from it, all roads leading to the classical stone buildings that made up the core of the university. More modern buildings, taller and built of wood and glass, filled the gaps between, housing the more intricate facilities for vapor chemistry or other high-tech disciplines. Even the dock yard had a way of feeling like university property, dotted with niche and incidental facilities as it was. The space felt like a world unto itself, with only the chill autumnal air and falling leaves tying it to the rest of the world.

The crowds bustling from building to building skewed young. Their wardrobes and demeanors had the tidiness of privilege with the smallest of rebellious accents--an exaggerated playful walk, or a willfully mismatched outfit, the kind of rebelling done by people who know they should but don't know how. Students of a particular nation tended to group together, clustering on more local or racial lines if enough were around to warrant it. Groups of Zeimatians, dressed in their nation's religious garb, walked and chatted as lightly as the secular Cymonians. Passing close in front of Tobias, a trio of gnolls hurried towards a building together. He noted the behavior: Gnolls always seemed to stick together on campus, usually three or four at a time, shying away from the other human species as if out of fear. Tobias had never heard of any incidents that would warrant such fear, he was quick to mention. He also noted that, while his students were mostly hunn and vian with a few gnolls, he never had any sahagin students. Officially, The University at Port Mab welcomed them, as it welcomed anyone who could cover the tuition. None ever came.

Tobias brought the group to the Miranda Hall, one of the older stone buildings, old enough that its vapor-driven heating system was once again on the fritz. The ground floor had little to show off, but upstairs was Tobias's office. He opened the door to reveal piles upon messy piles of papers and books. On the right side of the room was another elder vian, sitting at his desk and examining a neat stack of paperwork.

"Ah, Dr. Charmchi, hope I'm not interrupting," Tobias said.

The vian looked up and rubbed his eyes. "Always are, Fulton. I thought you were in Farolé."

"Indeed I was! And they snapped the border shut on me. But these three helped me get out in one piece."

Dr. Charmchi looked at the group and clicked his beak. "Ah. My sympathies."

Sheila chuckled, having found her favorite among the faculty.

"Elliot and I go way, way back," Tobias said. "We partnered on a project around sigil casting after I published that paper on familiars. If you want to know anything about military history and strategy in Linnute, he's your man."

"And if you need to know anything about familiars and summoning and all that," Dr. Charmchi said, "you're better off asking Cassandra. But I suppose Toby here could help."

"Appreciate it," Kell said courteously.

"Ah, of course. A vapormage," Dr. Charmchi said. "You're a long way from home, aren't you?"

"We'll be getting them back soon," Tobias said.

"'We'?" Dr. Charmchi rolled his chair back, laughing. "I'm sure the dean will be happy. You three can keep him as long as you need."

"But before I go . . ." Tobias ducked into the office, sliding aside piles of books as tall as himself and disappearing into a corner of the room.

"Now what are you doing?" Dr. Charmchi groaned.

"Do you remember that prop they brought around when we were doing sigil experiments? That we just kept hammering at over and over?"

"You kept that thing?"

Tobias emerged from behind a cabinet, triumphantly holding a spear in his hand. The weapon had been ornate, once, but Tobias's choice of words was no exaggeration. Its lines were crooked, beaten up. "Of course I did!" he called out.

Dr. Charmchi shook his head quietly, turning to Kell. "Careful. He's 62 years old, still acts like a damned boy. Though I suppose he'll need it. You folks look like you've seen a fight or two."

Alejandro quickly buttoned his jacket, covering the stains of battle. "Indeed."

"It was a summon, Elliot." Tobias's voice was the most serious it had been.

Dr. Charmchi sighed and rolled back to his desk, unconvinced. "Just be careful, Toby. You don't know as much as you think. Oh, and maybe leave that thing with the others if you're going to the dean's office. Don't want you killing her."

The dean's office sat in the next building over, a modern structure with elegant architectural lines and vapor heaters that actually worked consistently. As Tobias approached the office, he handed Alejandro his spear with the casual attitude of a man checking in his coat at the theater. He sauntered confidently into the office, closing the door behind him, muffling the sounds of conversation. The tone, though, was still clear. The conversation quickly turned into an argument. Between the shouts, Kell heard their mobile going off.

"Hello?" they answered. They put the call on speaker; nobody was around to eavesdrop anyway. The buzz of the campus had retreated to the classrooms.

"Kell?" a tired voice responded. "Good. Omar. Word from Banner is you and your buddies are hired." His tone was matter-of-fact, routine. He had done this too many times before.

"Hired? For what?"

"Depends what you don't fuck up. Crystal's show is pretty well-tuned."

"Crystal?" Alejandro said, suddenly excited. "Greene?"

"Whoever that was," Omar said, "don't throw your pants off. You're at Mab, right Kell?"

"The university? Yeah."

"Good. Be down at the main quad tonight. Someone'll point you to me."

Omar hung up abruptly as another shout echoed out of the dean's office.

Kell sighed. "You'd think people would explain things more."

"That's rich, coming from you," Sheila said.

Kell had no interest in telling Sheila, yet again, that they had reasons to keep secrets. Instead, they turned to Alejandro, who was subtly bouncing on the balls of his feet. "Crystal fan, are you?" they said.

Alejandro blushed and stood still. "I'll do my best not to gush," he said with a chuckle. "It'd be very boring, I'm sure."

Kell grinned under their helmet. "It's fine. We're stuck together for now, might as well get to know each other."

"We're stuck with him too, aren't we?" Sheila gestured towards the dean's office.

Kell nodded weakly. "Banner knows he's with us."

"Hell, he knew who doc was, didn't he?" Sheila said. "Seemed a bit strange."

"To be fair," Alejandro said, "he is well-known in his field. And Banner makes the most reliable summoning toolkits out there. I wouldn't consider that much of a stretch."

"So how'd you know about him?" Kell asked.

"I'm so very interested in his work," Alejandro said, before smirking and shaking his head. "After the Winters' War, he was called upon as a consultant. We were trying to start our own vapormage unit. Nothing came of it, and I have no idea why his name was on the list."

"That sounds like a Farolian government secret," Sheila said.

A smug grin from Alejandro. "And if I were still a Speaker, I would keep it."

With a final shout, Tobias walked out of the dean's office and retrieved his spear from Alejandro.

"Well?" Kell said. "What's the story?"

"I think it's safe to say things have worked themselves out," Tobias said as a door slammed behind him. "Do we have a plan?"

"We're going to the Crystal Greene show tonight," Alejandro said, barely hiding his excitement.

Tobias chuckled. "Those are meant for students, but I suppose we've earned a bit of fun."

"No fun allowed," Sheila said. "Seems Banner's big plan to get us into Cymona without anyone noticing is to shove us on the road crew."

"That could still be fun. We have until this evening, yes? There's something I should grab from my office."

"Weren't we just in your office?" Kell said.

Tobias held up a feathery finger. "I have a much better one. Come along, kids!"

E

As they crossed the campus, Tobias told the story of his true office. Many years ago, the administration of The University at Port Mab agreed to spend some of the amassed tuition money to build the campus outward, to the east. The campus already reached to the shore, but there was a modest-sized island not far away, on the other end of a short archipelago. A set of bridges could easily be built to span the chain. After years of funding mishaps and mismanagement, the Ferdinand Hamee Memorial Bridge System finally opened. The student body hated it. There was little of any value on the opposite side, the construction quality was slipshod, the bridge's path was meandering, and to top it all off, the name was laughable. Dr. Hamee would've liked it, but the students had never liked Dr. Hamee. Of the many nicknames, "Great Bridge Ferdinand" was the least vulgar to stick.

One of the few buildings constructed on the other end of the Great Bridge Ferdinand was a circular facility wrapped in dark metal, supposedly to make some kind of architectural statement. Whatever the statement was, it had immediately been ignored and lost. Everyone simply called The Wallace J. Umbreal Memorial Library and Laboratory "The Puck" instead. The administration, naturally, tried to enforce the proper names. The Umbreal estate had paid quite a lot. But when the student body sensed a directive, it only made them rebel louder against it. The Puck was open to classes for hardly a year before the administration effectively abandoned the building, ending the argument while never admitting they had lost it.

While the rest of the faculty departed, Tobias only dug in harder. He loved The Puck. It was isolated and quiet, even more so as his colleagues left. He could stretch the practice of conjuring familiars and summons in relative peace. Sure, if anything were to go awry, he would be all on his own. So, he decided he would simply never have anything go wrong.

He opened the front door of The Puck with the ease and satisfaction of someone returning home from a long vacation. The lights inside came on quickly. Despite being abandoned, the building still looked clean. The bookshelves visible from the foyer were stocked and orderly, the many doors down the hallway all shut. It was easy for Kell to imagine lectures or experiments taking place behind any of them.

"So I must warn you." Tobias's voice echoed through the empty halls. "We're here to pick up a prototype. Everything will be fine, nothing to worry about, it just might act erratic."

Sheila rolled her eyes. "What are we fighting this time?"

"My summon! Though we won't be fighting it. Shouldn't. It's possible we will."

"You don't remember how it's programmed?" Alejandro said.

"It's a summon, not a familiar," Tobias said. "Must I go over the nature of my work?"

"We have a show to get to tonight," Sheila said, trying to dissuade him.

"Oh, then I have plenty of time!" He started walking, ignoring Sheila's implied request.

"Now, then. Familiars are masses of vapor woven into a tangible thing. You could have a familiar that's, say, a lamp or a broom, but for a long time that was it. A really skilled mage could make a broom that did its own sweeping, but when I started research, making familiars that actually resembled living creatures was so unreliable. I say, we've come a long way in forty-odd years!

"But that was just the first step, you see. Familiars don't have instincts like real animals. Like you or me. We have to program them. Oh, but what if we didn't? What if a familiar *did* have instincts? Why, you'd have a real creature, made of nothing but vapor!

"So where do instincts come from? How does even the most anatomically primitive creature have them? Jellyfish have them, you know! We spent ages digging into the question, because if we could figure that out, we could give familiars instincts of their own. But then, oh. Oh. We did one better."

"You're scaring me a bit, professor," Kell said.

"I'm sorry," Tobias said, "it's just so exciting! And it was right in these rooms that we pieced it together. We were able to find not just a driver of instinct, but that kernel of consciousness, that sense of the self, that great cosmic mystery of what makes you *you*. And it's in everything! Everything alive, I mean. We call it the canopic. And once we found it, that meant we could use vapor to interact with it. We could build spells around it."

"Like mind control?" Kell exclaimed, their visor's eyes lit wide.

"What? No, no, obviously not! The sense of self is immutable. Make all the fuss you want, a person knows who they are. If you want to change someone's mind, you don't go putzing around in there, you . . . I don't know, deliver a convincing argument or something."

"Copying, then?" Alejandro said.

"We could never quite get there," Tobias said. "The canopic is immensely intricate, and everything that has one has a subtly different one. Every person's canopic is a tiny, tiny bit different. So there were those old lock-and-key kind of spells, once you get the canopic involved those become much better. Very easy, obvious application. But even with the subtleties there are general patterns. And once we worked out patterns, we were able to . . . define fragments, if you will. Then, separate those, work with them in focus. A sort of horizontal slice isn't very handy to pull out, but vertical--"

Sheila stopped in her tracks, her eyes wide. "Hold on. *Pull out*? You were ripping apart people's souls?"

Tobias scowled. "They are not 'souls'! The canopic is a discrete concept that has nothing to do with those metaphysical rules!"

"They're souls, doc!" Sheila shouted. "What the hell were you people thinking?"

"We were advancing science!"

"This is insane! It sounds ridiculously dangerous!"

"And in the wrong hands, it is! What our paper described was subtly, intentionally, incorrect. It would keep your everyday spellcaster from copying us, unless they had our level of mastery. The six of us, we could construct a summon with only eight parcels of the canopic, and a person can go without fifteen before even the slightest ill effects. But if you don't know what you're doing, then yes, a person creating a summon from themselves would greatly damage their psyche until they're reunited."

"And you didn't see a problem with that?" Sheila stood face to face with Tobias, unable to tower over the vian to intimidate him. "Did you people never think to ask what would happen if someone got their hands on something so powerful?"

"Of course we did," Tobias said, indignant. "Which is why we protected it."

Rather than stare Sheila down, he turned to unlock the door behind him. He swung it open and brought the lights up in the room effortlessly, illuminating a small laboratory with equipment and papers thrown haphazardly throughout. Sitting on the floor amid the lenses and grimoires was a feline creature, slightly smaller than a human adult, colored dark green with brown tiger-like stripes. Its texture was more lichen than fur. It slept quietly, its short tail flapping back and forth, until Tobias's approach woke it. Its silver eyes focused on the professor.

"Chapalu," he called, "it's time to come home."

The creature let out a ghostly purr, followed by a deeper growl.

"Oh, naturally," Tobias muttered. He held out his spear. "I never was a morning person," he said as he readied his first lunge at the summon.

The rest of the group stayed out of the battle. Kell kept their rod at the ready, just in case, but there seemed to be a silent agreement that this was a Tobias problem.

Tobias, to his credit, handled the problem quickly. After batting Chapalu's claws away, he pinned it down with his spear and started waving a hand in the air. The spell began its work and Chapalu, with a growl shifting from pained to relieved, dissipated into a yellow and white glow. It floated in the air for a moment before wafting to where Tobias stood, seeping into his body.

Tobias shifted on his feet as if cracking his back and clicked his beak in victory. He grabbed a pile of papers from a table behind where Chapalu previously sat and stuffed them into a pocket on his vest. "Right then. Shall we eat before the show?"

F

An elaborate stage sat in the middle of the university's campus, massive orange and blue banners flanking either side. The banners portrayed Crystal Greene in appropriately larger-than-life fashion, full of visual contrast and accent. Her flashy yellow outfit balanced out the subtle dark backgrounds; her dark skin and large blonde hair contrasted perfectly with each other. The imagery was meticulously designed, the same as every other element of the show. The biggest pop star on Banner Music's roster, the biggest pop star on the continent--when her rank wasn't under attack by the sultry and surreal Cigarette Wife--demanded such a precise production.

And yet, four travelers with no sense of anything related to theater production wandered the quad, asking anyone they could if they knew where the show's producer was.

Eventually, they found success and were pushed towards a large gnoll man guarding the invisible line that defined backstage. He held them there until a stout, scarred hunn man with sharply trimmed brown hair finished a conversation near the stage and approached.

"Kell? Good. I'm Omar. Welcome to hell."

Sheila laughed at the blunt introduction.

Omar took that as a cue to size her up. "You can lift stuff. Go talk to Dani, red hair. Take the little squirt with you." He turned to Tobias. "You're too old for this. You a professor?"

"Sure am. Faculty of sciences."

"Whatever," Omar said, unimpressed by the specifics. "Go talk to Ben. Big vian, real pale. You're on security. You'll scare the kids." He turned his attention to Kell. "Fishbowl. Walk with me."

Kell accepted that Omar was in command and stuck close to him as they walked to a distant, quiet corner of the quad.

"Little birdie tells me you're in charge of the group," Omar said.

"I wouldn't say I'm in charge," Kell said.

"Responsible, then. Look. This whole crew's made of folks who need to disappear. We ain't gonna judge. But I need to know what y'all are running from."

Kell paused to consider their words. "I have a bunch of people hunting me down, trying to kill me, and I don't have an answer why. There are three people dead in Farolé because of this. We need to get to Cymona so I can get some real answers. We're just here long enough to do that."

"You're here 'til boss says you're gone," Omar said. "You knew that was the deal when you went to him."

"He came to us."

Omar's eyes narrowed. "That so?"

"You don't trust us?"

"I don't think you're lying, if that's what you're asking." Omar glanced around at the clamor. "Go make yourself useful, just keep it backstage. Away from the crowd."

Omar's warning of an introduction had been aimed at those desperate to disappear. For a group of experienced fighters and soldiers, it proved to be a bit melodramatic. Sheila handled her tasks faster than Dani could provide them. Alejandro repeatedly allowed himself to sneak glimpses of the show from behind the scenes, a privileged perspective for any fan. Tobias took to his security work with considerable zeal. It wouldn't be until the next day that the students would learn why he was acting as if he was no longer part of the faculty.

The production ran late into the night, and the mass of reveling students took even longer to disperse. Dawn had already broken by the time the crew--several dozen people, and *only* people, no familiars in sight--finished dismantling and preparing everything for shipment. The reinforced wooden containers were wheeled to the docks and handed off to a Banner cargo ship and the scurrying band of jaculus-style familiars that made up its crew. A second boat was docked nearby, a smaller liner resembling the fishing boats that toured from Gauvencia. That, Kell learned, was their ride. The four were given the same rundown as the rest of the crew: The next port of call was Candhall. Travel time was a day and a half. All matters regarding border crossing had been taken care of. The crew had an opportunity to rest, and the veteran hands took eager advantage.

The group got their own rest, scattered across several cabins thanks to the limited available space. Even after waking, they mostly remained separated during the trip.

Sheila mingled with the road crew, immediately making friends when she pulled some provisions out of her bag. Food was available on the ship, the group learned, but it was provided by Banner Goods. Much of the crew wanted to rely on the company as little as they could.

Tobias spent much of the trip playing quiet rounds of card games and Twenties, as any of his attempts to discuss his work were quickly rebuffed.

Alejandro, visibly cautious in his movement, routinely dipped in and out of the common areas throughout the day. When confronted about it during lunchtime, he acknowledged that he was not the first Speaker to want to disappear. He claimed to be confident that one crew member was a former colleague, and he simply did not want to be in the same room with them.

Kell, for the most part, kept to themself, watching shows on their mobile while surrounded by other quiet crew members. After wandering aimlessly for a change of pace, they found themself on the deck. The afternoon had grown thick, the sun well into its descent. They watched the Vesper Sea roll beneath and gulls fly overhead and rubbed their aching right arm idly.

Omar approached, claiming their attention from a distance. He stood near Kell and watched the sea with them.

"Is something up, Omar?" Kell said after a moment. So far, Omar had only ever made his presence known in order to give directions.

Omar kept staring out to sea. "It's not urgent." With three gruff words, he had set the terms. Kell could keep watching the waters as long as they wanted, but the moment they moved, something was waiting for them.

"Fair enough." Kell took in the serene, nearly nostalgic view. "Appreciate the hospitality."

Omar's brows turned in weary curiosity, before falling to just weary. "Ain't my call."

"Yeah, I figured. Sounds like everything here's 'cause of Banner, at the end of the day."

Omar huffed out a small laugh. "Don't you know it."

"Rough guy to work for?"

"There's worse," Omar said. "You're military, right? You've been there."

"Yeah," Kell said warily. "Command is . . . strict. But, it's what I do. It's what I know."

"Lot of folks here said that, once upon a time," Omar said. "Hell, I did when I got wrapped up in all this."

"What was your line of work?" Kell asked. "Before you came to run things here."

Omar shook his head. He didn't seem upset by the question, but it would remain unanswered. "I never signed up to run anything," he said. "But things happen."

"Doing a good job of it," Kell said.

"Well, y'know how it is. Can't just let any old asshole do it. Gotta be the right kind of person to hold things together. Gotta be willing to take the punches. Take care of yourself last, after you've taken care of everyone else. Last to eat, last to leave. It's the only way."

"Must wear on you after a while," Kell said. They got the sense that Omar rarely had a chance to just talk to someone without the weight of leadership bearing down on him. Kell could listen.

"You say that like you don't know."

"It makes sense, sure, but . . ."

Omar finally turned to look at Kell. "You really tryin' to tell me you ain't the leader of your little band?"

Kell shrugged. "Not like I tell them what to do."

"That ain't leadin'," Omar said. "That's having people under your thumb. You wanna keep your crew together? Trust 'em. Be firm if you gotta, it sets the ground rules. But don't start actin' like you're a god or something. Banner does that. I don't."

"I'm sure the crew appreciates that."

Omar's gaze out to sea remained stoic and calm. "They oughta have one good thing in their lives. 'Bout all I can give them, but I can give 'em that."

Kell nodded and fell silent, letting them both relax for a moment longer.

Omar broke the silence. "Alright kid," he said, walking away. "Follow me."

The two walked to the lower deck, where the cabins were. Omar turned a corner and immediately started making shooing gestures.

"Crew cabins are starboard," Omar said.

"Yes, sorry." It was Alejandro, moving aimlessly a few doors down. "I get a bit lost in here. Ah, Kell, was wondering where you went off to."

"Yeah, just been talking with Omar." Kell turned to him. "Is it alright if he tags along, or is this private?"

Omar stared at the two for a moment before shrugging. "C'mon, squirt."

A nondescript locked door down the hallway opened to Omar's key, revealing more of the same kind of space. None of the cabin doors up or down the ship had anything identifying about them. Omar knocked gently on one. Crystal Greene opened it.

"Ah, you brought a buddy!" she said. "Thanks Omar, owe ya."

Omar bowed like a butler and stepped away, leaving Kell and Alejandro. They peered inside; other than the cabin having a single bed and not a set of bunks, and its own bathroom, it was no different from the cabins where they had rested earlier.

"You wanted to talk to me?" Kell asked, baffled.

"Yep." She waved them into her cabin. "Heard about ya. Banner's *really* interested."

Alejandro stepped inside, dumbfounded and starstruck. Kell's confusion was more pragmatic. They had some kind of celebrity, sure, but only in Cymona. They were nothing compared to Crystal Greene. Why would she care?

"So, you talk with him?" Kell tried to keep the conversation moving, since Crystal wasn't volunteering much.

"All the time," Crystal said with a laugh. "Guy needs to learn to delegate. He actually cut our release meeting short when you showed up."

"Sorry about that." Kell felt compelled to be polite. "I don't get why he bothered. I'm not anyone special."

"No, no, no." Crystal shook her head. "No saying that. If you say you're nothing special, you're saying they can swap you out whenever. And we aren't just some parts for him to throw out."

"I guess."

"You guess?" Crystal chuckled to herself. "C'mon, man. Banner doesn't just grab somebody if they're nobody special. I mean, he grabbed me!"

"Yeah," Kell said, indifferent. "Biggest pop star in Linnute, right?"

"*Two* biggest." Crystal and Alejandro corrected them in near unison.

Kell cocked their head. "What?"

Crystal grabbed a rough metal box sitting on a nearby table. She held one end up to her mouth. "You don't listen to much music?" Her voice, going through the box, shifted from a friendly tone to a gruff one with a sultry, alien undertone. "Everyone knows Cigarette Wife is just my alter ego. It's all an act."

"I'm more of the film type. Alejandro's the music guy."

"Clearly." She smirked, the face of a playful cat.

"So, okay," Kell said warily, "what do you want with us, then?"

"Think about this, Kell." She nodded to Alejandro as well. "Banner doesn't delegate. He's gotta control everything. So he's stretched thin. Honestly? He's not doing much for the show anymore. Omar runs the logistics, and I keep things going creatively. We can keep things going just with folks on this boat. Who needs Banner?"

"He's not paying for stuff or anything?" Kell asked.

Crystal scoffed. "Please. I ran the numbers, guy takes more than he gives. So let me ask you. What's Banner got you two doing?"

"We need to figure out what Prime Minister Lyon has been up to," Kell said. "Figure out why a bunch of people want me dead."

Crystal was skeptical. "That's what he wants?"

"That was the deal."

"Staying safe, good thing for you to get," Crystal said with a confident grin. "So what's *he* getting out of it?"

Kell thought for a moment before shrugging.

Crystal turned to Alejandro. "Any guesses, little guy?"

Alejandro was at a loss for words twice over.

Crystal nodded. "There's no way you guys are getting the better end of a deal with Banner. I know how he is, he thinks he's got the whole script figured out already. And it's *his* story. It's the Banner Show, not the Kell Show. You staying safe must mean *he* gets something better."

"It means I get to stay safe, though," Kell said. "I'll take it."

"You don't need Banner for that. Banner didn't build this, I did." She waved the voice changer in demonstration. "Banner doesn't write my songs. And he doesn't cast your spells. He's not gonna save your life or whatever. You are."

"How, though?"

"Good question," Crystal said. "If you want some advice? Keep flexible. Keep honest. And, you know what always works for me." She raised an eyebrow in conspiracy and held the voice-changing box in front of Alejandro's face. "Improvise."

People of Cymona, I thank you for your patience. And I thank Mayor Hardwick for the introduction and the coordination.

The memories of the Winters' War linger heavily on our hearts. Many thousands of our brethren fell to defending our land from the aggressions of our neighbors. It was the bravery of our knights, and the power of our greatest weapons, that spared communities such as the one I stand in today.

I know there have been desires to punish our foes. But that is not the way of Cymona, is it? That is not who we are. We claim our greatness on our wisdom, and on the protection of our cities' leaders, and on the guidance of Owain. We do not claim our greatness on the back of striking out at others.

But we do protect ourselves. We must. For we know, all too well, that our neighbors see our humility as weakness. They see Owain's patience as indolence. They believe us to be easy targets. We are not, Cymona. We are not. [*applause*]

Now, I know that rumor has a way of carrying on. People have spoken of seeing summons around Rijest, summons that should not be. Summons that moved to attack.

In the time since the first appearance of these creatures, our knights have investigated their origins. Their appearance here, near our border, and not to the south where the sahagin scourge has plagued our communities . . . all this has raised their concerns. I have been informed of suspicions.

Let me speak plainly, Cymona. If these summons are a show of force by an outside foe, then it will be met. If these are their best weapons, then they will be met by our greatest weapons.

We are a humble people. A modest people. For many generations, we have been known on the world stage to be the quiet ones. But to those who see humility and assume weakness, who see modesty and assume vulnerability, I remind them of the lesson of the Winters' War:

Fear the quiet ones. [*applause*]

— excerpt; speech delivered by
Prime Minister Mitchell Lyon
in Rijest, Cymona, delivered 12/10

CHAPTER SEVEN

S moke rose in patches from the Candhall skyline, as if the entire metropolis was slowly smoldering. The heart of the nation was perpetually busy, throbbing with activity. The richer ambient vapor made it an appealing center of Cymonian life, even if that same energy meant the city walls were practically useless. Any sort of unattended pet or wild animal could easily find itself poisoned with vapor, needing to be put down by knights on patrol. The knights were violent, and sometimes, it was warranted.

As Crystal's crew arrived in port, Omar gave Kell a tap on the shoulder. The four were dismissed. Fired, if anyone asked. Boss's orders. He slipped them a piece of paper with the word "improvise" written on it, along with a number--Crystal's, in all likelihood. They tucked it in a pocket with a nod, opting not to tell the rest of the group about it. It felt too much like a personal missive, as though Crystal and Omar were inviting them--and only them--into the crew long-term. Kell didn't need the invitation. They had a base to get back to. But, they didn't mind having a souvenir.

Alejandro's mobile buzzed, so he stepped away from the group. He stood out of earshot, but still visible, and Sheila made sure that remained the case. Kell gave him the occasional glance, watching him pace anxiously, as they let their own worries simmer.

Banner's stated motives for hiring the four were simple enough, but they were too simple to be believed. Lyon was making speeches, all the time. Kell had overheard one the day before, broadcast into the boat's canteen. Even if Banner didn't have a direct line to the Prime Minister, he could still know what Lyon wanted. He could watch the news. He owned the news service, after all.

So why us? Kell thought, sitting on a bench in the quiet afternoon of the dockyard, idly rubbing their wounded arm. *Got to be something. Has to be--no, Kell, stop it. This isn't Trouble in Paradise. You're not in a damn detective show. This is serious.*

Sheila took her eyes off Alejandro for a moment and noticed Kell. "You look lost in thought."

Tobias looked up from the newspaper he was reading. "Hmm? We have ideas to discuss?"

"No, no," Kell said, "I'm just trying to come up with a plan."

"Plan is, we get in Lyon's face and get an explanation," Sheila said.

The simplicity left Kell unimpressed. Sheila was just that straightforward of a person, it seemed. "You're just gonna break into the castle and barge into his office? Gonna kill Owain on the way? C'mon. That's not a plan."

"Agreed," Tobias said. "Though perhaps it helps that he's not in his office. Paper says he's giving a speech tonight in Rijest."

"Another?" Kell said.

Tobias nodded. "Apparently. And it sounds like he's rather unhappy."

"Typical." Kell stood and read over Tobias's shoulder, confirming what he had said. "Hold on, what am I missing here? If Lyon's giving so many speeches, why does Banner even need us?"

"Probably figures Lyon's hiding something." Sheila started reading as well. "For once, I hope he's right. Feels like Lyon wants another war."

Kell gestured to hold their chin in thought and got a handful of helmet. "Well if he does, he's not going to say it. Nobody in this country says what they mean. Does at least mention he'll call on 'Cymona's greatest weapons' if he has to. So that's reassuring."

"Reassuring?" Sheila said.

"That's always meant us. He wouldn't be calling on the vapormages if we weren't a unit anymore, right?"

"Yeah, maybe Al's info is all trash."

Alejandro, having finished his call, rejoined the group. He wore worry on his face as he approached, but Sheila's comment quickly turned it into annoyance. "If you prefer," he said, "I could keep my information to myself."

"Are you saying you have something for us?" Tobias asked.

"No, simply business. I didn't exactly tell my sources that I left the Speakers. And I've had quite a few sources, hiding in niches all across Linnute. That call was keeping me appraised of some rebellious activity around here. Hopefully, nothing we need to worry about."

"Hopefully," Sheila cautiously echoed. "Hopefully they don't have it out for folks like Kell. Gonna make it harder for us."

"That's quite unlikely," Alejandro said. "You saw those kids gawking. The people love the vapormages. They're not what I'm concerned about. And unlike some people here, I trust my sources."

"We should just head to the armory, then," Kell said as they began down the street. "Where I was stationed. I should debrief command, at least." *And I just wanna get home.*

"Are you sure about that?" Alejandro said. "Will they approve of your new mission?"

"Won't know until I talk to him," Kell said. "Besides, my commander has a direct line to Lyon. Might know what's going on, solve the whole thing right there."

The sky started growing dark as Kell led the group towards Candhall's walls. Days were growing short, and the metropolis was dense and winding, its streets intricate enough that understanding them was a small source of local pride. There were dominant avenues to follow, but even those wound conspicuously around forgotten plazas and trails. Simply crossing the city took far too long, even when using the covered and doored-off alleyways between old buildings that provided shortcuts to knowing locals.

To make matters worse, the knight guarding the gate refused to let them through. He offered little explanation for the delay, causing Kell to quietly panic. If Alejandro was right, if everything they'd heard was true--that the vapormage unit was disbanded, but that fact was not yet public knowledge--then the knight would know Kell was a fugitive. They had reached the end of the line.

Alejandro took over negotiations. The conversation stayed civil, but twisted and spun like a leaf in the wind, and soon Kell had no idea where things were going. Suddenly--or perhaps not--the knight stepped aside to let them pass. As the group walked out, gesturing thanks, the knight flashed a smug smirk to Kell. The small action told Kell all they needed to know about the entire engagement. All of the delay and roundabout negotiation was pointless. The knight had held up Kell and the group simply because he could.

B

The armory was far past the city walls. The woods to the west of Candhall perked up quickly, eager to overhang the wide road that emerged from the city. Situated among them, for about a kilometer past the city's gates, were wooden beastwatch towers. Someone would be posted in them to keep an eye out for large vapor-addled creatures approaching the city. From the ground, it was hard to see if anyone actually was stationed inside. Alejandro had the faintest unconscious sense of a presence, as though he was being watched. But considering what he knew from his sources, it was likely mere paranoia. The beastwatch towers eased public fears simply by existing. Why bother employing someone to make them functional?

Another kilometer passed. Kell held their rod out, lit with vapor flame since the group lacked a proper lantern. A misty rain steadily soaked the night sky. The vapor flame disregarded the moisture, generously giving its pale orange light.

After enough walking to be properly tiresome, the four branched off from the main road. The path to the armory had started to grow soft and marshy from precipitation. Tobias took to wiping the rain from his goggles repeatedly, to Sheila's petty amusement.

A ways up the road, Kell silently veered towards the left side of the path. The rest of the group didn't bother to follow until they stumbled at the dip in the road. Kell's movement was instinctive, so much so that they no longer realized that they were following an instinct built up from experience.

How long has Kell been here? Alejandro thought as he wiped damp hair from his forehead. *Briefing said they were recruited after the war. Rather savvy with the area, I'd expect a few more years on them. Still, plausible, I suppose. They do act green enough. Must've been a small band, though. Never caught wind.*

The armory was barely visible, its perimeter blending into the foliage and the night sky. Kell's gait picked up as they approached. Being a military base, but also being home to the much-beloved vapormages, the armory was largely split between the private and public segments. A large rectangular building, styled almost but not quite like a gatehouse, served as the publicly accessible portion; beyond that was a sprawling, walled-in compound. It had the feeling of approximating a castle, as though whoever had built it was aware of the concept but had never seen a real one.

To see anything of the deeper compound, one needed to be with the mages. A broad variety of machines and purpose-built familiars stood guard to make sure of that. There may be interesting sights or resources within, Alejandro figured, but they could remain points of curiosity if Kell was unwilling to share. If Alejandro were still a Speaker, he would feel obliged to gather the intelligence. A part of him, he knew, still did.

Kell swung open the door and tapped a few buttons on the wall, signaling their arrival. The heave in their shoulders declared they were home. They started taking steps farther into the building, well past the rest of the group, before awkwardly stopping in the middle of the room. They had forgotten themself in the moment.

"Never actually visited this place," Tobias said half to himself as he looked around. "A lot of vapor chem folks have stopped by, apparently."

"Your colleagues?" Alejandro asked. His words echoed around the hollow gatehouse.

Tobias nodded. "You and your comrades are quite fascinating, Kell. I'm glad to have met you."

Kell took the compliment with a shrug. "Well. Hope you learned stuff, I guess."

"And if we learn what we need about Lyon," Tobias said, "all the better."

The group took to leaning on tables that were lined against the walls as they waited. Kell tapped the buttons again, nervous that the signal may have been missed originally.

"Was yours the only unit posted here?" Alejandro asked to fill the air.

"For the most part," Kell said. "Used to be some knights posted here too, years ago, but that had to stop. Things got a bit . . ."

Alejandro nodded knowingly. "Did you not get along?"

Kell shrugged, stepping anxiously around the open room. "There were fights. Most of them didn't like us. Honestly, we don't like them."

"Happens a lot, huh?" Sheila said.

"Yeah. That's what took out your Burgundies back in the day, right?" they continued, looking at Alejandro.

"No," Tobias interjected, "retiring that force was a tactical consideration. To hear Elliot tell it, at least. Jack of all trades, master of none--"

"Is often better than master of one," Alejandro cut in with an annoyed fry in his voice. His point made, the tone abruptly disappeared. "All that was before my time, Kell. I won't pretend to know about it. I never kept close to the military side of things."

"You're not former military?" Tobias asked.

Slow steps could be heard approaching outside, from the opposite end of the building. Alejandro used them as cover to dodge the question.

The door leading to the armory's interior opened. An older hunn man in basic fatigues approached, a lit cigarette in his hand. He walked firmly and proudly, the march of a seasoned soldier, though his face and hair looked aggressively aged.

"Commander!" Kell perked up and stood at attention. "Private first class Kell Rusalka, reporting, sir."

The commander stared for a moment. He took a sluggish drag from his cigarette. "Well that solves that mystery, kid," he drawled before glancing at the rest of the group. "What are you people doing here?"

"Sir, the mission was interrupted. These three helped me survive and extract."

The commander tossed aside his cigarette and rubbed his eyes. "Fine. Commander Vance Fontaine, of Cymona." He elbowed a button near the door frame. The click of a locking door echoed through the room. "Tell me why you people should leave here alive."

"Commander?" Kell said, shocked.

Sheila reached for her sword. "Excuse me?" she growled.

Alejandro stepped forward, an arm out in front of her. "Very well. I'd be happy to. Alejandro Quintana, he of Lusaber Leather Works." He turned his voice friendly, dropping the confident creak. He whispered to Tobias as he stepped forward. "Hold Kell back."

Fontaine scoffed. "You expect me to believe you're a leatherworker?"

"Hadn't said I was," Alejandro said. "I'm in charge of sales."

"Really?" Fontaine looked Alejandro over, noticing the bloody shirt peeking out from beneath his jacket. "You look like something mauled you. What are you people doing in a decommissioned military base?"

Alejandro's skin flushed with a chill. *Decommissioned? Then Sully's right.* He paused a beat before calmly continuing. "We had some incidents, sure. But it's as Kell said. I ran into them at a pub over in Farolé. We wound up having a conversation, and eventually my colleagues and I pulled a few strings. Got them out of town with . . . well, for the circumstances at the time, I'd say relative ease. They did shut the border for a bit."

Fontaine's eyes narrowed. "What kind of conversation? What did they tell you?"

"Oh, I was going on and on about my business, absolutely," Alejandro said with a chuckle. "They only mentioned being separated and cut off. Didn't need to say more, frankly. Vapormages are quite distinct, and I understand quite beloved? Am I right? I'm certainly impressed. So I offered to help, both as a kindness and, honestly? If it brings the Lusaber brand up in Cymona's mind by association, then I've done a damn fine job." He punctuated his sentence with a salesman's smile.

"So they dragged you here, then?"

"It would appear so. Quite the adventure. And I'm surprised by the reception. Kell's been quite distressed that they were separated from command. I thought you'd be happy to have them back."

Fontaine smirked. "Gotta hand it to you, kid. You got balls."

Alejandro responded with a friendly shrug. "I'm used to tense negotiations. I *do* work in sales." *And how many sams have I run this cover on by now . . .*

The commander turned his attention to Kell. "This the kind of company you've been keeping?"

"I . . . I suppose so, sir."

Fontaine turned back to Alejandro and scoffed. "Let's get this straight. This isn't a negotiation. And I don't really like talking with salespeople." The commander reached for a knife holstered on his leg. He brought the point to Alejandro's chin, grazing the stubble. "Start telling the truth, or I slash that shirt up more."

On his muscle, then? Alejandro widened his eyes in false fear. "Commander, please," he said politely, "did you not want to handle this through conversation?"

"Not with a liar," Fontaine said. "Besides. You're armed."

Alejandro glanced back at Sheila. She still had one hand on her sword's grip. "True," he said. "We've had a rough road, after all. But we should all be safe here, correct? So then." He drew the two knives kept under his jacket, one at a time with a feigned amateurish fumble, and placed them on the ground. His eyes remained on Fontaine as he held a hand up, gesturing for the others to do the same. After hearing three different clatters of steel and wood against the stone floor, Alejandro held his hands out, palms open, inviting Fontaine to make the same move.

The commander sized up the situation, his attention lingering on Kell. Eventually, he threw his own knife behind him. "There," he said. "Now talk. Start telling the truth."

"Sir," Alejandro said with a hint of courteous impatience, "nothing I've described has been false."

"Then why are you still with the runt?"

Alejandro shrugged. "Why not? We have been traveling with Kell for some time now. Hard not to be friendly."

"They're not your friend," Fontaine sneered.

Alejandro glanced back at Kell, as if Fontaine's words mattered. "You think so? Er, sorry, do you mean just Kell or all of the vapormages? Because I'd heard rumors of the group closing up."

"What makes you believe that?" His voice started rising. "What makes you think they're a vapormage at all?"

Alejandro felt calmer than he looked. It was far from the first time he had to keep cool while someone grew angry before him. "They were just rumors. But I have no reason to doubt they're a mage; we've seen them do some impressive things. They reattached their own arm with vapor. I've never seen someone who could Mend so easily and powerfully, not even a nurse."

"I don't train medics," Fontaine said. "I train killers."

"I've seen that as well. Our whole adventure had us . . . off the beaten path a bit." Alejandro grazed the slash on his shirt as a demonstration. "We were even set upon by several sahagins at one point, and Kell handled them admirably. And . . ." He let out a small, almost playful laugh. "I can be a bit of a cock sometimes, and Kell was more than able to set me straight, as it were."

Fontaine smirked and chuckled, smoke still in the timbre of his voice. "Then you should be dead."

Alejandro took a small, incidental step towards the commander. "Should I be?"

"You spin a good story. But no vapormage of mine would hold back against foreign trash like you." Fontaine stepped forward, closing the gap, standing over Alejandro. "Neither would I."

"Commander," he said kindly, "if we're to remain civil, it would be best not to bring in such a harsh tone."

"Stop me, you Farolian fuck."

Alejandro abruptly hugged Fontaine with his right arm, pulling him in close, his body obscuring the movement of his left arm, where a hidden blade emerged from his sleeve, cutting into the side of the commander's fatigues, piercing his lung before he could feel the steel moving. Fontaine's eyes widened, his breath suddenly painful.

Alejandro's calm, pleasant face suddenly turned into a bitter scowl. "Gladly," he whispered in his creaking, professional voice. "You listen, Fontaine. The Speakers know your work. I know your methods. I know the Masks were your responsibility. I know mages have died to your training. I know there was no 'maritime accident.'"

"You . . ." Fontaine wheezed. He coughed, spraying blood onto Alejandro's face.

"You're not the only one who trains killers," Alejandro continued, twisting his left arm. "And Cymona isn't the only one to wage wars. But I swear, by whatever gods there are, I *will* be one who ends them." He twisted his arm again, dragging blood out of Fontaine's side and down his leg. "You have already embraced death. When the burning in your chest ceases, I will have made peace."

With a final wheezing breath, Commander Vance Fontaine's body went slack and fell to the floor.

Kell, who only saw Alejandro's back and could hardly hear the whispered indictment, shook as they realized what happened. "Commander!" They lunged forward, into Tobias's outstretched arm.

Sheila grabbed her claymore off of the ground. "The hell did you just do?" she shouted.

"My job," Alejandro said defiantly. A rich red drop of Fontaine's blood fell from his hand.

Kell struggled against Tobias's restraint and quickly broke free. They ran at Alejandro, throwing their full weight and momentum into a left hook aimed squarely at his jaw. He recoiled backwards but kept on his feet. Kell rushed over to the fallen commander, their visor blinking back and forth rapidly. They knelt down, putting a hand in the pooling blood, shuddering over the corpse as their body glowed faintly in the overbearing light. "You bastard!" they shouted, their breath heavy and panicked, before running off into the armory's fields.

Alejandro spit out some of his own blood and straightened himself out. "I deserve that," he muttered, rubbing his jaw.

"You deserve this." Sheila pointed her sword at him. "You're lucky they freaked out and didn't vaporize you. Former military my ass, you're not even a former Speaker, are you?"

"If you insist," Alejandro said, standing stiff. "Obviously I've not been forthright, but you could let me explain first."

"You better have a damn good explanation."

"You killed a commanding officer," Tobias said, his voice suddenly stern. "You've started a lot of trouble here."

"Any trouble here had already started." Alejandro knelt down to examine Fontaine's body, leaving the back of his neck exposed. If Sheila was going to render a hasty verdict with her sword, then he had decided to accept it. Every mission could be his last.

Alejandro pulled a keyring from the corpse's pocket and stood up with silent relief. "My source's updates were not limited to the rebels. Whatever Lyon is planning, Fontaine was enabling. I don't have all the details, though. He was clearly never going to tell us himself, but he will have them documented. If you won't believe me, then believe him."

C

By the glow of a flame of vapor from his thumb, Alejandro found a sign pointing to the administrative offices. He led the way down the hall. The familiars protecting the armory were on minimal patrol here; when one did appear, Tobias had little issue handling it from afar. Alejandro stopped at each door along the hallway, looking for Fontaine's office with Sheila breathing down his neck. Once found, he calmly selected the right key and unlocked the door. He was practiced enough to keep his hands stable, showing as little fear as he could, as every doubt about his source's revelation shouted in his head. He could not show weakness. Sheila was going to jump on it. He breathed deep and kept his nerves boiling beneath his skin.

Commander Fontaine's office was orderly from every angle. A row of cabinets, all closed and clean, lined the left wall. Even the stacks laid out on his desk were neatly piled in boxes well-suited to the task. Only one stack could be described as "loose," as it sat near the side of the desk with a few stray pages in imperfect alignment. Alejandro scanned each stack as he walked past, circling the room. Expense reports, personnel logs, training results, procurement requests.

"Anything?" Tobias asked from the doorway. There was a curiosity to his voice, but also a subdued aggression. Alejandro's work was being judged.

"Looking." Alejandro struggled to hide his uncertainty. The loose stack on the desk grabbed his attention. "Form 14-6," he read off. "Retirement request."

"Keep looking," Sheila said.

Alejandro focused on the sheet. "Subject: proudsteel longsword, 40 units," he read off before grumbling. The numb weight in the pit of his stomach grew heavier.

"I said keep looking," Sheila insisted.

He slammed the sheet on the desk. "I am." He dug through the loose pile, scanning the details on each one. "Subject: Basilisk-3 model personnel vehicle. Subject: Banner brand consolidated cooking surface, 2 units. God dammit." He held up a sheet pulled from the pile. "Subject: Vapormage Rusalka."

"So they were retiring, then?" Tobias said.

"Were you not listening, professor?" Alejandro snapped before pulling more sheets from the stack. "Vapormage Dylow. Vapormage Shen. Vapormage Morgan. This is the entire bloody unit, isn't it?"

Sheila looked at Kell's sheet that Alejandro had slid aside. "This was signed the day I found them," she said, confused.

Alejandro felt himself getting angrier. He never liked Cymona. Suddenly, the reasons were stacked neatly before him. "That call earlier," he began in his briefing voice, "was from a chap I know as Sully. He had corroborated some murmurs about Fontaine's actions. The moment the commander said this base was 'decommissioned,' all the pieces fell into place. These documents?" Alejandro slapped the pile on the desk. "These are just the coup de grace."

"And why the hell would you trust this Sully guy?" Sheila said.

"I will not burn my sources, Sheila," Alejandro hissed before collecting himself. "When I was told about Kell's arrival in Farolé, I was told the vapormages had been retired. This is Cymona. I *knew* it was a euphemism. I assumed, initially, they were being assigned to a different unit. The evidence I had at the time pointed to that. But you don't reassign a stove. These forms, that Fontaine signed off on over and over, for every last vapormage? They're for destroying equipment."

D

Kell came to at the entrance of the base's mess hall, sprawled out on the ground, exhausted and furious, their limbs weak and filled with static. The door of the mess hall had been shattered open, the thick planks of metal barely holding onto their hinges. Kell couldn't remember how they got there. The last thing they remembered, before the world saturated itself into an indigo blur, was throwing their weight into a frantic punch at the first villain they could find.

Alejandro. The bastard. They should never have trusted him. They should have killed him when they had the chance. It was never going to be easy, but it should have been done. It had to be done. It was their duty, it was who Kell was. A soldier. A killer. Cymona's greatest weapon.

Kell slowly got up and looked around at their dark surroundings. The mess hall felt unfamiliar, as if the architecture had shifted. They had been in that building for so many meals. They had spent so much time there with the other vapormages. They knew the space. It was home.

But they knew there was something wrong about it now, something invisible, some ghost haunting the tables. They grasped for a light switch. The electric lights burned their eyes. When they finally opened them, they saw blood.

The metal walls were dotted with dark red stains and the marks of spells: chars of flame and electricity, pinpoint holes from blasts of water. Tables were overturned, used as shields or thrown up by shaking earth. The far wall was lined with a grid of wood, long rectangles lined up evenly halfway to the hall's ceiling. Kell recognized them immediately, their stomach turning as they approached to confirm. They were makeshift coffins for the remains of fallen soldiers. The boxes were unmarked, but Kell knew what their contents had to be. They found one they could open and peeked inside. The outline of a leg, saturated and coated with dried blood like a second skin, was enough to confirm the contents of all the boxes. Their comrades, their friends, were inside.

They leaned against the wall of coffins, sank to the ground, tore their helmet off, and wept.

E

Sheila, Tobias, and Alejandro all sat, quietly and uneasily, in the gatehouse entryway. Alejandro scanned through the documents and contacts on his mobile. The fear in his chest refused to go away. He had never wished to be wrong so badly before, even after hearing the words and seeing the documents that proved him right. The vapormages were beloved in Cymona. A cultural touchstone. If word got out that all of them had been murdered, the public would want the heads of whoever did it. The papers Alejandro found, combined with Sully's information, pointed him to only one conclusion: Lyon would frame Farolé.

The failures of the Winters' War would be forgotten. The public would demand revenge. The papers Alejandro had were the best hope of stopping it. He sent photographs to Sully, but more needed to be done. He got up to leave.

"You're not going anywhere," Sheila demanded. "We're waiting for Kell."

"We need to distribute these documents," Alejandro said. "And Kell needs time. They're smart. Surely they've worked out what's happened. I'm letting them grieve."

"You made them grieve!"

"He didn't kill the mages," Tobias said.

"I don't care."

Tobias glared at Sheila. "If you care about Kell, you should care about facts. Do you or do you not, young lady?"

Sheila's aimless anger focused into indignation. "Don't lecture me. I'm giving them time. But I'm not leaving."

"Then perhaps this is farewell," Alejandro said, stepping outside, Tobias following behind. A third pair of footsteps joined them in the mud. He didn't care who they belonged to.

The three approached the intersection with the main road, the misty rain now dissipated, night fully fallen. Tobias abruptly held out an arm. "Think I see something," he whispered.

Alejandro saw nothing, but yielded anyway. Speakers were unlikely to come here of their own accord. Working outside of Farolé was riskier, and while Fontaine was known and tracked as a likely target, he was never an officially sanctioned one. So if a Speaker had made their way to the armory to take out a vicious commander--and the former member of their ranks who happened to be nearby--it was either going to be a renegade or one of their best. A renegade might be handy to have around, but Alejandro didn't want to meet one of their best.

Shifting shadows soon made themselves known among the trees. They clarified into a human figure as they approached.

"Halt! Who goes there?" Tobias shouted.

Sheila sighed angrily. "Really?"

The figure continued its approach, walking casually, making no gesture towards a weapon or anything of the sort. Alejandro slid a hand under his suit jacket, just in case.

"Are you with Lyon?" a young masculine voice called out.

Tobias turned to the group. "Are we what?"

Alejandro sighed and righted himself. *This is why I work alone*, he thought. "We are with Owain," he called out.

The figure stopped. "I didn't expect friends."

"We are interlopers," Alejandro said, "but we are friends."

Sheila jabbed him with her elbow. "The hell are you doing now?"

The figure stepped closer, lighting a small lantern, rendering himself visible. He was a young-looking hunn man with ashen hair, dressed in a dark, ratty overcoat that obscured a small sword at his hip. The lower part of his face was masked by a light neckerchief. "How are you with Owain, then?" he asked, skeptical.

"I am Alejandro Quintana, he of Farolé. Formerly one of Her Majesty's Speakers, but no longer."

The man looked at the group and nodded, satisfied with the explanation. "Fair enough. Call me Grey."

"We shall. I take it you were expecting to find someone?"

"I was afraid I would."

Sheila stepped forward, grabbing Alejandro's shoulder. "You two mind cutting this spy shit? Who are you?"

Grey laughed. "Sorry, I thought you were all on the same page." He extended his sword-drawing hand to Sheila. "I am one of the Faces Behind the Masks."

Sheila stared at him and blinked. "So?"

" . . .Are none of you native? Huh."

"I have heard of you," Tobias said. "You folks were mentioned in today's paper."

Grey scoffed and shook his head. "Guess Lyon did something, then. Our whole mission is to help Cymonians in all the ways Lyon won't. Which is a lot. Guy doesn't give a damn. But that means going over his head, or going against the law. Far as I can tell, the locals know what we're about. But the papers work for Lyon. Any of his cock-ups, we get the blame for. Anything good we do, he takes credit for."

"The unloyal opposition," Alejandro said.

"If you could have a real opposition here, we wouldn't need these." Grey rustled the neckerchief over his face. "Lyon's not fond of opponents."

"Sounds familiar," Sheila said.

"You Farolian?"

"Bessetran. Same thing though, start shit against Bathroy or any of the Secretaries and see what jail they throw you into."

"Exactly," Grey said. "Hence all the 'spy shit.' But a little bluebird told me Lyon's got something brewing. And it means getting new weapons. Figured, if that's the case, I should pay a visit to the old ones."

Alejandro quietly processed the news. Lyon had something brewing, indeed. "Commander Fontaine is dead," he said.

Grey nodded slowly, as if he had expected to hear it. "That why you three are here?"

"It's why I am here. If Lyon is intending to start another war, then I intend to stop him. These two simply came along with the last vapormage."

Grey's eyes widened. "The rumor is true? But you said there's a vapormage left?"

"Indeed."

"Unless . . ." Sheila looked back at the armory. "Fuck this, I'm finding Kell," she said, running back towards the base.

"Sheila! The familiars!" Tobias shouted, running after her.

Grey and Alejandro remained standing in the dimly lit road. "Kell? Rusalka?" Grey eventually asked. "They're alive?"

"They are." Alejandro paid little mind to his companions running off. He was not about to join them. He was likely not needed in the armory, and certainly not wanted.

Grey looked around, improvising a plan. "Alright then. Alejandro, was it? Keep Kell safe. Please. And, when you see them again? Tell them that we know Rocko is alright. They'll know who that is. As for the rest of you, you have a friend in The Faces. You all do."

With that, Grey retreated to the shadows. Alejandro slowly walked back to the armory, the worry in his chest shifting, nearly easing.

F

Some time passed. Kell didn't know how long. They didn't care. Between their exhausted, tearful breaths, they could hear Sheila and Tobias breach the gatehouse. Sheila shouted for them, indifferent to the alarms of familiars that she had alerted. The familiars could only let out one or two cries before Tobias's spells handled them, but each was loud enough to warn Kell. They hastily wiped their face down and snapped their helmet back on before they could be found.

Within a few moments, Sheila found Kell meandering in the dark yard of the armory, their visor's yellow eyes small and downcast, their shoulders hunched low. They saw her approach but refused to acknowledge her. They didn't need her help. They didn't want it.

"Kell. Kell! You alright?"

"Where is he?" Kell said, not looking up.

"Outside," Sheila said.

"Alive?"

"Yeah."

"Good." Kell pushed past her, towards Tobias and the gatehouse.

"Why?" Sheila said. "You going to talk to him or fight him?"

Kell barely looked over their shoulder. "Do you care?"

"Yeah." Sheila's response was stiff, annoyed. "Yeah, I do."

"About him?"

"About you. Okay? Look at you, you've been through hell. You're muddy, you're pissed, your arm's gonna fall off. And you're part of this team, Kell. I swore I was gonna look after you."

"I can look after myself," Kell hissed.

Sheila grumbled. "Yeah, probably. I don't know, maybe you are tough enough. Maybe you don't need us. Maybe you can scrape together a little home, and trudge along, and . . . Vakonivak willin' and the creek don't rise, you live another day. But trust me on this, Kell. It takes a lot to look after yourself all the time when nobody's got your back. It's a lot of focus. You slip up once and everything starts falling apart. Pretty soon you're losing sleep. Picking fights. Doing things you're gonna regret."

Kell shuffled on their feet, their anger stirring, unsure what direction to head. "This your way of apologizing?"

Sheila hesitated. "Yeah. I guess."

The answer only made the taste in Kell's mouth more bitter. "So what about Alejandro? Is he part of the team?"

"He knows an awful lot," Tobias said. "I don't exactly agree with his behavior, but he clearly understands what's going on. He's handy to have around."

Kell scoffed. "So he's a tool."

"I don't know that I'd put it like *that*," Tobias said.

"He would."

"Look," Sheila said, "Alejandro's a piece of shit, but he knew what Fontaine was up to. He went and found those . . . 'retirement' papers. It had *your name* on it, Kell. They had everyone's names. Yeah, he should have told us before we went, but--"

"Are you on his side or not?" Kell demanded.

"I'm not on Fontaine's side! A commander going and killing off his own unit? We both know that deserves punishment, Kell. Don't act like it doesn't."

"So is that your plan?" Kell growled. "Murder? What crusade do you think you're on?"

"Is your plan to just look at the guy who killed all your friends and say 'oh well'? Just stick your head in the sand, not do anything about it? Fuck that!"

Kell glared at Sheila, shuddering in exhausted rage.

"I have seen some monsters in the military," Sheila said. "But as far as I'm concerned, what your commander did beats them all."

Kell slowly shook their head. "Fontaine wouldn't do something like this without orders."

"From Lyon," Tobias said.

"Yeah," Kell said. "If you want your justice or whatever, go to him. And good fucking luck with that."

"Thanks." She radiated sarcasm. "Where is he?"

Tobias winced. "Sheila, are you seriously planning to assassinate the Prime Minister?"

"*Someone* has to stop him."

"Yes, *stop him*," Tobias emphasized. "Take away his power. Corral his knights. Bury him in scandal. If you kill him, you're justifying starting a new war. And you'll deserve it."

Sheila barely held back hitting Tobias. "Fuck you."

Her words froze the conversation. Kell noticed the energy rapidly leaving their body. Rage and adrenaline only provide so much power. Theirs had run out.

Haltingly, they looked up. "Sheila?"

"Fuck you!"

"Sheila!" Kell barked out the last of their energy. "Can you drive a Basilisk?"

Sheila looked around for the garage. "Hey, last time we stole a vehicle--"

"We're not stealing," Kell said. "If it's on base, vapormages have the right to use it. *I* have a right to use it. And it's not like anyone here can say no."

"Does it seat four?" Tobias said. Kell shot a glaring look at him. "Kell, you know why I'm asking. We need to bring him along."

Kell stared down the pleading professor, only to slowly relent. They had no fight left in them. Their visor went dim as they walked.

Alejandro was pacing around the gatehouse when the three entered. Kell greeted him with a punch to the gut. Alejandro buckled but didn't protest or retaliate. He simply stood and adjusted his suit jacket as he regained his breath.

"Fair," he eventually wheezed.

Kell grabbed the rod they had set on the ground when their commander was still alive. "We need to leave town." Their voice found a stern, commanding tone. "They'll find out what you did."

"We have a vehicle," Sheila added.

Alejandro nodded subtly, carrying himself with the weight of a shackled prisoner. "Kell?" He was immediately met by narrow lights on Kell's visor. "A gentleman called Grey wanted me to tell you that Rocko is alright."

Kell stared him down, refusing to respond.

"And when did he say that?" Tobias asked.

"After you two ran off to find Kell. He also said the Faces are our allies."

"We'll see about that," Kell said. "We're taking the road north. And Alejandro? I'm not letting you out of my sight."

Verse

We have a night

In mind but we both know

We could be so much more

Make up your mind

To not decide until we're

Dancing off of the floor

Chorus

Play with fire 'cause you're

Hot enough inside you

Throw out all our plans and

Feel me out, feel me out, feel me

Verse

I play both sides

Sometimes it's wise to lie

Get by, but only just

You know the truth

We came to do magic

We shouldn't, but we must

Chorus

Play with fire 'cause you're

Hot enough inside you

Throw out all our plans and

Feel me out, feel me out, feel me

Bridge

Look into my eyes

Tell me lies

Like you don't know what you want to do

Look into my eyes

Improvise

Our hearts will ache for something new

Look into my eyes

No surprise

I know what I really want

And so do you

Chorus

Play with fire 'cause you're

Hot enough inside you

Throw out all our plans and

Feel me out, feel me out, feel me out,

Feel me out, feel me out, feel

Like I'm fire 'cause you're

Hot enough inside you

Throw out all our plans and

Feel me out, feel me out, feel me

— "Improvise"
by Cigarette Wife

CHAPTER EIGHT

L ight bled out of the seam in the armory wall as it parted. Inside the opening garage, a Basilisk rumbled. It was a bulky, boxy vehicle, all sharp lines and sudden edges, painted in the same deep Cymonian green as Kell's uniform. It could move a dozen soldiers if they were willing to be cozy. Since there were only four passengers, there was plenty of space to stuff it with supplies: spare jerrycans filled with fuel and water, a small vat of Pemmash that would last Kell several more weeks, and whatever dry, ready-to-eat provisions the rest of the group could use. More than enough for the trip north.

To the north was Dayton Point. The city marked the northern end of Cymona's coastal route, only a few kilometers from the border with Farolé. The trip would easily take a few days were they to travel on foot. Traveling on a Cymonian train would be faster but, with the crowds, far too risky to have Kell or Alejandro around. The Basilisk was the best, and only, option. The group would be there by the afternoon, without worrying about exertion or detection.

Instead, they worried about sleep. The sun was threatening to rise. Alejandro, seated at the front of the vehicle, dozed off with relative ease. Sheila, as was her wont, refused to fall asleep, even with the monotony of a drive. The road would offer little to challenge her skills in the driver's seat: Traffic was minimal, the weather was agreeable, and the barriers along the route were keeping away hazardous beasts.

Tobias took his rest, the roll of the road offering a soothing rhythm. Just under halfway to Dayton Point, he woke. He saw that the other two passengers were asleep, and that Sheila, for all her stubbornness, was inching towards the point herself. He reached up to quietly get her attention. "Are you holding up alright?" he asked.

Sheila rubbed her eyes. "I'm fine."

"I do know how to drive, you know. I'm happy to let you have some rest."

With a sigh, Sheila pulled to the side of the road. "Fine. I'll watch Al."

Instead, she fell asleep in the back, leaving Tobias with a few hours of road to himself. It had been a long time since he drove. Like so many cities, Port Mab didn't allow private autocars, and most of the university campus lacked the space for them anyway. Fortunately, the road remained largely barren, shared only with methodical waves of Banner shipping vehicles. The sun climbed patiently up the sky. Tobias had plenty of room for his mind to wander.

He found himself recalling the last time he had driven Route 12, decades ago, back when his feathers were still richly red and his eyes hardly needed goggles. He was returning from a freelance job in the far south of Cymona. A quick government gig, just something that would prove applications of the sigil and canopic research he had been involved in. The rest of the research team had no interest, the money was good, and he had little else to occupy him that particular summer. He gave little thought to it at the time, but as the years went on, he found himself missing the casual, loose freedom that came with freelancing. There was instability, sure, but there was adventure. Those days of exploration and field work agreed with him far more than an office, even the one in The Puck.

Tobias was lost in nostalgic daydreaming. His mind suddenly remembered that was a bad place to be when driving.

Th-thump. Th-thump.

The jolt woke Kell. They shuffled around briefly in the back of the vehicle, getting their bearings. "Morning," they quietly said to Tobias.

Tobias glanced in the mirror. Sprawled out on the road behind him, rapidly vanishing in the distance, was a massive snake emitting a plume of vapor smoke. "Morning," he said, gathering himself. "Sorry about giving you a start there."

"It's fine," Kell said. They sharply nodded towards Alejandro. "Is he up?"

"I am," Alejandro said, still reclined in his seat as if he were asleep.

"Great," Kell grumbled.

An awkward gap emerged in the conversation. "We're only a couple hours outside Dayton Point," Tobias said. "What are we thinking of as a plan when we get there?"

"I don't know," Kell said. "Find The Faces somehow."

Tobias had a few tools he would pull out during lectures, in the hopes of making an uncooperative class participate. "Very well then, Kell. Al, how would you build upon that?"

Alejandro finally opened his eyes, staring narrowly at Tobias as he rolled his head. "I'm your prisoner, not your student."

Tobias sighed. "There's no need to be melodramatic."

"Agreed," Alejandro said. "This is voluntary." He suddenly jumped in his seat. Sheila had kicked it from behind.

"Keep that shit up, doc'll run you over too," she said.

"Oh, so you've selected a punishment for me?" Another kick to his seat.

"Quit it, you two!" Tobias barked. "I thought we were all adults in here."

A buzzing sound from Kell's satchel interrupted the silence that had filled the Basilisk. They answered their mobile.

"What do you want?" they said flatly before putting the call on speaker.

"I want you to explain what happened at the armory." Banner's voice was stern, yet more condescending than angry.

"How did you know about that?" Alejandro said.

"Never mind that, I asked you a question."

"I will not 'never mind' that," Alejandro insisted. "You acquired that information very quickly. It would do us no good if we're simply overlapping your other resources."

"Our assassin is just dodging the question," Sheila said.

"Assassin?" Banner said. "So that was your work?"

"The vapormages were dead long before we arrived," Tobias said.

"Lyon's starting a war, Banner," Sheila said.

"And what makes you say that?" Banner's tone was filled more with curiosity than accusation, like a teacher dropping a pop quiz on their students.

"We have the papers," Alejandro said. "We've gathered all the proof that was there."

"Even if Al fucked things up and got rid of the commander," Kell added.

Alejandro turned in his seat to silently glare at Kell. They shot back with razor-thin lights on their visor.

"Is that proof of Lyon's plans?" Banner asked.

"It's proof of what happened to Kell's unit," Alejandro said.

"Then it's not what we need," Banner said, the condescension making it clear the group had failed the quiz.

"With all due respect," Tobias said, "Lyon's speech yesterday sounded pretty clear. Considering the usual Cymonian roundabouts."

"I've done enough business with Cymonians, professor." Banner sighed overtly. "Fine, then. You lot are convinced there's a war brewing. Any ideas why?"

A pause. Even Alejandro had no answer.

"It's Lyon," Kell eventually said. "Probably still bitter about the Winters' War."

"'Probably' isn't going to fly, Kell," Banner said. "Find something concrete."

"That's what we're off to do!" Tobias said, growing faintly frustrated. "We're headed northbound right now."

"Good, good. Towards Rijest?"

"Dayton Point," Tobias said.

"I see." Banner's tone brightened. "Good neighborhood, good people. Shame that the old lighthouse there has been a wreck forever, makes the coast hell to deal with. Tell you what. I have to go handle other business. I'll be in touch this evening. If that lighthouse happens to be in good order by then, well, perhaps I should consider that a favor, no?"

With a click, the line went dead.

"Perhaps he should," Tobias griped. "I swear, he's more pig-headed than the faculty."

"He really thinks he can give us orders?" Sheila said.

"He's changing the contract," Tobias said. "You'd think a businessman would have more respect for a deal."

"I knew we shouldn't've trusted him," Sheila muttered.

"Shut it with the 'told ya so's," Kell said.

Tobias huffed in frustration. "Well, if he's this stubborn," he said, "we'll play along just enough to get him off our back."

B

The smell of salt and sand in the air was apparent long before the hills parted and the low walls of Dayton Point came into view. The city was a fishing town at its heart, thanks to the shoals and reefs just off the coast. A wide array of small ocean fish and crustaceans loved that part of the sea, in part because the larger predatory fish hated it. Even at low tide, the locals could take a sloop out for kilometers, practically out of view from the shore, before hitting the kind of deep ocean one could shout to from the steeper coasts of Linnute. The waters were tricky, to be sure, but the locals had learned over generations how to master their slice of the sea.

Mastery, though, does not guarantee control. Seasons wavered and waned, as all things do, and the seas held final verdict on a year's harvest. The residents of Dayton Point long since learned to only expect the success of a poor year. Everything beyond that was a bounty to be grateful for, not a profit to feel owed. A good year was a great year. A poor year was fine enough. To the ever-busy residents of cities like Gauvencia or Candhall, the people here would seem poor and quaint. Yet, on the whole, they were content.

That was a problem for Prime Minister Lyon. His capital city had been growing relentlessly, as had other cities that escaped the Winters' War unscathed. The growth illustrated a new image of Cymona, Lyon's image, one that passed off shows of wealth as signs of modesty. It was, so it went, no sin to build the continent's largest prison or tallest tower if one only acknowledged the fact with a sheepish Cheshire grin. And so the money went: Labor cost marks, materials demanded all manner of currency, and Lyon would happily spend it all to show Cymona's strength.

The sense of competition and envy that permeated the air of the capital was never stated as a goal, but there was no way it was an accident. With no outside foe to fight and few politicians qualified to tackle beasts and sahagins and the like when they showed, the mayors of Cymona would battle each other for what money they could plunder from the treasury. Naturally, with the locals uninterested in such squabbles, none of that money ever made its way to Dayton Point.

Where Lyon's money went, so too did Lyon's eyes. In cities like the capital, The Faces couldn't identify themselves as such without immediately causing a scene. In cities like Dayton Point, their operations could be an open secret. Kell, having lived so long in and around Candhall, hardly had chances to interact with The Faces. But perhaps "Grey" could introduce them to the order. Assuming Alejandro was telling the truth. Assuming he was worth trusting.

As the group passed through the town's lightly guarded gate, they quickly agreed to split up. The lines were easy to decide: Kell and Alejandro had to be kept apart, and Sheila would rather keep an eye on the former Speaker herself than trust the task to the professor. Tobias found a spot near the inside of the city wall to leave the Basilisk, and the groups went on their separate routes.

Kell led the way to the shore, sliding down the shallow incline on the other side of the beach dune. An array of haphazard docks and jetties jutted out into the bay before them, many of them with boats freshly back from a day's fishing tied up alongside. Kell had never been there before, yet the shore felt faintly familiar.

"Well then," Tobias said, scanning the horizon, "any thoughts on how to begin?"

Kell found a log of driftwood embedded in the sands and sat on it. "We don't."

"That's not exactly going to get us information," Tobias said.

"Sheila will get it." Kell's frame collapsed in on itself.

Tobias remained silent for a moment. "Are you alright, Kell?"

Kell barely looked at Tobias before silently turning back to stare at the sand.

"I'll gladly listen," he continued.

"It's all too much," Kell eventually muttered.

Tobias looked out at the sea. "I can understand that." He sat on the log, to Kell's left. "Would you like to talk about it?"

Kell exhaled deeply, slowly. Tobias was the only person they could talk to about anything, if they were being honest. Especially since Rocko still wasn't picking up his mobile. "Before I was conscripted," they said, "I barely saw my dad. Ever. Mom passed when I was young. Just, cancer. Dad was all I had, and I barely had him. Then I got pulled into the vapormages. And I was in the armory for years and years. It was home. The other mages, they're the closest thing I have to a family. . . .Had." Kell sighed. "So Fontaine was the closest thing to a father that I had."

Tobias nodded.

"And yeah, he's been harsh, but . . ." Kell's thought faded into the ocean air.

"Kell," Tobias said in a hushed, sympathetic voice, "he signed the order for you to die. That's beyond 'harsh'."

"I get it. I know. But he was still the closest thing I had." Kell paused, composing themself. "It doesn't matter if he was a monster. I know I'm supposed to be . . . at least okay with it when a terrible person faces justice. But I can't. He could be the worst person in the world, it doesn't matter. It still hurts. I just can't be happy he's gone."

Tobias gave them a consoling pat on the back. "You don't have to," he said softly. "It's okay."

Kell sat still for some time. "Careful. About the arm."

Tobias recoiled. "Oh! Sorry."

Kell chuckled in soft relief. "You're fine. I know you're not trying to hurt me." Exhausted defeat bled into their voice. "You're the only one of us who hasn't."

"Really? Strange bedfellows, then. Though I suppose that's more common in your line of work than mine."

"Yeah. University sounds real relaxing right now. Nobody trying to kill you."

Tobias clicked his beak. "I suppose. I doubt Elliot would actually try anything."

"Dr. Charmchi?"

Tobias nodded. "We have a long history. Not all of it pleasant. The administration knew that, it's why we share an office."

"So you'd learn to get along?"

Tobias burst into laughter. "Of course not! We both knew they were trying to break us. Get either of us to quit. We're tenured, you know. At this point, the only thing either of us dislikes more than the other is the administration. Helps to have a common enemy. Truthfully, I don't mind Elliot's barbs, even if I know in my heart they're genuine."

"Damn." Kell shook their head. "Guess I'm lucky I never got stuck with . . . certain mages."

"Do tell." Tobias gave Kell a pat on the back, keeping wide of their injured arm. "Even bad memories can be worth keeping, after all."

Kell rubbed their right arm. The professor was right enough. "Guy named Klein. He was the type that . . . well. If you were better than him, you were a showoff, and if you were worse than him, you were a waste."

Tobias chuckled knowingly. "Ah, that type."

"Yeah. And he was always a better mage than me. I mean, everyone was. I was bottom of the class. So he gave me a lot of shit for not being good enough. Saying I never should've been a vapormage."

"Well if you ask me, you're doing better than him at being a decent person."

"Because I'm still alive," Kell said dryly.

Tobias sighed. "That's not how I meant it."

Kell watched a small sloop dock. An old hunn in a worn coat tied it to a post. "I just think I could've done something."

"To save them?"

"Yeah. Maybe the little runt would finally get their day, y'know?"

Tobias nodded. "You're reminding me of a student I had years ago. Maximilian Eames."

Kell couldn't help but laugh. "That is a fake name."

"It was his real name! Very Goldstone, very cinematic, I know. Point is, he was having a rough time, caught up in a bad project. He came into my office, we had a talk. But he turned down my help! He just said, 'Dr. Fulton! By the gods I'm going to save this project!' Slammed his hands on my desk and everything."

"He sounds like a film character."

"Oh, he was very dramatic, certainly. He needed to be the hero." Tobias threw his head back and let out a melancholy sigh. "The stress broke him," he said. "Complete breakdown. Dissociative episode, I think they called it. Never saw him again."

Kell quietly stared at Tobias, unsure where the professor was going with his story.

"Kell," Tobias said, "not everything in life is going to go your way. You can't control it all. I've only lasted as long as I have by learning to roll with the punches. If you three hadn't found me when you did, I would've been stuck in Farolé for a while. And it would've been fine, really. You just take the situation for what it is and move on. Even the painful ones. You can grieve, you can take forever to accept them, but the moment you start saying 'oh, I should have done something different' . . . You're trying to take control you could never have. Eventually, it destroys you."

He wasn't helping. Kell's eyes focused on the seashells they moved around as they idly kicked their legs. The salty air collected on their visor, leaving streaks across their face. "I just know there's a world where I was there. Where I did something about it."

"If there is, then . . . In that world, are you alive right now?"

Kell looked at Tobias, his expression kindly requesting an answer. They had none. They turned and looked at nothing in particular, staring towards the sea before them, its tides calmly lapping into broad pools along the shore.

"And either way," Tobias continued, "you're here. *This* is what you have to work with. You're too young to worry about your past and your regrets so much. Save that for when you're my age," he said with a chuckle.

Kell nodded quietly. They didn't want to agree, but all the same, they didn't want to argue. "You have a lot?"

"Hmm?" Tobias sounded pulled from somewhere else.

"Regrets."

"Oh." Tobias sighed deeply. "I suppose. Hard not to. Plenty of years I can look back at and say, what was I even doing then? Got old much too fast, you know. We had that grand tale of sorting out summons, and then that was it. I've hardly done anything as a professor. Haven't put forth anything new. Couldn't even bring myself to settle down with someone. Found myself just sitting outside of everything and watching humanity go, from time to time. It's a strangely compelling perspective."

"You're as human as the rest of us," Kell said.

Tobias waved them off with a laugh. "Oh, you know what I mean! And at the end of the day, there's no point lingering on it. Just keep looking forward, to the next thing." He nodded towards the lighthouse off in the distance. "Like figuring out how we'll fix that lighthouse."

"Good luck with that." A dockhand was standing near the driftwood Kell and Tobias had sat on. Kell quietly flushed with embarrassment. They had no idea how long she had been standing there, eavesdropping.

"Oh? Why's that?" Tobias asked. Whether or not he was genuinely curious, he certainly sounded the part.

"Been shut off for years," she said. "Big ol' bird started nesting there."

"That's not so bad," Kell said. "I've handled some big birds before."

"He ain't that big," the dockhand said, gesturing at Tobias and drawing an offended look. "Hold up, though. What's a mage doing up here? Thought y'all were dead."

Kell perked up. Of course they knew what had happened, but they didn't know anyone else knew. "Dead?" They had hoped to sound surprised, but the word came out curious.

"Yeah, you must be lucky as hell. We heard the news when we were coming in. Someone attacked the capital, got all the vapormages. You didn't know about it?"

"I've . . ." Kell stalled. They couldn't admit that they had seen the evidence first-hand. It could raise questions they didn't want to answer. "My helmet's been busted since our mission started, I've been driving blind. We had no idea."

Tobias gave Kell a sympathetic, if exaggerated, pat on the back. He seemed in on the act. "Sounds like the mission's off, then. Any word yet who was behind it?"

The dockhand shook her head. "No idea. They said there were sahagins spotted, but like, c'mon. We get 'em now and then, they're not that organized. Some minister said it was probably The Faces, so you know that's bullshit."

"Oh, naturally," Tobias said.

"Well then, maybe they're not all gone! One lie begets another." Kell immediately regretted reaching for a Bryn Achterberg line. It wasn't going to make their act more believable.

The dockhand shrugged sympathetically. "I guess. Just hope there's nobody comin' here after your heads. Last thing we need."

"The Faces wouldn't be after our heads, correct?" Tobias asked.

The dockhand glanced around. "I wouldn't know. But I wouldn't worry."

Tobias nodded. He waited until the dockhand was well out of earshot before laughing to himself, the tension released. "We are dreadful actors."

"We really are," Kell said. "I actually said 'one lie begets another.' Gods. She probably thinks I'm not even a vapormage."

"But it does sound like we'd be safe here. So I'd say we've done our jobs. Shall we figure out how the others are getting on, or just watch the docks a bit?"

C

Sheila and Alejandro made their way west. Dayton Point's open-air marketplace stood there, as it had for generations, streets lined with freestanding awnings and tarps where farmers and artisans could establish a presence. Most towns in Cymona--as well as Farolé and Bessetrae, for that matter--had similar locations that once saw much of their local trade funneled through them. Those marketplaces gradually fell out of fashion over the years. There were always different reasons given for that, but Banner Goods had a habit of showing up on the list. People could get most of their essentials that way, without travel or haggling, and often those essentials came from the same source at the end of the day. As Banner grew, the marketplaces shrank, the lifeblood of cities flowing away from their once-beating hearts.

Dayton Point was an exception. Its marketplace still operated with the same gusto it had in decades past. If anything, it had become more lively, more festive. Traders barked their offers into the air, weaving them into rhythmic chants as if they were trying to summon their customers. Bards performed on the corners, hats overturned to await coin from their audiences. Butchers and fishmongers prepared their goods in the open air, leaning fully into the spectacle. A butcher who could juggle knives as he worked, or provide some other sort of intriguing flourish, was bound to draw a crowd. That crowd of tourists and travelers would only grow as more stopped at its edge, craning to see what the commotion was all about. When most potential customers couldn't tell one lamb shank from the next, any marketing trick was worth trying, even if the bulk of the crowd offered applause and not marks.

A few blocks from the marketplace, Sheila abruptly grabbed Alejandro's arm and pulled him into a narrow alley between a vandalized Banner storefront and a stout stone pub. She pushed him against the wall with some force, even though he had been complying as gracefully as he could. Alejandro could already feel himself smirking; Sheila was far from the first person to threaten him in such a way.

"A barney, then?" Alejandro said.

Sheila's stern expression flipped to confusion.

Alejandro scoffed. "Going to kill me or not?" he said.

"You're acting like you want me to."

"It'd get the Speakers to stop twigging me."

"What, you can't deal with the consequences of your actions?"

Alejandro bit his tongue. "I can handle them perfectly fine," he said with a growl underneath. "But ask my last boyfriend how well people around me handle them."

"Bad breakup?"

"He's lucky that's all it was."

"Sounds like his problem, then," said Sheila with a shrug. "Don't fuck around with a spook."

"A spook?" Alejandro resented the term.

"Yeah," Sheila said. "Government guy. Obviously sketchy."

"*I'm* obviously sketchy, am I?" Alejandro said.

"Haven't you looked at yourself?"

Alejandro just scoffed. "You must not trust anybody."

Sheila shook her head. "Of course I don't. If I trust someone I shouldn't, it's my head."

"Really? You're afraid of getting killed?"

"Who isn't?"

"You think you couldn't handle them?"

Sheila paused, her eyes narrowing.

"You're good with your sword." Alejandro went sly. He was winning. "If you tick someone and it goes south, you could certainly defend yourself."

"Of course I could."

"Then what are you afraid of?"

Sheila held eye contact as she thought. "I'm not telling you."

Because you don't know, Alejandro thought. "It's not me then," he said confidently, "I presume?"

"I'm not going to kill you yet," Sheila said. "But I will if you make me."

"If you can kill me, you can trust me."

Sheila's head shook quickly in confusion. "What? That doesn't make any sense."

"If you can do something extreme," Alejandro said, "you can do something simple. Makes perfect sense."

"Maybe I don't *want* to trust you."

"What we *want* hardly matters at this point. I didn't *want* to confront Fontaine the way I did, but it was his head or ours. And for as much as I *want* to spend the rest of my days on some tropical island out in the Frontiers, that's not where we are. And we certainly won't get there if we're biting each other's throats out, now, will we?"

Sheila pushed off the wall she had been leaning on. She smacked Alejandro in the face, with no explanation or warning, and leaned back against the abandoned Banner building.

Alejandro claimed it as a victory. "Now then," he said, "you have some kind of plan?"

Sheila nodded towards the marketplace. "We ask around."

"About an illegal underground rebel organization? Thought you were more savvy than that."

"So what, you're just going to spy on people?"

Alejandro rolled his eyes. He would, gladly, but eavesdropping alone could never be enough to do the job. "You use your sword. I use words. And it happens I know the words for this. Allow me to demonstrate."

He brusquely walked towards the marketplace, putting a cluster of locals between himself and Sheila. By the time she started to catch up, Alejandro had breached the marketplace proper. He wove his way into the wider crowd and blended in. That part of his job would be easy here. A surreptitious conversation, though, would be much harder to achieve in a crowd thick with barter.

Working his way to a less-trafficked corner of the marketplace, Alejandro spotted a lanky, aging hunn man alone selling wood carvings. He was plying his trade behind a table, dressed as if he had just stepped out of bed, chipping away quietly at a block of wood. His hands moved subtly and confidently, but his eyes were scarcely on the task. His behavior caught Alejandro's attention. The man was making no effort to sell his products because, Alejandro hoped, he wasn't actually there to sell.

"Ahoy, omi," Alejandro said with a casual brightness, "would there happen to be anyone at this market offering Alvacin dragonfruit?"

The woodcarver set down his block and looked Alejandro over. "You don't seem like the cooking type. Why's a fella like you buzzin' about for that?"

Alejandro shrugged. "Are they poisonous or something?"

Sheila pushed through the crowds to Alejandro's side and gave him a shove. "Stop running off your leash, asshole."

The man at the table chuckled. "Oh, did your lady put you up to this?"

"The hell are you talking about?"

"No, a pal of mine did," Alejandro said, ignoring her. "Guy named Grey. You happen to know him?"

The woodcarver stood up with a smirk. "Ain't seen that bloke around in ages. But a friend of his is a friend of mine."

"Good to hear." Alejandro handed him a thick envelope. "I'm sure he'll want a friend to have these."

"Sure thing," the woodcarver said with a smile. "Have a good afternoon, you two."

With a cheerful nod, Alejandro walked back into the mass of market-goers. Sheila followed, grumbling, and gave his shoulder a sharp shove once the two had enough air around them.

"Next time someone acts like we're a couple," she said, "you tell them otherwise."

Alejandro chuckled, feeling oddly smug about the demand. "What, am I not your type?"

"I don't have a type. And I'm sick of your little games."

"The proof of Lyon's plan is in the Faces' hands. My 'games' just stopped a war."

The group reconvened in the central town square. Sheila and Tobias did most of the talking. Alejandro couldn't see Kell's face, but he could sense their expression. He didn't want to make them angrier.

The four agreed that, while they would be best off keeping to the shadows, Dayton Point would be safe enough. They could stay a while, let things calm down, plan out the next move. Eventually, conversation moved to the lighthouse. None in the group had any mechanical experience, but if the issue was simply that a massive bird had taken roost, then the four could help.

As Tobias laid out what he and Kell had heard of the building's condition, a fisherman entered the square and approached the group. He was a strong-looking brown vian with confidence in his stride, flanked by a comparatively anxious pair of hunns.

"Thought we'd find you out here," he said as a greeting. "You're the vapormage, right?"

Kell started slowly reaching for their rod. "Why do you ask?"

"Don't want no trouble. Name's Douglas. Just heard you were askin' 'round about fixing Pharos."

"The lighthouse?" Kell said. "Yeah. Trying to help out."

"Don't."

"You already have a crew on it or something?" Sheila asked.

Douglas shook his head. "Ain't nobody fixing that thing."

"We can handle it," Kell said. "Whatever's going on, we've seen worse."

"Oh, I don't doubt that. I know y'all are some tough customers. Thing is, we don't want it fixed."

Tobias tapped a finger on his beak. "Why would that be? These are rough waters, surely you'd want the safety."

"Sure. But look at that thing." He pointed to the lighthouse in the near distance, perched on one of the lower cliffs that sat to the town's north. "It's only any good if you're coming in from far out. The way it's placed doesn't help us at all."

"Well it couldn't hurt, could it?" Kell said.

"Who asked you guys to fix it?" Douglas asked, scanning the group. There was a bitter tone to the question. He knew the answer already.

Kell didn't answer. Neither did Alejandro. A cover story was never going to pass muster.

"Only one who cares about that lighthouse is Banner," Douglas said. "You guys workin' for him?"

Alejandro had to do his job and speak up. His professional voice returned. "We owe him a debt."

"Quiet, Al," Kell sternly interrupted. "Sorry, Douglas. We're just . . ."

"Just doing odd jobs," Tobias finished for them. "As we pass by, you know."

Douglas huffed in doubt. "Really? Just a couple of ol' travelers? With a vapormage in your little party?"

"You heard what happened to us, right?" Kell said. "Not like I have anything to go back to now."

"So I heard. Pity the bastards who did it."

"Exactly. I'm just trying to get by, like everyone else. Right now, that means fixing Pharos."

Douglas loomed over Kell. "If that thing kicks back up, you're not gonna make a lot of friends 'round here."

"Now, hold up," Sheila said. She stepped between the two as though she could be the voice of reason. "Our job was to fix that lighthouse. Right? So once it's fixed, we're done. If it doesn't *stay* fixed, that's not exactly *our* problem."

"Banner will make it your problem."

Sheila scoffed. "I'd like to see him try."

Douglas couldn't loom over Sheila, but he made an attempt. "If he tries to make it *our* problem, we'll make it yours." The younger of the hunns behind him cracked his knuckles to accentuate the threat, though the worry in his movement betrayed him.

"Douglas," Kell said kindly, "we don't want to make enemies, okay? Of you or Banner."

"Well you're gonna have to pick," he said. "I don't know if you noticed, but this town ain't fond of his bullshit."

"Then we're out of here the moment we're done," Sheila said. "Look, we're sticking with our plan. We'll shoo that bird away or whatever. Get Banner to leave us alone. If that bird comes back, or the thing gets broken again, whatever. He can give us shit about that. We're more worried about Lyon, anyway."

"Lyon?" Douglas scoffed. "If you're with Banner, you're with Lyon."

"We're with Owain." Alejandro had a guess about Douglas's allegiances.

He was met with glares.

"Don't need a dragon's fire coming for you either," Douglas said.

Tight beak on him. Fine.

"Then let us get this over with and we're gone," Kell said.

Douglas scanned across the group once more before turning sharply on his heel. He walked off stiffly, one hunn following close, the other mumbling something about an autograph to Kell before being tugged along to follow.

D

The stone path up to the lighthouse was matted with damp autumn leaves. It made for a slick route. If the slope up had been much steeper, it would have been dangerous, but instead it was just another nuisance to add to the list. The path wound to the overlook where Pharos stood, unguarded and unlocked. Anyone could walk right in, if they wanted.

The four began their climb, preparing to battle the bird above should it prove to be poisoned with vapor. Their heavy footfalls on the stairs alerted it early, however, and by the time they made it to the watch room, they could see it flying off towards the mainland. It left behind a large nest of branches and scavenged strips of canvas with some broken eggshells inside. With a collective shrug, the group set to inspecting the state of the lighthouse.

Damage to Pharos was limited. There were broken windows around the lantern room, and a gear for the rotating mechanism had been dislodged and cracked. While Tobias inspected the fuel and power lines, Alejandro went to the cellar storeroom to find replacement parts for much of the lighthouse's mechanisms. Sheila kept an eye on him.

The glass would have to remain broken, ultimately, but the lighthouse would be functional. The whole project was surprisingly simple. Most of the effort and time came from going up and down the building's narrow, spiraling stairs.

With the replacement gear in place, Tobias worked to verify the mechanism. He paused while rotating the lens by hand to acknowledge the buzzing sound coming from Kell's direction. Banner was calling.

"Evening, Kell," he said when they picked up. His voice was strangely bubbly, as if he had just closed a good deal. "How goes the lighthouse?"

"We're there now, Banner," they said. "Making sure we did the job right."

"Diligent. Good to hear. It's not going to last a day or so and get busted up again, is it?"

"We'll see." Kell sounded cagey. "There was a bird nesting here. No guarantees it won't come back."

"Not if you don't kill it," Banner said, matter-of-factly.

"We're all good!" Tobias shouted from the lantern chamber. "Turning it on."

"Did I hear right?" Banner said. "Excellent, excellent."

With the flip of a few switches, a wide beam of yellow light shot out from the lighthouse and slowly panned across the ocean.

"There," Kell said as Tobias joined the group on the balcony. "That's our deal done. Ledger's clear."

"Hold on now." Banner's voice had a sudden bite. "Taking care of that lighthouse hardly makes up for the fact that you never dug into what Lyon's up to."

"We dug." Kell, frustrated, tried to return the bite. "We told you what we know. We sent you the proof."

"Answer me this, then. If Lyon's going to war, what weapon is he going to use?"

The group remained silent for a moment. "We don't know," Kell finally said.

"I thought not." Banner chuckled bitterly. "You're not the only team on this, you know. According to another group, Lyon's already been testing his new weapons. Has been for . . . a few weeks now? Kell, when was your little incident?"

Tobias's eyes went wide. "What are you implying, Banner?" he demanded.

"I think you already understand."

The eyes on Kell's visor widened as well. "Are you telling us Lyon is using summons?"

"That is my theory," Banner said. "It might not be him, but certainly someone is doing--"

"How?" Tobias shouted, slamming a fist into the metal railing. "We hid it! The paper does not work!"

"Perhaps someone sold you out, professor," Banner said calmly. "Or someone cracked your code. There are plenty of smart people in Linnute."

"This is a huge problem, Banner! You don't understand!"

"Dr. Fulton, I agree that something has to be done about this. I do have a proposal, though it's quite a long shot."

"Anything. Let's hear it." Tobias looked as desperate as he sounded.

"Are you four familiar with the Psamathene?"

Sheila reflexively groaned. Banner was telling ghost stories. "That haunted bit of the ocean? What's that got to do with anything?"

"Haunted? *Really*?" Alejandro said.

"I agree," Banner said, "it's not haunted. But it is troublesome. We would have an excellent shipping line along the coast if it weren't for the fact that, every time a boat gets near it, we lose it. Having to swing away from it costs millions in fuel every year."

"That's your problem, Banner, what's it got to do with us?" Sheila's patience was worn thin.

"Well, the last boat we lost from getting too close managed to provide readings about the vapor there. It's off the charts. Unnatural. As if something was down there, pumping vapor out."

"What kind of something?" Tobias was intrigued.

"Professor, what do you know of vapor's origins?"

"Origins?" Tobias said. "I mean, I know plenty of its nature, and its applications, but . . . what do you mean, origins?"

A sigh of concession came from the other end of the call. "I know this is going to sound ridiculous. But in all my years, trying to understand why some places are more dense with vapor so that our business could take better advantage, I've come to a particular view. I don't believe vapor is a natural part of this world. This . . . miracle has a source. Which could very well be in the Psamathene. If you managed to go there, you may find it. If you can find it, you can destroy it. And if you destroy it, vapor would disappear from the world."

The lighthouse fell silent. The four, surrounding Kell's mobile, exchanged baffled and surprised looks.

He's bluffing, Sheila thought. *This guy's run out of tricks. Right? Nobody's buying this?*

"That is insane," Alejandro finally said. "That is some conspiratorial nonsense. You might as well say we could turn gravity off and float about everywhere."

"I agree," Banner said, "it sounds preposterous, but I can hardly ignore evidence when it's put in front of me."

"I would very much need to see this evidence, then," Tobias said. "But, even so, how would that help?"

"Well, professor, consider this. The average person doesn't use much vapor to live their life. Sure, it affords a few conveniences, but people are resilient. They'll adapt. There are other ways to power mobiles or cook food or what have you. Summons, meanwhile, are entirely vapor. No vapor, no summons. No vapor, no war."

"And what would happen to Kell?" Sheila said.

They perked up. "What? I'm not made of vapor. I'd live."

"Exactly," Banner said. "If this worked, people would live. That's what we're all after, right?"

"If we want to live," Sheila said, "we can't be going to the damned Psamathene. You said it yourself, Banner, you can't get a boat close."

"Well I'm sure that--"

"The caves!" Tobias blurted out, drawing the group's attention.

Kell sat up. The eyes on their visor went wide and lit brightly.

"Caves?" Banner asked, taken aback.

"The Psamathene is a few kilometers off the coast," he explained. "Surprisingly close. And I've been down at that coast before. Fishing, you know. It's interesting terrain, a lot of caves and whirlpools and such."

"I see where you're going, professor." Banner sounded nearly impressed.

"If you had asked me yesterday, I would've said the Psamathene is just some nasty whirlpools made by all those caves. And I'm not against taking a chance to prove it."

"We're not going!" Kell barked. "Do you guys even realize what you're talking about? This is the Psamathene! People don't come back! I knew you all wanted me dead, but I didn't think you'd try and kill yourselves to do it!"

"Kell!" Tobias was plainly offended by the notion. "Calm yourself!"

"We're not going to risk our lives at your stupid whim, Banner!" Kell shouted towards their mobile.

"Do you have a better plan, mage?"

"Anything's better than that."

Alejandro stood up. "If I may--"

"No!" Kell interrupted.

"Let him speak," Sheila said before thinking.

"We can settle this," Alejandro said. "Banner, we don't have time to be following your every whim. But we acknowledge that we still owe you a debt for the rescue. So here is what I propose. We will go down to the shore. We will *not* go by boat. We are not going to endanger ourselves. Once there, we'll investigate, speak with locals, do whatever we can to get proper proof of whatever the Psamathene is. At the same time, we'll be gathering resources to deal with Lyon. We will report that knowledge of the Psamathene to you, and then whatever that knowledge is, we are done, Banner. The ledger is clean. No more fucking about. Whatever you do with that knowledge is your business, not ours. Are we in agreement?"

Tobias silently nodded his agreement.

This is stupid, Sheila thought, *but it'll get him off our ass.* She nodded as well.

"You drive an interesting bargain, Speaker," Banner said. "But I can work with those terms."

All eyes turned to Kell as they looked out to sea, through the bars of the balcony's railing, watching the lighthouse's lamp sweep over a Banner cargo ship as it sailed by. Eventually, they quietly sighed. "Fine."

Thank you, thank you for the introduction. You flatter me.

My colleagues, I will naturally address the elephant in the room. It has been many, many years since I spoke to you all in this Forum. Historically, I had done so as a faculty representative, whether with Zeimatic National or with Port Mab. But, I have taken my pension and taken my leave, and taken some long-overdue time off.

And so today, I speak to you as an individual, to address a topic that has become near to my heart. Sailing. I have so many photos . . . I jest, I jest. But I have spent much time on the waters, and that does bring me to why I asked to speak today. Because, my colleagues, as they say . . . I have one last heist in me. Next slide.

I need not run down the list of anomalous locations and phenomena that have plagued our community for ages. Be they the near-perpetual Typhoon, or the lack of precipitation in Farolé's Tabrill Pass that should, by all models, not be the case. There are plenty of exceptions that serve only to prove the rules that we know. Next slide, please.

These past few years have found my curiosity focusing on the anomalous weather surrounding the Psamathene. And, yes, I will note that I said "surrounding." Bringing vessels and crew closer is a fool's errand. Next slide.

In the last 172 years, as far back as reliable records go, there has not been a ship that has entered the area we currently describe as the Psamathene that has come out . . . at all, let alone intact. The only verifiable material we have is footage from the *Ace in the Hole*, Mr. Kingley's ship. Attempting to research the Psamathene from within is a death sentence, and there is no science worth such a cost. Next slide.

But a death sentence only applies to the living. This, you see depicted, is the *Holford*. And her crew. And you will notice: There is not a soul among them. Many vessels on the waters today are piloted primarily by summons, but they always require a human captain for oversight. Next slide.

However, I have been approached by researchers with the Banner Companies, who have been devising the next generation of summons. Ones they claim could man a boat entirely on their own. Their application is limited thus far, and we will be pushing them far beyond what they've demonstrated, but the opportunity is still clear. We can examine, up close and personal, the strangest parts of our world without risk to human life. Risk to property, sure, but who among us hasn't left gear out to ruin on accident? Property is nothing compared to lives.

The *Holford* sets off this summer, pending final logistical checks. I look forward to sharing what we discover, both about the Psamathene and about this new process of data collection.

— Comments by Dr. Boyko at the Weather Investigation Forum,
Delivered 18/04

CHAPTER NINE

Tobias was the first to wake, stepping out to the balcony around Pharos's lantern to take in the salty air. A swarm of gulls dove across the surface of the shallows below, tracking their morning meal. The nest on the balcony remained undisturbed. He took a curious look over it, idly wondering where the canvas and other materials came from, what had happened to the offspring in the eggs, when the bird would come back. *The bird will be back*, he thought, confidently, without proof.

The group soon left the lighthouse, Kell reluctantly bringing up the rear. As they walked down the slick stones, Douglas and his compatriots approached, holding clubs. Tobias greeted them cheerfully and wordlessly. Douglas returned the gesture. They each understood the other's plan, and nobody had any desire to interfere. Pharos belonged to Dayton Point. The locals would take care of it, whatever the locals decided that meant.

The road to Reeseport, the nearest town to the Psamathene, was long, more than a day's drive. Sheila and Tobias agreed to shifts, while Alejandro--who, he confessed, never learned to drive--kept in the back. Kell sat in the front passenger seat, their hood drawn up, quietly brooding and retreating into themself. They were clearly not a fan of going south.

"This situation keeps getting more complicated," Alejandro said idly, poking at his mobile. "So much for our plans."

"I wouldn't say it's getting more complicated," Tobias said, seated beside him. "It just keeps shifting. At least we'll have Banner away from us soon."

"Hopefully. Then it's just a small matter of Lyon's super weapons," Alejandro said dryly.

Tobias nodded. "Right surprise he got his hands on it."

"You knew there were summons out there, doc," Sheila said. "We fought one."

Tobias sighed. "Well, yes, I had just guessed that it was Santhrupta. Or *maybe* Cassandra, low chance as that is."

"What do you mean?" Alejandro said.

"Well," Tobias said, "Cassie always hated the strix design. Said it was unsettling."

"No, professor, I mean why did you think it was Santhrupta?"

Tobias shrugged. "A summon has to come from *somebody*. And that strix was smart enough, it was reacting and observing. It was definitely a summon, it just wasn't all there. As if whoever made it wasn't all there themself. Which would be Cassandra, last I heard. But I simply can't imagine her making a strix, even involuntarily. Santhrupta, he's always been a bit . . . leaning overboard, as it were. Entirely possible he'd become more and more unwell in the last few years. And summoning is just a spell at the end of the day, so there could've been an accidental discharge."

"So your guess," Sheila said with a grumble, "is that this guy accidentally made a summon, it walked to Rijest, wandered into the mountains to fuck with Kell, then went to Gauvencia for us to fight it?"

Tobias nodded. "The distances aren't impossible."

"They might as well be," Sheila muttered in disbelief.

"So who else could've made them?" Alejandro asked.

"The rest of the team have all passed," Tobias said. "They were much too old. I was the chipper young chap of the lab, I'll have you know."

"You're sure they never taught anyone?"

Tobias chuckled. "Obviously I don't know that, Al, but I would be surprised. Nobody was ever interested in learning."

"Who did you try to teach?" Sheila accused.

Tobias shrugged off being caught. "Dr. Charmchi, if you can believe it. I was quite eager to share when we first worked it out. He wasn't eager to learn."

"Better not be eager now," Sheila said.

"Certainly not *that* eager," Tobias said. "Willing, though, absolutely. I always figured, when the day came, it'd be my job to pass the technique along to someone I trust not to misuse it."

Kell scoffed. "You trust us?"

"Why wouldn't I?"

"'Cause we're a bunch of killers, liars, and assholes," Kell said flatly.

"Have you not been to university, Kell?" Tobias chuckled. "A doctorate doesn't mean you're a good person. I'd trust any of you three over much of the faculty I've worked with.

And it's a bit of a moot point besides," he said, leaning forward to tease Sheila, "given that some of you aren't too keen on the idea."

"You're not messing with my soul, doc," Sheila said.

"Ah, some students simply refuse to learn," Tobias said with a laugh. "Kell?"

They shook their head quietly in response.

"I'll try," Alejandro offered. "If there are no objections."

"Don't," Sheila said, barely taking her eyes from the road. "That cat was huge. You won't have enough space back there."

Tobias waved off Sheila's words. "Oh, there's plenty. Chapalu's only as big as I want it to be."

"*Don't*," Sheila repeated.

"We'll be fine. I *am* the expert on this, after all. Shall we?" Tobias held an arm out stiff in front of him. "Al, take my hand."

"You're a bit old for me, professor."

Tobias's arm sagged as he laughed. Kell, for all their brooding, couldn't keep themself from huffing out a small laugh as well. "Serious, Al. Please."

"I know, I know." He grabbed Tobias's wrist and relaxed his posture.

"I'll do something very simple, I'm sure you'll feel what's going on. Just focus."

Tobias removed his goggles and placed them in a pocket on his vest. He closed his eyes and started the spell, the loose vapor sweeping through the Basilisk coalescing in a small, barely visible ball in his lap. He exhaled deeply and fell silent. The movement was familiar, but familiarity is not ease, and he still had reason to focus. With a sudden gasp and a squirm in his seat, the mass of vapor started to turn green and solidify, stubby limbs stretching out from its center. Chapalu, as small as a kitten, looked around from Tobias's lap. It took a look at its summoner and batted at his goggles.

Tobias released his grip on Alejandro's wrist and put his goggles back on. "There's a lot there to explain, I know, but I've always encouraged the hands-on approach."

"You just made a familiar," Kell observed.

"That is the starting point, yes. The rest is . . . quite a bit more than that, Al, I'm sure you can tell?"

Alejandro's arms hung limp in surprise. "*That* is what you do?"

Chapalu let out a soft, ghostly purr as Tobias idly pet it. "Have you made a familiar before? I should've asked that first . . ."

"Of course. With kits. I've done it enough, I know their shortcomings and quirks and all that. But this?" Alejandro slumped in his seat. "It reminded me of having food stuck in your throat, how it was lodged in there as you moved the vapor, it seemed so . . ."

"Dense?" Tobias asked.

"Unnatural."

Tobias sighed. "And that was with the smallest bit of canopic I've successfully used. Quite proud of myself."

"Kudos, I'm sure," Alejandro said. He watched Chapalu laze about for a moment. "Why was the vapor so turbulent? Do you not define the form in there?"

"The canopic defines it. There's a bit of influence you can exert if you want, but . . ." He gave the summon in his lap another pet. "What can I say, I like Chapalu."

"Is that what would show up if you evoked?" Kell asked.

"Wish we knew. Never found anyone capable of it."

"Sheila can do it," Kell said flippantly.

"Kell, come on." The end of her rope was in sight.

Alejandro sighed and righted himself. "So then. I'll start with a familiar, and just . . . follow that technique you demonstrated."

"That'll get you started." Tobias offered his arm and watched Alejandro's hesitation. "Nervous?"

"You weren't?"

Tobias's beak tapped. "I'm right here to clean things up if anything happens. Don't worry."

The reassurance seemed to float past Alejandro, his face and arm remaining as anxious as before. Chapalu let out another purr. The sound stopped the subtle, rapid shuddering of Alejandro's arm, allowing him to grab Tobias's wrist.

Alejandro closed his eyes. Tobias watched intently, listening as closely as the engine and the road passing underneath would allow, as his student began forming the barest shape of a familiar. He tugged gently at Alejandro's arm, trying to steer his progress. Gradually, the vapor coalesced into a chunky, rabbit-like form with stubby antlers and small, bat-like wings on its back, its brown fur matted and swirling like a wood grain. Alejandro gasped for air and jostled, dropping the creation to the floor of the Basilisk, where it stayed unmoving.

"There you go, there you go!" Tobias cheered with fatherly pride. "Still with us, Al? That was a hearty chunk."

Alejandro shook the stunned look from his face. He was a touch pale, his light blue eyes even fainter. "Yeah, yeah. Just a bit . . ." He trailed off, the sharp edge in his voice having dulled away.

Tobias chuckled. "Dazed? Confused? I know. You were on the upper end of safe, there, almost had to pull you back."

"Thank you for not making a mess," Sheila snipped as she rapped the steering wheel, "but don't do that again."

Alejandro nodded and gathered himself, looking at the summon on the ground. It had rolled over and was flitting its wings rapidly to no effect. A hint of a smile appeared on Alejandro's face. "Dolly little thing. Not really what I figured would come out, though."

Tobias set Chapalu on the floor. It regarded the other summon like it was a new, lazy playmate. "It was your first go at it! Be proud of yourself!" He took another look at the new summon. "Oh, you can tell it's yours, has your eyes and everything."

Alejandro chuckled to himself. "Never planned to be a father."

"What're you calling it?" Tobias said.

"I don't know. I'm bad with names."

"Any Crystal songs to go with?" Kell heckled.

Alejandro blushed and shook his head. "Why'd you go with Chapalu?"

"The wildcat," Tobias said. "That old rhyme?"

"Oh, right, duh," Alejandro said. He stared at his summon in quiet thought as it lethargically looked around.

Kell stared as well, from the front of the vehicle. "Raurack," they eventually said, as if the summon's name was already decided fact.

Alejandro smiled. "I guess it does look like one. Huh. My own Raurack for a cull, that's good." He gave Raurack a pet between its wings. "I swear I can almost see the world through its eyes," he added in placid wonder. "Like I'm down there."

Tobias worriedly shuffled in his seat. "Oh, that's not good," he said. "Let's get that dispelled, just to be safe."

Alejandro watched Tobias intently as he held a hand over Raurack, slowly turning it into a glowing mass of vapor that retreated into Alejandro. Dispelling was an easy spell, even on a proper summon. Alejandro cast the same spell on Chapalu with little difficulty. Tobias gave him a friendly pat on the back and relaxed into his seat.

B

The south of Cymona was dense with bitter swampland. Travel would've been difficult without the centuries-old web of roads the group found themselves on. The barriers flanking the route were tall and spiked to better deter whatever was hiding in the sawgrass. The trenches in the macadam were deeper thanks to the softer earth, with occasional puddles seeping up from underneath. Sheila and Tobias had traded off driving duties, pushing his mind closer to the nature and state of the road the Basilisk drove upon.

Long stretches of the route, where the road stopped its meandering weave and stiffened out straight, had an unnatural rigidity in the ground that refused to absorb the rumbles of the Basilisk's engine. They were the result of experiments in earth-aspected vapor. Made perfect sense to Tobias. Most spells that aspected towards earth dealt in attraction and repulsion. A vapormage could use them to shake and unsettle the earth from beneath their foes; for everyday folks, the spells made for a decent short-term adhesive. Using that idea to tack down the ground itself was clever. Good for them.

The main route branched off to the east, with a narrow channel heading towards Reeseport. The offshoot continued directly to the town's gate, its barriers splaying out to meet up with the town's outermost wall. The gate itself barely existed, just towers marking the corners. There was nothing that could be closed. The city, with its architecture, trusted anything and everything that happened to come down Route 14.

Reeseport was a younger city, relatively speaking, one of the few that had managed to thrive in the southern fens. The popular opinion held that it thrived entirely because of its textile trade. The ground was better for it, and some enterprising locals managed to convince others that their quality and process was especially strong. Treating the process as some highly secure trade secret certainly helped the mystique. Fabric from Reeseport was good, sure, but it was the adamant promotion that made it a coveted commodity.

The locals, and die-hards to the brand, would naturally never stand to hear such a negative claim. To them, real Reese cloth was something special, and anything made elsewhere was a pale imitation unworthy of the name. After the factory owner became mayor and sold the concern to Banner Goods, those imitations--like the vest Tobias was wearing--became all anyone could find. At least they were cheaper.

Traffic that day was sparse. The older cities to the north grew before Banner's fleet of delivery vehicles, forcing them into single-file columns as they snaked perpetually through the streets, but Reeseport was younger. Its roads were wide, wide enough that vehicles could sprawl out and pick up speed, wide enough that Tobias could steer the Basilisk without difficulty. He drove through the city center, past buildings that once held tailor's shops and hat makers and a dozen other sorts of business, but now held little if anything of interest. The only facades that appeared to be taken care of were Banner's.

"Not much chance for a quick shopping trip," Tobias said, craning his neck and glancing around as he drove.

"As much as I don't want to involve him further . . ." Alejandro trailed off, poking at his mobile.

"Would prove we're on it," Sheila said.

"True. So much for their 'rapid delivery,' though. We'd be stuck waiting at least a whole day."

"Well, yeah," Sheila said. "That's only in the big cities. If I ever ordered anything back home, it'd be two, three days before it shows."

"Bit obnoxious."

Sheila laughed dismissively. "You're even more of a city boy than I thought! Figured a diplomat would get out of town once in a blue moon."

"You may be surprised to learn," Alejandro said dryly, "that people who want power over people tend to congregate around other people."

The lights of Kell's eyes narrowed in blunt displeasure with the two. "What do you even think you need for this?" they said.

Alejandro shrugged. "Something for excavation, I would assume."

"We're not digging a hole. Diving a cave is like climbing a mountain. You need ropes, anchors, grip. Unless you're gonna crawl like an animal," Kell said.

"Kell's right," Sheila said. "We have enough supplies already. Long as we're not idiots, we'll be fine."

Getting into Reeseport by the main road was simple. Getting out towards the coast was trickier. There were no other gates, it seemed, certainly none large enough for a vehicle. Tobias followed signs to a small locked gateway in the city wall. It had a guard station but no guard. Tobias parked in a nearby lot and led the way, letting out a satisfied sigh as he looked around and waited.

"That's the sigh of a man who's finally come back home," Alejandro said in reply.

Tobias chuckled. "Suppose I have, in a sense. My brother lived down here for quite a while. I'd come down and visit now and then."

"I presume he was here for the clothworks."

Tobias nodded. "Vaporless materials science expert. At it for years until they laid him off." He casually turned to Kell. "Imagine what they could've done with your kind of training."

Kell barely looked back at him. "What are you talking about?"

"Just trying to involve you in the conversation. You've been awfully quiet."

"I know." Kell wanted to keep it that way.

"Well." Tobias's train of thought derailed but quickly found the tracks again. "Well then! I can't imagine we'll need to be at the shore for very long. Shall we continue waiting for a guard, or perhaps head to a tavern and gather information?"

"Might as well hit the shore," Sheila said. "Not gonna be anyone at the tavern."

"There's nobody here," Kell said.

"There's gotta be someone on duty."

"You don't know that," Kell muttered.

"What? Of course I do," Sheila said, "it's the middle of the day. Gate's gonna be staffed, tavern's gonna be dead. There were fuck-all people at that one in Vaaland around this time."

"We're not in Vaaland, are we?" Kell grumbled.

"Kell, *come on.*"

"Fuck this." Kell abruptly started walking away, their pace accelerating as Sheila gave chase.

Tobias and Alejandro, meanwhile, stayed put and watched with a shared sense of confusion.

"Well they seem a bit displeased," Tobias eventually said.

"I've set them in a bad way," Alejandro said with a sigh.

"Doubt it's just you. Very sudden from them. Must be something more to it." Tobias took a deep nasal breath. "The vapor doesn't feel all that different here to you, does it?"

Alejandro stood stationary for a moment. "Not that I can tell. Could that induce something like this?"

Tobias laughed to himself with a hint of bitterness. "The fact you have to ask."

"Pardon?"

Tobias shook his head. "When I was young, we had very different materials for learning how to interact with vapor. We had the green book when I was a student, Porter and Swift's second edition. They're up to . . . well, I'm guessing you're in your mid-30s, Al?"

"I turned 30 a few months back," he said.

Tobias thought for a second. "So you probably had an orange-covered book when you were learning to use vapor, right? Eighth edition?"

Alejandro took his turn at thinking. "Believe so."

"My sympathies. Somewhere around the sixth edition, the Porter and Swift just turned to rubbish. That was the first moment that took the glamour out of academia for me. It was one thing for them to take such an interesting book, so very well written, and turn it into such a sterile piece of pulp. There were spells in the second edition that kids simply aren't learning these days! Some of it I understand--we should not have been learning to do a whirligig. Still have a scar on my leg. But there were practical things, and now they all say, 'oh, just use this kit,' you know. And my department gets off easy! Dr. Charmchi has the more recent history books, and by the gods. No wonder there are kids who don't know Alvacii even existed."

Alejandro's head tilted as he looked at Tobias. "Seriously?"

"Seriously!" Tobias was flustered by his own story. "I'll grant you, they were Zeimatian students, but still. That empire covered nearly the whole continent. How could you not know about it? And I'll tell you how, it's rubbish textbooks. Whoever's writing them or funding them, if they don't like a bit, they just don't put it in! And then we're left having to tell people basic things about how the world works, all because some priest or president doesn't want people to know you can flick a damn flame!" Tobias's shouting suddenly cut to embarrassed laughter. "I'm sorry, I apologize, I'm working myself up here."

"You've thought about this a lot," Alejandro said.

"Of course. I try to take pride in my work." Tobias shrugged. "Don't you?"

Sheila and Kell were approaching, and neither seemed happy to be doing so.

"Can't say that I do," Alejandro said quietly.

Sheila rejoined the group, arms crossed, her attention centered on Kell. The vapormage was watching the guard station with their head hung and their hood up, their posture unwilling to shuffle any discernible amount. They made no apology, or if they had, it was too muttered and quiet to be heard. The two had clearly gone through quite the argument, but it had just as clearly been settled. Tobias had no reason to linger on it. When Kell was in a better way, he decided, perhaps he'd try to speak with them about it.

The group loitered in an uncomfortable silence for some minutes until the door on the guard station finally opened. A hunn knight emerged wearing a clean uniform and a baffled expression.

"Who are you lot?" the knight said, eyeing the four suspiciously.

"Oh, hello there," Tobias said. "We're travelers. Headed down to check out the caves along the coast, if we may."

"With a Basilisk?" He gestured at the nearby vehicle.

Alejandro stepped forward, straightening out his suit as he had every time he was about to speak for the group. Kell held their good arm out in front of him, knocking him in the chest as they took command. Their hood was still up, so they let it down and stared at the knight, keeping their head hung. Presumably, they meant for their helmet to do all the explaining.

"Who do you think you are?" Either the knight didn't understand the explanation, or he didn't buy it.

"The last vapormage. What does it look like?" Kell sounded exhausted, and addressed the knight as if he were the only thing between them and a comfortable bed.

"It looks like you stole a bunch of equipment." He reached for his sword.

Kell clenched their left fist. In an instant, their entire left arm was engulfed in a swirl of wind and lightning, vapor sweeping and crackling around their body. "I don't want to do this," they said, staring squarely at the knight.

The knight paused, worry written on his face. He hesitantly returned his sword to its scabbard. "Fine. Then tell me why you're off to the coast."

With their gaze still fixed on the knight, Kell released the vapor around their arm, bouncing on their feet slightly as the wind aspect pushed into the ground. They stiffly readjusted their posture, punctuating their annoyance. "We're settling something with Banner Goods. It doesn't concern you."

"I've been down there before," Tobias said, hoping to reassure the knight. "We don't need a guide."

The knight unlatched the gateway. "Good. Get out of here."

C

Much of the coastline outside Reeseport was cliffs of limestone and rhyolite, a sharp striped fissure dropping to the sea. But some points saw the ground dipping towards the water as the surrounding terrain formed natural bridges over it. Tobias led the group to one of those lagoons, where a narrow path opened to a small beach surrounded by curiously smooth and geometric walls of basalt.

The lagoon offered a view of the ocean and the many islands and spires that stood in it. They jutted sharply out of the water, sheer walls of rock a dozen meters high standing proudly, while equally tall but far thinner pillars looked as though they could fall over with a sharp enough wave. The waters surrounding them churned, lapping at their edges, exposing submerged surfaces when they dipped even slightly lower. Despite the tumult of the waves, the spires acted like breakers that kept the water closer to shore foamy yet calm.

Tobias let in a thin hint of nostalgia as his hand graced the rock wall. "This would be the mouth of the cave."

"So where's the rest of it?" Alejandro asked. "Underwater?"

Tobias chuckled and knocked on the rock. "Right here."

Alejandro stepped closer to inspect. "Doesn't quite look like a cave-in."

"Nor should it." Tobias cracked his knuckles. "I'm sure I mentioned, when I first described my work, that you could use someone's canopic as a sort of identifier. Yes?"

"Something like that," Sheila said. "I wasn't listening too closely."

"Well, not to go on too long, but that was one of our first breakthroughs. If you cast a spell, Sheila, and I cast the same one, they'll be subtly different. The more it interacts with the canopic, the more obvious that becomes. Follow that logically until you have a spell where the whole point is just to shout who you are. Pair that with sigils and you get a sort of lock and key with vapor. But the early prototypes were quite imprecise. Almost any ol' fool could get in."

Just glad Chapalu's back with me, Tobias thought. *Wouldn't work if it was hogging my canopic.*

Tobias leaned back against the columns of basalt, his hands held flat against the rock. With a steady grinding sound, two columns nearby started to retreat into the wall. The adjacent columns followed, fanning out until the full mouth of a cave was exposed to the beach. When the grinding stopped, Tobias gestured to the opening and bowed with a proud flourish.

Sheila sighed. "You never fished here, have you?"

"Not once."

"Nice work, professor," Alejandro said. "What's down there?"

"I don't actually know. The Environment Minister was curious about our work and asked for a prototype here, said there wouldn't be much impact to the local ecosystem."

"And you just believed them?" Sheila said.

"She certainly knew what she was talking about."

"Should be simple to explore quickly, then," Alejandro said as he peered into the darkness of the cave. "But if it isn't much deeper than it looks, then what do you suppose that gets us?"

"Well, consider the state of the water and just how many spires are out there." Tobias pointed to the ocean. "It looks unpleasant out there on a clear day. Doubt even a Dayton Point sailor would take that on. And with the ground this broadly porous--" he gestured towards the cave-- "clearly, there's a geological phenomenon here. That's all the Psamathene is."

"What if the cave's deep?" Kell said, staring at the abyss in the rock.

"What do you mean?" Tobias asked, genuinely confused.

"Cymona doesn't pick things at random." Kell was still staring. "They'd want a lock because they'd want to keep something out. Or in."

"Such as?"

Kell sighed. "Cymona hates sahagins, right?"

"Nobody likes sahagins," Sheila said dismissively.

"But Cymona *hates* sahagins. They see one, they kill 'em. But sahagins have to live somewhere, right?"

Tobias, concern bearing down on him, looked into the cave. "You think there could be a sahagin settlement down there?"

Kell rubbed their right arm. "I think you should be ready for that, yeah."

Alejandro took the first steps in, holding out a flame of vapor from his hand to illuminate the cave as it twisted away from the sunlight. As the path sloped downward, the columns of basalt that composed the cavern's walls were replaced by jagged, porous rock. Tobias wasn't much of an expert on the subject, but he guessed the area had once been volcanic. It would lend credence to his theory for the turbulent waters above. He turned around, considering if more exploration was even necessary, only to see Sheila taking up a distant, hesitant rear.

"Are you alright, Sheila?" he called. "Come along."

"I'm coming," she snapped back.

"Afraid of sahagins?" Alejandro teased.

"Afraid of cave-ins," she said. "This is just some hole in the ground. It collapses, we're dead."

Alejandro felt his way around a corner, where a strip of pale green glowed in the rock. The light it gave off was dim, its color producing a peculiar sickly air, but it was bright enough to aid in navigation. Not much farther down the path, more green rocks glowed in the walls and roof, illuminating square columns of metal.

"There are support beams," Alejandro said. "This is more like a mine than a cave."

"Well I'll be," Tobias said before turning to Sheila. "How are you about mines, then?"

"Still would rather have the open air." Despite the protest, Sheila hurried herself along, pressing against the sharp wall for stability on the increasingly polished and slick rock ground.

The twists in the cavern continued for what felt like kilometers, never staying too steady, never staying too narrow. The pale green glow came and went, staying rare enough that Alejandro refrained from extinguishing his flame. Flat portions of the ground gathered thin pools of water. Stalagmites reached up along the walls, some reaching their destination and becoming thin columns, but the middle of the cavern remained consistently free of obstructions. Soon the echoing drips of water ahead carried a more airy timbre. The group found a large, open chamber in the cave, dotted with older and thicker mineral columns and very few glowing rocks. They stepped in cautiously.

Looking around, Alejandro gestured for the group to go silent. He extinguished the sizzling flame in his hand. After a moment of nothing but darkness and echoing drips, he reignited the flame in his right hand. Alejandro and Sheila were both looking up.

"You hear it too?" Alejandro said quietly.

"Hear what?" Tobias said, cursing his age for the first time in a long while.

Alejandro pointed to the top of the chamber, shrouded in shadow. "That humming. Tobias, can I borrow your goggles for a moment?"

"Sure, why?"

Alejandro held Tobias's goggles in his left hand. "I should've paid more attention at the lighthouse," he muttered. He surrounded the flame with his left hand, goggles pointing upward, and tried to focus the flame so it would give off more light than heat. The effect barely shifted, but it focused enough light towards the top of the chamber that a large mechanical fan could barely be seen, spinning rapidly and almost silently.

"There's a fan up there," Sheila said.

Alejandro nodded and returned Tobias's goggles. "Ventilation. Kell, you were on to something."

Kell gave a small, indifferent nod to the praise as they continued past the chamber.

The hum and hiss continued as the four wound through the passage, their weapons close at hand. After many more minutes, the workings of the ventilation system started emerging even among the narrow corridors. The hum held steady, but the hiss increased in volume, oscillating regularly. Tobias shrugged it off as mechanical noise. It hardly bothered him, though apparently, his hearing was starting to go. He wondered idly how annoying everyone else found it.

The hiss started to turn erratic as the group found their way into another large chamber, the third along the seemingly unending passageway. The mineral columns here were thick and old, wider than a person, and the glowing green rock was plentiful in the walls. Alejandro finally extinguished his vapor flame. There was no need for it anymore; the glow was so even that shadows struggled to form anywhere. There was little clue that, behind a thick column deep in the chamber, a large white serpent was waiting. The group only knew of its presence as it slithered out slowly.

Sheila and Alejandro quickly grabbed their weapons. Tobias followed suit, but Kell stood steady, unarmed. "I know what this is," they said.

"Well?" Alejandro said.

"If we're going to a sahagin city, then this would be their Guardian."

Tobias glanced at Kell, then at the serpent steadily approaching. "You know their Guardian?"

"Yeah." They stepped ahead of the others. "Caduceus?"

The serpent's head twitched in recognition. It focused on Kell as it repositioned its lower body. The serpent was long, the length of three adult humans if not more. Much of its body was coiled around itself like a noose made of scales. It had some fins along its body, but they were small and sparse enough that it was unclear whether land or water was the creature's domain. The fins along its head rippled with a pearlescent shimmer as it moved. Its head tipped down in front of Kell.

INTERLOPER.

"What was that?" Alejandro said, his eyes gone wide. The word rang in their skulls, though the serpent had not spoken, its face staying still, fixated on Kell.

"You heard it too?" Sheila said, her stance loosening. Tobias nodded as he glanced around, his beak separating with awe.

Caduceus slowly brought its body closer to Kell, who remained rigid as they stood--whether from bravery or fear, it was impossible to tell. After a lingering, silent standoff, Caduceus abruptly lunged forward, ramming Kell in the chest, knocking them to the ground.

Sheila's sword moved instantly. "Get the hell away from them!"

The swing connected solidly with Caduceus's body. When Sheila pulled away for a second swing, however, there was no sign of injury on the serpent. No blood, nor vapor smoke, emerged from where there would be a wound, should be a wound, but there was no sign of injury at all, just the smooth rippling of scales under a pervasive pale green light.

Sheila stepped back, defensive. "The hell? How tough is this thing?"

As if to answer, Caduceus swung its neck and head at her, knocking her off her feet and onto the ground with a thick sloshing thud. Tobias, swinging his spear to make any room he could, rushed over to help. Caduceus responded with a lunge that Tobias could easily dodge, allowing him a scraping strike with his spear that had as little effect as Sheila's sword.

"Kell!" Sheila shouted as she stood. "Fire!"

Kell staggered to their feet. "Can't! There's nothing!"

"The vapor is damned thin," Tobias said. "Save it for defense!"

The serpent lunged at Tobias again. Alejandro stabbed at its tail, shouting for its attention. His hits, too, had no impact, but he was able to dodge as Caduceus swiped at him multiple times. The others used the time to recover. Alejandro's dancing dodges inched towards where Kell stood, forcing them to back up towards the wall. Caduceus swung, pushing Alejandro into Kell and both into the wall. After a quick nod of apology, Alejandro spun around the serpent to redirect its attention. Kell, lacking their usual offensive options, kicked at Caduceus, falling off balance as their boot bounced off the serpent's body.

BETRAYAL.

The voice--for as much as a soundless sensation could be called a voice--rang bitterly in their heads. The serpent focused on Kell, biting at their good arm, the strikes only barely deflected by the rod Kell held out ahead of them. Alejandro took advantage of its focus, plunging his knives in behind the fins on its head. The move drew a pained reaction, the serpent's skin reacting as if it should be bleeding, though even then, neither blood nor vapor smoke emerged from the creature.

Kell whispered something, or perhaps just exhaled loudly and rapidly, at the serpent only centimeters from their visor. After a pause, Caduceus slumped to the ground. Alejandro gave it a few more stabs to confirm the kill before falling backward to the wet ground.

The four took a moment to recover and acknowledge what had just happened. They killed a Guardian. Worse--or better, depending who you asked--it was a sahagin city's Guardian. Regardless of the allegiance, a Guardian was nearly impossible to kill, and certainly not by a meager group of four. Either Caduceus was less than they had thought, or they had gotten incredibly lucky.

Tobias slowly stood. "Are you okay, Kell?" he said between gasping breaths.

Kell was whispering something under their breath as they collected themself. They leaned against the wall of the chamber, their visor blank. "I'll be fine," they eventually said. "Not hurt. The vapor's way too thin though. I need a bit to recharge."

"Alright," Sheila said, "we'll recoup here real quick."

"You three, go on ahead," Kell said. "I'm gonna be a while."

Sheila shook her head. "I'm not leaving you."

"I'll be fine." Kell gave the serpent's head a soft pat. "If you don't see me in, say, ten minutes, then worry. Just . . . if there is a city down there, try talking with them first, okay? We can't win that fight."

"We can just turn back," Tobias said.

Kell shook with a small laugh. "Can you, doc?"

Tobias nearly argued but instead hung his head and chuckled. Kell had the right of it. His curiosity was too strong. He was too committed. There was no world where he turned back.

"We won't stray too far, Kell," Alejandro said as he tapped the others on their shoulders.

Kell rubbed their right arm and nodded. "Appreciate it, Al."

D

After sliding through a tight corridor and rounding a corner, Sheila held an arm out to group the three up, close to the wall.

"The hell kind of unit are we here?" She spoke barely above a whisper. "Are we really leaving them behind?"

"Sheila." Alejandro glanced back up the tunnel. "Did you look at them? Did you listen to them? Kell is terrified."

"Of sahagins? Doubtful." Tobias glanced deeper down the tunnel, the luminescence waning in the near distance. "What would a vapormage be terrified of?"

"Better question," Alejandro said, "what would *Kell* be terrified of?"

Sheila scoffed. "Everything?"

Alejandro glared at her. "They're the anxious sort, yes. But this is *fear*. What could a sahagin city possibly have that would push them over that line?"

Tobias shrugged. "Only one way to find out, right?" He slid away from the others and started down the cave.

Sheila sighed lightly. "Curiosity killed the cat, didn't it?" she called out before following.

The glow in the cave walls picked back up, showing clean staircases and hand railing grooves in the rock. The ventilation system ducked in and out of the ceiling. Rectangles were chiseled out of the rock along the stairway, remnants of frames that now held nothing. Occasionally, a rectangle held a decaying sheet of wood inside. Soon the grooves in the walls were replaced with railings of petrified wood and chiseled stone. Their footfalls softened as the group saw more and more evidence of civilization.

Tobias led the group around a corner and slid to a stop. Alejandro and Sheila ran into him as he stood, frozen in place, before two sahagins holding their weapons out at him. They were dressed in simple, clean uniforms and standing before a wooden gate that reached to the height of the cavern. They had been waiting, ready.

"Hands up," one guard demanded. "The elder will see you."

The group complied. One guard opened the gate as the other led the three down another staircase, taking another twist before opening into a massive chasm. The exposed walls were saturated with luminescent rock, giving the entire space a rich, surreal glow. Stone structures, built in cascading tiers, climbed in curving rows much of the way towards the ceiling nearly a hundred meters high. A thick, spiraling column stood near the middle of the cavern, giving the impression it supported the entire ceiling's weight. Barely visible in the heights, a complex ventilation system hung, circulating the dense, cold, stale air. A number of simple, freestanding metal structures, three or four storeys tall at best, stood in front of the stone structures along what resembled a narrow road. Lanterns glowing orange with vapor flame hung from tall nearby poles, barely balancing the overwhelming green light.

The guard walked the awe-struck trio up to an older sahagin waiting in what resembled a town square, surrounded by three others. He wore a simple, sharp rope that seemed white, though the dominant green glow made true colors harder to identify. He stood with seriousness, a hint of a smirk on his flat, scaly face.

"Found them, Cyprin," the guard said to the robed sahagin. "Walked right up to the gate."

Cyprin's yellow eyes narrowed. "I see. Thank you, Val." His voice carried the gravitas and weariness of age. "Welcome to Sao Neso, you three. What did you do to Caduceus?"

Sheila and Tobias both looked at Alejandro. He silently accepted the assignment. "The serpent, you mean?" he said.

"Of course." Cyprin's scaly brow furrowed. "What have you done to her?"

"Caduceus attacked us, sir." Alejandro was stalling.

"Of course she did. She's supposed to." Cyprin was diplomatically impatient. "How did you get past her?"

"We came down as a group of four, sir. Our fourth . . . remains behind." Alejandro decided the full truth would not help their situation. He was probably right.

"A distraction?" Cyprin sounded surprised.

"Caduceus was quite focused on them, sir."

Cyprin approached Alejandro. The sahagin was tall, taller than Tobias, yet alienly thin. His lanky frame easily towered over Alejandro. "You're the leader, then?"

Alejandro swallowed a lump in his throat. "Yes, sir."

"Interesting. I'm not seeing much leadership out of you," Cyprin said.

"I am not our primary leader," Alejandro said humbly. "Our leader was the one who stayed behind." Sheila shot him a quick, curious glance. Tobias nodded. *Kell is a leader, I suppose,* he thought.

"Did they? Hmm." Cyprin stepped back and looked the three over. "You do realize I don't believe a word you're saying?"

"Plainly," Alejandro said. "But that doesn't change the truth."

"Caduceus has been our Guardian since time immemorial," Cyprin said bitterly. "We know her far better than you. She would not let you three slip by and sacrifice one of your own. She does not abide such cowardice."

"What I have described is true," Alejandro insisted.

"Then we shall prove it! We're going up to Caduceus. Unless this mysterious fourth of yours"--his voice rose as if calling for someone at the gate--"intends to show?"

A beat of silence. Cyprin scoffed at the expected absence and had the three turn around to walk towards the gate. As they did, a faint human shadow began to appear in the walkway.

"I'm over here," a voice called out.

Steps echoed. A scrawny hooded figure walked down the steps leading to the entry plaza, slouched and stumbling, their dark cloak dragging against the ground. A twin-headed rod stuck out behind them. Their right arm, covered in bright green fabric and bandages, cradled a large, glossy helmet. Their golden yellow eyes nearly glowed beneath their hood, catching the light as they stood tall and raised their head. With their left hand, they pulled their hood back to expose scaly ridges that nearly resembled hair and a flat, purple-tinged face.

"Dad."

For the professional football team, see Farrill Guardians.

The earliest known record of any of the creatures known as Guardians dates to the *Historia Linutia*, written around the year 829, and describes the first interactions between the Zeim hunn tribe and Owain several hundred years prior. The *Historia* describes the Zeims as having "reacted with great fear, and thus conspired to slay the beast, only for it to reappear in haste, indifferent to death." The tribe's migration into what is now Zeimatia is believed to be a result of fleeing Owain. (See Zeimatia → Founding.) *The Ballad of Avalon Chase* in 914 is the second extant record of Owain's presence that is widely agreed to refer to the Guardian directly.[1] The veracity of its details are disputed, however, and it is generally considered to be an iteration of regional folk legends as opposed to an authoritative historical record. Despite this, it has remained influential in cultural depictions of the Guardian.

The four Guardians known to date--Owain, Hakuta, Vakonivak, and Gauven--are first described as a group in René McNeill's *Overlay of Linnute Upon the Fall of Alvacii* (pub. 1170). None of the Guardians beyond Owain had been recorded in surviving material prior to McNeill's work. McNeill describes the Guardians as "influencers of the new order; they are tasked, whether by themselves or by their patrons, with exerting quiet control when it is needed." McNeill describes several traditions related to the Guardians that continue to this day; he describes King Julien I riding Gauven "as a demonstration of his power and worth as a sovereign", for example.

The process by which Guardians reincarnate has not been publicly documented[2]; however, experiments conducted with Vakonivak by Dr. Yvonne Felse have resulted in the general scientific agreement that such a phenomenon does in fact occur. A Guardian's death has been described in several sources as resembling the death of a vapor-poisoned animal in both observable artifacts and vaporic effects. The Guardian then returns within 3-12 days with no evidence of injury or ill effect. They do, however, demonstrate awareness of their prior life and subsequent death. There is debate whether the new Guardian is the same creature or if it only shares a consciousness.

In most cultures, communication with a Guardian is done through an official interpreter, who is tasked with examining the physical movements of the Guardian to determine their desires and intentions. In Farolian governance, this is considered an official duty of the sovereign; other nations use appointed or elected officials. Guardians are not known to be capable of direct speech, although both Owain and Vakonivak have been shown to understand human language.

------

1. Fragments of *The Grand Westerly* have been dated to before 914, but extant fragments do not reference Owain by name and many scholars believe they refer instead to an unspecified sea monster.

2. Cardinals of the Zeim High Church have claimed to have observed Hakuta reincarnating, though descriptions of the event are considered highest holy text.

— Excerpts from *Lucan's Grand Reference,*
8th Edition, article on Guardians

CHAPTER TEN

The entry plaza of Sao Neso fell silent. The sahagins standing guard said nothing. Kell's allies, visibly stunned by the mage's appearance, said nothing. Cyprin Rusalka, town elder, was too overwhelmed with emotion at the sight of his child to say anything. The cool air was thick with silence, hanging motionless as if the oxygen and nitrogen were themselves surprised.

Cyprin took slow steps towards Kell, a shocked smile growing on his face. Kell's frown held. They grabbed the rod on their back and wordlessly pointed it at their father. Cyprin froze in his tracks.

"Kell . . ." he managed. He sounded tired, the authority of a leader absent from his voice.

"We're here on a mission," Kell said as calmly as they could, their stomach turning in constant knots. "We need to get through the locked door."

Cyprin's face, cascading through a barrage of emotions, settled on a sad confusion. "The locked door? Why? Kell, what's happened to you? We have so much to catch up--"

"I don't want to catch up with you, dad."

"Why not? I haven't seen you since you were nine."

Kell refused to answer. The explanation could come later, when they were finally ready.

"Then how about a meeting with the town elder?" Cyprin paused, leaving a hopeful space for Kell to respond. "Well," he conceded, "when you do want to talk, I'll be in my office. Same place it's always been. See you there, kiddo." He smiled weakly and started walking away.

"Dad."

Cyprin froze instantly.

Kell swallowed their anxiety. "I gave Caduceus her last blessing."

Cyprin nodded. "That's . . . good. I appreciate you doing that."

Kell silently watched as their father left, his feet dragging against the cobblestone street, slowly turning past the stout metal buildings that stood alongside the plaza. Scattered signs of life showed themselves down the connecting roads. Kell sighed and turned away from them to face their party, who were all still standing in obvious shock. They stashed their rod in its holder and meekly rubbed the nape of their neck. The knots in their chest were releasing, but slowly. "I'm sorry, guys."

Sheila coughed out a pitying laugh. "The hell are you sorry for?"

She's right, I guess. "I didn't want you to get involved. I didn't want you to come down here, but it's not like I could've said why. I thought I was in the clear after the armory, but then Banner mentioned the Psamathene, and you mentioned the cave . . ."

Alejandro stepped forward. "Kell, we need to apologize. *I* need to apologize." He emphasized his words but couldn't look at Kell for more than a moment. "For a start, we killed your Guardian."

A start, sure. "Well, she'll be back," Kell said. "Besides, respect where it's due, but she's not really my Guardian at this point. Owain is. I've been living up there for the last decade."

"Decade?" Alejandro said. "Your father just said you left when you were nine. You seem about my age, not that young."

With a small laugh, Kell gave themself to nostalgia. "Y'know, they always say that very little changes in Sao Neso. Folks here like consistency, like to take it slow. When I got up to the surface, everything felt fast, like nature was in a rush. Eventually, we realized why." They gestured at a clock hanging from a building that flanked the plaza. Its face showed a rotation of 24 hours, pointing solidly at 7:30. "Days are just longer down here. We worked it out and, yeah, to the surface I'm coming up on 30." They sighed. "And Dad would still treat me like a teenager."

"Oh, of course," Tobias said. "Without a frame of reference, circadian rhythms keep extending. So being isolated like this--"

"Doc, could you not?" Sheila said. "Kell's kinda having a moment."

"Oh! Sorry, sorry. You're right, now's not the time."

"It's fine," Kell said, privately relieved that Tobias was still his old self. They lightly jostled their helmet, hunting for some kind of physical comfort. "We're committed now, huh. The four of us."

"That we are," Alejandro said.

"Can I ask something of you guys, then? No secrets."

"Absolutely," Tobias said. "That seems like the least you could ask of us."

Alejandro hung his head for a moment before nodding. "I will do my best."

Sheila was biting her lip anxiously. She had secrets.

"Sheila?" Kell said.

"What?" She was trying to play innocent, and failing.

Kell nodded. *When you're ready.* "You alright? I know you don't like caves."

She looked around at the vast chasm. "It's a lot."

"It is, yeah." Kell tucked their helmet under their right arm and waved the others along as they started to walk. "I'll show you around."

B

The gate plaza opened up to three narrow streets, roughly following each cardinal direction. The northern road led mainly to markets and the like, with homes towards the south. That was more of a tendency than a rule, as with any city. Kell grew up closer to the northern side of Sao Neso, their childhood home sitting among the city's oldest freestanding residences. Not the absolute fanciest of houses, but their father had been the town elder for most of their life. They grew up well enough.

The road to the east, opposite the gate in the western cave wall, pointed at a massive column of rock deeper in the cavern. The column had the look of a pillar built in some ancient temple. Windows in the shaft made a steady, spiraling impression, with ornamental trenches emphasizing the illusion, while the cave's ventilation system wove around and through thick, uniform swirls of stone that made up the pillar's capital. The windows existed because the column was hollowed out long ago and turned into the city's seat of government. Cyprin's office was there. Kell led the group north, avoiding the column for the time being.

Even though it had been a decade since Kell went up to the surface, their memory of shops and restaurants remained accurate. Indeed, little changes in Sao Neso. The schoolhouse they attended as a child was still there. The marketplace where they would hang out when skipping classes and causing trouble with friends was still there. Perhaps one or two shops had changed, but to Kell it felt the same as it ever was. Quieter, perhaps, but in Sao Neso the day was just beginning.

The streets were too narrow for the four to all comfortably walk side by side. Tobias kept to the front with Kell, turning and peeking at every stall and shop the group passed, his beak parting in impressed awe. Even the closed shops, marked by thick curtains hung over their facades, drew a look of wonder.

Kell noticed a similar look of wonder on a blacksmith's face as he stepped out of his workspace nearby. They gave him a slight, polite wave. "They're with me," Kell said. The blacksmith nodded, keeping his watch while the group passed by.

"Not a lot of visitors down here, I take it?" Tobias said.

"Nope. Some Cymonian officials, rarely, but that's all there ever was." Kell chuckled to themself as they glanced around. The blacksmith wasn't the only one watching. "And they probably never came to the markets."

"Why not?"

Kell shrugged. "Why would they? They've got everything they need."

"Need, perhaps," Tobias said, "but who wouldn't want a little souvenir from a trip? Even if it's for work." He ruffled his vest as he spoke, as though it were an example.

Kell couldn't disagree, but they also couldn't relate. The life of a vapormage offered little chance for casual travel, less than even some civilians. Yet it was far more than any other resident of Sao Neso. At least Kell got to see the sun.

Their idle glance upwards turned into an idle glance behind. Sheila was following along close, holding a worried expression and posture as she walked. Alejandro was not close; he had stopped outside a tailor's shop, looking at some of the shirts on offer. Unsurprisingly, he had stopped at one of the fancier options in the marketplace.

He was nearly embarrassed when he noticed the others waiting. "You don't suppose they take credit?" he sheepishly asked Kell.

They shook their head. "Banner's not a thing down here."

"Hmm. Should've freshened up in Reeseport."

The tailor, an older lady, poked her head out from the rear of the stall. "Can I . . .?"

"They're with me," Kell said.

The tailor smiled. "Kell? Kell Rusalka, is that you? Oh my, you've darkened up, look at you. Still the spitting image of your father, though!"

The scales of Kell's face took on a redder shade of purple. "Thanks Maera. Glad to be back."

"Not causing too much trouble, are you?" Maera chuckled. Her attention turned to Alejandro. "This one's got good taste, I see. I'm sure we have something to fit you."

"Oh, no, it's quite alright, miss," Alejandro said politely.

"Please, please, I insist," Maera said. "I'm sure Kell's father won't mind covering things."

Kell could only offer a small smile. "Just go along with it."

Alejandro shrugged back and stepped into the tailor's shop. The rest of the group meandered to the nearby intersection, where a circular planter had small mossy plants growing in its center and benches carved into its stone perimeter. Kell took a seat on one bench and dropped their helmet in their lap. Tobias casually sat next to them, treating the seat like any other park bench. Sheila sat on the bench at its far end, leaning into the corner. She took silent looks around the plaza, still on her guard.

"So what was all that about a door, Kell?" Tobias asked.

"Hmm?" Tobias's easy air surprised Kell.

"Earlier. With your father."

"Oh, right." Kell turned towards the far eastern end of the Sao Neso cavern. They gestured vaguely at it. "So, way down that way, there's this archive place. Probably a lot of old legal documents and records and all that. Only been there once; I don't really remember what's in there. But there's supposed to be this door in there, right? A big, important, scary door. And you just . . . you don't open it, or else some creepy thing is gonna come crawling out."

Tobias looked intrigued. "What sort of creepy thing?"

"I dunno," Kell said. "I don't actually believe in it. It's the kind of stuff you tell little kids to make 'em shut up."

Tobias nodded. "Like a folk legend, then."

"I guess. But they told us all sorts of stories growing up about the surface, and half of those weren't true, so who knows. I just figured, if this cave does go all the way down to the Psamathene, it has to keep going somewhere. Right? Maybe it's behind that door." Kell chuckled to themself. "And, I mean, it got Dad's attention."

Tobias chuckled back. "I think you showing up did that well enough! The look on his face. Suppose we'll head that way when you're done with the tour, then."

The archives were ultimately Kell's destination, but their surname alone wasn't going to get them in. They would need registered permission. For that, sadly, they would have to talk to their father. So when Alejandro rejoined the group, dressed in perhaps the finest deep purple shirt Sao Neso had to offer, Kell led the group down a perpendicular street towards the stately column at the middle of the city.

The lobby inside extended to a dizzying height upwards. A clockwork web of lifts and pulleys hung from the distant roof, offering access to the upper storeys. After eagerly receiving directions from a clerk, the four rode up one of the lifts. The knots in Kell's stomach returned with each meter passed. Once at their stop, they explored the drab walkways until they could lead the group into Cyprin's office.

The town elder was doing a poor job of looking busy. He sprang to his feet the moment Kell opened the door. "There you are, there you are!" he called out with enthusiasm. "Sit down, Kell! We have so much to talk about!"

"No we don't, Dad." They could only be businesslike. "We just need to get through the locked door."

Cyprin laughed. "Whatever happened to you, being all stern and serious? You used to be so playful all the time. That from your vapormage training?"

"Every vapormage is dead," Kell said. "All of them."

"All of . . .?" He sounded more dejected than surprised, as if he'd expected it to happen eventually. "You're sure? All of them?"

"I saw their bodies."

Cyprin dropped into his chair. "I see. We get word from Cymona every so often. We've heard about losses, but all of you? Had to have happened recently. Within the last few weeks?" Kell nodded to confirm. "Oh, dear. Do you know what happened? Did Bessetrae finally invade?"

Sheila perked up. "Invade? What?"

"Well, the war," Cyprin said. "Been smoldering for years at a stalemate."

Sheila and Alejandro looked at each other, baffled. "The Winters' War ended years ago," she said.

Cyprin's eyes narrowed in skepticism. "Are you sure?"

"Of course I'm sure," Sheila said. "I'm *from* Bessetrae. Yeah, we don't all like each other these days. There's resentment and anger that pops up, and some people just hate foreigners. But there's no war."

"Except Lyon's trying to start one," Kell added.

"Lyon?" Cyprin let out a confused laugh. "What are you talking about? I have regular conversations with his advisers! They have no desire to keep fighting. It taxes their resources!"

"And you trust them?" Sheila said.

"Why wouldn't I? Lyon is trying to lead his people in a difficult time, the same as I have. I understand the challenges." He tone steadily stiffened, as if he had been talking to children and was now talking to adults.

"Dad," Kell said, "you *understand* what his people have been telling you. What we're talking about is what's actually going on. They aren't the same."

"Well, perhaps I should go see for myself, shouldn't I?" Cyprin said. "I'll go visit Lyon in his office."

Kell grimaced, annoyed. "You know that if you go up there, someone's gonna see you and try to kill you. They don't care if you lead Sao Neso. If anything, that just puts you at more risk."

"Then it's your word against theirs, I'm afraid." His voice struggled to be impartial, unable to hide the dismissive undercurrent.

"You'd trust them over your own child?" *Of course you would.*

"Consider this," Alejandro said, leaning on Cyprin's desk. "Whether the war has been continuing non-stop or it's about to start again, it is in *everyone's* best interest that something be done to stop it. That should be reason alone to help us."

Cyprin returned the gesture, leaning against the opposite side of the petrified wood plank. "And what makes you so sure opening that door would help?"

"What makes you so sure the war is still on?"

Cyprin stared at Alejandro for a tense moment.

"What's behind that door, sir?" Alejandro asked. He seemed genuinely curious, even if asking would put pressure on Cyprin as well.

Cyprin remained silently glaring for a moment longer before blinking, sighing, and righting himself. "There are three keys," he began. "We gave them to communities on the surface. That way, it would be very difficult to open the door, but not impossible. Just in case it was necessary someday. One went off to what is now Farolé, one to Zeimatia, one to Bessetrae. This was ancient history. I don't know what the keys look like, I don't know what happened to any of them. I don't know if they even exist anymore. But if you were to open the door, you would need them."

"Then we'll leave as soon as we're rested," Kell said. "And when we come back, we'll have all of them."

"Are you listening to yourself, Kell? How in the world do you plan to pull that off?"

"We'll figure it out as we go along," they said as they stood. "Y'know. Improvise."

C

Kell left the column with exhaustion bearing down on their shoulders. Standing in the plaza outside, they threw their head back and let out a hearty groan of frustration.

So many years spent resenting their father. So many tasks and redirections they were being forced to follow. Of *course* that door would have some immensely elaborate security. Of *course* it would demand all sorts of travel and trouble to get through. Of *course* it couldn't just be simple.

Tobias gave them a pat on the shoulder. Rather than ask about the outburst, he kindly suggested finding something to eat.

The restaurant they walked to was one Kell remembered fondly from their youth. It wasn't particularly fancy or even especially good, but it was comforting, generous, friendly. Thanks to generation after generation struggling to survive in the underwater caverns, there was a robust system of farms and growhouses that produced food that could handle the limiting conditions. An intricate network of watertight traps, thick pipes, and heavy machinery allowed for accessing the seawater above to support farms of laver and mollusk. Easily-grown mushrooms rounded out nearly every meal.

The four had free rein of the menu, thanks to the Rusalka family's status. Kell was less interested in taking advantage and more interested in having their first solid food in weeks. They'd been sick of Pemmash since the second day.

"Kell," Tobias said, "I didn't want to interrupt talking with your father, but was I reading between the lines correctly? The vapormages were all from here?"

"We were, yeah," Kell said sadly.

"As if killing the whole unit wasn't vile enough," Sheila said.

"Indeed," Tobias said, his voice balancing awe and analysis. "Imagine if Cymonians knew their beloved vapormages were all sahagins. The soldiers they love are people they hate. Imagine the scandal."

Kell nodded, not wanting to dwell on it any more than they already had. "I'm surprised you didn't know, Alejandro."

"As am I. Usually the intercepts are quite thorough. Either they didn't know or they didn't care."

Kell poked their fork at a slice of mushroom. "Probably didn't know. Even when we shared the base with some of the knights, there was a lot going on that . . . I mean, it was obviously all just to keep up the secret. No other reason. Full uniform, all the time. Only dropped that after they left. And not much chance to leave the base, either. Maybe once a month. I'd call Rocko every so often, but beyond that it was always just us mages."

"Damn sight nobody screeched the rose," Alejandro muttered to himself.

Tobias quirked his brow. "Pardon?"

Alejandro smirked playfully. "Screech the rose? Let out a big secret. Speaker lingo, professor. I been a bene cove this whole naff boat even when you lot chirped me mogue, and if you hear anyone *else* talking like that, you know they work for Her Maj on the slip."

Kell chuckled. "Damn, got more slang than us."

"Can't be too easy to follow, our marks would catch on."

"Wouldn't hurt to teach us," Sheila said.

"Gladly," Alejandro said. "No secrets, right?"

"No secrets," Kell said.

"No secrets," Tobias echoed.

Sheila's eyes darted across the rest of the group, each waiting for her to commit. She slumped her shoulders in defeat. "I ran."

"You ran?" Alejandro said, confused.

Her hung head turned towards Kell. "Remember when I dragged you through Windglade? That was my home. My unit was there the day it got destroyed. But when we got our orders, with what I saw on the ground and what I heard from my superiors . . . I knew it was hopeless. That's what I told myself. Maybe I was just too much of a coward. So I ran. Abandoned everyone. My squad, my family. After the dust settled, I was declared dead with the rest of my unit. And I've been running ever since."

The group stayed silent. Kell nodded. The actual details were fine to know, but not important to them. It mattered more that Sheila opened up for once.

"No secrets," she affirmed.

"Well, good. Good," Tobias said. "But we have no clue where to start, either."

"Okay, first off, are we sure this is even a good idea?" Sheila said. "We're only down here because Banner pointed us this way."

"I don't think he knew," Kell said. "Probably thought he was just sending us on a snipe hunt. Like, 'go down to the Psamathene?' C'mon. That's how you get people killed. But I've always figured, you don't get so many stories and legends and whatever about that door if there's nothing behind it."

"What do *you* think's behind it?" Sheila asked.

"No clue. I don't think anyone knows, but it's gotta be *something*. Maybe it'll help." Kell slouched a little. "Right now, I just wanna know."

"Sounding like a scientist there," Tobias said with a chuckle.

"More like a desperate idiot," Kell said. "Look. Unless we get back to Reeseport and find out they've run Lyon out of town 'cause he killed us all, we're not done. There could still be a war. And what can *we* do? We're nobody. We need some tool. Some trick. Something to even up the game. I'll take anything that'll get us that."

"Well then, if we're going with the door, then we're looking for keys, right?" Sheila said. "So we look for keys. Easy."

"No guarantee they'll look like keys," Alejandro said. "Could take some artifact and enchant it for the purpose, like a sigil."

"That's a good point," Kell said. "If these things are ancient, then they're artifacts. Like what you'd have in a museum, or an archive."

"The door would give us some ideas, no?" Tobias said. "Let's get over there and hear its side of the story."

"They'll only let me in. Place is locked down, definitely no surfs. Er, surface folks. You guys."

Tobias offered no resistance. "Fair enough."

Alejandro held a finger up as he chewed on a chunk of crab. "I have a thought. I don't like it, but I have it."

"Oh, this must be good," Sheila said.

"Museums, yes?" Alejandro began. "The rebels in Farolé. Not long ago, they plundered a museum in Stanton, in the midlands. One that had all manner of archaeological artifacts. Those folks had been staying under the radar perfectly, then they pop out to do that, of all things. They took a lot of items, as I understand it, but nothing that came from Farolé itself. And to top it all off, they put out this manifesto, all about returning nations and histories to the people they belonged to."

"They would certainly be against the monarchy," Tobias said.

"They would know a few things about ancient items," Alejandro said. "That's what we care about. Slim shot they'd have any of these keys, but they could point us the right way better than anyone I can think of."

"So what's the problem with this idea?" Sheila asked. "Seems good enough."

"This is Farolé I'm proposing, Sheila."

An amused smirk grew on Sheila's face. "Oh. Are they not fond of you, Speaker?"

Alejandro glared and stabbed at a mushroom with his fork. "A lot of people aren't fond of me, soldier. Some for good reason. That includes the Speakers, but those are my roughs to handle, not yours."

"We can handle it if it gets to that," Kell said, more to defuse the banter than exude confidence.

"What about you, doc?" Sheila said. "Doesn't the university have a history department or something?"

Tobias chuckled. "Hardly! Nothing worth slapping the name on, if you ask me. Since they closed The Puck, it's felt like nobody cares to do actual field research anymore. If it's not in a textbook, it's not getting covered. And you show me the textbook that knows about this place!"

"Then it's Farolé," Kell said. "Any clue where the rebels are hiding out?"

Alejandro shook his head. "I would've heard something. We never did know for sure where they were hiding. I don't know their rituals, their shibboleths, anything that would endear us to them. Best I have is an educated guess. It would put us a bit outside Vaaland, but even that could be wrong."

"Better than nothing," Sheila said. "Long drive, though."

"Can we get the Basilisk over the border?" Tobias said. "Vehicle like that would draw quite the attention."

"Right," Sheila groaned.

"I'll call in a favor with Crystal," Kell said.

Alejandro blinked. "A favor? From her?"

Kell smirked. "She offered, didn't she? Probably have to play road crew again, but it's Crystal. She can get us just about anywhere. Might as well take her up on it."

D

After dinner, the four settled into a group of suites in the column. The rooms were set aside for when Cymonian delegates visited, so they were done up fancier to meet expectations. Tobias eagerly embraced the higher standard, while Sheila gave Alejandro a lighthearted ribbing about landing in such posh accommodations. Kell could have slept on a box of hay for all they cared; they were just happy to sleep under the faint green glow, beneath the endless waves, for the first time in far too long.

When they woke, their mobile claimed it was late the next morning. They did the groggy arithmetic; for the schedules of Sao Neso, the evening had rolled in. The column was likely emptied out. Still, they found themself reaching for their helmet before going anywhere. There was no reason to hide their identity, but the habit was too deeply ingrained. The first thing Kell had done every morning for the better part of a decade was hide what they were.

They stepped out of their room, wearing the simple--if slightly baggy--short-sleeved tunic that had been provided with the room. Their scaly, purple skin felt alien and hypersensitive without their vapormage uniform pressing tightly against it. Their right arm was still a miserable sight, the wound obvious and painful, but at least they could refresh the bandages and give it some air. They felt like a patient in a hospital, stripped down to such lightweight clothing and wandering into the airy, abandoned hall with a certain aimlessness.

Down a ways, Alejandro and Tobias were chatting at a small table set off to the side, a kettle settled between them. "Morning, Kell!" Tobias said cheerfully. "Tea?"

"Sure. You two been up long?"

"I have, at least," Tobias said. "Too worried I'd sleep for far too long, I suppose."

"As was I," Alejandro said. "Time feels quite strange here. The thin vapor doesn't help. I had wanted to practice bringing out Raurack, but I can't hardly."

"A shame," Tobias said. "Feeling rather well rested, though, that's what matters."

"Wish I could say the same," Alejandro said. "The one place I can be sure there'd be no Speakers, and yet . . ." He set down his cup and looked Kell in the eye. "I need to apologize, Kell. For as much help as Tobias has been, I still should have spoken with you and Sheila before recruiting him. And . . . I'm sorry about how I handled things around your commander. Given the opportunity, I handled it like I was still a Speaker: Get in, do the job, get out. I didn't give you any thought."

Kell nodded thoughtfully. It was a start. "I notice you're not apologizing for killing him."

At that, Alejandro dropped eye contact. "I still believe it had to be done. By having the vapormages murdered, he put himself beyond redemption. I do apologize for *how* it happened. Not *that* it happened."

Kell stared into their cup of black tea as if reading the leaves. "I can't entirely disagree. Much as I want to. Guess I just want to think people can redeem themselves."

"Noble."

Kell huffed in faint dismissal. "I just don't like to think about it. I end up thinking, where's that line? Have I crossed it?"

Alejandro nodded calmly. "You've seen action."

"Yeah." Kell sighed. "Late in the Winters' War. When things were pushing back into Cymona. It was going bad enough that they even called me up. Three confirmed."

"It's a heavy burden," Alejandro said solemnly. His eyes fell on Tobias, across the table. "I'm sorry, we're being a bit morbid."

Tobias shook his head. "Not a worry. It's understandable, given your lines of work."

"Well, former line of work," Kell said.

"Yes." Alejandro exhaled. "Finally."

His choice of phrase caught on Kell's scales. They stared, inquisitive. After a moment, Alejandro's head dipped.

"I must apologize again," he said quietly, exuding shame.

Rather than say anything, Kell let their expression ask him to elaborate.

"I *have* left the Speakers," he said. "But it took speaking with Crystal to finally convince me."

Kell's cup clanked dully against the wooden table. They stared at Alejandro's ashamed face. "You . . .?" They trailed off as Alejandro nodded slightly. A quiet glance to Tobias's expression seemed to confirm he was thinking the same thing: Alejandro had not been on their side the whole time.

"I . . ." Alejandro pushed to compose himself. "I needed to know. What you were. And I couldn't take both you and Sheila, alone. So I tried to put a plan in motion. Reveal you before I . . . took care of you. But before I could find an opportunity, I realized what I had become."

Kell let out a slow, long exhale. They were angry at him, undoubtedly, yet they couldn't seem to hate him.

"I hope I am not beyond redeeming myself," Alejandro said, faint cracks appearing in his composure, "though I can't argue I deserve the opportunity."

Kell wanted to hate him. But he wasn't Lyon. He was showing remorse. "You're done?"

"I promise." Alejandro finally lifted his head and looked Kell in the eye. "No secrets."

A moment of heavy silence passed. Kell looked at Tobias; his expression was trusting the matter to their hands.

"Alright," Kell said. They could trust Alejandro, for now.

The relief on Alejandro's face came instantly. He cautiously held out his left hand. "I don't expect any of you to forgive me. We don't have to be friends, Kell, but we can at least not be enemies. Right?"

With a slight nod, they shook Alejandro's hand with all the awkward softness of two people using their non-dominant arms. "I think there's a world where we'd be friends."

"I hope so. You do get along well with Sheila, after all."

Kell glanced around. "Speaking of, have you seen her?"

"She's probably still asleep," Tobias said.

"Good," Kell said. "She's earned it. Been running herself ragged."

"That sort of thing happens when you care too much," Tobias said.

"Or when you're too stubborn to trust anyone," Kell said.

"That does sound more like her," Tobias said with a small laugh.

Kell tried to relax in their small, metal chair. It would be hard to consider either Alejandro or Tobias a friend, each for different reasons. Tobias, even at his cheeriest, always carried the distant air of a scholar. And Alejandro . . . *I hope I'm right*, Kell thought.

Yet even Alejandro's confession hadn't erased the faint feeling of being among friends. The same feeling that came when venting with Jeng or flirting with Rey hung in the hall--a familiar camaraderie, a sort of trust and comfort that was less about faith, or even liking somebody, and more about having experienced so much with another person.

After some time, Alejandro excused himself. Kell watched him walk back to his room with a weight still lingering in his shoulders.

"I'll admit, Kell," Tobias said quietly, "I'm surprised you let him get away."

"I'm surprised you taught him how to summon," Kell said.

Tobias sighed with a tinge of guilt. "Well, I was telling the truth. Have to pass the art on to someone. Sheila would never go for it, and you were . . ." He trailed off.

"I was just afraid," Kell confessed. "Of everything going on. I needed some space."

"And Alejandro needed a friend," Tobias said.

Kell chuckled reflexively. "I think we all do, doc."

"Can't deny that," Tobias said, his head dipping. He perked up abruptly. "Well then, in the spirit of befriending, may I ask something?"

Kell looked up at a clock on the wall. "As long as it's fairly quick," they said. "Don't know how long someone will be at the archives."

"Well, I was just wondering, did you always have more of a purple color?" Tobias asked. "I haven't seen anyone down here like that, but that lady didn't seem too shocked by it. I'm wondering if it's unusual or something."

Kell shook their head. "This happened gradually. To all of us. Think it's from being in the sun a lot. Once the knights were reassigned, we kinda got free rein. As long as it was just Commander Fontaine around, it was fine. So any chance we'd get, we'd be outside. No uniform, no helmet. I remember just being . . . in love with seeing the sun, you know? You don't get that here. And skin changes color when you're in the sun a lot, that just happens, right?"

"Yes, yes," Tobias said, "I used to start turning a little pink after a few days' vacation myself. And then the sahagins that *do* brave the surface would surely live hidden, only coming out at night, so less of a reaction could occur. Sounds perfectly reasonable. And here I was, worried it'd be a sensitive topic."

Kell smiled. "If you ask me something rude, I just won't answer."

Tobias chuckled. "I apologize in advance if I do. Curiosity gets the better of me, always has."

"Well," Kell said as they stood, "if you can sit still long enough, I'll let you know what I find out with the door."

Tobias raised his cup of tea in a cheerful toast. "I'll be right here, friend!"

E

Kell stepped out into the streets of Sao Neso without any of the equipment that would mark them as a vapormage, save for the strap hung diagonally across their body that held their rod on their back and a handful of small pouches on their front. The staff at the vault would probably know who they were, but there was no harm in carrying some identification. Besides, the tunic didn't have pockets, and they needed to carry their borrowed mobile somewhere. Bringing the rod was just another force of habit. Unlike on the surface, there was little reason to remain armed in Sao Neso. The vapor was thin, thin enough that it seemed to put the lie to Banner's whole notion about the Psamathene. It was thin enough that vapor poisoning was nearly a non-issue. The few creatures that shared the cave with sahagins were almost certain to remain healthy and tame.

The front of the vault building had the texture of corrugated metal, like a downtown shop closed for the night. They knocked on the door and reached for their identification, but the caretaker who answered waved them in without hesitation.

"Your father warned me you'd be coming by," she said, excited by the fact. "No grabby grabby!"

Kell shook their head, exasperated. "I'll behave."

"Good!" the caretaker said. "So what are you after? Not legal documents, I'm guessing. Maps? Grimoires? Old reels?"

Kell paused. "You keep old reels here?"

"Keep just about everything. There's a really interesting one, from the 300th Tideday festivals, they made a musical version of *Grand Westerly*!"

Kell held in a laugh. "That sounds terrible. I need to see it, but some other time. I'm here to check out the locked door."

The caretaker's eyes lit up. "Ooooh, spooky! This way."

She led Kell past the stacks to a dim, neglected corner of the archives. Set into the far wall was a plain metal door. She gestured at it, smiling, clearly trying to fool them into thinking it was *the* door, despite her giddiness giving the plot away. Kell smiled and quietly gestured. O*n with it, please.* With playful disappointment, she unlocked the door and swung it open, revealing a second door behind it.

The locked door was made of dark, dense-looking metal inscribed with lines and shapes across its entire surface. There was no handle or latch visible. It stood imposing, a monolith stuffed in a cramped nook. Dotted among the channels and chisels were deeper depressions, twelve in total. They appeared on the door in a seemingly arbitrary pattern--a few clustered in the top left, one far at the bottom center. A group of three made for a neat line along the full height of the right side. Kell carefully inspected the details. The top and bottom were cleanly round, while the middle was more of a lumpy circle. They noticed that many of the depressions were smooth shapes, except for four of them spread out across the door. Along with the lumpy circle and a second nearby with more of an egg shape, one pit had a triangular shape, while another pit in the door seemed especially deep and jagged.

As they reached into the pouch that held their mobile, they felt the shard they had recovered from the statue in Cuesta. They never had the chance to hand it over at the embassy.

Their eyes widened. *Wait a second.*

They pulled both items from the pouch. The caretaker raised an eyebrow at the yellow fragment but said nothing, acting innocent as Kell noticed her interest. They ignored her and held the fragment near the jagged pit in the door, though not inserting it. The shard felt ever so slightly warmer to the touch.

Of course, Kell thought as they used their mobile to get some quick images of the door. *Extra security. This thing is trying to lie. All the identical ones are probably fake, right? So then there are four keys. Not three. Does dad know? He has to. He's trying to stop us without saying it.*

Kell left the archive building with what they hoped was enough information to work with. It was certainly more than their father had to offer, and far more accurate.

The direct route back to the central column passed by a cluster of shops that was as bustling and active as anywhere in Sao Neso would get that day. Even here, without the signature helmet and cloak of the vapormages, their presence would turn heads and draw comments. By now, everyone had to know that they were the only surviving member of the unit. In a city where very little happened, when something did happen, everyone knew about it. Kell was never fond of the fawning attention above the surface. They didn't want to receive it here either, back home.

Was Kell home? The thought dragged their feet at an intersection. Everything was familiar--truly, little changes in Sao Neso--but the familiar doesn't make a home. They wandered aimlessly, lost down side streets and alleys.

They ran into Sheila on the way. She was trying, and failing, to get used to Sao Neso. They suggested, as kindly and earnestly as they could, that she get Alejandro's story herself. She agreed but seemed wary, wandering opposite the column's direction.

Kell's path back took them through a residential neighborhood. It wasn't the one Kell grew up in, but they knew Rey and Klein and several other vapormages did. The street was quiet. One door, with its lit lantern, carried enough familiarity to grab their attention. They slowly approached it, chills of anxiety forming in their body. They stopped at the bare wooden door. *Alright. You can do this, Kell. They need to know. It's the right thing.*

Knock. Knock.

A woman in a simple gown answered. "Yes? You're . . . are you Kell?"

They nodded. "This is the Kemeny house, right?"

"Always has been. Why?"

Kell exhaled slowly. "It's about Nina."

The woman gave them a curious look. Her husband joined her at the door. "What about? We heard what happened, Cyprin came around and told us."

Kell nodded, a small shiver running through their body. "Did she ever send letters back home?"

"A few. Hadn't heard from her in months, though."

"Did they mention anyone called Scar? Or Havoc?"

The husband chuckled. "Those the kinds of nicknames you folks gave each other?"

Kell shook their head. "I never knew anyone with a nickname, myself."

"She never mentioned anyone by name at all," the woman said. "Why?"

"Well. She went missing a few years ago."

"Years?" The Kemenys were baffled.

Kell nodded. "She ran. We all kinda figured she would." They held up their hand and gestured to the Kemenys to calm down, even though the couple had barely shown a change in expression. "But, when I was out on my last mission. With the surfs I came in with. We got stuck in Farolé and had to sneak out. And, while we were doing that, we ran into her. With two others, calling themselves Scar and Havoc. She didn't have a nickname. I can't imagine she was around them very long."

"Is she alright?"

Kell swallowed a lump in their throat. "They attacked us." They reached behind their back and snapped Nina's rod out of their holder. They held it out in offering to the Kemenys. "I got this off her body. You should have it. Something to remember her by."

The couple stared at the rod. They stared at Kell. "You . . . you killed her?" the woman said.

Kell nodded solemnly. A hint of tears formed in their eyes, despite their efforts. "I did, yes."

The couple exchanged mortified looks. Kell tried to stand as stoic and steady as possible, though the chills in their legs were starting to betray them. After a moment of tension, the woman stepped behind her husband, who pushed away the rod in Kell's hand as he stepped forward.

"Get that thing out of here," he commanded behind gritted teeth. "Who do you think you are, Kell? Huh? You barge in here, bringing surfs, causing a whole damned commotion. Always acting like you can just do whatever the fuck you want. I don't know what you did to Caduceus, but Val made it sound like you killed her, too! You think we're just gonna, I don't know, shrug it off? You've always been a damned punk, Kell! You've always been trouble! Stealing and breaking things and hiding behind your father! How dare you come back and give us this sorry-ass pity party! Our daughter is dead, our Guardian is dead, and it's *your* fault! Murderer!" His words came out with a mist of spit. His arm came up, ready to strike Kell, but with a shaky hesitation it returned to his side. "You better not show your face in Sao Neso again. We don't want you, and we don't want your fucking weapons!"

Slam.

The Kemenys locked the door loudly, leaving Kell standing in the street, soundly rejected. They slowly returned Nina's rod to their holder and walked away, their head hung. *It had to happen,* they tried to reassure themself. *They needed to know the truth.*

May your flesh become the rocks
And strengthen our path ahead
May your blood become the water
And cleanse your heart's regret
May your bones become our shelter
And protect all that you loved
May your ghost become the wind
And breathe into us all

— Sahagin funeral blessing, traditional

CHAPTER ELEVEN

The midday sun battered the Cymonian coast. A day spent in Sao Neso--or two days, however long it was, Alejandro wasn't keeping things straight--was all it took to dull the eyes and accustom them to the soft green glow. Outside of the cave, colors were brilliant and vibrant, at least when they weren't burning his eyes into a squint.

The group took their time getting used to the surface. Kell took one last nostalgic breath of ocean air before putting their helmet back on. Whatever protection it afforded their eyes meant they could actually see where they were going, so they led the way to Reeseport while the other three re-acclimated to the sunlight. Prior to the excursion, Alejandro might have described the dark underground as his natural habitat, but after seeing Sao Neso, that idea felt too self-centered.

The Basilisk was where the group had left it, though not in the same state. The rear window had been shattered, glass piled up on the ground. The body of the vehicle had been scratched in a wordless message of anger and insult. The food inside was all gone, though it was just as well; every bit had tasted slightly off, as if the cans had been debating if they should spoil or not.

Tobias treated the situation as little more than a curiosity, while Sheila treated it as the aggravation it was. The vehicle was still drivable, but the trip would be noisy and unpleasant. Kell, after a period of commiseration about the problem, retrieved the slip that Omar had handed them and called the number on it.

"Hello, Crystal here." As predicted.

"It's Kell."

A loud gasp. "Kell! You guys are still kicking? That's amazing!"

"Thanks. We need some help, though. Think you can help us get from Reeseport to Vaaland?"

"Hmm, maybe? What are you guys doing down there?"

Alejandro only realized he was bouncing lightly on his feet when Kell silently gestured at him, as if to say, *I can handle this one.*

"We're done with Banner's little story," Kell said. "Working on our own. Trying to get into a place down here that should help us stop Lyon, but they spread the keys all over Linnute."

"A scavenger hunt? Fun!" Crystal's enthusiasm for the idea was clear. "But, you know about the Psamathene, right?"

"Of course. We can get around Cymona, but we're not making it through borders."

"Not without getting *somebody* curious," she said. "Think you can make it to Candhall in, like, two days?"

"Easily. Let Omar know to expect us." Kell hung up and looked around the group. "We are *not* telling her about Sao Neso," they said, as though anyone present would.

The four left the Basilisk outside Candhall and snaked their way towards the castle, just to scout it out while they waited. They could only do so at a good distance, two or three blocks away, before the rotations of guards made the idea unpalatable. A covered alleyway in the old town, near the docks, kept them out of sight until Crystal's crew could arrive to pluck them from the urban thickets.

Making their way back to Vaaland would cost the group several additional days. While the boat entered Grann Bay and started traversing the Purro River, the four found themselves space in the canteen. Alejandro and Tobias silently took positions around an available Twenties board. As they set up the match, Sheila and Kell each took seats at the table besides them, Kell pulling out their mobile in the process.

"Okay, smart guy." Sheila was testing Alejandro, ever so slightly. "You got a plan?"

"For the game or for our mission?" Alejandro couldn't help himself.

"If it's for the game, don't be telling me," Tobias said.

"Agreed," Alejandro said, claiming the dice. "Remember that forest we went through?" He rolled a 3. "There's a few acres there. Special acres, legally speaking. I won't pretend to understand all the legal minutiae. That stuff becomes nonsense too quickly. But someone did bother, a gentleman known as Barlow. He headed to that land and started farming, outside of royal control. And royal taxes."

"Clever." Tobias rolled a 1.

Alejandro nodded. He rolled a 0, with a sigh. "You can imagine how well that went over when it was found out. By the time Barlow got his farm set up, the Royal House had closed the loopholes. Shut the whole thing down. Very publicly."

Kell looked up from their mobile. "Made an example of him?"

Alejandro finally rolled a 4, removing one of Tobias's pieces from the board. "Could say that. People really liked Barlow. Still do. So, the Speakers were called in to . . . clean up the situation."

"You killed him," Sheila said.

Alejandro rolled a 3, a useless roll for the positions of his pieces. "I didn't kill him," he said as flatly as possible.

Sheila glared. "I know that tone, Speaker."

Alejandro set the dice down to glower back. "Yes, I know. Whatever I emphasize will make you think I mean something else. But no, soldier, I meant exactly and only what I said." He rolled a 1 and advanced a piece. "With Barlow gone, the farm was claimed by the Queen. She said she'd open it as a public facility. And then she didn't. Of course. Officially, it's been abandoned since."

Tobias rolled a 2, his hand already hovering over a piece before the dice settled. "Officially?"

"Officially. *Un*officially," Alejandro said, "I suspect that's bollocks. Perfect place for a rebel hideout. Would like to verify first, though. Remember that tavern?"

"Where you tried to kill me." There was no anger in Kell's voice, but there was clear accusation.

"Yes," Alejandro stammered. "That one. Would be a good place to ask around."

"No, it's not," Sheila said. "They know us. Hell, they think we're a couple."

Tobias dropped the dice as he reflexively laughed. "You two? Have they not met you?"

Alejandro could almost laugh as he glanced at Sheila. Her expression was much the same. "It's Vancius. Southwest Farolé. Plenty of people there who think everyone from Gauvencia is gay as daisy."

"That's . . ." Kell sounded suddenly unsure of the plan.

"I know," Sheila said. "How'd we spend a whole day there without getting hassled?"

Alejandro shrugged off a poor roll. "Perhaps I'm just paranoid, then. Still, best to work with a ruse. Assuming Sheila's comfortable with it?"

Sheila knew she was gathering a stack of favors to redeem at her will. "I'm punching you if you try to kiss me," she joked, almost the way a friend might.

Vaaland was buzzing like a cheap light bulb. The four disembarked from the ship with the rest of the crew before, at a silent nod from Omar, they split off into town. Alejandro led the party towards the Fogbank Tavern, which was some blocks away.

"Busy day today," Tobias observed. Raucous noise was radiating from the tavern, audible well before the place was in sight.

Alejandro checked his mobile. "Bloody hell," he sighed, "it's Founding Day already. Of course." His adventures thus far must have changed him, to ever lose track of time like that.

As he turned down a west-facing street, Alejandro finally caught sight of the Fogbank Tavern. Unlike during the previous visit, its exterior was decorated. With the old Vancius flag. A sharp, reflexive chill hit his spine. It was a very particular kind of crowd that still flew old colors. The Four Kingdoms of Farolé unified generations ago, and those who held on to the old nations were . . . traditionalist, to be Cymonian about it. Alejandro had been briefed about Barlow. Barlow was not traditionalist.

He could see some of the crowd, milling about outside. Sharpies and pigs, the lot of them. Leather armor and open swords. A Vanciot stronghold, the sort that the Speakers would want to put down, the sort that looked eager to put down a Speaker themselves. And anyone he associated with.

"Change of plans," Alejandro said tersely, pushing north, away from the tavern and towards the edge of the city.

"I thought we wanted information?" Tobias said, glancing between the two directions.

"I would also like us to live," Alejandro called out, waving at him to hurry up.

B

The four moved quickly. The autumn chill hit shortly after they exited the town gates, gusts of wind tossing hair and shaking leaves from the trees. A long harvest caravan rolled towards the town, clogging the main road and pushing the party to the edge of the path. The route only cleared as they worked their way into the Felmata Forest, following the same road they had used previously.

After hours of traversing the old road and handling the few bits of hostile wildlife that crossed their paths, they made their way to the site of the makeshift buildings that Alejandro had spotted on their previous pass. He paused to examine them more closely. They were built of sheets of discarded metal and loose piles of rocks and contained a few old, sealed boxes. It seemed nobody was using them as shelter, or if they were, they were remarkably tidy.

The buildings flanked a faded trail that ran along a hilly valley. With some assistance from Tobias, Alejandro brought out his summon. Raurack led the group through the woods. Alejandro scanned the tree bark for any splashes of paint or other markings that would indicate the trail's intended path. There were some, scarce and hard to see as the sun continued setting, but enough to forge ahead.

Raurack stopped abruptly at the sound of cracking wood and rustling leaves. Near where the group stood, a nuck had stumbled into a trap. It dangled by its forelegs, neighing, emitting wild bursts of fiery vapor. Alejandro sighed in relief. The noise was a startle, nothing more.

He turned his attention back to the trail. The blade of a glaive jutted out in front of him. Its holder was a camouflaged hunn standing to the side of the trail, wearing a patterned cloth mask that loosely covered the upper half of her face. "You folks gotta watch your step," she said.

Of course this whole area is trapped, Alejandro thought as he put his hands up. "We're that close? Terribly sorry."

"Yeah, the road's way over there." She pointed to the main road, which the group had intentionally broken off of. "What are you doing out here?"

Clearly a guard, but too bene. Playing at hunters? "We're looking for the Barlow farm."

The woman's amateurish mask didn't completely hide her eyes. They went wide, enough for Alejandro to notice her surprise. "Why would you want to go there?" She kept her voice impressively calm. "It's been abandoned for ages."

Alejandro straightened out his jacket. The guard wasn't a political power player, but she deserved professionalism. "I am Alejandro Quintana, he *formerly* of Her Majesty's Speakers. We're trying to stop a war from starting. We think there's someone there who could help."

The guard looked them over, her glaive sagging towards the ground in indecision. "Nella!" she shouted. A second camouflaged guard emerged from the underbrush nearby, appearing as if from thin air. "Go get the captain."

Nella ran off, weaving between trees and invisible traps. Alejandro watched her path as he kept still with the rest of the group. They had no reason to be uncooperative prisoners, and the guard's uneasy behavior made it clear she could be easily overtaken if the group wanted. But rushing the farmland, armed and screaming, was not the way to make allies.

The guard pointed her glaive at Raurack. The summon had been standing, forelegs raised, at Alejandro's feet. "The hell's that thing?"

"It's my summon," Alejandro said.

"Dispel it," the guard said.

Alejandro hesitated but complied without arguing. He picked up Raurack and dispelled the summon, letting its vapor waft back into him. The confusion in the guard's eyes was clear, even behind her mask, but she said nothing about it.

The nuck caught in the trap neighed loudly. With a violent, full-bodied kick, it broke free, landing on its side with a hard thud. It got up and dashed towards the guard.

She swung her glaive towards it, more frantic than firm. The beast finally got the message and pivoted towards the road, but not before getting close enough to make the guard backstep away. She tripped in the process, falling into Alejandro's waiting arms. She looked embarrassed about being so green. Alejandro kept his eyes kind. He'd been green, once.

The guard righted herself and retrieved her glaive from the moss. All the stoic authority she had been hoping to build up had run off with the nuck, and she knew it. "You guys swear you're alright?" she asked.

Alejandro held up a hand. "On Gauven."

"Alright. Come on."

The path wound through dense clusters of oak before revealing a clearing. A trio of silos stood in a line, each taller than the previous one. A small complex of buildings, built with a mix of stone and wood, stood a short ways away. The central building was a broad wooden structure only a storey or two tall, with pillars of stone and wide doorways alternating along its face. A few scattered groups of people moved about busily. If it weren't for the masks and uniforms they were wearing, there would be little to make the place seem any different from any other busy farmland in Farolé.

The guard led the four to the central building. A blue-feathered vian in a simple khaki uniform--and no mask, Alejandro quickly noted--approached from inside.

"You brought them here?" they said with kind surprise.

The guard hesitated, as though she was about to be punished. "Yeah."

Alejandro stepped forward. "We understand you have some artifacts we're . . . very interested in."

The vian looked intrigued. "Really? You four don't believe the news, then?"

Alejandro wasn't positive what they were referring to, but he could hope it wouldn't matter. "The news would say all of Cymona's vapormages are dead," he said, gesturing at Kell. "I think we're right to be skeptical these days."

"Good point. Captain Sleetre, they of Barlow's Bread." They bowed in welcome.

Alejandro nodded in relief. Aligning so closely with Barlow? This was a group he felt he could trust.

The four went around, introducing themselves. Alejandro began explaining the situation while a masked pair stopped to listen. As he told it--with the occasional interjection from the others--Lyon was planning to weaponize Tobias's research, and he could likely be stopped if the group could access a facility deep in southern Cymona that only vapormages would have access to. The artifacts they were looking for were disguised keys for the facility. All of the information was true--it simply left out Sao Neso and the sahagins, so that helping the four out would be less controversial.

The captain stood, arms crossed, listening with curiosity. "Okay then," they said, "I think I get how this all came together." They gestured at Kell. "You're the mage, obviously. You're the brains." They gestured at Tobias. "And you're . . . muscle." Sheila chuckled at her label. "But you. Alejandro, was it? How did you fit into all this?"

"Oh, I just stumbled into it, frankly," he said. "Right place, right time, sort of thing."

Captain Sleetre tapped a finger against their arm rapidly. "I know you four mean well, but come on. Be honest."

Alejandro sighed. *More savvy than they let on.* "Fair. I used to be one of Her Majesty's Speakers."

"Oh!" the guard exclaimed with a small panic. She had been lingering quietly with the rest of the audience, only to suddenly make herself known. "Right, you told me that, I'm sorry."

The captain's beak tapped in buried frustration. "It's alright, Rachel."

"We should get back to post," a young man who had stopped to listen said. He waved the guard towards the woods. "Get along, lil' lunan."

The turn of phrase stuck suspiciously in Alejandro's ear. Speaker lingo. The man could've overheard it somewhere, though. As the small cluster dispersed, Alejandro made note of people's appearances--as much as he could, given the near-uniform outfits and masks. He was compelled to investigate, if he had the chance.

"She's pretty green," Sheila said.

"A lot of them are," the captain said with a nod. "They're not fighters like you folks. I was in the army, at one point, but the recruits? They're just here 'cause they want something better."

"Can't blame them," Alejandro said. "This country has quite a few messes that need cleaning up."

"That it does." There was a knowing undercurrent of blame in the captain's voice.

Alejandro's head dipped. "I've been part of a few, I know."

"Well, we're here now," the captain said. "If you want to talk about the artifacts, we should go talk with Captain Kearney. Follow me."

The group followed into the central facility. Alejandro's guard was up. The captain seemed a bit too forgiving, too willing to ignore his former employment. They had to have known what actually happened to Barlow. They had to have known that his blood was on the Speakers' hands.

C

The inside of the central building had been gutted of whatever machinery and farm equipment it once possessed, leaving the space open for a sprawling, ad-hoc base. A few bunks stood in a corner, and an extensive nook was occupied by a mess hall, all with lines of barrels and shelves acting as both dividers and storage. There was no armory that Alejandro could see, but there were other buildings in the compound. Perhaps the weapons were kept there. Or, perhaps the people would fight for their cause with shovels and scythes. Alvacii fell to less.

A portion of the building had been relieved of whatever duty it once had and now housed dozens of stone and crystal objects, laid out like a market vendor's offerings. A small cloud of people stood around them, slowly moving together as one. They inspected the figures, comparing them, taking notes, having quietly intense conversations. They were dressed no differently than the field workers outside, save for one hunn woman in a khaki outfit much like the captain's. She spotted the group of visitors escorted by Captain Sleetre. Her eyes went wide. She shoved the statuette in her hands into a nearby researcher's grasp and stormed towards the four.

"Who the hell are they?" she demanded of the captain.

"It's okay, Rowan," they said calmly, "they want to talk about the artifacts."

"I don't care what they want, who are they?" Her attention, and an accusatory finger with it, chose Tobias. "How did you get here?"

"We walked," he said, taken aback.

Sheila stepped forward. "Look. Rowan, was it?"

"Captain Kearney!" she barked.

Sheila exhaled and righted herself to a vaguely sarcastic attention. "Captain Kearney. We're allies, ma'am. Trying to stop Cymona from starting another war."

The captain rolled her eyes. "At ease. And get your story straight, this about the artifacts or not?"

"The artifacts are key to stopping the war," Tobias said.

Captain Kearney glanced at the collection of figures and the cloud of people examining them. "I'm not buying it. Besides, we've got our own problems." She lowered her volume for Captain Sleetre. "You read the wire, right, Em? She's rounding up troops in Nohlgara."

The volume wasn't low enough. Alejandro perked up. His sources had been quiet since Sao Neso. Burned, probably. He was not happy to be caught off guard by Queen Eileen's moves, even if he was happy that the captains had no information protocol whatsoever. "Are you sure?" he said. "Nohlgara?"

"Quiet!" she barked. "You look like one of her lap dogs anyway."

Alejandro glared. "I was," he said stiffly. "But no longer."

Captain Kearney froze, before aggressively getting in Captain Sleetre's face. "You brought a Speaker here?"

"I have left!" Alejandro interjected.

"Bullshit!" The captain was nearly yelling. "Get them out of here. Now!"

She turned and rejoined the cluster examining the artifacts, leaving Captain Sleetre to usher the four out, an apologetic look on their face. They grabbed Tobias's arm, tugging at him to move. He stood, rigid, staring at Captain Kearney.

"We're not leaving," he declared. "This is too important."

Captain Kearney ignored him.

Captain Sleetre tugged at his arm again, the kindness in their face dissipating. "Nope. Come on."

"Does Barlow's Bread not want recruits?" Alejandro asked.

"We do," Captain Kearney yelled from the cluster, "but not you."

"From the sounds of it," Alejandro said, "you folks need anyone you can get. Unless you're working with those Vanciots."

Captain Sleetre's beak pinched in indignation.

"You can take our weapons if it'll make you feel safer," Kell offered.

A muted groan from the table. Captain Kearney walked back to the group, her gait dragging slightly. She loomed over Alejandro. "Why are you here?" She spoke slowly, looking him in the eye.

He matched her gaze. "I have fought too many battles on the wrong side. The world demands better of me." *A bit melodramatic there, Al.*

It was enough for the captain. She turned to Kell. "What about you, mage?"

"My unit is dead on Lyon's orders," they said. "I want justice."

"Then talk to Gauven," the captain scoffed.

Captain Sleetre, joining the interrogation, grabbed Tobias's shoulder. "This is an academic thing for you, isn't it, professor?"

"Hardly. Lyon's perverting my work. Better that I'm here doing something about it than boring my students in a lecture."

"And someone's gotta keep these three from getting themselves killed," Sheila added without being prompted.

Captain Kearney gave the group a stern look over. "Alright. Here's the deal. We're wrapping up within the hour. Birdbrain, you're sticking with me. Look, but do not touch. The rest of you, make yourselves useful. You can sleep in the infirmary, you're gone first thing in the morning."

The four exchanged glances and nods. "Deal," Sheila said.

"Your weapons," Captain Kearney added. The group complied readily, pulling scabbards and straps off of their backs and belts.

"One more thing," Captain Sleetre said before standing squarely in front of Alejandro. "Your mobile."

He pulled it from his pocket and held it in front of him. *They don't know what to look for on it.*

The captain tugged it out of his hand sharply. They grasped the device as firmly as the shape would allow and, with a sudden windup, hurled the mobile at the wall. It hit a stone pillar and shattered with a sharp metallic ring.

The sound reached Alejandro's ear as he realized what was happening. He kept his gaze fixed on Sleetre's steely, stoic face. *Don't react. Don't.*

"She's not hearing anything," the captain said.

"Dennie! Raji!" Captain Kearney shouted towards the mess hall nook. "You've got help."

Kell joined Alejandro in walking to the mess hall, where two masked hunns--a young, pale man and a motherly woman with dark skin--were cleaning mismatched pieces of kitchen equipment. They may well have been among those who stopped by to listen outside, but Alejandro wasn't positive. Not quite yet.

He subtly nudged Kell's left arm as they walked. "We may have a rat," he whispered. "Hear any lingo I taught you, you tell me."

Kell nodded as the man looked up and acknowledged their presence.

"Oh. Ahoy." He spoke as if an opportunity was walking in.

"I take it you're Dennie?" Alejandro asked.

"That's what I'm known as," he said. "Here to help clean?"

"It's that or hauling stuff around," Raji said.

"If I could," Kell said, "I'll stick to cleaning. My arm's busted up, can't carry that much."

"I'll do the carrying, then," Alejandro offered.

Raji quickly confirmed his guess that he'd be working alongside her. Which was good. Dennie seemed like he wanted to be alone with Alejandro, and not for enticing reasons.

Alejandro and Raji started walking to the granary. On the way, Raji made eye contact with Captain Sleetre, who was at a table tending to some sort of administrative business. The two exchanged silent nods. The quiet trust between them was reassuring for Alejandro. Sure, it had been Dennie that threw around lingo earlier and not Raji--if he had his marks right--but Sleetre didn't seem like the kind to dole out trust freely. Neither Speakers nor Vanciots would earn it. After all, Alejandro had only just started to earn anybody's trust, and even that came with conditions.

"You seem on quite good terms with the captain." After the first round trip, Alejandro decided it was time for small talk.

"I'd hope so," Raji said earnestly. "Been here long enough."

"How long, if you don't mind?"

Raji sighed. "Two, three years now?"

"Quite a long time."

"Well, it's just a week at a time, then I'm back home. Less suspicious. Looks like I'm just a Banner courier."

Alejandro thought as he dragged a barley sack. "I hadn't really considered the logistics of the whole place. Figured a farmland might be self-sufficient."

"We're almost there," Raji said. "Until then, it's like this." She tapped the mask across her eyes.

"Aliases, too?" Alejandro said, knowingly.

"Always. No mobiles, no faces, no names. Captains are the only ones who don't, and they never leave, so it doesn't matter."

With a heave, Alejandro finished his delivery. "Bit surprised you're telling me all this. A former Speaker and all. I get the sense information is fairly casual around here."

Raji smirked. "We trust each other. And, come on. No real Speaker is ever gonna admit it. You're not even the first recruit to act bigger than they are."

They stepped into the main hall, sweaty from exertion, to find the space calmly quiet. The cloud of people examining artifacts had all but dissipated, leaving Captain Kearney with Tobias and a couple others. Kell and Dennie swept up quietly.

"'Bout time, you two," Dennie scoffed.

"Glad to be of help," Alejandro said politely, hoping that would end the conversation there. He turned to Kell, about to ask where Sheila happened to be, when a door down the hall creaked open.

Sheila, flanked by Captain Sleetre, waved for their attention. "Hey Kell!" she yelled. "You still have that thing from Cuesta?"

"Should, yeah," Kell said.

"Wait," Alejandro said, patting his pockets. "I might have it on me." Between pats, he subtly gestured at Kell to come closer. They got the cue.

Once close enough, Kell ducked their head as if they too were examining Alejandro's pockets. "He muttered something about you having awful riah," they whispered.

Knew it. Nobody but a Speaker's tossing that around. "Good work," Alejandro whispered back.

"Told you," Kell said loudly towards Sheila, "must be with my rod. Why?"

"Your professor friend thinks the Kaguya piece is related," Captain Sleetre said. "Want to compare. Let's go get it."

Kell handed their broom to Alejandro. "If you don't mind," they said, "I'm gonna go over and see what they're looking at."

Alejandro was left with Dennie in an empty hall, as Raji had seemingly vanished into the night.

"They sure are concerned about a bunch of rocks," Dennie grumbled.

"You're not?"

Dennie shrugged. "More concerned about other things."

Alejandro swept nonchalantly. "Such as? If you don't mind."

Dennie glared, leaning on his broom. "I *do* mind, Speaker."

"Ah, my reputation precedes me," Alejandro sighed. "But as I've reassured everyone, I left that job."

"Nobody leaves that job."

"That's what they say." Alejandro's sweeping steered him closer to where Dennie was working. "But then, in a way nobody ever leaves their jobs. Doesn't matter what work you do. The things you see and learn, you can't simply forget them." His tone dipped slightly. "They stick with you. The language. The secrets."

Dennie stared at Alejandro. "Do they, now?" His question lacked curiosity. "How about sharing some of those secrets?"

Last chance, Dennie. I hope I'm wrong. "You first." Alejandro smirked.

Dennie clearly smelled blood. Catching Alejandro would be a great career move for such a rookie. Impossible to resist.

"I don't know what you mean," Dennie said with a lying grin.

Poor little idiot. "You know I know," Alejandro hissed.

Dennie's eyes narrowed. His grin turned bitter. He pushed himself against Alejandro, his mask smearing into his face. "Know what?"

"Our job."

Alejandro stiffened and swung his left arm across his side, deflecting Dennie's incoming punch. Dennie, unfazed, swung with his left, but Alejandro ducked below and jabbed his forearm quickly at Dennie's shin, disrupting his footing, before taking a step back.

"The standard? Really?" Alejandro mocked. "Against a former Speaker?"

Dennie righted himself. "A posh hog like you? Like you've fought."

Alejandro took off his suit jacket and threw it aside. He glanced around. Nobody was watching the two. *This will be a scene the moment someone notices. Don't over-commit.*

"A barney, then?" Dennie said, clearly aware he was blowing his cover.

He lunged at Alejandro, leaving the question unanswered. Alejandro caught his weight and pivoted, sending Dennie rolling over the nearby table, landing smoothly on his feet. Dennie threw his mask off and vaulted the table, connecting an opportune punch to the gut on his landing. Alejandro bent at the impact and watched Dennie's feet. He had landed awkwardly. Alejandro took advantage, spearing into Dennie's midsection, pushing him off his feet and crashing through the table.

The noise gathered attention. Tobias and Captain Kearney ran over while the current and former Speakers traded punches, Alejandro barely retaining the upper hand in the grapple. The captain clawed her way between the two to separate them.

Alejandro stepped back, his body aching and bruised. "You have a rat," he said to Captain Kearney.

"Yeah, and it's you!" The captain shoved Alejandro aside. "The fuck are you doing?"

Dennie, bloodied and sitting on the floor, started laughing an adrenaline-fueled laugh.

Alejandro breathed heavily. His lungs burned. He wiped sweat and blood from his face. "Why are they in Nohlgara, Speaker?" he demanded of Dennie.

Dennie laughed bitterly.

"Why?" Alejandro shouted.

"You know why, traitor."

Alejandro angrily kicked him in the leg. Captain Kearney made no effort to stop him. "We need to evacuate," he said to the captain. "They're coming."

Captain Kearney's eyes darted warily between Dennie and Alejandro. "When?"

A chime played from the floor where Dennie was lying. He ignored his mobile going off. "No time like the present," he said with a snide grin.

In the rafters of the hall, an alarm began to sound.

Bastard.

D

The pitch of the alarm rose, bringing Captain Sleetre into the main hall carrying something small and red wrapped in a cloth. Sheila and Kell followed.

"Em, what the hell's going on?" Captain Kearney shouted. "Where's the breach?"

"Northeast," Captain Sleetre shouted back. "Everyone, move! Safe room, now! Come on, we practiced for this!" The handful of people now in the hall responded to their directions quickly, dropping whatever they were doing and rushing to nondescript doors or running outside. Sleetre set the bundle they were carrying on a table and ducked out of the hall to repeat their orders.

"Where's Raji?" Alejandro shouted to Sleetre. He had a sense of where everyone else he met that evening went, more or less, but she had vanished. It had him worried. He couldn't entirely justify it--these were people he had only just met, and only loosely aligned himself with--but he couldn't deny a need to make sure she was safe.

"She had a key to the armory," Kell said after Sleetre, too busy with their duties as a captain, failed to reply. "Locked up our weapons before hiding."

Alejandro grumbled. He pushed a mess of hair back and bit his split lip in frustration. It still tasted of blood. He looked across the faces of his comrades. Sheila, naturally, was angry about the situation. The professor held himself with the eager pivot of a man who wanted to help, *somehow*, if only he were given the direction. And Kell. He couldn't see their face, but he knew how they carried themself when they were relaxed, and how they did when they were enveloped in righteous fury. Kell was furious.

He knew them well enough. He could trust any of them with his life.

"You guys trust me, right?" Alejandro quietly asked.

The three quickly glanced at each other before giving small, wary nods.

"Captain Kearney!" Alejandro called to the captain, who had sat down on the floor to restrain Dennie. "Get us our weapons. Now."

"The hell?" she said. "That's the army, you idiot. We're not fighting that."

"*You're* not. We are. Get us our weapons."

"You have a death wish? We have a safe room. Go."

"You have an army at your gate," Sheila said. "This is war. And we're soldiers. We need our weapons."

Captain Kearney looked at the tied-up Dennie lying on the ground, grinning weakly. She reached into her pocket and tossed over a keychain. "It's your funeral."

After gathering their equipment from the nearly empty shed that was the facility's armory, the four rushed in the dark towards the northeast corner of the compound. There could be a full, proper unit approaching, at least a hundred Farolian soldiers, possibly more. If so, Alejandro had put the group up to a tall order. But then, if Dennie had been feeding headquarters the truth, a group that large would be overkill. The Queen, ever tight-pursed, would send only enough to deal with the expected, limited, amateur resistance. Hopefully.

The group stopped on a small mound of compacted dirt just off the edge of the forest. A short line of lamps was in the wooded distance, steadily approaching. "There should be more than this," Alejandro said. "Professor, keep ready on triage. Nobody's dying today."

"Keep yourself back," Kell said to him. "You look wounded."

You've got one arm, Kell. You're one to talk. "Fine. I'll keep eyes and call positions. Can you two handle the vanguard?"

Sheila drew her claymore and held it loosely, the tip digging into the dirt. "Easily. Kell and I? We make a good team." As if to agree, Kell grabbed their rod and wrapped the claymore's blade in flame.

The Farolian captain leading the force emerged from the woods. He raised his lantern, turning the flame brighter, and paused in trepidation. Rows of soldiers, three or four wide, stayed among the trees behind him. The captain looked around at the four, illuminated by Sheila's burning sword and a ball of vapor flame on Kell's rod.

"Right then," he said, clearly not expecting the audience. "Put down your weapons!" he ordered. "By the order of Her Majesty Eileen II, this facility is shut down! You are coming with us!"

Kell took a confident step forward. "By the order of the last vapormage," they shouted, "go fuck yourselves!"

Alejandro smiled to himself in the shadows. *There's the storm, Kell. About time.*

The captain had no response beyond tossing his lantern to the ground, drawing his sword and shield, and calling for the soldiers to attack. At this, Kell swung their rod in a wide arc before them, the fiery vapor spraying across the attacking force. Those who didn't find themselves in flames were intercepted by Sheila's sword. Within seconds, a half dozen

Farolian soldiers were injured, reeling into defensive positions they had not expected to take.

Alejandro scanned the surroundings. "Ten o'clock!" he called out, spotting a pair of soldiers attempting a flank. He swept around Tobias and threw out a dagger, followed by a small burst of watery vapor. Neither were bound to do much damage, but they were enough of a distraction that the soldiers couldn't interrupt Kell's spellcraft. They were knocked off their feet by Kell shaking and lifting the earth beneath them, followed by broad sweeps of Tobias's spear forcing them into retreat.

As the battle progressed, the group holding their ground against more than two dozen soldiers, one finally slipped through the cracks. By the time Alejandro spotted him, his sword was raised high, primed to strike at Sheila, who was too focused on another attacker to defend herself. But the arm dropped the wrong way, away from both Sheila and the soldier's body, as a wooden arrow pierced the skin. Another came flying, hitting the soldier in the torso, dropping him to the ground. Approaching from the complex, lit only by the moon, was Captain Kearney, bow in hand. Captain Sleetre followed close behind, their sword and shield already drawn.

The defense felt like it took hours. Alejandro and Captain Kearney each shouted out advances and sniped at soldiers that had fallen out of position. Kell blasted out waves of vapor at groups of attackers, while Tobias used what other vapor was available for shoring up defenses. Sheila and Captain Sleetre kept up the physical blockade against anyone who got too close. Eventually, a call for retreat came from the depths of the woods, granting the six a chance to catch their breath.

Captain Kearney, gathering herself, draped her bow across her body. As she rubbed the fingers of her drawing hand, a concerned look covered her face. "Are all your flames out?" she asked Kell.

They looked around. The vapor flames exhausted themselves quickly as usual, and the few lanterns left on the battlefield were crushed and extinguished in the brawl. "Looks like."

"So what's burning?"

Alejandro took a deep breath through his nose. He could smell wood burning, as sure as he could smell the blood and sweat of battle. He turned to face the farm complex. The main hall glowed a violent orange.

"Shit." Captain Kearney dashed towards the main hall, the others following close behind. Flames flickered out of the broad side doors, accompanied by loud crashes. A trio of well-armored soldiers holding torches stepped out from the flames.

"What in the hell are you doing?" Alejandro called out.

The soldiers gave each other quick glances. One threw his torch into the smoldering hall before the three ran off into the night.

An arrow from Captain Kearney's bow landed among the fresh footprints behind them. "Bastards!" she shouted. A beam inside the hall gave way with a loud crash. Captain Kearney stared at the burning hall in distressed awe as it crackled. The roof collapsed. Her posture, her heart, sank with it.

Kell began blasting the burning building with watery vapor in an attempt to quell the flames. They were having little success; their spells, like the ones Alejandro knew, made focused jets of water. Tobias tried to offer wind, but his limited control over the element hardly helped. After a lengthy, fumbling effort of spellcasting and tossing loose dirt, the fire finally receded into embers.

Alejandro's body wanted to give up. He had managed to avoid taking any blows during the siege, but he spent the entire time on high alert, which tore at his energy just as well. Spending so much vapor likewise taxed him. It didn't help that he had been running on adrenaline all night, and the crash was surely coming. But when Captain Sleetre, with no regard for their feathers and skin, climbed into the remains of the hall and started pushing around smoldering rubble, he felt compelled to join them.

"Over here," Captain Sleetre said, gesturing to their position. "The hatch."

Alejandro didn't ask questions. He helped pull away destroyed furniture and fallen wood until a wide square of stone in the ground became visible. A handle was chiseled out of the rock.

With the stone cleared off, Captain Sleetre gave it five quick, rhythmic knocks. They waited, kneeling over the hatch, their lower beak trembling in barely contained anxiety.

Silence.

Knock knock, from within the hatch.

"Oh, thank Gauven," Captain Sleetre exhaled. They grasped the handle, stood, and pulled.

E

Captain Kearney was relieved to finish her headcount. Everyone was accounted for. There were some injuries that came while getting everyone into the safe room or in the hidden hutches outside, but nothing serious. Even Dennie wasn't that hurt. Physically, at least. He seemed to have given up, barely struggling against the restraints that Raji held.

"Now what?" Raji asked, sitting on the cold grass outside the hall.

"I don't know," Captain Kearney said, sounding defeated as she glanced at the burnt hall. "I don't . . ."

"You've assigned out enough beds underground, right, Raji?" Captain Sleetre said quietly.

"Aye, captain," she said.

Captain Sleetre sank at the title. "Alright. We can sort this out in the morning."

"Who's keeping watch?" Raji asked as she stood.

"I'll do it," Alejandro said. "I'll need to keep an eye on Dennie."

Captain Sleetre took a look at him, then at their prisoner.

"I'll do nothing more to him," Alejandro continued. "Just keep an eye on him. I promise."

"He's good for it." That the words came from Sheila shocked Alejandro.

The captain nodded. The rebels slowly got up and stepped over the rubble, into the underground safe room. Sheila and Tobias followed, with Kell bringing up the rear. They seemed uncertain about joining. Perhaps they were concerned about being spotted as a sahagin, perhaps they didn't want to claim any more of the rebels' hospitality even after saving them. Knowing Kell the way Alejandro now did, either seemed likely.

Alejandro sat on the ground, leaning against a warm stone segment of the hall's outer wall and looking up at the cold, clear moon. Dennie, his wrists and ankles bound, had been propped up similarly at the other side of a wide doorway. The two remained silent for some time, with only faint clamor from the safe room or the neighs of wild horses for company.

Dennie rolled his head towards Alejandro. "Alright, booly dog. Where'd you find the rose?"

Alejandro's gaze stayed towards the sky. "Didn't. We got lucky. We came for the artifacts."

"That's a lousy cover," Dennie said dismissively.

"The truth can be boring. It has that luxury."

"We do know all about luxuries." Dennie squirmed against his restraints. "So when are you gonna bother?"

Alejandro shook his head. "I'm not going to kill you. Promised I wouldn't."

"Bull. It's what Speakers do."

"I'm not a Speaker," Alejandro said. "Not anymore."

"Then I'll just break out," Dennie said, more a weak observation than a promise or a threat.

"You're not my prisoner." Alejandro turned to see Dennie's head hung. "Look at me, Dennie. Listen. These people are going to do to you whatever they think is right. You're *their* prisoner. Now, if you want to stay alive, I would suggest cooperating. And if they do let you live? Run. Change your name, change your clothes, change your haircut. Run until your legs burn to cinders below you. Get out of Farolé. Go to Zeimatia if you want. You can breach the wall, I *know* you can.

"I don't care where you head, it doesn't matter, just . . . get out of this life while you still have one. You'll spend every day haunted by the damage you've done, and you'll deserve it, but you'll get to have those days. Because you know what will happen if you stay here. You know that the Speakers demand perfection and precision and *you fucked up*. You got cocky. You are a dead man if you stay, Dennie, they will make sure of it. Maybe you think you want that, maybe you think you've accepted that every mission could be your last, but once the blade is at your throat? It changes. Suddenly you're looking forward to every breath, every heartbeat, as cursed as they are. So if they let you live, then by the Guardians. Live."

Dennie stared at Alejandro with hollow acceptance. Eventually, he turned away, having no words to speak.

Sleetre was the first to emerge from the burnt-out barn the following morning. They clearly hadn't slept either. They stood between Dennie and Alejandro, looking out at nothing in particular.

"Morning, captain," Alejandro said quietly, not wanting to wake Dennie.

Sleetre sighed. "Please don't call me that."

"Ah. Apologies." Alejandro stood. "Are things alright?"

Sleetre hung their head. "The queen didn't have an heir," they muttered.

"Pardon?"

Sleetre pulled a mobile from their pocket and tapped it a few times. They handed it to Alejandro. "Founding Day parade yesterday. Watch."

A video began playing on the mobile's screen. Even sleep-deprived, Alejandro quickly recognized the scene: a marketplace in Gauvencia, close to many of the old estates. Holiday parades frequently went down that road. Judging by the golden streetlight bathing the scene, it must have been late in the parade route, into the evening. The crowd was large.

Queen Eileen II rode into frame. She was on Gauven, the pale brown horse-like Guardian of Farolé, the namesake of its capital, trotting along regally on his six legs. She always rode on Gauven. She was the Queen, after all.

The parade crowd muddied the sound. As the Queen approached, she could finally be heard enough to be understood. She had been making a speech the entire ride. " . . .But today, we honor the Four Kingdoms of Farolé, and their history, and their Guardian, and their most loyal people. And we honor the strength of their fleet, as they lay low our enemies. Those seeking to foment chaos have been laid low today, plucked from hiding in the Felmata Forest. I assure you, Farolé, there will be no chaos so long as I reign!"

The applause befitted a smaller crowd. Gauven looked around as he walked. His head dipped. A confused murmur broke out in the crowd. "What was that?" the person recording the video said before Gauven suddenly jostled, neighing loudly. The queen, flailing in surprise, was launched off his back. He reared, kicked, and stomped the ground. A body flew out of frame.

Someone screamed. The Queen was dead.

Chaos erupted in the streets of Gauvencia.

The video ended. Alejandro stared at his face reflected in the screen. It sagged, tired and confused. He offered Sleetre their mobile back. They took it, in return handing over a mass of cloth with a small, red lump of some glossy material poking out from its center.

After a moment, Sleetre exhaled. "You four should leave Farolé."

"Yes cap--" Alejandro caught himself. "Thank you, Sleetre."

Long ago, before man, Vakonivak kept watch over the beasts of the land. One day, she bid the beasts gather around her home, for she had something to say. "My friends," said she, "I fear a great curse will befall this world soon. Our eyes will cloud and our hearts will ache." The beasts were terrified by her words, but Vakonivak reassured them. "If you work together in kindness, then we shall continue to live on." As her wisdom had been true before, the beasts agreed and sought to make their plans.

Soon, one beast, the serpent, approached Vakonivak. It held its head low in sadness. "Great Vakonivak," it said, "this plague worries me. I wish to help the other beasts, but I fear I cannot."

"Why not?" Vakonivak asked.

"I am seen as deceitful," the serpent said. "I slip and hide among the grasses as I fear the dangers of the world. Yet they believe I hide as I plan to betray their trust."

"Is that what you intend to do?" Vakonivak asked.

"No," the serpent replied, "but it is my nature to be vile thus."

Vakonivak considered these words. Soon, the wolf approached Vakonivak and quietly sought to speak to her. "Oh dear Vakonivak," the wolf said, "the other beasts have been planning well, but though I wish to help, I find I cannot."

"Why not?" Vakonivak asked.

"I am seen as prideful," the wolf said. "I walk through the world alone, as I do not wish to burden others. Yet they believe I am too proud to give aid, and will only bring argument."

"Is that what you intend to do?" Vakonivak asked.

"No," the wolf replied, "but it is my nature to be vile thus."

Vakonivak considered the wolf's words. Later, the crow perched near Vakonivak. "Mother of skies," the crow said, "the other beasts have prepared greatly, but I fear I could not help them to do so."

"Why not?" Vakonivak asked.

"I am seen as greedy," the crow said. "What others leave behind, I take for myself, as they have no desire for it. Yet they believe I will take from them what they require to survive."

"Is that what you intend to do?" Vakonivak asked.

"No," the crow replied, "but it is my nature to be vile thus."

Vakonivak considered the crow's words. Having done this, she summoned the lion, as he was respected among the beasts.

The lion answered Vakonivak in worry. "Great Vakonivak," the lion said, "we have prepared ourselves as much as we can. Yet there is worry that it will not be enough."

"You have done all you can?" Vakonivak asked.

"Indeed we have," the lion said.

"And how did the crow assist you?" Vakonivak asked. "Or the wolf? Or the serpent?"

The lion thought. "They did not," he said, "for they are too greedy, too proud, too deceitful."

"They are not," Vakonivak said. "They are tidy, lonesome, afraid. Speak to them, and listen to them. Only if you do will you be prepared."

The lion trusted Vakonivak and followed her words.

Some time later, Vakonivak bid the beasts gather around her home. "My friends," said she, "I am pleased to see you work together wisely and well. I do not see our world falling to darkness anymore."

"Are we truly safe?" the hedgehog asked.

"Yes," Vakonivak said, "for you have cured yourselves of a great curse of misunderstanding."

Many beasts were confused by her words. Soon, the lion spoke. "Was there no darkness? Were you untrue to us?"

"I was not," Vakonivak said. "The curse would scatter and cloud us, but you joined as one. Even the beasts deemed vile were of help. Without them, the curse surely could not be broken."

The beasts understood. Yet the lion said, "You did speak true, but we feared greatly at your words."

Vakonivak shook her head in apology. "Then it is my nature to be vile thus."

— *Fable of the Vile Beasts*,
Author unknown

CHAPTER TWELVE

S heila was the last to sleep and the first to wake. The group had made their way far north, spending a day and a half following a footpath that pushed past the edge of the forest, until exhaustion and a howling windstorm forced them to pause and camp among some boulders on a plain along the Tabrill Pass. The pass stretched for kilometers in nearly every direction, blanketing the visible landscape with an unremarkable sprawl of small, unstable rocks. It was a notorious part of Linnute's terrain, whether notoriously difficult to traverse or notoriously boring to look at.

The area the four had stopped in could have been worse. It was largely lacking in features to draw the eye or many natural resources to work with, just dull and flat with occasional patches of grass. At least the ground made for even terrain, the rocks small enough that walking took an almost ordinary amount of effort. The rocks they had settled among provided middling shelter, but shelter all the same. It was as good a place to rest as they were going to get. Sheila tended to the modest fire she had lit, huddling against its warmth.

Kell woke with a start, catching Sheila's eye. They rubbed fog off their visor and sat up. "Hey. Did you sleep?"

"A little," Sheila said quietly. "Mostly been keeping guard."

"My turn, then."

Sheila shrugged and stood up. "You know me, Kell. Once I'm up, I'm up. You can cover tonight."

"Good." They retrieved their mobile from their satchel and gave their attention to the screen.

Sheila watched quietly long enough for a smile to show up on her face. "New episode?"

Kell dropped their mobile, embarrassed.

Sheila laughed. It was so easy to tease Kell just by bringing up Bryn Achterberg. It was practically a game. "Signal decent up here, at least?"

"Seems okay." Kell gestured with their mobile. "Wanna watch while we wait for the guys?"

With a shrug, Sheila sat down and obliged. She didn't care about . . . any shows, really, but for a friend, she'd watch for a bit. When the bit passed, Sheila started looking around. A patch of vegetation caught her interest. Some small bushes still had red berries on them. Might be edible. It'd help the group survive a little longer.

"How's your arm?" she asked as she went to collect the fruit.

"Kinda numb. Aches a lot. Think the vapor's finally starting to give out. But the cold helps."

"Makes sense." She brought a handful of berries back to the fire and grabbed her mobile. She was used to foraging farther south, back home, so she wasn't positive exactly what they were.

"Trying to get used to the thought that it'll fall off someday."

"How's that working out?" Sheila meant it kindly, even if she could hear the sarcasm in her voice.

"Yeah, I know," Kell said with a chuckle. "But, hey, we're alive. That counts for something."

"You certainly fight like you wanna live. Put on a hell of a show at the farm."

"Same to you. Great job."

Sheila shrugged. "Lighting the sword makes it easy. I don't--" *Shit, I don't wanna go down this road.* "Never mind."

Kell set down their mobile. "You alright?" they asked, earnestly.

Sheila gave their visor a glance. If Tobias or Alejandro asked the same thing in the same way, she'd doubt they meant it. But Kell? They were too soft for a soldier sometimes. "I don't do well with lots of blood. It's the smell. Bad memories."

"Your periods must suck."

"Always have. A burning sword means less blood, at least, so it . . ." Sheila knew the words, but couldn't find herself saying them. Juice gathered on her fingers. She had been squeezing the berries without realizing it. "I don't think I could fight this much if you weren't helping," she eventually said.

"Part of the job." Kell sighed. "Not that I really ever wanted to do it before. But that fight? I guess that was what I was always supposed to be as a vapormage. Bold. Unstoppable. Power overwhelming. Never felt it before."

"Not the sort of thing you can just pull out. You gave a damn."

"Of course. They're good folks."

Sheila tossed the berries aside. Everything pointed to them being poisonous. "Yeah. We didn't spend long there, but Kearney and I got along good enough. And I've been thinking. Think I get what Sleetre was talking about, with recruiting."

"Oh, all that about leftovers?"

"Yeah. Look at us."

At Sheila's prompt, Kell did. They looked at Tobias, spread out lazily on a patch of grass; at Alejandro, curled up tightly, using a satchel as a pillow.

"There was no way we'd ever run into each other if it wasn't for this," she continued. "Not like we have much else in common. Just like the folks Sleetre was talking about, how they don't get big batches of recruits, just us weirdos. The scattered bricks."

"The scattered bricks," Kell repeated with a nod. "Hope they can build something good with theirs."

Sheila pulled some flatbread from her bag. She broke off a piece and offered it to Kell, who refused. "Kell, come on," she said. "There's nobody up this far. Have some food."

Kell peered around the boulder they were leaning against. Sheila took her own look to confirm. The barren, rocky landscape stretched forever without another soul in sight. Hesitantly, Kell unlatched their helmet and set it to their side.

The group was slow to get moving. The days of tense travel, spent in fear that more Farolian soldiers would track them down, had burned through their bodies. Now their muscles and bones were charred with exhaustion. Tobias, from all his groaning and creaking, easily had the worst of it. He had to push to keep up with the others, and so had definitely pushed past his age.

His mind was seemingly well-rested, though, as he started trying to plan the group's next steps far earlier in the morning than Sheila had any interest in doing. She couldn't bring herself to feel the urgency. There was some, sure, but they were doing much better than she had expected. If the little chunks of whatever they are that the group had been gathering actually were keys--and Kell seemed convinced they were--then the group already had two, when she had only figured they would find one. Or, if she was being frank, none. Cyprin, the twat that he was, at least was right about how impossible the whole plan sounded.

"I'm going to assume none of us are familiar with the terrain," Alejandro said, warming himself against the fire.

"Nope," Sheila said. "It's rocks. We get rocks."

"Just what I always wanted," Alejandro quipped.

"Entirely possible the last key is one of them," Tobias said, lost in thought.

Kell rubbed their eyes, still adjusting to the clear autumn morning. "There's two left," they said. "Dad was lying. Or mistaken."

"I'd bet he was lying," Sheila said.

"Malice or not," Alejandro said, "we know he doesn't have the facts. What else *do* we know?"

"We know the Guardians are involved."

Alejandro tilted his head. "How so, Sheila?"

"So, okay," Sheila said, sitting up a bit taller. "That video that Sleetre showed us, right? Gauven's marching around, then all of a sudden, people are acting like they heard something that wasn't on the video. Like they heard something that wasn't a sound. Like what Caduceus did. Guys, Gauven *talked*. And then he flipped his shit."

"That doesn't mean it has anything to do with us," Kell said.

"Yeah, but it's *weird*. Guardians don't talk."

"Hakuta talks," Tobias said.

Sheila rolled her eyes. "To the priests. Do we look like priests?"

"That's their story, anyway." Alejandro was simmering on the topic. "I keep coming back to that speech the Queen was making. She set herself up as a bulwark against chaos, which is an utter farce, frankly. But it seemed as if Gauven was reacting to that. As if he . . . *wanted* chaos." He spoke as if he disbelieved his own claims. "If I still had my mobile, I could contact my sources, find out what was said. So much for that. To be blunt, this is where I worry about our mission. I don't know what side the Guardians are on here."

"Caduceus is on our side," Kell said. "We didn't defeat her. She surrendered. I tried to tell her why we were there, and I think she understood."

Alejandro closed his eyes in thought. "But if Caduceus and Gauven are on the same side, then . . ." He tapped the ground with his hand rapidly. "I don't like this. The Guardians are a wild card here."

Sheila stared off to the west. The peak of Mt. Grann was barely visible in the mist of the atmosphere. It was better than nothing. "So here's what I think. The army uses Mt. Grann for a training ground. But, Vakonivak lives in the top of it. We can get there. And we don't leave until she tells us what's going on. If she doesn't know, then maybe they're not working together. Maybe Gauven's just a dick. But if she does know, then we get the truth."

"If she speaks honestly," Alejandro said.

"I have faith. She will."

B

With a final check of their supplies, the group broke camp and started on the long march west. Grann Bay, and the mountain that gave it its name, was only a few kilometers from the border, but reaching the edge of Bessetrae would take a full day on foot. Possibly longer if the weather finally broke. Thick grey clouds taunted their every move.

Even if the group was able to reach the border without too much trouble, crossing it was going to be a different story. They didn't have Crystal to help them. Maybe Banner could. Crystal worked for him, at the end of the day, so any trick she could pull he probably could as well.

But that bridge was burned. After the group left Sao Neso, they sent Banner a carefully arranged set of images and details that would, technically, fulfill their agreement. Along with it was a diplomatically phrased missive, reminding Banner that the group was done working with him. Sheila wanted to send her original diatribe, unedited, full of the vulgarity and anger the group all felt. Banner could close her account in retaliation for all she cared. She didn't need him. Resting everything important in life on the whims of one guy was a bullshit idea anyway.

The weather cooperated. The sky competed with the rocky terrain to see which could be greyer, but there was no precipitation. The boulder fields could be traversed with something resembling speed. Even so, the border remained out of sight in the distance when the sun set far enough to force them to make camp.

Sheila and Alejandro took another attempt at foraging. It had happened that the group went farther north than they intended, coming close to the coast. The two stumbled upon a long inlet where a moderately sized canoe had washed ashore beside other trash and flotsam that, collectively, implied the sailor hadn't survived very long. The canoe looked like it could seat five or six people, but its hull was in no condition for any passenger count. Still, Sheila and Alejandro agreed to lug it back to camp. At worst, it would be a supply of firewood. At best, a bearskin and a bit of work could make it viable for reaching the mountain in the bay.

The next morning, Sheila woke to aching muscles and the sight of Kell practicing their spellcraft in the distance. They were jostling boulders into the air, one at a time, each of them larger than they were. Kell let them land and then looked them over for . . . something. Sheila couldn't tell what, but she could tell they looked somewhat discouraged by what they found. Maybe the rocks were supposed to fly higher, or shatter when they landed, or just be rockier in some way. She ultimately decided not to interrupt. She wouldn't listen if they told her how to train, so of course they wouldn't listen to her either.

The sun was almost at its highest when the four arrived at a small shed, sitting just off the border between Farolé and Bessetrae. A second shed sat a few meters away, with a low and worn fence sitting between the two and stretching off into the horizon. They had gone days without seeing any other humans, and the border crossing would prove no different. There was nobody there, on either side. The whole station felt like a forgotten formality, something that existed because it had to and not because anybody particularly wanted it to. Whoever had been stationed there was clearly being punished for something, and by their absence, had decided that the punishment did not fit the crime. The four rushed through the crossing, not expecting the good fortune of an unguarded border to hold, the boat skidding along the waves of rocks behind them.

On the Bessetran side, sparse signs of life began to reappear in the terrain. By mid-afternoon, the remnants of a road headed south appeared. Sheila led the group along the road, northwest-bound, towards the bay. They found the corpse of a lavender-tinged arth just off the trail, but between the decay and vapor poisoning, the former bear's skin was too brittle to be useful for the canoe.

The path curved past a sizable thicket and down a stepped hill, at the bottom of which was Grann Bay. Granberg itself was easily visible across the water. On a flat layer of the hill, three tiers above the land that sat flush with the water, was an old cabin of logs and sheet metal. If anybody was there, then a light would be on. The absence was a strong indication that the cabin was abandoned.

Sheila knocked on the door all the same. The group would have to set up camp nearby, and any resident was going to see them. The wood creaked open with her second knock, exposing the darkened interior. Kell's vapor flame illuminated the cabin, revealing it as a cluttered mess of strewn housewares atop primitive furniture. Half of the cabin was dedicated to a workshop, with tools and large sheets of canvas and metal and other materials laid about in the barest semblance of order.

The four agreed to leave the place be. The cabin's owner was probably out hunting and could be back at any moment. Better to set up camp away from their property and make introductions when they returned.

Night fell and the cabin remained unoccupied. Tobias and Alejandro tried to work out what they could do with the skeletal canoe to make it useful for reaching the mountain. Neither of them was a handyman. It was painfully obvious.

Kell quietly excused themself from watching the two fumble about. They returned to the campfire a few minutes later, carrying large tanned hides draped over their shoulders as though their uniform wasn't providing enough of a cloak for their tastes.

"You guys think these'll help?" they yelled as they dropped the hides on the ground, next to the canoe.

Sheila stood to inspect the hides. Bearskin. "Where did you get those?" she asked.

"Don't worry about it," Kell said.

"Don't--?" Sheila grumbled lightly. "No secrets, Kell. You took those from the cabin."

Kell, indifferent, sat by the fire. "The *abandoned* cabin? Yeah. No sense in it going to waste. And if I'm wrong, I'll figure out how to pay 'em back."

Alejandro and Tobias must've agreed with the logic, since they took the hides and starting working out how to sure up the canoe with them. Sheila didn't have issues with the idea either, in principle. She was just surprised Kell actually was the kind of punk they claimed to be.

Mt. Grann jutted sharply out of the bay, the tide lapping against sheer rock faces for most of its perimeter. If it had been deeper in the winter, the group could have crossed the ice that formed in the bay and stepped up one of the low cliffs. Approaching by boat that autumn morning, however, meant rowing around to the southern face, where the flowing water had worn the land down into a low beach. At least they were approaching from the east. The channel on the mountain's west side was much wider, so all of the commercial traffic took that side. Dodging Banner's cargo ships in such a small, languid vessel was never going to happen.

Kell and Tobias pulled the canoe ashore, wedging it between some rocks on the beach in case they were there long enough for the tide to roll in. Farther up the shore was a low channel that carried on as the mountain turned steeply upwards. A uniformed hunn man sat in the channel, near a door that led into the mountain itself. He spotted the group and stood quickly, drawing his crossbow.

"Hey!" he shouted. "I need you to back away! This is government property!"

"We don't want any trouble," Alejandro said politely.

"Hold on." The guard pointed his crossbow at Kell. "Who are you? What are you doing here? I was told all the vapormages are dead."

"You were told I was dead, too." Sheila marched in front of the group, pulling a small, worn fold of paper from her bag. She unfolded it and held it up in front of the guard's face. "Sergeant Sheila Takeda. Stand down."

The guard did not stand down. "You're joking. Where did you get this?"

"Central command," she said, "the same place you got yours. You *do* have yours, right, private?"

"Of course."

Sheila gestured for him to retrieve his documents.

The guard grumbled and complied. "What about them? They got their papers?"

Right. Shit. "They're War Department agents," Sheila said. "Not army. Got fake civ IDs on them."

"Really?"

"Are you doubting me, private?" Her voice was growing stiff. If bluff failed, bluster would have to do.

"I'm asking why the hell the Department is sending secret agents in here without warning. Surprise inspection or something?"

Sure, let's go with that. "Sort of. We're here to visit Vakonivak."

"Vakonivak?" the guard asked, incredulous.

"The larger details are classified," Tobias said, making it sound as though Sheila was close to overstepping some bound.

Sheila feigned annoyance at Tobias before turning back to the guard. "If it's a problem," she said, "take it up with the oberst, or the Secretary, not with us. Alright? Now can we just get in?"

The guard hesitated before withdrawing his crossbow and taking a reluctant step back. Sheila rewarded his cooperation with a salute. The guard gave a half-hearted salute back.

C

The staging area was brutal in its simplicity. Bare concrete lined the walls, painted with cleanly visible primary colors that directed the eye towards the different channels that branched from the room. Supplies were piled neatly along the walls: stacks of crates, racks of swords both sharpened and dulled, wooden targets for the archers. The place felt recently used, but of course it would. The Citadel was still an active training ground, last Sheila heard.

The volcano that was Mt. Grann was long extinct, so the site was stable. Its location made it naturally secure, perfect for storing expensive military gear and letting recruits use it when it sat idle. And, most importantly, there weren't any Secretaries pushing to get a new one built for their own benefit.

Kell gave Sheila a light jab with their elbow as she looked around the chamber. "Did you just pull rank on that guy?" they said, amused.

"Indeed, quick thinking on that line," Alejandro said. "But to have the papers for it, even?"

"'Cause it's not a line." Sheila handed him her identification. "5th Infantry Division. Would've been staff sergeant if I survived Windglade. Not like it means anything."

"Got us in," Tobias said. "That's something."

"Now, you're the one with the quick thinking," Sheila said. "Cut him off before he could ask anything else. I didn't have anywhere to take that."

He chuckled. "Guess I'm still enough of a civilian to want to jump on any sort of cloak-and-dagger pretend that I can. Al here is such an influence." He gave the hunn a friendly pat.

"So where to from here?" Kell said.

Sheila started pacing around the staging area. "Give me a sec, I'm trying to remember where everything is. We wanna go up, eventually."

As she craned her head down the hallway marked with red, an indistinct shout echoed from a distant part of the facility. *Shit.*

"We could follow that," Alejandro offered.

"They're training here today?" Sheila said in a hushed, exasperated tone. "Why didn't that guy say so?"

"I wouldn't be talking back if I was in his position," Tobias said.

Sheila pulled the group into a huddle. She would have to reach for a plan B, which would be difficult, given there was no real plan A. "Look, just stay close. Follow my lead. If anything happens, stay calm. These are rookies. They won't want the real thing."

Sheila butted herself against the wall of the staging room, between the hallways marked in green and blue, squatting cautiously as if the threat was nearby and not a distant echo. The shouts came again. Green hall. Revel, celebration. Good shot, whoever it was. She slid to peer down the hall. It quickly curved upwards, steep enough to require stairs, with the impression of a doorway to the right at the top of the slope.

Details flooded back. Green was the way to head. *Blue is supplies, curves down . . . right. Great.* The door at the top of the slope led to a lancers' yard, where the mounted soldiers trained for maneuverability and finesse. They had horses in there, once upon a time, but these days those soldiers used a sort of personal, saddle-seat cart, like a unicycle so broad it required a second wheel. They looked damned foolish, despite how fast they were. They were also noisy, which would have been an asset if they were being used by the fresh recruits that were definitely around. It would have given the four some cover should they not step lightly enough.

Past that--and now in sight, as Sheila led the slow stealthy climb up the stairs--was a specialized target range. Most of Bessetrae's archers used crossbows. They had downsides; as one of Sheila's instructors had put it, longbows were better because a longbow only needs two parts: the long, and the bow. But crossbows shot just as hard, and could be easily handled while prone, and their proponents had the ears of the right people. So a target range was set up in a broad, low-ceiling chamber that was now echoing with orders and shouts of success.

A single guard, a fresh officer judging from their uniform, sat outside the range. They were glancing lazily up and down the hall, probably waiting for someone. Sheila could barely lead the group in close enough, ducking between crates and nooks, to see inside the target range. Several soldiers were cramped inside, the ones not actively firing either sitting on the ground or doing a low, nearly crawling walk around.

The officer would be a problem. Sheila sat on the ground to think and collect herself. Tobias and Alejandro huddled close beside her, while Kell watched from the periphery.

Alejandro was making small, sharp, tactical hand gestures that nobody in the group understood. Eventually, he conceded and leaned in to whisper. "Chapalu? Raurack?"

Tobias was considering the proposal when a shout came from the target range that lacked a victorious undertone.

"Hey! Careful, Berkeley!" a masculine voice yelled.

"What are you talking about?" another replied.

"Don't give me that!" the first voice shouted.

The room quickly descended into clamor and chaos. The officer outside, visibly upset, got up and went to investigate. The coast was clear. Sheila started hurrying down the hall, waving for the others to follow, barely seeing Kell return their rod to its holder.

A bend in the hallway gave the group enough cover to continue in the open. The chambers ahead were either unoccupied, judging from the quiet and lack of lights, or had their doors closed, which was just as well. Sheila hurried her way to the lift at the end of the hall, moving as quickly as stealth would allow. The last leg of the journey was blocked by the lift operator, who didn't notice the group approach but would certainly notice them boarding. Sheila cursed under her breath. They were stuck.

Hiding behind a stockpile of supplies, Sheila silently tried to devise a plan. It wasn't coming easy. Kell could make another distraction, but that would be more likely to set off alarms than anything. Summons almost felt like a good idea. The group could just storm in and take out the operator. Not like the lift was hard to operate or required a key or anything along those lines. Really, the operators were unnecessary. Didn't matter, though. A group was approaching.

With them, suddenly, came an idea. Sheila tried to gesture a silent reminder to follow her lead, but she knew no gesture for that, so she wound up making small flailing motions at the group before standing to confront the approaching officer and his trio of recruits. "Ahoy there, officer!" she called out, saluting, startling him.

"Who the hell are you?"

She waved for the other three to emerge. "Sergeant Takeda, 5th Infantry." She pulled out and quickly flashed her identification. "Sorry for the surprise there, sir, but none of your recruits spotted me or my team."

The recruits were more ashamed than confused, while the officer was leaning more irate. "I beg your pardon?"

"I know, sir. Your captain wasn't supposed to tell you, don't want anyone getting nudged about the test."

"What test? And they have a sergeant running this?"

Fuck. This is gonna fall apart fast. Sheila exaggerated a sigh. "I'm with you on that, sir. This hasn't been going over very well. We should talk with command about this. Mind if we ride up with you, sir?"

The officer grumbled his acceptance and waved her and the others along. As the lift rose, he peppered the group with questions about who they were and what business they could possibly have. Tobias and Alejandro held to the cover, claiming to be with the War Department, with specializations that fit neatly with their actual skills. It surprised Sheila a little bit--surely Alejandro would make something up entirely, if only out of habit--but she couldn't deny that it worked. One of the recruits was more interested in Kell and their "recovered" vapormage uniform. Kell mostly kept quiet, insisting that the uniform was real, difficult to take off, and uncomfortable to wear. They'd be out of it as soon as they could be.

D

After the recruits disembarked and the lift continued upwards, Sheila relaxed against the lift wall. *Man. Al makes being a liar look easy.* The remaining meters upwards were taken in silent satisfaction, a sense of rest that lasted only until the group reached the top of Mt. Grann and was met with a confused lift operator who quickly interrogated their presence. Tobias offered to explain, but was interrupted by Sheila pressing forward. There was no ruse that was going to work here. Not worth bothering.

Up a sloping, unadorned passage sat a chamber with a natural skylight. The walls were smooth but bare stone, the pipes and wires that would be nestled between layers of brick or wood left exposed to the slightly chill air. The hole in the ceiling was covered from the outside with a pane of glass that was clearly not well secured, as wafts of volcanic dust slipped in from outside with the wind.

To the left when entering the room was a massive pile of dried reeds, hay, and branches. On top sat a similarly massive bird, the bulk of her feathers plumed in either orange or green. Even curled up as if resting, Vakonivak was far larger than any human. She kept still. Numerous wires, hanging from the ceiling, were attached to her broad, thick wings and her calmly rising and falling torso. They looked thick enough to hold her in the air, if necessary, though their ends seemed barely attached to the Guardian.

On the opposite side of the room was a bank of machines that the wires ran to and from in faintly organized cross-hatches. A trio of monitors, spread across the bank, lit up with frequent information that a pair of hunns, dressed like technicians, kept close watch on. Overseeing things between them was a slick, tan-feathered vian man in a well-tailored outfit. The operators and the vian all turned to see Sheila barging in, her allies and the lift operator all in tow.

"And what's the meaning of this?" the sharp-dressed man demanded.

"You're not supposed to be up here!" the lift operator huffed as she caught up.

Sheila ignored them both. She stepped in front of Vakonivak, bending down to see her closed eyes. The Guardian was beautiful, up close. No better word.

"Vakonivak," Sheila said. "Please, Vakonivak. We need to talk to you."

"You want to *talk* to her?" the sharp vian said. "You can't just *talk* to a Guardian! Who do you think you are?"

"Sergeant Takeda, 5th Infantry," she said, dismissing him. "Vakonivak, please, we need help--"

"This area is for commissioned officers only! Get out of here at once!"

"Fuck off!" Sheila shouted. "You a Secretary or something?"

"In fact, I am!" the vian shouted back, puffing out his chest. "Interior Secretary Blondin!"

"He is," one of the technicians said offhand.

Tobias perked up, as if he was surprised by the confirmation. "Quinn?" he said to the technician. "That you?"

"Professor Fulton?" Quinn said sheepishly. "Hi. Small world."

"We need Vakonivak--" Sheila started.

"None of you are authorized to be here," Secretary Blondin said, ignoring everyone else, "*especially* a vapormage. However, I *am* authorized to have you arrested. You there!" He gestured at the lift operator. "Take these louts away."

"Wait, are you a vapormage?" Quinn said to Kell.

Alejandro stomped his foot. "Could we all stop for a second?" he yelled. "You're worse than Cymonians, talking past each other."

"Who are you to give orders?" the Secretary barked. "I am the highest-ranking authority in here."

"I respect her authority more than yours." He pointed to the resting Vakonivak.

"She does not *have* authority," Secretary Blondin said. "All she has are secrets that she *refuses* to give up."

"Is that what this is all for, then?" Sheila sharply gestured at the wires and machines.

"We're just trying to understand her," Quinn said. "She's interesting."

"That's enough from all of you!" The Secretary was at his wits' end. "There will be no more until these four are removed, is that clear?"

THEY MAY SPEAK.

She spoke. The Mother of Skies opened her white eyes and lifted her head to just above the Secretary, who had his own awestruck look on his face. She glanced slowly around the room, at the wires and machines surrounding her, at the mix of humans before her. She lifted a wing a short way, tugging and shuffling the wires that were surreptitiously connected to it.

Sheila raised her arm, lifting her hand slightly, as if the Guardian had waved in greeting and she was to return the gesture, before quickly putting it all back down at her side. "Thank you," she said.

"Was that . . .?" Quinn was baffled.

Sheila righted herself and pretended she was calm. "Vakonivak, we beg for your help. You know what Gauven did, right?" Vakonivak slowly lifted her head. "Why? Why did he go wild?"

HIS MOTIVES LONG ESCAPE ME.

Sheila let the words rattle in her head. She didn't doubt Vakonivak, but there were reasons she could be lying. Maybe she wanted to protect Gauven. Maybe she did know his motives and found them suspect. Maybe she never wanted to understand him in the first place. But any of those would mean Vakonivak was hiding something. She couldn't be. If the gods were liars, then what good were they?

"Do you know about the door?" Kell spoke up. "Has Caduceus told you about it?"

"What's Caduceus?" Quinn asked quietly.

"How are you doing this?" Secretary Blondin demanded, having conquered his awe. "What kind of magic are you doing? Vakonivak, how dare you not speak to us!"

The Guardian turned her head to stare at Secretary Blondin, leering with her pale eyes.

"You are not better than us, beast," he continued, riled and indignant. "We're the ones that build this country and keep everything going. You just sit there, refusing to earn your keep. You fought *one battle* for us. That does not make up for not telling us your secrets. We *will* get them!"

Vakonivak closed her eyes in thought.

MY NEST.

Her nest? What? Before Sheila could ask aloud, Vakonivak began to stand, swinging her wings in a jagged, sharp, one-two motion. Her talons left the ground. The wide beating of her wings tugged at the wires that circled the room. The wires, in turn, tugged at the machines and the stone walls they were attached to. Part of the wall, near the skylight, gave way.

Everything crashed in an instant. Rocks split and fell, violently ripping wires from machines, sending sparks across the ground and machinery toppling. Glass shattered. A loose wire cracked the air in front of Sheila's face. She dove to the ground. Rocks and debris pelted her back, knocking her air away, filling the room with the smell of dust and electricity.

When the cacophony settled and the ringing left her ears, she pushed off the floor to see a small stain of blood.

"Help!" Quinn was shouting.

Sheila rolled, feeling something trickle towards her eyebrow, and spotted the technician stuck under a pile of machinery. She wiped the blood from her forehead and scrambled over to help. "Doc! Al! You alright? Help me out here!"

Alejandro groaned loudly from the ground, holding his leg right above his knee. "I'm wounded. Kell?"

A pained yell came from Vakonivak's now-empty nest. "Landed on my arm! Shit."

Tobias, disheveled and covered in dust, started pulling sheets and boxes of metal off of Quinn, straining to move the hefty machinery. With Sheila's help, he lifted the portion of the central console that had pinned down Quinn's legs, letting him slide out. "I can't do much, Quinn, but you'll live," Tobias said under his recovering breath. "The others?"

Sheila looked around the dusty room, the wires dangling off the walls and roof like loose ivy. The lift operator was frozen in place by shock and terror, but since she had been near the doorway when Vakonivak took off, she was physically unharmed by the collapse. The second technician had been crushed fully by a falling machine, their outstretched arm the only sign anyone was there. Sheila touched it to verify. The life had left it.

Sheila and the lift operator helped tend to Alejandro's wounded leg while Kell recovered themself in the nest and Tobias wove spells to stabilize Quinn. Once Tobias was done, he moved to a pile of rocks that had fallen off the outside wall. "Sheila!" he said. "Over here! Help me dig him out!"

She glanced again at the fallen technician's arm. "Who?"

"The Secretary," Tobias said, pushing a rock off the pile.

Sheila started moving before she wanted to, crunching broken glass beneath her feet as she stood beside the pile of rocks that was once the wall. The cold wind batted around the dust. Sheila started to pull back a larger rock, only to see a smear of tan and red and pink beneath it. She immediately dropped the rock and turned away. There wasn't a smell. She paced her breathing and soon felt her muscles return to her. At least there wasn't a smell.

An officer, his sword drawn, ran up the sloping hall towards the room. "What the hell's going on up here?"

"Vakonivak . . ." the lift operator started, her voice wavering.

Sheila swallowed and stood at the best attention she could muster. "Fled, sir," she finished. "Two dead, several wounded. We need to leave, get the recruits out of here."

The dazed eyes and fearful nods around the room were enough for the officer to accept the story.

E

The beach buzzed with confusion under the midday sun. Packs of fresh-faced recruits huddled together like penguins, one or two splintering off at a time to join another circle, all in the collective pursuit of finding out what had caused the roaring noise. The six witnesses, meanwhile, stayed off to the side of the yawn that led into the Citadel. The officer had ordered them to stay while he managed the evacuation.

They could have run. The canoe wasn't far. There was even enough space to squeeze in Quinn and the operator. But those two hadn't signed up to be fugitives. Well, not so far. Quinn could probably be convinced. Curiosity and recklessness are neighbors. But he was in too rough of a shape for travel, with what happened to his legs. He could hardly stand, preferring to sit in the dirt as he made small talk with Tobias.

Sheila kept looking out at the sky. Its Mother did this. Vakonivak tore out of Mt. Grann and killed her own people in the process. Was it on purpose? Did Vakonivak only contribute to the Winters' War so she could let out a bloodlust? She wasn't around to answer questions, so Sheila had to work with what she had seen. Everything she had seen felt like a betrayal. Vakonivak couldn't be trusted.

The officer emerged from the Citadel with the weariness of a job completed. Alejandro gave Sheila a soft jab to get her attention. "Let me handle this," he whispered.

"No, Al," she said, "this is my problem."

"It's ours." He glanced quickly at the officer. "I have a cover. It should work. Trust me."

"Alright, you punks," the officer said, "get to explaining."

"We have no idea why Vakonivak flew," Sheila said.

"We'll get to that. Start at the beginning, who are you?"

Sheila looked over at Alejandro, who had already straightened his posture and prepared to speak, even as his wounded leg threw his professional stance off balance. She slightly bit her upper lip and nodded to him. *Fine. You take it.*

"I am Alejandro Quintana, he of Her Majesty's Speakers." He flashed a small identification card. The news surprised the officer. "Kell over there is a true Cymonian vapormage. The last. They defected when they found out Lyon intends to start a war with Farolé. Since then, the four of us have been seeking a way to stop it. We belie--*I* believed the Guardians could be allies, and that Vakonivak would be the most amenable to aiding us.

You've seen the news; Gauven already proved he was not. But it is clear at this point that I was mistaken, and now people died for it." He had an uncanny melancholy to his voice.

Sheila listened, surprised and still. Alejandro's cover story was . . . the truth.

The officer calmly considered his words, the pause giving worry a chance to spread its tendrils through Sheila's stomach. "Sir," she said, "they need to continue. I'm the only reason those three were able to get inside the Citadel. It was my ID, my cover story that got them in. Court martial me for it if it means letting them go." A court martial was the least of what she deserved, but whatever got the others out of there was worth doing.

The officer stared her down. There was a familiar weariness in his eyes, a look Sheila had worn too many times herself, the look of a man stretched like he were made of taffy. He turned to look at Kell, who was leaning against the rocks, head hung, rubbing their right arm. "That guy telling the truth?" he asked.

Kell nodded without any energy. "Yeah."

"And you're Sergeant Takeda, right?"

"Yes, sir."

"A Speaker, a vapormage, a . . ." The officer's shoulders slid, possibly in relief, possibly in resignation. Either would do. "I'm talking to ghosts," he said. "Nobody made it out of that room alive. Understood?"

"Sir!" the lift operator interjected.

"Would you like to explain how they got through, then, private?"

The operator stepped back, still upset. Quinn did his best to console her from the ground. A silent anger lingered for some time. The six were being discarded, thrown away because it was easier for the officer. It wasn't fair to be written off as dead just because some guy didn't want to do paperwork. Paperwork wasn't *that* bad.

"Now what do we do?" the operator said, almost to herself.

"We'll get you to the shore," Sheila said. "I know a good place. Milend."

"I don't want your help!" she said with a shove.

"We don't have options, Mia," Quinn said. "Let's just go." Tobias helped him up and supported his weight all the way to the waiting canoe, its hull still damp from the arrival trip.

The canoe ran aground downriver of the cabin, a short ways from a small skiff that was already beached. Kell and Tobias climbed out and dragged the canoe farther up the shore, Sheila and Alejandro belatedly getting out to help. A younger man with ashen hair and a scarf across his face watched from outside the cabin. His overcoat looked nicer than what Sheila remembered.

A red-haired hunn woman was also around. She approached the group slowly, curiously.

"Hey there!" she called out. "You folks alright? We saw what happened, were you in there?"

"We were in there, yeah," Sheila said, loud enough to ensure everyone heard. The captain wanted them to deny ever having been near Vakonivak's nest, and she would do no such thing. "We're lucky to be alive."

"Says you." Mia was ready to pick a fight.

"Are they hurt?" The red-haired woman was dressed somewhat like a physician, with a pocketed tan vest bearing a handful of tools. If she was offering to help, the aid may actually be competent.

"Quinn is," Kell said, "and Alejandro took a hit. Mia's a bit shocked. Rest of us are fine."

"I've tried to patch them up," Tobias added, "but I can barely Mend. Quinn needs much more."

As the red-haired woman started examining Quinn's wounds, the masked man casually walked up. "Leena does insist on being helpful," he said.

"She a friend of yours, Grey?" Sheila asked.

"We've been traveling. Busy with things. What brought you folks around?"

Kell approached, holding a small, light blue, egg-shaped mass in their hand. "We were looking for this." They turned to Sheila. They probably expected her to have questions, and they were right. "It was in her nest. Feels right."

Grey's scarf shifted, betraying the smirk underneath. "Back on a mission, then, vapormage?"

Kell put the key--hopefully, it was a key--back in their pouch. "Not back on it, Grey. Still on it." Their voice had a sly friendliness, one Sheila had never heard from them. They knew Grey. No doubt.

She could press them on that later. "This her cabin?" she asked Grey.

"Nope." He nodded towards the boats on the shore. "The, uh . . . former owner was in that skiff when we showed up yesterday. Looked like vapor poisoning."

"Oh, damn," Kell said, with fitting sadness for the death of someone they'd never met.

Grey nodded. "Yeah. But, boat's still good to cross the bay."

Sheila turned to look at the skiff. Her heart felt tired. Her body soon followed. "That can fit three, four people, right?"

"Should," Grey said. "You guys need to cross the bay?"

"I do," Sheila said. "I need to get Mia and Quinn to Milend."

"Sheila?" Kell objected.

"I'm not running, Kell. But, this shit's my fault. I need to make sure they end up somewhere safe."

Grey peered over to watch Leena tending to Quinn's leg, testing its motion with an experienced ease. "Don't break up the band," he said. "Leena and I can take care of them. Where's Milend?"

Sheila gave Grey and Kell alternating looks. She had a responsibility. A duty. She couldn't just hand it over to someone she barely knew. That would be running away. A betrayal. Like Vakonivak.

Sheila watched Leena help Quinn stand and take a hesitant step, cradling his leg like she was teaching him to walk for the first time. Her manner exuded professionalism and compassion.

Kell, Tobias, Alejandro... they could stop Lyon without her. But Sheila knew she'd regret it for the rest of her life if she didn't make sure they *did* stop him.

"It's far south," Sheila finally said. "Near Bellum. If you don't have a vehicle, the guy's gonna need a hand."

Grey nodded. "That's fine. I'd been meaning to get to Bellum at some point."

"Take care of them," Sheila said. "Alright? For me."

KAHLER (guest): This is the sort of thing that too many parents and politicians are not paying attention to. This year, Crystal Greene accounted for a full 22% of spending on music.

SACCO (host): She's quite popular.

KAHLER: It's absurd! And it's dangerous. One woman should not be the entirety of the youth's culture. It's too much influence.

SACCO: It is easy to believe that whatever she suggests would be picked up widely and quickly.

KAHLER: Absolutely, Clarissa. And we're already seeing this. The disruption in Vaa-land this week was clearly the result of her incitement.

SACCO: It should be said, Gregory: Cause has not officially been established.

KAHLER: Officially, sure. But the likelihood.

SACCO: Of course.

KAHLER: And the thing is, with so many people she can influence like that, you have to assume that it turns into control. That they're organized in some fashion, at her beck and call.

SACCO: Now there are claims of people thought to have gone missing showing up in her orbit.

KAHLER: That as well, that as well. It needs to be said that any person getting too close to Crystal Greene is going to have some trouble for themselves.

— *The Voice of Farolé*, aired on BV2 25/10

CHAPTER THIRTEEN

E ight souls, soggy and weary, disembarked at a public dock in the city of Granberg. They had crossed in two boats that had no business traversing the bay, with the constant parade of Banner Goods ships chopping up the waters.

After the customary, uneventful interrogation from a familiar acting as a gate guard, the cluster split in half to go their separate ways. Grey's group was headed south, towards Milend. Kell's group wound their way into the city itself, though they did so aimlessly.

Tobias proposed the next stage of their plan. When talking with the Barlow's Bread captains, he explained, they mentioned a professor who worked at Port Mab. Tobias finally followed up, calling the professor and weathering his mockery. He ended the private call with satisfaction on his beak.

"Well then," he announced, "how shall we get to Candhall?"

"Think there's something there?" Sheila asked.

Tobias huffed jovially. "Certainly not suggesting it out of recreation. Place is dreadful. But I'm told the National Gallery there has the largest collection of . . . how did he put it? Artifacts of unclear provenance."

"Stolen stuff," Kell said.

"Some of it, certainly," Tobias said. "Think it's a good lead, though. Yes?"

It was better than anything Kell had. And unlike the ones they'd found so far, if Cymona did have a key from Sao Neso, they wouldn't be surprised.

Their mobile buzzed. They didn't recognize the line, so they ducked into an alleyway before answering, putting the call on speaker as a matter of habit.

"Kell."

Banner. "What are you--"

"I see you're not in the mood for pleasantries either." Banner's voice was stiff and violent. A new tone, but not much of a stretch.

"We did our job," Kell sneered.

"Not if I say otherwise."

"We agreed to terms," Alejandro said, "we met the terms. The information has been in your box. Goodbye."

"You have not met my terms," Banner barked. "I know you didn't do your job! There is something under the Psamathene, and you have not told me what it is!"

"Then go find it yourself!" Tobias shouted back. "We have more important work to do!" He grabbed the mobile and forcibly ended the call. "As we were saying."

"Doc, you sent him our message, right?" Sheila accused.

Tobias's brow furrowed in offense. "Sheila," he said firmly, "you know I did."

Alejandro stepped between the two. "Both of you, focus," he said. "Banner has a history. He has been messing with us every chance he's had. Don't let him under your skin."

Kell tried calling Crystal. Surely she could help the four travel. No answer.

Tobias fidgeted in his own impatient anxiety. "Al, tell me you've heard of the Blue Cruise."

Alejandro blinked in surprise. "How have *you* heard of it?"

"Some talking head gits, acting like Crystal has you all in her thrall."

Alejandro's short laugh almost agreed. "It's just a fan club. But, if she's not picking up, it's worth a try. We *are* in Granberg."

There was a café in Granberg that an early Crystal Greene song centered on. Thanks to that, it had become a pilgrimage site of sorts for her most ardent fans. No surprise, then, that it was unspeakably busy. Alejandro went in alone; there was virtually no space for the other three, even if they were so inclined.

He emerged a suspicious amount of time later with a cup of tea.

"Couldn't get some for the rest of us?" Tobias joked.

Alejandro casually tossed a vehicle's key towards the professor. "Sorry. That will have to do."

Sheila looked impressed. "That's a key for a Montaville."

"Do be careful driving it, you two," Alejandro quipped. "We're only borrowing it."

A Montaville was a boat of an autocar, taking up more space than a Basilisk while having less room inside. Any private car drew attention, but a Montaville had a way of doing so even with its limited ornamentation. They were all but exclusive to people like Crystal, after all. Tobias was utterly giddy to drive one.

The group detoured to try to find Quinn and Mia, to deliver them to the safety of Milend. But they, and Grey, had faded into Granberg like wafting smoke. Only four were in the vehicle when it stopped that night outside Windglade. Sheila insisted on keeping watch. There were zombies around, she said.

The following morning, an aged professor drove his life's accomplishments through the freshly reopened tunnel to Cymona. That was how Tobias framed it to the skeptical guard on the border. He wasn't arriving via Farolé, a country that the news claimed was sliding deeper into chaos each day, so he didn't capture much of the guard's concern. She didn't even inspect the pile of supplies in the back, a relief to the three people hiding there.

The drive east was long but uneventful, ending with the Montaville being left in a posh garage within Candhall that seemed to expect Crystal's vehicle arriving with a mystery driver. It really appeared that nobody asked questions of Crystal Greene. Kell knew some strong spells, but Crystal had real power.

Kell spent the travel time scheming privately. They wouldn't be able to visit the Gallery itself; that was a public space, and vapormages were, publicly, all dead. They found that the Gallery had an annex building somewhere in the city, storing things that couldn't fit in the museum itself. But such a place was bound to be hard to break into. Not impossible, just harder than what they were used to.

That would be the plan, then. As twilight fell, Kell traced shadows towards the annex, ready to sneak in while the others checked the public Gallery. Alejandro, however, followed Kell. Their stride stopped and their eyebrow bent as they noticed.

"What?" he asked innocently.

"Aren't you going with the other guys?"

Alejandro shrugged. "The three of us agreed. It's an important job. You should have a partner."

His offer sounded earnest, even serious. Kell couldn't help themself.

"I dunno, I've been fine being single," they said with a smirk.

Alejandro moved around to Kell's left so he could give them a friendly shove without hurting their injured arm. Kell laughed, relaxed.

"We'll be fine," Kell said, resuming the walk to the annex. "Not like I haven't broken into places before."

Alejandro smiled. "When you were a bit of a punk, as you put it?"

"Yeah. And, man, there was a lot more than what I told you guys." A small laugh escaped Kell's helmet. "We were bored, y'know? Nothing happens in Sao Neso, had to make our own fun. And it was fun. Nothing serious. Long as we cleaned it up when we got caught, it was fine. Dad was too busy to give me hell, and Mom was just like, 'stay out of trouble and trouble won't find you'."

"Trouble finds what it wants," Alejandro said.

"It sure does," Kell said with a sigh. "Might as well find it first."

"I'm with you there. We're birds of a feather, no?"

B

The annex was just as Kell expected, an unremarkable stone box about three storeys tall with the only windows appearing near its roof. From a brief walk around, there was no back or side door that they could spot. The front door was unguarded from the outside, but there was no reason to believe the two would be able to slip in through it without drawing an alarm.

"That's too high for a vapor jump," Kell said. They looked out into the street and got inspiration from a storm drain. "Sorry, the sewers are gonna be worse than Gauvencia."

The two scurried across the quiet street and worked the drain cover out from its position. Kell slipped down first, landing in what they told themself was mud. As Alejandro replaced the drain cover to hide their entry, Kell looked around for an indication of a door. The oldest parts of Candhall were low and lacked good drainage, so new surfaces were made and the old roads became sewers. Old buildings turned their ground floors into basements, and the doors sometimes remained if nobody could be bothered to seal them away.

Alejandro spotted a metal door, covered in grime and fungus. The handle had sheared clean off, leaving only the rusty gunk-filled indication of a lock. Kell squared themself in front of the door and blasted the lock with a thin jet of aquatic vapor. It shattered. Alejandro pushed the door open, something heavy sliding away in the process. He stopped when there was enough gap to slide through.

Kell's flame revealed a number of crates spread across the room and behind the door, all of them appearing sealed. A stairway sat in the back of the room. Alejandro approached the stairs cautiously as Kell checked a few crates, hoping to find some indication of their contents. The boxes, stained with waste, only bore painted notes about their age and provenance. All were Cymonian, centuries old. The crates were probably sitting there, sealed and forgotten, when the sewers were built.

Alejandro rejoined Kell from the stairway, stepping lightly all the way over. "Right then," he said quietly. "Door seems to work."

"Do you wanna send Raurack out?" Kell asked.

Alejandro hesitated. "No, let's not. Having more actors only complicates things." He sounded disappointed by his own judgment.

"You're the expert." Kell approached the stairs and climbed them slowly, trying to minimize the creaking of wood and having little success. They opened the door at the top enough to peer through. The inside of the building was all but hollow, with no walls they could see save for the exterior, though catwalks criss-crossed below the rafters. Massive shelves, easily taller than a person, formed the aisles and gave the space some sense of structure. From behind one shelf, halfway across the chamber, a bearded hunn man appeared and marched past the shelf.

"Shit," they whispered, ducking back. "Guards."

Alejandro took point and peered through the crack as Kell sat on the stairs and thought about how to approach the guards' presence. A rhythmic clomp of footsteps approached. With it, Kell's visor warned of increased vapor density. The warning receded with the footsteps.

"That thing's a summon," Kell whispered.

"Are you certain?" Alejandro had the faintest shake to his voice.

"People don't make this go off." They tapped the side of their helmet.

Alejandro shook the implications from his face and refocused himself. "We'll worry about that later. For now, follow me."

Alejandro slowly opened the door again and looked around for the guards' positions. He abruptly dashed to duck beside a table stacked with documents. He silently gestured for Kell to join him. They took gradual steps together, quietly approaching the building's opposite corner. Kell kept one eye on the vapor indicator projected on their visor. Things were holding steady.

Leaning against a cabinet, Alejandro signaled to wait. His index finger tapped the air rhythmically. On the third tap, a trio of loud pops rang from near the staircase they had ascended moments ago. Alejandro used the distraction to cross a wide, central aisle and reach an array of cabinets and shelves housing old stone and clay pieces. He quickly set to work, opening drawers with an uncanny dexterity, as so few people ever have a need to practice opening drawers with both speed and silence. Kell wasn't such a person, so they kept an eye out for the guards.

There were four in total, looking virtually identical, each looking around the site of the distraction with the uniform rhythm of familiars. Perhaps that was all they were. Familiars made to look like people would be unsettling, but only at a distance, and only while they were still on their programming. But the guards, having decided the noise warranted investigation, huddled together with the look of a party making a plan. They were not simply returning to their programming, Kell realized. They were not familiars.

The vapor density increased. Kell ducked under the table that Alejandro was crouching near and pulled at his wounded leg to get his attention. He inhaled sharply before joining Kell, giving them a silent glare. A guard walked past, oblivious to their presence.

Once the guard was far enough for them to feel safe, the pair scrambled for a ladder built into the outside wall. It led up to the catwalks. Alejandro climbed it at a good clip; Kell moved slower, due to the stabs of pain pushing through their wounded arm. They started to panic about being spotted. Once they were close enough to the top, Alejandro pulled them up the rest of the way. A guard walked past below them.

The shift in elevation let the two see the archives from a better angle. Many of the shelves were tall enough to have built-in ladders or steps, and neither Kell nor Alejandro had much chance to get a good look at the upper levels. Even the middle levels of the shelves rose taller than either of them.

Kell gently walked along the catwalks, looking down at the shelves, crouching by instinct to offset how high up they were. They stopped above a cabinet that they had passed by earlier, in an area that one guard had kept under tight patrol. The lower shelves held items of obvious monetary value, sparkling as they were in untarnished silver and gold. On its top shelf, nestled between ancient-looking figurines, was a turquoise object resembling two triangles intersecting each other at a perfect perpendicular angle. Nearly pristine, though a little shard had chipped off. The shape and size looked right. The material looked right. Kell waved Alejandro over. They wanted to go for it.

With a few hand gestures, the plan was silently agreed upon. Alejandro would make a diversion while Kell grabbed the stone. The question was how. Grabbing it straight from the shelf was too risky. They didn't know any spell specifically for levitating an object, but they knew the next best thing. Properly focused, gusts of vapor wind could carry an object through the air. The turquoise stone looked light enough that Kell could conjure enough vapor on their own. All they needed was precision.

A pair of pops went off in a far corner of the annex. Alejandro had done his part. Kell focused vapor towards the stone, slowly whipping up a pad of wind beneath it. They gave it a gentle push up to get it moving, but the push also nudged the figurines neighboring the stone. One teetered over and rolled to the edge of the shelf. As it started to fall, Kell abandoned any hope of precision and launched the turquoise stone towards them. They caught it against their chest as the figurine fell to the ground with a clang.

The guards decided that sound was more important. Kell put the stone--the key, it had to be a key, the material was too perfect--in their satchel and hurried over to where Alejandro was, on a catwalk inches from a row of windows. One guard seemed to notice them. Kell started to panic. The two of them would not win a fight with all four guards, and they saw no way to pick the guards off one by one. Alejandro, meanwhile, calmly opened the window outward, over an alleyway.

"Have enough vapor to stick the landing?" he whispered.

Kell leaned over to look out the window. The smoke of panic cleared enough for them to see what Alejandro meant. "Right. Should."

They churned a wide pad of yellow-green wind in the alleyway that they hoped was thick enough to safely stop a fall. Alejandro slid through the window and tumbled smoothly out. The catwalk started to sway. A guard was climbing the ladder. Kell followed through the window, landing face-first on the pillow of vapor, then the ground. It felt like they had belly-flopped into water. Their body was stinging, their arm worst of all, but there were no new injuries. Alejandro helped them up and found the door back to the street. The faint sound of an alarm followed them as they scurried off.

C

The four regrouped in an alley near the Gallery. Kell broke the good news to Sheila and Tobias as the group piled into the Basilisk. The Montaville was a comfortable ride, but an uncomfortable presence. Even Alejandro felt too low-class for it. The Basilisk, beat up and workmanlike, fit the four better.

Kell spun their heist tale with full, genuine enthusiasm. They were proud of their work, in a nearly sinister way. They got one over on Cymona. The runt of the vapormages, a little punk from Sao Neso, got one over on the big guys. They won.

Tobias listened to Kell's story, attentive and pleased, as though they had defended a thesis with flying colors. He was first to make the declaration: The four had finished their mission. It was time to go home. They would head back to Sao Neso first thing in the morning.

In the Basilisk, Kell couldn't catch their sleep. They won, sure, but what were they winning? They still weren't sure what would be behind the locked door. It had to be something important, and was probably something dangerous. Otherwise, it wouldn't be sealed away. It wasn't going to be whatever Banner thought it was. Couldn't be. But that didn't mean it would help. Kell imagined opening the door and finding some long-forgotten weapon, too impractical to actually use. They imagined opening the door and finding their own sudden demise. They imagined opening the door and finding nothing at all.

Kell caught up on sleep as best as they could during the uneventful drive down to Reeseport. They slept through much of Alejandro and Tobias discussing the summons in the annex, waking to a groan of frustration from the old man.

"Ah, Kell, you're back with us," he said quickly, as if changing the subject.

"Yeah." They reached to rub their eyes, forgetting their helmet for a second. "How are you guys holding up?"

"We should be asking you that," Alejandro said. "Are you alright returning to Sao Neso?"

"Not like we have a choice." Kell slumped. "Can't get close to Lyon. Can't just let this all go. Guess I'll put up with Dad if it helps."

"Of course it'll help," Tobias said with a laugh. "We're in brilliant shape here, yes?"

Kell refrained from answering. They weren't sure. Based on Alejandro's hesitant glances, he didn't seem too sure either.

Hours and kilometers passed. Sheila parked the Basilisk in the same place the four had left it the last time they went to Sao Neso. Shattered glass, left where it fell, crunched underfoot. The streets of Reeseport were always a bit quiet, especially compared to the busier cities the four had gone through, but on that rapidly darkening afternoon, the town felt deceased. Even the few storefronts along the way that claimed to be open felt like memories, places that *were* rather than *are*, with no signs of life to bring them into the present tense. At least Windglade had the good sense to start falling apart. Kell stepped out of the Basilisk feeling as if they were being watched by ghosts.

Seated in the guardhouse by the coastal gate was a hunn man, dressed like a guard, hunched over and still. His personal effects were scattered across the guardhouse: some books, some open tins of food, a powered-off mobile. He didn't stir with the group's approach. He didn't stir when Alejandro spoke up to get his attention. Only when Sheila poked him in the shoulder did his movement confirm he was alive. He looked up at the group, his eyes glassy and tired, before faintly gesturing towards the doorway and returning to his catatonic pose. Sheila poked him again. He repeated the gesture.

"That guy is a mess," Kell said once on the other side of the wall.

"Like he's a familiar or something," Sheila said.

"He may as well have been," Tobias said, despondent. "But how would . . .?"

The question lingered in the air as they hiked to the shore and, after Tobias opened the rock door once again, down to Sao Neso. The climb down the cavern went faster than before. They knew what to expect. All four of them did, this time.

Kell removed their helmet as they slid on water-slicked stone into Caduceus's chamber. The Guardian was lying on the ground, sprawled out and restful. Kell knew she would be back, even though the group had killed her before. That was the way of Guardians. It did make them seem quite a bit like gods, but then, people once thought the sun was a god, didn't they? As good of a sight as it was cracking through the clouds on a misty, wintry morning, it was still just a big ball out in space.

Two sahagin guards were tending to Caduceus. One noticed the party's arrival, bending her arm back for her spear. "Hey!" she shouted. "What are you people doing here?"

"I'm Kell Rusalka," they called out as an explanation.

"I know who you are. I thought you were never coming back."

"According to whom?" Alejandro asked.

"We said we'd be back when we could open the locked door," Kell said. "Did Dad tell you we were gone forever?"

"He definitely made it sound that way," the guard said. "Guess he doesn't have much faith in you--hey!" She turned to yell at Tobias, who was kneeling in a puddle in front of Caduceus. "That's our Guardian! Keep away!"

"Caduceus." Tobias spoke kindly, as if asking a grandmother for advice. "What do you know about Vakonivak? And Gauven?"

"Are you trying to talk to her?" the second guard said.

Sheila scoffed. "You haven't?"

Kell joined Tobias in front of Caduceus, who slowly looked up at the pair. "Caduceus. We're going to open the locked door. If that's a really bad idea, please, stop us now." They looked into Caduceus's black eyes. "Okay. Can I ask what's behind the door? If you don't know, that's fine . . ."

Caduceus slithered lightly.

DESTINY.

"Could've been more ominous, perhaps," Alejandro muttered.

"Leave her alone," the female guard said. She seemed unfazed by Caduceus's comment. "Your dad's gonna want to see you."

"I know," Kell said. "Caduceus, please. Any idea what we'll find?"

"That was an order," the second guard added. "Get going."

"We just want to talk."

"Then talk to Cyprin," the guard said. "Now. Get down to Sao Neso."

NESO.

The guards ignored her echo, though they gave enough of a glance at Caduceus to imply they had heard it. Kell looked again at the Guardian and sighed in concession.

"Fine," they said as they stood. "Next time we talk, Caduceus, I'll show you what we found down there. How's that sound?"

Caduceus glanced back with a tired, neutral look. Kell could accept that. If anyone, anywhere, would know what was behind the door, it was her, and if she wasn't about to stop them, then they had to be on the right track.

D

The clock in the entry plaza claimed it was late afternoon when the group passed through the gate into Sao Neso. The streets were beginning to come alive with evening activity. Shop lights glowed, illuminating the first batches of Tideday decorations--special streamers and chains of beads hanging from wires criss-crossing above the street. People were getting at it early, it seemed. *Good for them.*

The clusters of locals that Kell approached on their way to their father's office split and stepped back as they got near, like wood confronted by an axe. There was a clear unease to their presence. Kell couldn't imagine their father telling everyone about their deal. What he probably announced was the same as what the guards believed: that Kell would never return. And now they had. Kell was an ill omen in Sao Neso.

The four waited in the column's lobby as a lift was called down to pick them up. Sheila tapped Kell on their left shoulder. "You sure about this?" she said.

"Not like we have a choice," they said.

"We could just go straight to the door. Forget him."

Kell hesitated, giving the illusion of considering the idea. "No. I want to talk to him. There are things I need to hear from his mouth." They looked up at the descending lift. "We'll do this right. Get the permits, get it over with. But we're not playing his game. Just follow my lead."

As they rode up the lift, Kell distributed the keys. Tobias took the red lump, swaddled in cloth and oddly warm to the touch; Sheila took the blue piece, the egg Vakonivak had been guarding; and Alejandro held on to the yellow shard, still clinging to tiny flecks of stone. They all agreed to keep the keys hidden in pockets or satchels until Kell gave the signal. Even then, they agreed, they wouldn't let the keys go under any circumstances. Kell didn't have a plan for when any of that would happen, if at all. They were more focused on the conversation.

That, it turned out, would have to wait a moment. Cyprin was out of his office, dealing with some suddenly urgent matter, though the four were told he would return shortly. When he did, he offered no explanation. He simply apologized and gestured at Kell for a hug. They did not oblige.

"Well then," Cyprin said as he sat at his desk, "you decided to come back, I see."

"Sounds like you're surprised." The years of resentment were bubbling up again. Kell was doing a poor job of keeping it out of their voice. They almost didn't want to.

"You did say you wouldn't be back unless you found all the keys to the locked door." Cyprin chuckled. "I appreciate you coming to your senses and dropping it."

Not yet. Not yet. "Dad," Kell said, "I have some questions for you."

Cyprin leaned back. "Well, shoot."

Kell started clenching their fist, hoping to release some of the knots in their chest. "Why. Why did we have to go and fight for Cymona? Why was there a whole unit of us? Why was that the only way?"

Cyprin seemed almost relieved at the question. "Well, kid. It's part of the deal. Cymona provides us with protection and resources. Sends goods regularly, sealed off the cave so nobody can attack us. We don't exactly have a lot down here. Have to pay our dues."

"With our lives."

"Kell, I . . . I can't put into words how sorry I am. What happened to all of you was a tragedy."

"It was murder." Their body warmed with anger.

"Kell, now, keep calm. Save that fury for the battlefield. You don't want to hurt anyone here."

He still thinks we're at war. I'm never gonna get anywhere. "Dad. We have the keys."

Cyprin's eyes widened. "Are you serious?"

"Very. Guys?" They raised their left hand with a slight flourish. That would be the signal. The rest of the party responded, pulling out their keys and holding them up for the elder to see. Cyprin gestured for them to put the keys on his desk, but all three refused.

"It's as if you don't trust me," he said, standing and craning his neck to examine the keys.

"We went through a lot to collect them," Kell said. "Can't have something happening to them."

Cyprin nodded and sat back down. "Simple sahagin wisdom, that's for sure. Can see why you lead your little band."

"We work as a team," Kell said. "And we're going to stop Lyon's war. We're off to the vault."

"To open the door?" Cyprin said.

"Obviously." Kell stared at their father, letting the word hang in the air. *Call my bluff, Dad.*

"Gail won't let you. It's part of her duties."

"We'll apologize to her," Kell said.

"That won't get you the last key," Cyprin said.

That's how you're gonna tip your hand? "So there are more," Kell said flatly.

"We kept the last one here," Cyprin explained. "Secure. In a sealed vessel since before you were born. You can dig around the vault all you want--you're not going to find it. And you shouldn't. That door should *not* be opened, Kell."

Kell unfastened a pouch on their hip, near their canteen. "One last question. What are you afraid of, Dad?"

Cyprin scoffed before briefly contemplating the question. "What do you think? I'm charged with leading this community. Sao Neso is mine to protect. I'm afraid opening the door would raise hell down here."

"Don't cause trouble, and trouble won't find you." Kell reached into the pouch and grasped the key. The flat frown on their face held steady.

"That's what your mother and I always taught you." Cyprin sounded pleased.

With a soft slam on Cyprin's desk, Kell revealed the key, inverting their father's smile.

"This was in Cymona. They stole it ages ago."

Cyprin stammered, at a loss for words.

"Lyon took us, and he killed us. We are disposable to him. All of us. Trouble is coming for us, Dad. Whether we like it or not, whether we cause it or not. We'd be fools not to be ready."

Cyprin grimaced and scowled. "Are you calling me a fool?"

Kell stared silently. *Of course I am.*

"Then remember, Kell. You're still my child. If I'm a fool, then so are you. Wisdom runs in the blood."

Kell stood, staring daggers at their father. "I've bled it out."

The group was on the lift, several storeys below Cyprin's office, before Kell could cough out a tense, disappointed laugh. "Of all the fucking times to quote *Trouble in Paradise.*"

"I was wondering if that was on purpose," Alejandro said.

"It was the only thing I could think to say. I just . . . Everything about me being a vapormage was his fault. And he'll never listen. Even if Lyon came to kill him himself, he'll always be sure he's doing the right thing."

"Are *we* sure we're doing the right thing?" Sheila asked.

Kell sighed and shook their head. "No. But we can't do nothing."

"If you ask me," Tobias started before chuckling softly to himself. "And I know none of you did. Even if nothing comes of this, pursuing discovery is a far better approach than just burying our heads in the sand."

"Spoken like a scientist," Alejandro said.

"Spoken like someone who wants to see this end in peace," Tobias said as the lift reached the ground floor. "Though any discoveries would be a lovely sight too."

"Then we're off to the vault," Kell said, walking with the purpose of a leader. They followed the direct route, their presence continuing to part any crowds in the street.

E

Gail, the vault keeper, was sitting near the door when Kell opened it. Her face plunged when she saw the group. "Wait, wait, wait!" She ran at Kell, arms outstretched. "They can't come in!"

"They're coming in," Kell said, firmly but kindly. "I need my team."

"For what?"

Kell pulled the turquoise key from their satchel. "We're going through the door."

Gail stepped back with a posture of worried surprise. "Where did--?"

"Cymona," Kell interrupted. "Who knows when they stole it. Surfs have been in here already. Sorry." They pushed their way forward, into the Sao Neso vault, Gail relenting in fright.

The locked door was still exposed, the plain steel door in front of it left open. Kell started with the jagged yellow piece. It felt warmer the closer it came to the slot that matched it. Kell felt it lock into place. They put their helmet on and adjusted the visor's sensitivity; the piece was glowing, ever so faintly, as it had been when it was inside the animated statue. They were definitely on the right track. Had to be.

One by one, Kell slotted the other keys into their nooks. Gail watched, shuffling and glancing about nervously. As Kell started to unwrap the lumpy red piece, Sheila tapped them on the left shoulder.

"We sure we're ready?" she asked, calmly enough. Kell nodded. They felt ready. They slotted in the key with their right hand, which was still alive enough to feel a hint of the key's warmth.

Some mechanism rumbled. The door squeaked. Gail squeaked. The door started sliding apart, scratching and squealing against the stone ground as it slowly swung open to reveal a clean, well-lit, perfectly round tunnel. The walls were smooth sheets of metal bent in perfect arches, with tubes of glowing white situated in the seams between them. A walkway of perforated metal offered an even, flat footing. The path broke off twice, once in each direction, before bending downward out of view.

The group stepped forward in awe, walking in the dry metal tunnel with more caution and care than they had walking the slick path to Sao Neso. Kell removed their helmet and smelled the air; they couldn't place the aroma, but the air was definitely different from what was in the town, and not for an absence or excess of vapor. Fresher, in some way, but it felt wrong to describe it as such. The air simply felt like it came from somewhere else, somewhere foreign.

At the junction, Alejandro left a mark on the wall before taking the corner, as an indication of what paths the group had already taken. There were already markings painted on the tube, but they made unfamiliar symbols that none of the group could recognize. Tobias mused aloud that it could be writing, given the regularity of the patterns, but nobody knew the language--though language, Tobias would admit, was not his strongest suit. The first junction the group took featured a sealed door along the wall before looping back to the original path. The second junction lacked a door, but likewise returned to the central path. There was nowhere to go but forward.

Kell led the steady, cautious march down the pathway. They felt as if they were being watched, but with no sense of what could be watching. The corridor felt so alien, so impersonal, that it felt like somewhere no ghost would even bother to haunt.

After a second dip downward, the tunnel came to an end at a large double door with unfamiliar writing on it. Unlike the writing along the tunnel, the symbols were a mix of crisp shapes and looser, hasty-feeling scrawls. It felt like a warning. Kell stepped slowly towards it, hoping to inspect it closer, only for the door to open on its own. Inside was a large chamber as clean and brightly lit as the tunnel. There were no signs of life anywhere, not even familiars scurrying about, yet the place felt more alive than The Puck that Tobias worked from.

"What in the hell is this?" Sheila said, her mouth hanging agape.

"*This* is what's beneath the Psamathene?" Alejandro said.

Tobias looked around, marveling at the pristine architecture. "Did Banner know this was here?"

"How would he?" Kell said. "Nobody in Sao Neso knew."

Tobias took careful steps farther into the room. From a dark recess near the ceiling, a small flying machine buzzed out. It looked him over briefly as he held still, breathing with a measured pace. The machine beeped. A blade emerged from its chassis. It dove at Tobias, who ducked and swatted it to the ground with his spear.

"We're not wanted." Alejandro spoke barely above a whisper.

"No alarm, though," Tobias said. "And just the one. There should be more."

"Precisely what I'm concerned about."

"Kell." Sheila was gripping their left shoulder firmly. "We gotta turn back. We're not supposed to be here."

She's right. They looked at Alejandro. He seemed as concerned as Sheila. Tobias looked up from the machine he had swatted down and broken to nod in agreement.

Kell slid their helmet onto their head and faced the far end of the room. "You're right. You guys should go. I'll take it from here."

"No you won't," Sheila ordered.

Kell let their visor go blank. "Guys, this is part of Sao Neso. Whatever this place is, or was. We've been living above it this whole time. Protecting it. Hiding it. Hiding from it. There's no way my ancestors made that city and had nothing to do with that door. Either they put it there, or they've opened it before. I don't know. I just know this place is part of me."

They looked around at the others. There was something they were trying to express, some unspeakable attachment, some gravity, some invisible longing that was being re-lieved. They felt pulled in to the facility. The others didn't seem to feel the same, so they should be spared whatever lay ahead. "You guys can go back. I can work this one alone. Maybe there is something that'll help us stop Lyon, but right now, this is just something I need to see for myself."

The group stood silently for some time. The building hummed a steady, almost in-audible note around them. Kell turned and started taking steps away from the front door, deeper into the building.

"Then we'll see it too," Tobias said with an almost stately confidence.

Kell stopped, unsurprised. "Doc?"

"Kell, we're standing in an incredible discovery. Maybe there's nothing in here, but its mere presence . . ." He chuckled to himself. "Regardless. You said it yourself: There wouldn't be so many folk tales about that door if there wasn't something back here. And I want to make sure you live to tell your people about it."

Kell smiled in resignation beneath their helmet. *They're not gonna let me go, are they.*

"Hey. Doc," Sheila said. "Keeping the kid alive is my job." She stepped forward and gave Kell a friendly knock on their helmet. "And if you're stuck on being an idiot, then I guess I gotta keep an eye on you."

"And I made a promise to Grey that I would keep you safe," Alejandro said. "I'm trying to keep my word. Be an honest man. So. Lead on, Kell."

F

The four moved past the lobby of the facility, through a door that led to a bare hallway flanked by several small rooms. Many of the doors were left open. Inside were machines, measuring devices, all the trappings of a laboratory setting. Tobias recognized some devices as tools for capturing and measuring vapor, though most of what was around was unfamiliar to him. A few notepads and other papers were left on tables, with writing fully indecipherable between the foreign script and the hasty scribbling. It quickly became clear that the group wouldn't work out what the place had been set up to study, but it definitely was set up to study *something*.

They were also unlikely to work out what had happened, though Kell could piece together a story. People had obviously been working here. People who probably lived in Sao Neso. Kell's ancestors. Why they stopped working there . . . It couldn't have been a sudden disaster, Kell figured. The rooms they visited were too orderly. Things had been cleaned up. When people left, never to return, there was time to leave. But the decision had to have been made suddenly, or else they would've taken their notes. Assuming, of course, the notes mattered. Perhaps, then, what happened had nothing to do with this place at all. Perhaps something outside caused them to lock the facility away, intending to come back. And until Kell got the brazen idea to open the locked door, nobody had.

The hallway snaked past another block of rooms. At the far end stood a large machine, nearly filling the space. A mechanical eye embedded in it gradually swept from side to side. A small cannon barrel pointed out from its middle. Seams along its chassis implied there may be more weapons hiding. Alejandro looked it over from around the corner and formed a plan.

"Kell?" He pulled out a knife and held it out. "Could you give me a charge? I think I can disable it."

Kell obliged, wrapping his blade in electrified vapor. Tobias gave him a shield of vapor as well, just to be safe. There was no harm in doing so. Plenty of vapor to go around.

Alejandro watched the eye's movements and slid forward out of its view, ducking gracefully into the open rooms along the way as he approached. Once close enough, he started reaching along the machine's seams with his free hand. The machine beeped. Alejandro froze in place until it resumed its pattern. He started using the electrified blade, jamming it in and sliding like he was filleting a fish. After another moment of dexterous handiwork and electrified stabbing, the machine made a mechanical groan. The sweeping eye stopped moving.

Alejandro wiped the sweat from his brow and chuckled, signaling all clear. "Tense work, that," he said. "Could you give me a hand? I suspect there's something behind it."

The machine made grinding noises against the ground as the four pulled and pivoted it away from the wall behind it. It had, indeed, been blocking a door. Kell pushed the door open, exposing the first darkened room they had come across in the entire facility.

They found a light switch as they entered. With a hum, the room lit up, showing a large machine composed mainly of thick looping pipes and cylinders, like a knot of intertwined serpents. The front of the machine had tight, nearly geometric writing on it, repeating several symbols that were in use across multiple signs they had already seen. There were unfamiliar symbols as well, arranged in crisp lines as if they were translating each other. Towards the bottom of the list, scrawled and unprofessional, was written the word "vapor."

The room was otherwise empty, with little space for there to be anything else. The four spread out in a half circle around the machine. Kell stayed put, staring at the machine, their visor's eyes wide. "What in the world?" they said.

Alejandro took a slow lap around the machine, examining it at all angles. "Impossible," he muttered. "This can't be . . . *making* vapor."

Tobias leaned closer to the pipes to listen. "Everyone, quiet, please?"

The group complied, holding nervously still.

"Nobody hears anything?" he asked.

After pausing a moment to confirm, the others each shook their heads.

Tobias gently put the back of his hand against the machine. "There's nothing," he whispered. "No noise. No heat. I don't think this is even on."

"Is this thing what Banner was talking about?" Kell said.

"How would he know about it?" Sheila said. "You guys didn't."

"Could be a coincidence," Alejandro said. "To my eye, this looks more like a reservoir or processor or something."

"Maybe," Kell said, not quite agreeing but not quite dismissing. They started pacing small circles to think. "Okay. Say we're right. Say this is a processor, and it's not on. If we turn it on, then it would suck up vapor, right? So we're done. Mission accomplished. We actually did it. But if this is what *made* vapor, then it's just gonna make more. It's gonna make it worse. And it won't help us at all. But we can't do nothing. That doesn't get us anywhere." They stopped and emptied their lungs of thought. "Okay. Banner wanted us to destroy whatever was down here."

"So that's the last thing we should do," Sheila said.

"Unless he's counting on us not trusting him."

Sheila blinked. "Shit, you're right."

"He doesn't know about this place," Alejandro said.

"He *shouldn't*," Kell said. "Maybe he does. I don't know. I don't . . ." Kell fell against the wall and sighed. "I just want this to work. I want us to do the right thing. But I don't know what it is."

"Look. Kell." Sheila stepped towards them, her voice softening. "Y'know something I've learned as a sergeant? You never get to make perfect decisions. You just make the best ones you can. You get the best intel you can manage, and you trust that intel, and you trust your gut, and you do whatever you can to make sure your squad trusts you. That they've got your back. And that's the really hard part. I could never do it. But . . . I'm not gonna speak for the boys, but I think they got your back. I know I do."

Tobias and Alejandro nodded in agreement.

The weight of the responsibility pushed on Kell, sliding them a few hairs down the wall. "Guys," they said with a restrained worry, "last thing we want is to cause more trouble. And this could easily go completely wrong! This is really old stuff. Who knows what'll happen. Could just blow up and kill us."

Sheila gave a quick, firm salute. "Then it's been an honor, soldier."

Kell stared at Sheila for a moment before slowly pushing against the wall. They took a deep breath and stood before the machine. An array of unmarked buttons was laid out in front of them, along with a pair of glassy rectangles. The machine, ominous and anonymous, gave them no direction. They exhaled deeply and pushed a button.

Nothing happened.

They watched the inert machine silently until they realized they were holding their breath.

"I don't see anything," Kell said as they started to pull back. "I'm not touching it again, I don't want to push our luck too--"

A rumble.

A flash of white.

Their vision went black.

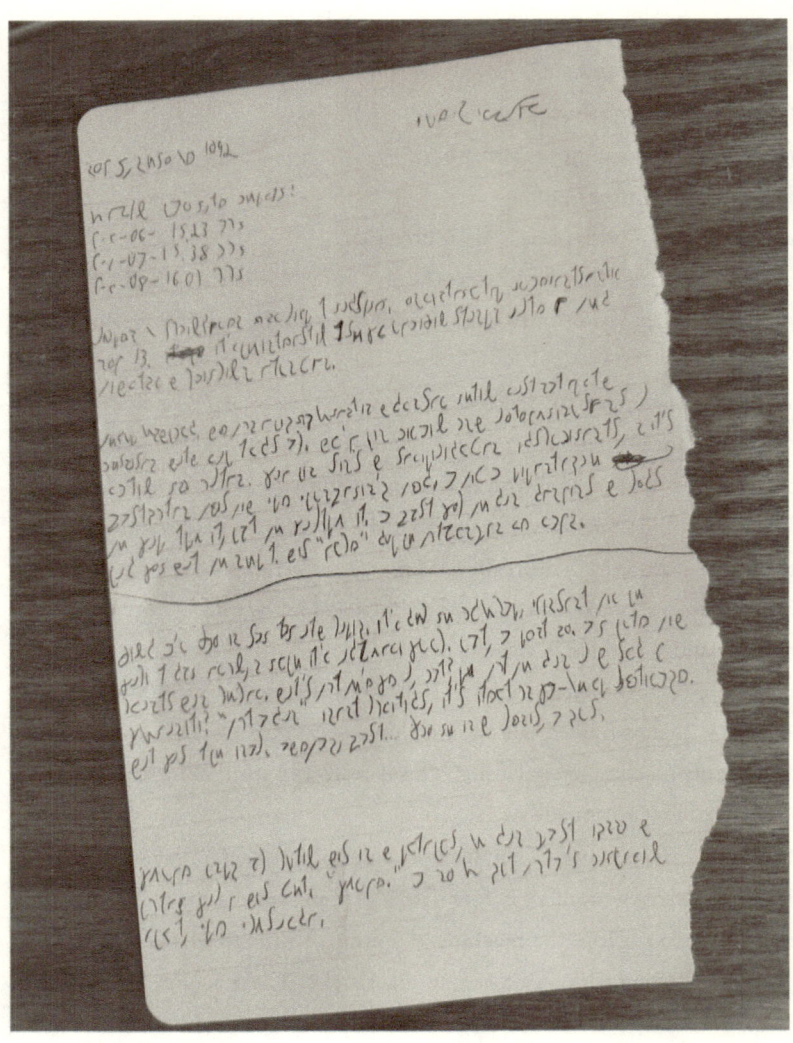

— note found in abandoned laboratory

CHAPTER FOURTEEN

The black gave way to a deep, steel grey. Sheila opened her eyes, or perhaps her eyes were already open, as an impossible landscape filled her vision around her. The sky was filled with wafts of platinum smoke appearing at all elevations, rising and sinking and appearing and disappearing with little apparent cause. The blue ground, its texture resembling neither stone nor water nor grassy field nor anything else she had ever seen, stretched in all directions with a gentle roll and subtle oscillation. The horizon where the two met was ill-defined, as if ground and sky went on in parallel lines forever.

Sheila had little chance to observe her surroundings before a beak barreled towards her. She instinctively threw an arm up to deflect it and reached for her claymore. The weight fell into her hands and her stance was readied before she could realize her assailant was Vakonivak, wings broad, standing confidently before her.

"The hell's going on?" Sheila shouted.

Vakonivak cawed. "Defend yourself!" she said, her beak moving, the sound coming from outside Sheila's mind.

"Are you serious?"

Another peck to deflect. She definitely was. Sheila pushed Vakonivak's beak to the side with her shoulder, easily, too easily, and followed with a wide swing of her claymore. The blade swept through where Vakonivak stood. The Guardian's body flickered out of existence around it, bending and glitching with an impossible geometry. Vakonivak was there, and Vakonivak was not there, and there was no *there* there, in the space that Sheila's sword accelerated through. She never made contact. The dramatic, wide arc of her swing passing through nothingness threw off her stance. As the tip landed on the ground, Sheila felt a sharp jolt of electricity run through her, making her convulse and scream.

"Is that how you defend?" Vakonivak said.

Sheila breathed deep and faced the Guardian again. "The fuck's wrong with you? What's going on? What are you doing?"

"Testing you."

Sheila regained her stance, holding her sword up defensively. "It doesn't really work if you tell me." She gently parried another peck without striking back.

"Is that so?"

"Of course, it's the whole point. Else I'll just do what I think you want me to."

Vakonivak swiped weakly. She seemed to give up the test a little too easily. "I see."

Sheila went through the motions of parrying Vakonivak, letting the occasional weak peck through out of boredom. "You could've just lied, you know."

"I could not."

Sheila huffed out a small, dismissive laugh. "C'mon, lying's easy. Everyone does it."

"It is not my nature to be thus."

Really? A drip of strength returned to Sheila's body. Her stance righted. Her boots held more confidently to the ground. "Alright then," she said skeptically. "I've had questions. What are you?"

"A Gardener," Vakonivak said plainly.

Not a Guardian. Huh. "Okay. So then, what do you garden?"

Vakonivak dropped the last pretense of testing Sheila and considered the question. "Worlds," she said. "Danger can happen to them, and we try to stop it."

"Is something dangerous going to happen to Linnute?"

Vakonivak's white eyes darted around, looking anywhere but in front of her. "It has. It will."

Sheila stood up straighter. "Well, if we've handled it before, we'll handle it again. Right? Get me out of this place and I'll show you."

"It is not something you can handle."

Sheila scoffed. "Says who?"

"Existence cares not of your strength," Vakonivak said.

The smirk on Sheila's face drooped. *She doesn't mean Lyon, does she.*

"Why do you strive so?" Vakonivak asked.

"What do you mean?" Sheila put her claymore away. She had almost forgotten she was still holding it.

"You fight, for what?"

Don't start with this. "Because I want to, okay?" Sheila said. "I know, I could've left. But I'm not gonna."

Vakonivak's head dipped in thought. "Ah. Them. Your . . . squad?"

A sudden heat spread under Sheila's skin. "What do you know about my squad?"

"Was that wrong?" Her voice was layered with apology. "What to call, your . . ."

Sheila wasn't about to wait for Vakonivak to finish her thought. "My squad is dead," she said. "How would you know them?"

The Gardener looked down at Sheila with a curious expression, almost as though she had never encountered a human before. An angry memory burned.

"I lost my squad in the Winters' War," Sheila went on. "'Cause I ran. 'Cause I'm a fucking coward." It came out as if she blamed Vakonivak. Maybe she did. Maybe her squad would be alive if she had a better Guardian to bow to.

"They live," Vakonivak said, lightly confused. "In nest?"

"They're dead--" The heat under Sheila's skin took a different tone, like the pleasant spice of a curry turning into a charcoal singe. *Shit. She means . . .* "You're talking about Kell and the boys, aren't you."

"The . . . friends? Is that their names?" Vakonivak's tone remained curious, oblivious.

"Fuck. Yeah, I thought you meant . . ."

"Who is squad?"

Sheila grumbled. "Don't worry about it."

"I do not worry. I love."

"Well I don't. So."

"Do you not care for friends?" Vakonivak asked.

Sheila threw her arms up. "Sure, I do. Okay?"

"You defend them, and not yourself," she went on.

"I guess?" Sheila hadn't considered her role in the group all that strongly. She just knew that she was trained infantry. She was the front line. Someone had to do it, and nobody else could.

"Is that not love?"

That word again. "Pal," Sheila said, "we've got very different ideas of what that is."

"I . . . sorry." Vakonivak's eyes sank, nearly closing. "Your language is confusing."

"You should hear Alejandro," she said with a scoff.

"Is that the like-me?"

The like--oh, vian. Duh. "No, he's the . . . like-me, I guess. Tobias was the like-you. The one you didn't kill, anyway."

Vakonivak's eyes shot open. "What did I do?"

Sheila rolled her eyes. Vakonivak was divine, wasn't she? Sheila shouldn't have to explain things to her like she was a child. "What do you think? You flew off, knocked out a bunch of walls, crushed the Secretary to death. Wasn't that your plan?"

"No!" Vakonivak cawed mournfully. "I left so friend could . . ." The thought remained unfinished, unspoken.

"Well, we did. Alright? Are you happy?"

Vakonivak's head shuddered. "No," she said.

You could've just--no, wait, you said you can't. Right. "Okay then." Sheila reached for Vakonivak's massive head and gently tilted it to look her in the eye. "The truth, Vakonivak. Why are you here? Why Bessetrae?"

Vakonivak easily pulled her head away, despite Sheila's grasp. Her beak pointed to the platinum sky. Some time passed, an uncanny amount, too long it seemed, yet Sheila couldn't bring herself to speak up again.

"Because," Vakonivak said wearily, "I love. As you do."

"Vakonivak," Sheila said, ready to lecture as the Gardener began to bend and flicker again, the way she had when Sheila tried to strike her, only now it was across her entire body. The sight left Sheila speechless. Vakonivak gave her one last motherly look before her head shimmered and collapsed in on itself, along with the rest of her body, leaving Sheila standing alone, lost in the endless blue plains.

B

Tobias's attention--and a fair amount of his vision--was consumed by the rust-grey dragon before him. His beak slowly parted in awe and satisfaction. He had never met Owain in person before. The creature was regal, commanding, imposing in all the ways that dragons of fiction and fantasy were, likely because they were all based off of him in one way or another.

"Funny seeing you here," Tobias said, seated on the ground, as he glanced around at the blue, alien landscape. "Though I do have to wonder where 'here' is."

Owain did not respond. He stared at the professor with burgundy eyes, sitting stone stiff. The vian got up and walked around, scuffing his boot against the blue ground, idly testing what materials it was made of. *Rather firm . . .*

"Hmm. I shouldn't assume you can talk. We haven't heard a Guardian actually speak aloud."

Silence.

"Besides," Tobias went on, "you could just as well be a figment of my imagination."

Silence.

Tobias sighed, with a hint of a laugh. "This isn't a lecture, Owain. I know I've not asked direct questions, but you're free to jump in."

"Patience." Owain's voice seemed to echo, even though he stood in a space with no walls for his voice to echo off of.

He does speak! "Very well," Tobias said. "Take all the time you need. I can't imagine I'm going anywhere."

"Patience," Owain repeated, his expression turning stoic and still once again.

Hmm. So it's like that, then? Tobias sat again on the smooth blue ground. "Understood."

Strange place, this. Not like anywhere I've seen or heard about. Not that comes to mind, anyway. Literature? Has anyone written about . . . Tobias took a deep nasal breath. *Oh that's a smell, isn't it. Smells like . . . endive, I believe. Or chicory. Interesting. References, references, what places would look like . . . Hmm, chicory, isn't the Zeimatic idea of the afterlife the plains of chicory and lavender?*

. . .Oh no.

No, no, no. No. This can't be. I can't be. I'm breathing. My heart is--well it's racing now. I'm not dead. I'm not. I'm alive. I'm--I have to be. I have to be.

Am I?

He looked up at Owain, the dragon still stationary, unmoved by the worried expression growing on Tobias's face.

Is that where I am? Facing my final judgment? . . .And is that really what Guardians are? Gods living among us? Truly? Well, if they were, wouldn't they announce themselves as such? They've not hidden at all. If they wanted to witness all our sins and failings firsthand, without influencing humanity, they've done a damn poor job blending in. So they can't--no, no, gods would be inscrutable. Probably some elaborate plan going on and it's a mark of human folly to try and understand it. That's every old fable I can think of, at the end of the day.

What is he waiting for, anyway? Am I supposed to do something? Blurt out every one of my sins? A massive confession? "Acknowledge, and I may absolve," that kind of thing? What would even count? If he's one of those old-fashioned, controlling, selfish gods, says you can't have sex or do anything fun . . . hooo, it'd take forever just getting through my 20s. Good times, those.

But I'm not--I'm alive. Right? How would I be alive, though? Be honest with yourself, Toby. You have the facts, trust them. You felt the earth, you saw the flash. Those split seconds, when you know before you can think, they tell you everything. Like when you saw Kell without their helmet. Like the first time you summoned Chapalu.

Summons. All this mess is because of summons. We kept chasing that dream. That nightmare. Damn the consequences, we weren't satisfied. We had to keep reaching. Keep ignoring every time we thought, no, this is a bad idea, this is too far, this is playing god. Whatever kind of god Owain is--or represents, maybe he's just an avatar--there's no way they're happy with us about summons. I know I wouldn't be if I were them.

"The threads appear," Owain said, slowly and abruptly.

Tobias opened his eyes. "Am I alive?" Only when the words came out did he notice how desperate the question was.

"How so?"

Inscrutable, indeed. "Am I alive or am I dead?" Tobias asked, standing to meet Owain's face, feeling more composed and scientific.

"Both. You lived, and you died."

"You're going to have to clarify what you mean."

Owain shifted subtly. "There are threads where you are gone. They have all returned. Yours? You are alive."

"What are these 'threads'?"

"Possibility."

"Possibility of . . . what?" Tobias asked.

"All things."

Tobias pinched the top of his beak. "We're getting well outside my specialist subject. You're saying, anything that *can* happen, you can see?"

Owain breathed a slow, deep breath. "We can."

"So you can see all the ways in which I've died?"

"If I looked."

"So I haven't died in that explosion."

"You have."

Tobias felt the blood flee his face. "But you just said I'm alive!"

"You are."

"I can't be alive and dead at the same time, Owain!"

"All things are."

Tobias dropped backwards to the ground. He could feel the firm terrain, though it barely registered in his mind. "Stop pulling me around, for gods' sake! You *must* understand my question, surely! Please, am I alive or am I dead?"

Owain tilted his head, leering at Tobias. "Why do you demand?"

"I need to know!" He lifted his goggles to wipe his eyes. "Must I repent for creating summons?"

"Why ask?"

"Because," Tobias said, "if I'm still alive, if there's still a Linnute to get back to, then . . . then I can *do* something! I can make things right, somehow, or at least make a damned honest attempt! This is the worst regret I have, and if I can't take some kind of action, then I'll repent as long as I have to!"

"Repent is action." Owain huffed. "The living act. The dead rot."

"Then let me repent!" Tobias shouted, pleading, praying in the face of what may as well be a god.

"There is no world," said Owain as his form flickered out of existence, "where I stop you."

C

Alejandro's eyes opened to a neutral grey sky, his mouth hung open in awe. The weight slowly returned to his body, dragging through his shoulders and chest and legs towards the ground. He dropped onto the blue terrain with a limp exhaustion. Only after confirming that he could still breathe did he sit up, the damp blue ground poking at his hand like freshly cut grass.

There was no wind. Alejandro felt a chill anyway, the stillness of the air--assuming what surrounded him was air--drawing the same shudders as a stiff breeze. He scanned the surroundings. There was nobody, no signs of life, no signs that the concept of life had ever touched the place before. It had been a long time since Alejandro felt so lost and alone, if indeed he ever had. Disorientation tumbled in his chest like a barrel going over a waterfall.

He found himself closing his eyes for long stretches. It felt like his eyes were closed for a long time, at least. When he opened them, he found Gauven seated on the ground, his forelegs crossed peacefully.

Alejandro stared. "Well." He could muster no other words.

"Well," Gauven echoed with a nod.

Alejandro stared at the Guardian, watching him breathe slowly and calmly. He realized that he, too, was still breathing steadily, that fear had not cut off the air, though no amount of effort could meet Gauven's serenity. "I'm not dead, then?"

"Of course not." Gauven's low voice matched the serenity of his body.

"Good. Good." Alejandro rolled his shoulders and looked around. A desperate part of his mind hoped that he would turn around and see the plains of Stanton, or the Felmata Forest, or even the swamps of southern Cymona. Anything he could recognize. "Where are we, then?"

"Our home," Gauven said calmly.

"Your home. The Guardians, you mean?"

Gauven shook his head. "We are Gardeners."

"Is that so?" Alejandro said. "My apologies."

"You are . . . steady," Gauven said.

Alejandro shrugged, sending a shiver down his back and through his limbs. He shook it out with a practiced affect. "I've learned to keep my cool. Some lessons you learn, you never forget. They become burned into your soul, as it were."

"The Gardeners know your soul," Gauven said. "You do not connect with your peers. We feel you should have none."

"I beg your pardon?"

"Your queen is dead. Those who lead Bessetrae are . . . indolent. Rinculo, impotent. Zeimatia, subordinate. You are determined to tear down Lyon. Chaos is coming to Linnute, child. You can connect them." Gauven lowered his body farther.

"Is that why you brought me here?" Alejandro asked, more in surprise than confusion. "You're offering me your back? You want me to lead Farolé?"

"Linnute," Gauven said. "Take the throne. Unite the nations. End the wars."

Is that their plan, then? Alejandro thought. *Have us get rid of everyone in the way, and then appoint me?*

Gauven's tail flicked subtly. "Alvacii is yours."

No. No, that doesn't make any sense. They've been getting rid of everyone, not us. Gauven killed the Queen. On purpose. This is a trick. There's something else here, Gauven's got a scheme. The hell with this. I'm not playing someone else's game.

Alejandro couldn't stop himself from flashing the smallest of smirks. "You said you know my soul."

"Indeed," Gauven said.

Alejandro nodded. "I do as well. I call it Raurack. I've held it in my hands." He gave Gauven's back a gentle, sentimental pat. "If I tried to take the throne, it would only raise further chaos. I would need to raise up my own army, there would be wars whether to secure me or depose me. I have no claim, no legitimacy, no trust with . . . anyone. I'm not a king, Gauven. I'm just a man. Alvacii fell for a reason. Linnute is not mine to rule. It's not anyone's to rule."

"Even if the people demand unity?"

"Perhaps they do. I haven't asked." He sighed. It was never part of his job to ask. "But if that is what the people want, then I'll help them. Openly. I will be among them, not their ruler."

Gauven exhaled deeply, his breath faintly visible. "So you refuse?"

Alejandro swallowed a lump in his throat. "I do."

"The Gardeners see all futures," Gauven said. "You do not have a happy future if you refuse."

"Then fate is cruel," Alejandro said. "But I would rather be a tragedy than a puppet."

"Stubborn." The peace in Gauven's voice had melted away.

"I had to learn to be stubborn, yes. It came with the job. You can't exactly impose someone's will otherwise."

"That is leading."

"That is ruling." Alejandro felt a bitter heat. "Controlling. Manipulating. Domineering. You're supposed to represent justice in Farolé, Gauven, where is the justice in that?"

"Justice takes many forms."

Alejandro sat cross-legged on the ground before Gauven, a scowl on his face. The fear that so often threatened to bubble up when he worked started to seep into his muscles yet again. *Don't show it, Al. Breathe. Gauven is not getting the better of you. Guardian, Gardener, he could be a god for all it matters. You are not going back to being someone's tool. Not when you've come this far. There are people who trust you now, Al. You have friends. There is no fucking world where you let them down.*

"How will you leave?" Gauven taunted, breaking the silence.

"Here? I don't know." Alejandro projected a false indifference. "Maybe I won't. Every job I took could've been my last, I made peace with that years ago. Life is fleeting, after all. And I will not betray my friends or my principles. If my options are to be a bastard king or die in some impossible land, then I guess I'll die."

"Dramatic," Gauven scoffed.

Alejandro chuckled. "I'm very dramatic. Why are you surprised? I thought you knew my soul."

The Gardener glared and began to stand.

"Either you're lying," Alejandro continued with a sneer, "or you knew this was futile. How long have you lived among humanity? Surely, you *must* have seen this coming."

"Are you testing me?"

"You're testing me," Alejandro said as he, too, stood. "And I don't take kindly to it."

Gauven sneered. "Defiant."

"I. Know." He spoke through gritted teeth. "I know what I am. I'm a defiant, lonely, melodramatic, violent little shit. I may not be happy with all of it, but I know what I am, and you didn't." He stared daggers at the Guardian. "Do you even know what *you* are?"

Gauven's breath on Alejandro's face, as he leaned forward and over him, was the first warmth Alejandro had felt since waking. "Do you intend to tell me?" he said.

"No," Alejandro huffed. "I can't tell you what you are, just like you can't tell me what I am. Only I can decide who I am. And I *have* decided. I am not a leader. I am certainly not a ruler. I am not your tool to be swung around. I am my own man. So either kill me already or send me back to my friends."

Rather than state his verdict, Gauven glared at Alejandro and started to flicker and disappear. Alejandro was left standing in the uncanny plains with only fury for company, until it forced its way loudly and wordlessly out of his lungs.

D

Kell's helmet gave them no readings of any use. Their array of sensors, which would provide detailed information on everything from vapor density to atmospheric pressure to temperature, could make no sense of the environment before them. They considered removing the helmet, but for all they knew the air surrounding them was toxic. For all they knew, there wasn't air.

They blinked repeatedly, their head aching as the uncanny colors of the landscape asserted themselves. Not far from Kell, waiting patiently and coiled around herself, was Caduceus, shimmering in her own impossible color.

"What . . . Where am I?" Kell gasped out. They faced Caduceus, worry on their visor. "Caduceus? What's going on? Did . . . did I die?"

"Living," the serpent said slowly, her mouth moving hesitantly as she spoke.

There's no way I am. Not after that. "Then where am I? What is this place?"

Caduceus looked around laconically. "Nowhere," she eventually said.

Kell's head rang with confusion. "Nowhere? That doesn't make any sense. Caduceus, where did you bring me? Did you bring me here?"

"Outside," Caduceus said.

Kell sighed. "Caduceus, I'm . . . I'm sorry for what happened back home. But I need your help. You can . . . you can put words together, right? You can make sentences. You don't have to say one thing at a time."

Caduceus dipped her head slightly, with a serpentine smile. "*Tssheh vokao geg-gguasd ahtheambn.*"

Kell stared blankly. They felt their mouth trying and failing to recreate the alien words, as if it would give insight to their meaning.

"Understanding?" said Caduceus with a playful confidence in her tone.

Kell exhaled with a faint groan and shook their head apologetically. "Fine. I'm sorry. I'll work with that. I have a lot of questions, though."

Caduceus nodded and watched as Kell paced small circles in the ground.

"That explosion. I caused that. There's no way we survived. Nobody could. I don't believe it. So . . . how? How did you get us out of there? Why?" Kell held up their hand. They were rambling, their mind racing, asking far more questions than Caduceus could possibly answer. "Okay. Caduceus." They knelt down to look the serpent in the face. "Why us? Me, Sheila, Al, Doc. What's so special about us?"

Caduceus set her head on the ground, rolling it side to side gently. Eventually, she lifted it to match Kell's. If a giant serpent could shrug, Caduceus had just done so.

Nothing? Kell stood. They unlatched their helmet slowly, with their left hand, and gradually removed it. They took a deep breath and looked down into Caduceus's black eyes as she peered up at them. "So we're just . . . This could've been anybody. Is that what you're getting at?"

Caduceus vacillated before nodding slightly. "Suitable," she muttered.

"Are we just your tools, then?"

The serpent's head whipped sideways. "Camaraderie!"

Does she think she's helping? "I just want to understand, Caduceus. I was willing to think that the Guardians are just some indifferent part of nature, like everything else, but . . ." They pivoted and gestured with their good arm at the surrounding landscape, as though its presence could speak for them. "I don't understand anything anymore. I don't know what to do anymore."

"Mission," Caduceus hissed.

"Well, yeah, right now I have a mission," Kell said. "It's all I have. You know what Lyon did to us vapormages, right? The whole unit's dead. My old friends are dead. I want revenge, I want justi--"

The word caught in Kell's throat until they choked on it. Their fist clenched around their helmet. A shiver ran across their skin.

"No," they confessed. "No, there's nothing noble here. I can't pretend there is. I'm mad, Caduceus. I've tried to hold it in, but I've been mad for weeks. That bastard had my friends killed and I want revenge. That's all. I want him to hurt, to know every bit of pain, and bile, and despair, that I've tried to just . . . push through and shrug off and I can't anymore, I can't, Caduceus, and I don't care if it means I'm a bad person, I don't care that it's not going to bring anybody back, it's not even gonna make me feel better, I *don't care.*" The shiver had grown into a shudder, shaking their body as they cried.

"Relinquish," Caduceus said softly.

"What?" Kell burst out before attempting to regain their composure. "Let it go? I can't! After that shit he did, how can I? How can you? Aren't you mad about it?"

Caduceus frowned and said nothing.

"Really? You're our Guardian! The vapormages were all your people. Don't tell me you're fine with what happened."

With the tip of her tail, Caduceus held up a small sword by the blade. She slithered to lay it at Kell's feet before sprawling out long on the ground. "Generous," she hissed softly.

Kell's confused expression jumped between the thin blade in front of them and Caduceus's prostrate body. They dropped their helmet and picked the sword up. It was a little large for their hand, but far lighter and shorter than Sheila's, not much worse than the rod they carried. A sloppy note, tied to the hilt, read "you are invited" and nothing more.

It was a sword Kell could use. If they had to. If they could hold it steady. Caduceus looked up and, on seeing them grasp the sword, stretched herself out wider on the ground.

She's getting ready--no. No. "No." The knot of anger shifted to a vague panic. Kell dropped the sword. It landed with an earthen thud. "No, Caduceus, I'm not going to hurt *you*. I can't."

"Generous," she hissed again, more aggressively.

"What? No!" A panic seeped into their breath. "Why? Why would I?"

Caduceus gave them a stern, commanding glare.

"Caduceus, I don't understand what's going on! I don't want to kill you! I don't . . ." Kell found footing with their breath. They weren't calm, but they were going the right direction. "I don't hate you, Caduceus. You're not the one who stole us. You're not the one who made me . . ." Kell trailed off, staring at the small sword on the ground, tears forming again. The anger holding their muscles up seeped away, leaving them sagging and exhausted. "When we're done with Lyon," they said, "once we know we've stopped the war. No more. I'm getting rid of the rod. I'm done being a vapormage. I can't live like this."

Caduceus slowly slithered to bring her face up to match Kell's. Her black eyes darted around, the movement barely discernible. She was trying to find the word. "Adapting," she eventually said.

"It's all I can do," Kell said. "I'm only human."

The smile on Caduceus's face, as she started to flicker out of vision, had the slightest hint of satisfaction on it.

E

In a blink, Kell was in Sao Neso, their back on the ground, their helmet on their head. They were groggy and disoriented, like waking from a fitful night of shallow sleep. It took some time to realize they were staring at the thin white lights of the vault's ceiling. They looked around to get their bearings; they were outside where the locked door once sat, though there was no clear indication in the rock that the door had ever been there. The once-lit channel beyond it was dark. The air was heavy with vapor, thick as anywhere on the surface would get. The vault itself was in disarray. Cabinets and shelves were toppled over, spraying books and film reels and a dozen other kinds of artifacts across the floor.

They slowly sat up and removed their helmet, taking deep breaths of the stale, dense air. The others were sprawled out on the floor around them, seemingly uninjured but still and lifeless, like lumps of wax in the shape of people.

Kell stared at them for several moments, unable to bring themself to check any of them for a pulse. The vault felt unreal, detached, a space devoid of life. It didn't feel how Sao Neso had when they went through the door. It didn't feel how that smoky blue plain that Caduceus brought them to had felt.

Had Caduceus brought them there? Those moments felt like real moments, the place felt like a real place, but how real could any of it have been? None of it followed any rules of existence that Kell knew. In one moment their hand was slowly retreating from a button in a sterile room, the next it was against the ground in a blue wilderness. There was no movement to justify it, no cause and effect, events attached by sequence but not by time, a run-on sentence of existing. It was a dream, even if it was real.

The confusion weighed on them, keeping them anchored to the floor. They saw Sheila come to with a jolt, the armor wrapping her calf clanging against the hard floor. She rolled over and gave Kell a confused look with dry, wide eyes.

"Where are we?" Her voice was hoarse.

"The vault," Kell said quietly. They paused to let Sheila rejoin reality. "Did you see it, too?"

Sheila's eyebrows jumped. "That blue place?" She sat herself up as Kell nodded. "Gods. Did you talk to Vakonivak?"

"Caduceus."

Sheila stared at the floor, her face stunned and terrified. "Did she try and test you?"

"I think. She wanted me to kill her. I think that's what she meant. I couldn't do it."

Sheila said nothing of her own experience. She stayed quietly hunched over until Alejandro and Tobias each came calmly back to life. The four sat in silence, disbelief and concern on each of their faces, for what felt like too long and not long enough.

"We're . . ." Alejandro muttered. "We're all alive, then?"

"Probably," Tobias said, drawing in confused looks from around the room. "I talked with Owain. It said it was Owain."

"I met Gauven," Alejandro said.

"What happened?" Sheila said. "Vakonivak and Caduceus tried to test us. Did they try to test you too?"

Alejandro nodded. "Certainly tried to test me."

"Owain didn't," Tobias said. He stood and started pacing in tight circles. "I was too busy fearing that I was dead. I was . . . I need to do something about summons. Before I die for real." He was shivering and pleading to no one. "They're the worst thing I've ever done, I have to fix this. I have to."

"It's okay, doc," Sheila said. "It's okay."

"It's not!" Tobias yelled suddenly. He quickly tried to compose himself. "I'm sorry. I was so certain. That I was dead. And it made me realize that, for all I've done, for all I've enjoyed of life, the only thing anyone's going to remember about me is that I helped make these damned summons! I've made the worst weapons the world has ever known." He tore his goggles off to wipe his eyes. "I can't let that be my legacy, I can't!"

Sheila stepped over to console Tobias. "We all had a fucking intense moment in there, didn't we?" she said kindly.

Alejandro nodded before looking across the room to Kell. "Gauven wanted me to rule Linnute," he said. "I told him no."

"The whole continent?" Kell said.

"Yeah. He wants to bring back Alvacii. I don't know about the other Guardi--sorry, Gardeners--but Gauven has a scheme. And I'm not playing." Alejandro shook his head. "I could lead if I must, but I won't rule. This world doesn't need rulers. And . . ." He laughed to himself. "I know how rulers are. How the Queen was, anyway. They're . . . miserable. Isolated. Lonely." He looked up at Kell. "I refuse to be lonely."

Kell silently nodded. Alejandro could have just as easily been talking about their dad.

"Everyone feeling okay?" Sheila asked. "You guys sound like they really got under your skin."

"Conveniently," Tobias said, almost calmly. "The more I think about it, the more it feels too subconscious. How would the Guardians--er, sorry, Al, you said 'Gardeners'?"

Alejandro nodded to confirm. Sheila's eyes went slightly wider.

"Hmm. Regardless, how would they know how to push our buttons like this? It doesn't quite make sense. What does it get us?"

"Nothing," Kell said weakly. "All that was pointless."

"If it was real, there must be a point." Tobias was trying to convince himself.

"You think it wasn't real?" As Alejandro spoke, he shifted where he was sitting, and a glint of light behind him caught Kell's eye.

"Al?" Their eyes were wide behind their visor. "Is that one of your knives behind you?"

Alejandro turned around to check. "No." He grabbed the sword that was behind him and held it out towards Kell. "Was it this?"

Kell grabbed it and held it in their good hand, feeling the weight of the blade and examining the hilt. Their surprise grew with each gentle motion. "Guys. Caduceus gave me this. That was all real. I don't know how, but. It was."

"Then . . . why would . . ." Sheila muttered as she dropped back to the vault floor. "She didn't have to . . . but she had to have known . . . and I . . ." The words poured out indistinct, like a thick slurry.

Kell slid over to Sheila's right. They rested their arm on her back, their hand on her shoulder.

She cracked.

Her eyes locked shut, her whole body shuddering, straining to hold back tears. Kell gave her a gentle pat and all the time she needed.

Sheila coughed out a small laugh.

"I love you guys," she finally said, letting her bloodshot eyes open behind a mess of loose hair. She looked around with a weak smile that Kell couldn't help but match. She added a light chuckle as she looked at Alejandro. "Not like that," she said, making him chuckle back. He draped an arm over Sheila's other shoulder, and Tobias sat to gently complete the circle, paying mind to Kell's tattered arm. The four sat on the ground, exhausted, alive, together.

F

Eventually, Kell stood and started leading the group out of the vault. They glanced at the sword Caduceus left them, only briefly, before carrying on. *I won't hurt her. That's not who I am. That's not why we're here.*

They opened the front door to find it taped over with a few yellow and black ribbons. The vault's attendant was nowhere to be seen. Perhaps she had put up the warning and ran off to tell someone. If so, she was doing it far away from the building, as the surrounding air--still stale, Kell noted, though less so than usual--carried no noise from anybody nearby.

"What time is it, anyway?" Alejandro said.

Sheila pulled out her mobile and tapped it. "Dunno, I'm out of charge."

Tobias and Kell checked their mobiles and found the same problem. They hadn't been down there that long, it felt like, but whatever happened in the lab could have drained their mobiles. It certainly drained their bodies. Kell felt their legs dragging as they walked towards a square on the northern half of Sao Neso, close to the column that held Cyprin's office. The square, devoid of holiday decorations, was empty save for a lone sahagin man shuffling aimlessly between the planters. *It must be pretty late,* Kell thought. *Not a soul around. 'Cept that guy. And he looks . . . drunk.*

The sahagin spotted the four and perked up cheerfully, stepping close enough to be identifiable. His air was alien, devoid of presence. "Ah, ahoy there folks! Fascinating afternoon, isn't it?" He spoke whimsically, as if he were discovering his words along with his audience. "Say, you wouldn't happen to know a good sushi place nearby, would ya?"

Kell stared. They could feel their throat being choked from the inside. "Dad?" they forced out.

Cyprin looked at his child askew, before looking at their concerned comrades. "Something wrong with the little one?"

Dad, you don't . . . ? Kell could put no sound to their breath.

"They'll be fine," Alejandro said. His whole demeanor had been softening, as if Raurack was out. His diplomacy was turning kind, rather than sharp. "But, no, afraid we don't know any sushi places. We're just visiting."

"Ah, rough luck." Cyprin was instantly back to the perky tone. "It's such a quiet town lately, must be a boring visit!"

Alejandro chuckled defensively. "Oh, no worries sir, we've found it interesting enough."

"Well, you kids enjoy! Hope you're feeling better," Cyprin said to Kell, who only felt more nauseous with each word. "Oh!" He perked up in revelation. "I hate to ask, but have you come across any good sushi places nearby? Been dying for some."

Alejandro gave a short apology and nudged the group away from the square. Kell resisted. *What did they do? What did . . .*

"Dad!" Kell managed to shout.

Tobias grabbed Kell's left arm and pulled them away, down the road. Kell was a storm on the inside, surging back towards the square where their father, what was left of their father, placidly sniffed at the grasses and shrubs in their elevated planters. Kell's breathing accelerated as their resistance faltered.

"Kell, calm down," Sheila said with compassionate command. "You're glowing."

Glowing? What? Kell took deeper, slower breaths until Sao Neso started to return to focus.

"Doc," they finally said, "what happened to my dad?"

Tobias gave them a gentle pat on the shoulder. His head hung. "Do you remember all of that about the canopic? The paper covered every safety precaution for working with it, and we determined so many of them. But if you disregard all that common sense, you could damage somebody."

"How bad?" Sheila asked.

Tobias sighed. "You were right to call me out for it. It can be bad. That dementia behavior, it's far from the worst that can happen. I've seen Santhrupta catatonic. Couldn't eat. I'm pretty sure that guard . . ." He knelt down to look Kell in their reddened, teary eyes. "I've been in the same state your father is in. It's terrifying, but it's completely fixable. Okay? He will be fine. Trust me. We just have to find the summon they made."

"The summon *Lyon* made," Alejandro said bitterly.

Tobias nodded. "Most certainly."

Kell stood, sputtering, staring at the road, feeling too many things at once. They felt a pull back to the vault, back to the sword Caduceus had bequeathed them. They didn't want to use it. They would never use it on Caduceus. But Lyon? Sure, killing Lyon would be a major crime, would throw Cymona into chaos, but did it matter? Sure, they hated their father for making them a vapormage, for sending them to what should have been their death, but did it matter? Did anything but revenge matter? Did anything but revenge even exist in their soul, their crushed and crumpled but still intact soul, more than could be said for--

Kell abruptly laughed at their own train of thought. They were sounding like a Bryn Achterberg show again.

"You okay, Kell?" Tobias still sounded concerned.

"I'm okay, I'm okay," they said weakly. "I'm just . . . melodramatic."

"And what's wrong with that?" Alejandro said with a reassuring smile.

Kell smiled back. Birds of a feather, the two were. "Yeah. Alright. Let's get that son of a bitch."

The four had barely gathered themselves when they heard footsteps approaching from a side street nearby.

"Hey!" A sahagin guard emerged from between buildings, looking worn down and exhausted. "You four? What're you doing here?"

"Leaving," Sheila said.

"No, I mean, we thought you died months ago."

Kell was out of emotions to feel. "What do you mean, months?"

"You're telling us," Alejandro said, "that we went through the locked door *months* ago?"

"Well, month and a half," the guard said. "Then there was the explosion, and all the vapor." He gestured around. "Place has been weird since."

"We... lost months?" Alejandro said in shock.

"I guess so. You don't remember Banner coming around?"

"Banner was here?" Tobias said. "Jakob Banner?"

"Is that the owner? Don't think it was him. Just a couple folks from the company, came down handing out a bunch of these." The guard pulled a small, sealed tin from his pocket. The top was stamped with the Banner Goods logo. He shook it gently, rattling the contents. "Supposed to have coupons and set-up info and all that. Music from this Crystal Greene person, whoever that is."

"May we?" Tobias asked, holding a hand out.

The guard handed it over, letting the vian examine the tin. Alejandro held a hand up, offering to examine as well. When Tobias was satisfied with his look, he handed the tin over.

"Guess you surfs aren't enough business for 'em anymore," the guard said. "They were all over, putting those in everyone's mailboxes and all that. Swarm of bugs, they were."

Alejandro, after scanning the outside of the tin, started to unscrew the lid. A sharp hiss came from inside, followed by a rush of vapor. His eyes shot open and went faint. He stumbled backwards, falling to the ground in a barely controlled fashion, a cloud of vapor swirling around him. The cloud coalesced into Raurack, standing as tall as a person on its hind legs. It landed on all fours and looked around, rapidly scanning for an exit. Tobias lunged, piercing its side with his spear. Sheila jumped at the summon to restrain it while Kell, half dazed themself, kept the visibly alarmed guard clear of the scene. Sheila wrestled the pudgy rabbit-like beast to the ground, letting Tobias hastily begin the spell to dissolve the summon. Raurack faded into yellow and white vapor that gradually, with gestures of coaxing from the professor, found its way into Alejandro's prone body.

"Waves above, what just happened?" the guard muttered.

"Those things are bombs," Kell said.

"Spellbombs are shit," Sheila said. "Who would make one that does *that*?"

"A goddamned maniac, is who," Tobias said, barely holding in his anger. He crouched down over Alejandro as he started to come to. "You with us, Al?"

Alejandro groaned and stared back. "Sorry. That was the stupidest thing I've ever done."

Kell turned to the guard. "How have you not seen that happening?" they asked, indignant. "It's been *months*!"

"I work nights!" the guard said. He gestured around as if the time of day was obvious in Sao Neso. "I've gone days without seeing anyone even before all this. And it's not like people are gone, they're just weird. Like they're stuck in a loop."

"They would be," Tobias groaned, his fists clenching. "That is exactly what would happen. Kell, once your mobile is charged, we need to call Banner. We deserve an explanation."

Alejandro started to stand. "The hell with an explanation," he said. "We need to get that son of a bitch too."

WAR!

Rising tensions between Cymona and the recognized governments of Farolé have boiled over into open conflict.

Boats filled with Cymonian knights made landfall near Dolya Bay in Farolé last night. At 19:17 that same night, Cymonian Prime Minister Mitchell Lyon issued a formal declaration of war against Farolé, accusing the nation of creating summons for the purpose of waging warfare.

[...]

— Banner News article announcing
beginning of War of the Summons

FAROLÉ FALLS!

War in Linnute has ended with Farolé's complete surrender. A public declaration will be issued by Prime Minister Lyon at 16:00 this afternoon.

At 8:39 this morning, the Provisional People's House of Farolé issued a declaration of surrender, effective immediately. This follows the Royal House's declaration issued yesterday. With the declaration, the two most widely recognized governmental bodies within Farolé have ceded the nation to Cymona.

[...]

— Banner News article announcing
ending of War of the Summons

CHAPTER FIFTEEN

The lines were dead.

Every line Banner had used to contact Kell produced nothing but dead air when they tried to call back. They tried to reach Crystal. Silence. Nothing from Rocko, either. They paced angrily around the lot in Reeseport, cursing Banner and Lyon and the chilly morning sun.

Standing beside the beat-up Basilisk, Sheila called Cory's line. He picked up, much to her relief, and gave the group the rundown of what had happened while they were in Sao Neso.

Farolé had fallen.

The news barreled into Alejandro, pinning him to the wall he was leaning against. He had never looked so afraid.

Cory shared the rumors that had made it over the border. According to them, the Farolian defense fought hard, valiantly standing against a wave of summons. Alejandro seemed to believe the stories immediately. Kell was prone to agree. The rumors sounded messy, human, real.

Lyon, to nobody's surprise, had been making proud, victorious speeches the whole time. He never said as much directly, of course, but it sounded like he had his eyes on Bessetrae as well.

Cory wasn't taking chances. He had retreated to Lake Goldstone, farther in the country's west, in the hopes it'd buy him some time. The rest of Milend was free to make their own moves. That didn't include Quinn and Mia, as it happened.

Sheila groaned loudly as the call ended. "Dammit! If those Gardeners hadn't kept us in their weird place for two--" She checked her mobile again. "Three months? Fuck, we could've done something. We could've stopped this."

"Maybe," Kell said. "But we didn't get that chance. So what do we do with the chance we have?"

"Not much in the way of options," Tobias said. "From what that Cory chap said, there are knights all over Farolé. With summons fighting alongside them. A proper mess."

"We *will* clean it up," Alejandro said, rich with determination. "*That* is my old job. If something's threatening Farolé, I *will* do something about it."

"But there's no point going up to the battlefields," Kell said. "We can't fight a whole war by ourselves. We need to get Lyon."

"Where would he even be?" Tobias wondered aloud. "Between Cymona and Farolé, that's a lot of ground to cover."

"We might have it." Sheila held her mobile up to the group. "News says a statement is coming tonight. Speech tomorrow morning." She put her mobile away and opened the Basilisk's door. "Gotta be Candhall. This is our one shot."

The group piled into the vehicle. "It's going to be busy," Alejandro said. "Head of state in town? More security."

"If he's there already," Kell said. "If not, he's in for a hell of a surprise when he gets back."

"Be better if he's not there," Tobias said. "Won't have to get through his personal guard. I presume he has one."

"Whatever he has," Sheila said as she navigated the Basilisk out of the lot, "we'll have to deal with it. Missed our chance to have options."

"Sheila, can I look at your mobile?" Alejandro asked. "There might be tourist maps of the castle. If we can get to him without a fight or a scene, it'd be far better."

Sheila, without taking her eyes off the road, tossed her mobile backwards towards Alejandro. "What's our plan when we get to him?"

"May I just say," Tobias started, "I know I'm the one here who's not a fighter. But if we can, I would rather we didn't fight."

Kell wasn't opposed to a fight. It would be the surest way to get revenge. Lyon had hurt them, hurt everyone they cared about, and the simplest answer would be to just dole it back in kind. "We might have to," they said. "He might force it."

"How did the papers not matter?" Alejandro griped. "Lyon killed the vapormages!"

"He killed sahagins," Kell said. "Cymonians wouldn't care."

"They damn well ought to," Alejandro said. "The man should be mired in scandals."

"He's too much of a git for scandals," Tobias said. "Man has no shame. He's after power, right? I could try to convince him that summons would turn on him and take his power. And I would be the person to know."

Alejandro quickly considered the plan. "I like the thought, but you're not a great liar. We'll need to hash out the story on the way."

"And if that doesn't work," Kell said, "we push the scandal. Better than nothing."

Sheila chuckled softly from the driver's seat. "You guys sound like my old squad."

Kell was suddenly ashamed for bringing up bad memories. "Sorry, I know that's kinda--"

Sheila waved them off, focusing on the road. "It's fine. Whatever you guys need, just tell me. I got your back."

B

The Candhall gate was sealed shut. Kell couldn't be surprised. The city was the seat of government for a country whose ruler was making no small number of enemies. Of course Lyon would be keeping people out. Or keeping them in.

A shaky older hunn in a Cymonian knight's uniform emerged from within the city wall. He confronted the group, sword drawn.

"Halt! Who goes there?" he shouted.

"Who does it look like?" Sheila barked back.

"Get out of here," the guard said, "the city's closed off."

"This is my city," Kell said, a stern anger in their voice and on their visor. "We're going in."

The guard's already shaky hand wavered as he looked at Kell. "Where did you get that? You're not a vapormage!"

The blade of Alejandro's knife appeared abruptly, pressing against the guard's throat. "They're more a mage than you are a knight," he said with a smirk. "And they have business to attend to. So if you don't mind stepping aside, we'll be on our merry way. Understood?"

The guard nervously wheezed out agreement, staying put even as Alejandro followed the rest of the group through the gatehouse and into Candhall.

The air inside Candhall's walls was dry and cold like spent ash. To the northeast, on a hill that broke into a cliff over the waters, the old castle's keep glistened in the falling light. Tobias and Alejandro broke off west to observe more of the locals. Sheila and Kell stuck to the old town's shadows and made ground on the castle. The group would reconvene at a square close to the castle, where the original barbican once stood.

Kell tested a rusting metal door that faced a quiet street. It creaked open to an alleyway. Such spaces criss-crossed the old town and were good for traversing the city without being spotted. That was Kell's plan for getting around, a plan they knew from experience would get them closer to the castle unnoticed. Indeed, one could travel Candhall with almost perfect stealth thanks to the many covered alleyways.

Kell and Sheila were only a few steps past the door when a mostly familiar trio emerged from a building's back door, speaking in hushed tones. They stopped once they noticed Kell and Sheila. Grey stepped to the front of the three, Leena to his side. A young, black-feathered vian woman took up the rear, her eyes fixed on Kell from the moment she spotted them.

"Well there's the spell," Grey said with a snide kindness. "Funny running into you two."

"Small world, huh?" Kell's visor lit up, showing their amusement. Of anyone they could run into, it managed to be Grey. They felt blessed.

"Are Mia and Quinn alright?" Sheila asked with earnest concern.

"Last we saw, yeah," Grey said. "Quinn had family in town. They stopped off there."

Sheila sighed in relief. "Alright. Good." She nodded towards the vian, who was still focused on Kell. "And who's that with you?"

The vian, startled, started to speak, but Grey cut her off. "My party. Thought yours was bigger?"

"The guys are scouting," Kell said. "We need to get the lay of the land."

"What for?"

Kell smirked. *The guy is Cymonian, after all. Talk the talk.* "Want the best seats for Lyon's speech, of course."

The scarf over Grey's face hardly hid his own smirk. "I see." He looked at his party. Leena nodded, an adamant look on her face. "Y'know, Kell, you might find this interesting, then. An old family heirloom. My great-grandma used to work in the castle, way back when. You might think this is cool."

Grey stepped forward and held out a closed hand. Kell held out their left hand. Into it dropped a small, dense steel key.

"She was a stablehand," he went on. "They still had the official horse and all that. Terrible hours, but since they built the inner wall right through the stables on the west side, at least she could go to work without dealing with the gatehouse."

"Must've been a relief," Kell said, pleased by the implications. "Sure you want us to have this?"

"Ain't mine, if anyone asks."

"Pity the cove who lost it, then," Kell said.

"You don't want to come with us?" Sheila said.

Grey shook his head. "Oh, I do. But Art's right." He gestured at the vian. "You get good enough seats and it's a hell of a show. Maybe I shouldn't see it."

Kell looked over at Sheila. She seemed to be biting her tongue. Maybe she was just sick of all the Cymonian euphemism. Kell wouldn't blame her.

"Grey?" they said. "Think we could have a word? Privately?"

He shrugged. "Sure. That's an old Annie's we just cut through, should be fine. Mind keeping watch, you two?"

Kell followed as Grey opened the side door. "Play nice, Sheila," they said with a tease.

Sheila laughed. "Oh, piss off."

It used to be, there was an Annie's on every corner. Now, most of those restaurants were like the one they had slipped into from the alleyway: abandoned, dusty relics, seats and tables piled neatly along the papered-over windows. A faint mix of street lamp light and the last of the sunset bled through the covering. Nobody outside would see the pair.

Grey shut the door behind him. "What's up, Kell?"

Kell stood in the middle of the empty dining room, their back to Grey, their hood still drawn up. They rubbed their right arm nervously. "Thanks for the update," they said. "At the armory. Alejandro got it to me."

"Glad I could help," Grey said. "Did any other Faces help you guys out?"

Kell shrugged. The Faces didn't matter to them. "Didn't run into any. But, oh well. Thanks for taking care of Quinn and Mia, by the way. Meant a lot to Sheila."

"She know them?"

"Naw." Kell chuckled faintly to themself. "I think we were the only ones there that actually knew each other."

Grey chuckled back. "I knew you had me pegged the moment you saw me."

Kell, with their left hand, started unlatching their helmet. "We should both drop our masks, Rocko."

Rocko Larson, the Grey Face, eagerly agreed. "Gotta put it back on before we go, though," he said, loosening the scarf over his face. "Folks are after me."

"I know what you mean." Kell popped off their helmet, showing Rocko their scaly, purple face for the first time.

He was as shocked as they had expected. Rocko dropped his weight backwards against the counter. "Tell me you're joking."

A sympathetic smile sat on Kell's face. "You know how bad I am at jokes, Rocko."

Rocko stared at the dirty floor, his head slowly swaying in disbelief. "I am such an asshole," he eventually said.

"You were nowhere near the worst."

"Still." Rocko paused and looked back up at Kell. "All of you?"

"All of us."

"Shit." Rocko struggled to keep his eyes up at Kell. "That . . . explains a lot."

"Sorry I never told you."

Rocko almost looked disgusted. "What? Kell, I'm just glad you don't have a death wish."

Maybe Kell did. They weren't sure. "Can you promise me something, Rocko?" Their eye contact broke at Rocko's nod. "We're going to go find Lyon. I don't know what's gonna happen. We might kill him. Maybe the Faces will be in charge, I don't know. But if you guys are? Please. Promise me you'll try to make it safe for sahagins." Rocko's eyes darted away. "I know, I know. It's not gonna happen overnight."

"Yeah," he sighed, "there are definitely people who'll still want to hate you."

"I know. I'm gonna be wearing this helmet the rest of my life. But I'm asking for the folks back home. They deserve better. It'll be years, sure, but someday." They took a short glance at the papered-over windows behind them. "I want them to see the sun."

"I wish I could make promises. But, we'll do what we can," Rocko said, putting his scarf back on over his face. "You'd be good for the Faces, honestly. But something tells me you're not interested."

Kell chuckled as they clumsily put their helmet back on. "I'm not cut out for politics."

"C'mon, Kell. I don't believe that for a second. Look at you, you're way more together than you used to be. You make a good leader." Rocko reached for the door. "Come home in one piece, alright?"

"I'll try."

C

Sheila and Kell lingered in an alleyway facing the barbican square, the old keep looming large in the near distance. There was nobody around to hide from--no locals meandering or knights on patrol--but that could change at any moment. Kell didn't want to get too comfortable, not with the castle this close.

Sheila turned from scanning the area around the square to look at Kell sagging against the opposite building. "You holding up alright?" she said quietly.

Kell nodded. "I'm fine."

"How's your arm?"

Kell rubbed the wound and hesitated.

"Hey. No secrets, right?"

Kell sighed. *Fair.* "It never stopped hurting," they said. "The whole time. Using it just made it worse. I never complained 'cause like . . . we've all got bigger things to worry about. So I just patch it up each night. Farther and farther along." They slowly dragged their left hand over the wound to illustrate what they meant. "Had to go deeper and deeper with the vapor to hold it up. More muscle split? Whatever. Bone broke? Whatever. Until . . . after that blue place? I realized I had patched my arm all the way across." They pinched their right hand, raising it and letting gravity drop it back to their side, slapping against their leg. "I don't feel it anymore. It's gone." Kell had come to terms with the fact.

Sheila looked like she hadn't. "Once this is over, Kell. We'll take care of it."

Kell nodded and glanced out at the square. *How? It's gone. There's no spell or surgery that's gonna fix this. But that's for later. Omar's right, take care of yourself last.*

Alejandro appeared from the west side of the square, stepping close to the buildings' walls. Tobias followed, taking alert glances around him as he moved. He was the first to spot Kell and Sheila. He gestured to Alejandro with professional confidence. The professor was taking things seriously.

Alejandro nodded to Sheila as he slid into the alleyway next to Kell. "Reconnaissance complete," he whispered. His professional, business-like tone was slipping back into his voice.

"What's the story?" Sheila asked, businesslike in her own ex-sergeant way.

"Quiet night out there," Tobias said as he took a position beside Sheila.

"City's under curfew, it seems," Alejandro said, slightly relaxing himself. "People seem a tad anxious, but they appear intact."

"Figures he wouldn't do anything to the locals," Kell said.

"Bastards are predictable," Alejandro said. "Any plans on getting in?"

"Should be good there," Sheila said. "Kell's got some friends in high places."

Kell looked around the square cautiously. "And some enemies in high places. We better move before any of them show up."

The flow of Candhall's streets was pushed around by the old castle's walls as they curved and swelled to encircle the courtyard and buildings inside. Close to where the eastern wall began to curve to the south, an unremarkable metal door with a small deadbolt lock and no handle interrupted the jagged pattern of old stones. A patch of land, almost barren of vegetation, sat between it and the street. As the group approached, weaving through alleyways one or two streets away to retain some distance, they continued to see and hear not a single soul. Even with light pouring out of nearby windows, Kell felt more like they were scampering around ruins than a nation's capital.

The rest of the group seemed even more on edge. "How is there *nobody*?" Alejandro whispered as the group came within a block of the door.

"This can't be right," Sheila muttered. "Knights wouldn't be on curfew. This is a trap."

"Or we're too early," Kell whispered, looking for signs of life. "Haven't locked down yet."

"Armor up the front, leave the underbelly exposed," Alejandro said. "Not exactly a sound tactic."

"Would be if he was out of resources," Tobias said. "Wouldn't it? Farolé may have bled him dry, fighting back so well."

Kell watched a lone pedestrian walk down the street several blocks away, eventually turning to go down a side street. "Maybe. But I'm assuming the worst." They grabbed the key from their satchel and clutched it tight in their hand. "Coast is clear."

Kell dashed across the street, their right arm hanging limply behind them. They pressed against the door and fumbled to slot the key into the lock. The key refused to turn. They wiggled the key slightly, hoping to line it up correctly, but they were having no success. They started to reach for their rod, content to blast the door open with vapor.

"Here," Sheila said quietly, watching over them. "Let me try."

Kell stepped aside. Their left arm, they realized, was shaking faintly. Sheila's posture was much steadier and more composed as she angled and adjusted the key, muttering curses and pleas for it to work. The door let out a hefty metallic thunk as the lock turned.

The door opened to darkness. The persistent, vague musk of the building's history rushed out of the door as if it needed air from itself. Stepping inside, Kell found that the old stables had been converted to a storage unit. They wrapped the end of their rod in flaming vapor, illuminating rows and rows of crates stamped PROPERTY OF BANNER GOODS -- NOT FOR RESALE. Tobias peered over and around piles of boxes, wary of an ambush, as he moved quietly to a door on the opposite side. It opened to the castle's courtyard, the rectangular keep towering overhead.

"Right," Alejandro said. "Map says the side buildings have ministers' offices. Assembly hall is in the keep. As is Lyon's office."

Kell looked around the open courtyard, lit a blazing red by the last of the twilight. "Did it say where Owain would be?"

"Throne room," Alejandro said. "Also in the keep. Don't know if he's always there or if it's just for tours."

"No lights on," Tobias said, giving the side buildings a distant look over. "Doubt the rest of the parliament's around. Shame, would've liked to pull some of his peers onto our side."

Sheila scoffed. "Guy probably doesn't think he has peers. C'mon." With a crouching run, she hurried along the perimeter of the courtyard, moving north towards the keep. The others followed, each taking their own cautious glances around.

How is there nobody here? Kell thought as they slipped past the front door of a long, low stone building. *He can't be this much of a fool.*

As she made it to the corner of the keep's exterior, Sheila abruptly pressed her back against the side wall and, with sharp shakes of her head, gestured for everyone to join her quickly.

"You spot the guard too?" Tobias whispered.

Sheila nodded. "Not in uniform though. Weird."

Alejandro cautiously peered around the corner. "Looks like the guys in the archives. That's a summon."

Kell took their own look. "Shit. Think it saw us?"

The group all stood silently and listened. "No," Alejandro whispered, "it'd be coming if it had. But it's too close."

"We getting rid of it, or distracting it?" Sheila whispered.

Kell gave Tobias a light prod. "Chapalu?"

"Raurack," Alejandro firmly whispered.

Tobias didn't like the plan. "Even after--?"

Alejandro looked both confident and resigned. "I have to. Just keep an eye on me."

He sat on the ground, back against the keep's exterior, and fell into a meditative stance. No sign of the guard emerged as he worked, drawing a small Raurack from his body. Alejandro stood, visibly pained but satisfied. Raurack stood at his feet, ready to run in an instant.

"It'll bolt around, behind the offices, towards the stables," Alejandro planned. "Should distract the guard long enough." He gave the group confident glances. "Ready?"

The others responded with a collective nod. The small rabbit-like summon bolted behind the nearby offices. It emerged from the other side, dashing into the courtyard, doing laps and leaping in the air.

Soon, the vapor density readings on Kell's visor rose. The guard stepped out into the courtyard with the methodical rhythm of a familiar and started to track Raurack's rapid movements. Alejandro's summon dashed for the stables, leading the guarding summon to give chase.

Sheila and Tobias quickly moved to the keep door, trying to open it silently. The door moved, the wood complaining softly through the entire process. As Alejandro slipped into the keep behind the others, he waved a hand out the door with a faint flourish. Through a window, Kell could see Raurack dash back through the courtyard and clamber up the small, irregular rocks of the castle wall until it was up and over.

"Good work," Kell said.

"I have a good teacher," Alejandro said, relieved.

"Hope that summon's not smart enough to realize that was a distraction," Sheila said. "If it does, we're screwed."

D

The keep's entry hall was an ornate stone chamber lit by lanterns along the walls. The lanterns held dim vapor flames, the colder sort that gave a steady washed-out light and required little upkeep. From a look around the carpeted entryway, there may not have been much upkeep going on. A hint of dust permeated the air. At the far end, an unfinished wooden platform stood between two curving stairways, each with planks of wood overlaid on the stone steps. The hall seemed to be in the midst of renovation. Kell approached the stairs cautiously; there was no sign how far along the renovations were or how stable the ground would be.

The small landing at the top of the stairs, above the entry hall, was cut off by a double door far too wide and tall to be anything other than ornamental. A pair of more reasonably sized doors flanked it on either side, close to the walls. All three doors were, at a first examination, locked.

Tobias's eyes, and soon his whole body, followed the sweeping lines of thin iron that made symmetrical patterns on the giant wooden doors. "Hmm. I wonder." He put his hands against the right door. "Al, would you mind touching the left door? See if you feel anything unusual."

As the two examined the door, Kell looked at the surrounding walls. There were no lanterns above the landing, so the area was somewhat dark. Kell had to adjust their visor to see well. When they did, they noticed a stone in the masonry, across from the large door, that protruded as though it were a button. A touch confirmed that the stone could move, so Kell pressed on it.

Clank.

Tobias stumbled in surprise as the door he was leaning against suddenly reacted to his pressure, moving slightly before he could back off. "Wait, did we . . .? Did that actually work?"

"Did what work?" Sheila asked.

Tobias righted himself. "Well," he said, "no handles, quite large, these patterns resemble a sigil. Thought it could be locked by enchantment."

"Makes sense," Kell said, "but no, there was a button over there."

Tobias laughed to himself. "Well. Thank you for humoring me. Shall we?" He rested his hands on the door again and looked at Alejandro. The two began pushing on their respective doors in unison.

The doors to the assembly hall groaned with weight as they opened. Flanking the sides of the room were elevated rows of seats and desks. There, ministers were meant to sit, and listen to arguments, and make arguments of their own, all in partaking in the grand tradition of democracy. Many of those seats had sat far too empty for far too long. There were ministers to fill them, but there were no traditions to uphold. Whatever Lyon wanted to do, Lyon would do. There would be no argument.

The center of the hall was left open as a stage for debate and presentation. Occupying the space, lit by the array of vapor-flamed torches that concentrated towards the spot, was a massive dragon with rust-grey scales. Owain slept soundly, claiming the space through his presence like a giant cat. He had sprawled out broadly enough to deny passage.

Kell stepped quietly, looking for a route that would get the four through without disrupting Owain. There wasn't one, as far as they could see. They turned back to the main door. Perhaps there was an unlocked side door they had missed, or one that could be cracked open with vapor without leaving too much evidence.

DEPARTING?

Kell froze in their tracks. *Guess he's not asleep, then.* They turned to see Owain still sprawled out, eyes closed, head down, the lift of his chest slow and steady. "Owain," they said softly, "we need to speak with Lyon."

Owain's head lifted slightly, his burgundy eyes opening. "Is that so?" he said, slowly and aloud, focusing on Kell.

Kell caught their breath. Of course the Gardeners could talk for real, as strange as it felt to witness.

"You only wish to speak?" Owain continued.

"We need to stop Lyon," Kell said. "Whatever that takes."

"Rarely is speaking enough," Owain said.

"We're ready for that," Sheila said. "If that's what it comes to."

Owain closed his eyes briefly. "It still may."

"You've seen the threads, haven't you?" Tobias said.

The short puff from Owain nearly resembled a scoff. His attention fell back onto Kell. "Where is her sword?"

Kell paused. They hadn't thought about the sword since leaving Sao Neso. The dragon's question came out flatly, but it had a sense of accusation about it. Kell couldn't help but feel a fleeting guilt.

"I left it. I . . . wasn't sure why she gave it to me. Either she wanted me to kill her, which, why? Because she trusted the wrong people? We've all done that. She doesn't deserve to die for it." The words, now freed, came out of Kell with rolling momentum. "So it's that, or she wants me to be her blade. And, no. I'm done with that. I'm done having someone control my life, deciding what I'm gonna do, what I'm worth. We're fighting for ourselves." Kell stepped closer to Owain's stern, scaly face. "It's not like I don't care about her, alright? I do. I want to understand her. I want to understand all of you. I wanna know why you helped us."

"Our story does not concern you."

Kell disagreed silently. It had to matter to them, or else the Gardeners would never have interacted with the four of them. But this wasn't the time. Lyon had to be dealt with first. "Well," they said, "*our* story involves us confronting Lyon. We know we can get to his office through that door behind you. So, please, would you let us pass?"

Tobias readied his spear. "If we have to fight you . . ." he said, resigned to the idea, the rest of the thought fading out.

With a weary breath, Owain closed his eyes. "This is not such a world."

Slowly, tediously, with groans of the wood below him, Owain's lower body shifted. His legs and tail pulled closer to the center of his body, creating a gap between him and the wall. Tobias was the first to slip into the gap and move towards the back of the hall. Sheila and Alejandro followed, while Kell delayed for a moment.

"I mean it, Owain," they quietly said to the seemingly asleep dragon. "I want to understand you. All of you."

"You will try," Owain muttered deeply.

Beneath their helmet, Kell bit their tongue. They hurried to rejoin the others, their left hand clenched in frustration.

E

The staircase beyond the assembly hall climbed two additional storeys before it would reach the throne room. The offices were above that, but the stairs that led to them were towards the back of the keep. The route the group had taken was more roundabout than necessary, but it was what the map Alejandro found provided, so it was the only route they knew.

By all official accounts, the throne room was only used for ceremonial purposes by the modern government. Beyond the occasional speech and signing of laws, the room sat unused. Yet the doors were already cracked open when Tobias, who had continued to take the lead all the way up the stairs, stopped beside them. With the four grouped together, he gave a silent nod with inquisitive eyes, as if to ask, *are we all ready?*

Kell glanced at the cracked open door and the yellow light bleeding out of it. *I'm leading this.* They stepped around the others and walked through the doors into the throne room.

Lyon sat there, alone, in the old wooden throne with the relaxed and spread-out poise of a man in his favorite armchair. The Prime Minister wore a clean, crisp suit and a matching grey beard. He barely moved as the party approached in a line before him, only bothering to shift his weight farther to the side of his seat.

"You finally bothered to show yourselves," Lyon said, embracing his contempt.

"How long have you been waiting for us?" Sheila said.

Rather than reply, Lyon smirked. "I assume you three came here to kill me." His attention fell on Kell.

"Oh fuck you." Kell tugged at the clasps of their helmet, loosening it enough for them to rip it off of their head. The helmet dropped to the floor with a hollow, metallic ring. "You're not turning us against each other," they said, scowling. "They know who I am already."

"So one did survive," Lyon said. "That asshole will be happy, then. Tragic."

"This isn't about Kell," Tobias said, stepping forward. "I'm Dr. Tobias Fulton, he of the University at Port Mab." He took a moment to gather his breath and steady himself. "My team conceived of those summons that you've sent off to fight your war. Sir, you must recall them and dispel them *now.* For your own sake."

Lyon's eyes narrowed. "Excuse me?"

"We knew summons had dangers to them," Tobias said. "The papers are intentionally flawed. We didn't want people making them. There's no way around it, Mr. Lyon. They fight back. If they haven't already, they will any day now." His words came out quick and nervous.

"You're bluffing," Lyon said with a dismissive wave.

"I'm afraid I'm completely serious," Tobias insisted.

"I wouldn't believe you if you said you were a vian," Lyon said. "So what, did you wish to hear the news firsthand?"

"What news?" Sheila asked, with a bitter undertone that said she knew it could be nothing good.

Lyon had a gluttonous grin. "President Bathroy has elected to step down. And after I did so well restoring order to Farolé, I'm clearly a good fit to do the same for Bessetrae."

Sheila glowered. "You forced her, didn't you?"

"She's her own woman," Lyon said dismissively. "She can make her own decisions for her people."

"Let the people decide for themselves," Alejandro said.

Lyon scoffed. "Were you not following the news? If the people could decide on anything, that whole setup in Farolé after the queen's death would've lasted more than a month. People don't know what they want. Somebody has to tell them."

"Bessetrae isn't going to just roll over," Tobias said. "You know they won't. You'll still have summons marching, and the longer they're out there, the sooner they'll turn on you."

Lyon sat up in the throne and shrugged. "They're cooperating quite well so far, doctor. And they're too useful. A single one can fight as long and hard as a dozen men. And they don't have conniptions over killing."

"Sir," Tobias said, "you're not listening! Those same summons will come to kill *you*!"

"Like you have?" Lyon sneered.

"We're not here to kill you," Alejandro said, gritting his teeth. "We came here to warn you."

"I don't need a warning," Lyon said. "Now. Out of my castle."

"No." Kell stood stiff and angry, glaring at Lyon. "Not until you give Farolé back to its people."

Lyon growled under his breath. "I had figured you'd run off your leash with Fontaine gone. *Sahagin.*" Lyon stood up and walked to a desk that sat at the side of the hall. "Very well." He reached into a suit pocket and pulled out three small tins. They resembled what the guard in Sao Neso had. "This castle is *very* well guarded, I hope you realize."

Lyon set two of the tins down on the desk and twisted the third. It began to spark. He tossed it over the desk, towards the party, as the sparks turned into a plume of green vapor smoke.

The smoke took form, solidifying into a massive winged figure. Its gold and blue feathers tapered off towards a torso that resembled a purple-skinned hunn woman. It landed on the ground and flapped angrily, cawing with a sharp, melodic cry.

Alejandro stared in worry, drawing his weapons slower than the rest of the party. "Crystal?" he murmured.

The summon looked at Alejandro. It let out a mournful note.

"Let's have another, just to be safe," Lyon said dismissively as he repeated the process with a second tin. The vapor smoke emerging from it coalesced into a stocky, vaguely reptilian creature with bright patches of yellow among its red-orange scales. The brightness and pattern resembled the skin of a poisonous newt. It stared at Kell, its head pivoting back and forth.

Kell stared back, looking in the summon's eyes. "Omar," they said to themself.

"Good. You two," Lyon said, "kill them."

With a twitch, the reptilian summon rushed at Kell. They dove away, landing hard on their side, near where Sheila stood. She helped them up and stood at the front of the group as they clustered together defensively. Tobias focused what barriers he could onto Sheila, as well as Alejandro, who had stepped forward with her.

Kell released a shockwave of vapor towards the two summons. It staggered them, allowing Sheila and Alejandro to press forward with their blades. They could each only connect a few strikes, drawing sprays of vapor smoke, before the summons retaliated. The winged summon let out a piercing cry that interrupted Alejandro just long enough to leave him open to a broad, swiping strike with its wing. The reptilian summon, meanwhile, weathered Sheila's claymore with hardly any concern for its own well-being. It reared up to ram her with its head, barreling into her chest, knocking her off her feet and sending her sliding on the stone floor.

The winged summon rose into the air. With a single, focused gust, it whipped up winds that picked up people and furniture across the room and threw it all any which way. The desk Lyon had been standing next to shattered against a wall. Sheila and Tobias collided as they landed beside a pillar, while Alejandro came to a rest behind the summons. Kell landed in front of the throne, their head knocking into one of the arms. The room went fuzzy and white. They slumped against the throne.

Alejandro regained his footing. The two summons were focused on Sheila and Tobias, leaving their backs exposed. As the winged summon gently landed on the ground, Alejandro leapt onto its back. He stabbed it repeatedly with one blade, using the other as leverage to hold on as the summon tried to throw him off. Tobias drove his spear squarely into the summon's midsection, drawing smoke and screams as it fell to the ground. The reptilian summon shoved Alejandro away with a stocky leg before lunging at Sheila again, knocking her back to the ground. She pulled herself up slightly, the summon looming tall over her. Its body dropped towards her, falling away as her claymore pierced it sideways. Smoke and roars poured out of the summon as it, too, ceased to move.

The cries echoed in the stone hall. As they finally faded, Tobias pulled himself up to his knees. "Al, quickly!" he yelled. "Help me contain them! We can fix this!"

Alejandro scrambled to his feet. He started mimicking the spell Tobias was in the midst of casting. The fallen summons began to dissolve into separate clouds of smoke. Alejandro and Tobias each tried to corral a summon, waving their arms slowly and calling out loose vapor that threatened to escape.

Sheila stood, panting and exhausted. She spat out blood. "Show yourself, you bastard!" she shouted.

Lyon emerged from behind a pillar near the exit, his hair and overcoat disheveled from the chaos. He chuckled as he straightened himself out and stepped towards the open door. "Quite the show," he said, "but I'm afraid I have to duck out. Very important day tomorrow."

"You're not going anywhere," Sheila commanded. "Not until you call back that announcement and call back your troops."

"Or what?"

Sheila took a glance at Kell, crumpled up as they were against the foot of the throne. "Or we tell everyone that *you* killed all the vapormages. That *you're* the traitor to the people, or whatever you called them. We have the proof."

Lyon shook his head dismissively in reply.

"Or," Sheila growled, "I could just kill you myself. Save us all some trouble. Whatever the fuck I have to do to protect my people from you, I *will* do it."

"You're Bessetran?" Lyon scoffed. "Thought none of you liked your president."

"Bathroy can rot in the dirt for all I care, at least she's *ours*."

"And here I am, trying to do you people a service." Lyon shook his head. "Well, she doesn't step down until midnight, so you haven't committed treason quite yet. But we'll see how I'm feeling tomorrow."

Lyon began turning to Tobias and Alejandro when his chest suddenly jutted forward. A spray of vapor and blood and bile shot out from his stomach. His eyes went wide. Another spray followed immediately from the base of his throat. He gurgled as if trying to scream before a final missile of vapor pierced his skull and dropped him to the floor.

F

Standing in the doorway, dressed in a lengthy overcoat and dark trousers, a waft of spent vapor drifting from his hand, was Jakob Banner. He stepped calmly into the throne room.

"The fuck are you doing here?" Sheila asked, equally riled and baffled.

"Sorry. Have I interrupted something?" A sly grin came over Banner's face as he stepped over Lyon's corpse.

Tobias, having finally secured Crystal's summon back into its tin, grabbed his spear and stood. "You were making these summons, weren't you?" He pointed his spear in accusation.

"Of course. Banner Goods sells everything. Who am I to turn down a customer?"

"Any reasonable human being would say no to such an idea!" Tobias said, his voice rising with indignation.

Banner shrugged. "Like you did, professor?" Tobias's glare was met by a confident smile. "I'd offer a demonstration, but it seems Lyon already took care of that."

"That was Crystal!" Alejandro grunted and secured the last of Omar's summon into its own tin, huffing from exertion. "And Omar! You've mutilated your own people!"

"There are penalties for insubordination." Banner looked around at the mess brought on by the fight. "Both at once and this was all they could muster? Sounds about right." He nodded towards Kell, who had stayed stationary, leaning against the throne. "Only one kill."

"I'm alive," Kell said weakly, slurring the words together. They couldn't quite gather the strength to stand.

Banner didn't care. "Congratulations, then. You do seem ill, though. Have you not been eating well?"

The question, and a realization, jolted Tobias. "What are you insinuating, Jakob?"

Banner grinned in reply.

"What did you do to their food?" Tobias shouted. "What did you do?"

Banner let out a hearty chuckle. "Are you, of all people, going to wave your feathery old finger about an experiment?"

Kell glared at Banner. Nausea and anger boiled in their gut.

"You can't just *teach* someone to be a vapormage. That power? No. Fortunately, my men were already studying vapor poisoning. A poisoned person can do incredible things, if not for the side effects. But perhaps those could be avoided. We just needed some subjects." He sighed wistfully. "And then Lyon had to go get distracted by this 'summons' idea before we could wrap up all the tests."

"You *poisoned* the vapormages?" Sheila yelled.

"I *made* vapormages," Banner retorted. "Yet the idiot couldn't manage to take Bessetrae." He kicked at the corpse on the ground beside him.

"Well apparently," Alejandro said, "he *did* manage it. Before you killed him. That's what the announcement is about."

"Oh, I know," Banner said. "That's why I had to come here so urgently. He'd gotten too big for his britches."

"You can't handle competition, can you?" Sheila said. "Someone threatens your little palace and you freak out, huh?"

Banner shook his head, rolling his eyes dismissively. "Look at him. Lyon was barely any competition in the first place. More of an obnoxious little rat. But he was right about one thing. This whole world, all of humanity, it's nothing more than a fight for power. The ones that have it are the only ones that matter. History forgets everyone else. Lyon wanted to claim more power for himself. Which is all well and good, but the greedy bastard went after mine. He could have his little politics, his little wars. But *he* wanted the economy. He wanted to *own* everything. Business, culture. Those are mine." He scoffed. "He should've gone after the Guardians. They know better than to fight back."

Sheila scowled. "You think you can just *own* everyone?"

"Can? I do." Banner pulled a mobile from his overcoat and waved it in demonstration. "Somebody has to. Somebody has to decide what everything is worth. That's my job. Just like your job is to kill people."

"And if someone's not worth it to you anymore," Alejandro said bitterly, "then you make someone kill them."

"So the vapormages just weren't worth it to you anymore," Sheila said. "And you got Lyon to kill them all."

Banner sighed as he put his mobile away. "Summons are more profitable, I suppose. But Lyon was his own man. He made his choices."

Banner punctuated his statement with a bitter scoff that was interrupted by a mass of bright green striking him in the chest. It fell to the floor with a wet thud as he reeled backwards in surprise.

Kell staggered to their feet, pulling themself up with their left arm, using the throne for leverage. Stray drops of blood and greasy, vapor-laden liquid fell from where their right arm used to be. Bright green remnants of the tarp that covered the wound hung loosely in its place. They drew their rod as they found their balance. A teal glow began to envelope their body and create a ghostly shark-like shape around them. The evocation followed their strained movement as they stepped forward, baring their teeth in fury.

"Do you own that, then, Banner?" Kell shouted. "What is it worth to you? What is my flesh, my blood worth to you? What about every vapormage, every person who's been hurt, and tortured, and mutilated, and killed for your schemes, what are we worth to you? How many corpses do you have to steal and sell and *make* to be satisfied?" With a shaking left arm, Kell pointed their rod behind them and gathered all the vapor they could. "You better know what your life is worth, Banner! Because *fuck you* I am going to make you pay!"

Kell twisted on their foot to launch the vapor they had collected, dragging their rod against the ground as if striking a match. The blast shot forward, flaming water swirling within a storm of whipping wind. Kell's evocation, their anger, their pain, pushed out of their body and spread into a school of shark-shaped ghosts. The blast collided with Banner in an explosion of blue-green smoke, hitting with a deep rumble. The smoke billowed out forcefully, pushing over the group and up to the ceiling. The throne room went quiet as the vapor slowly dissipated. Banner was pushed back, against the wall.

But he was still standing.

With a stomp, he stood up straighter, a furious glare on his face and a shield of vapor flickering around him. Banner shook the settling dust off his overcoat with a single sharp motion. "Did you *really* think I would walk in unprepared?" he said with a slow snarl.

Kell's legs began to betray them. They felt themself start to collapse in exhaustion and defeat.

"You four have not cooperated for a single moment," Banner said. "You were *supposed* to deliver yourselves to Lyon. You were *supposed* to get yourselves killed. I didn't particularly care how. But it seems you've finally made up your minds."

Banner reached into a pocket on his overcoat and pulled out a small syringe, filled with a dark fluid.

"The hell are you doing, Banner?" Alejandro said.

"An experiment." He calmly removed the safety cap from the needle. "I'll admit, Lyon was right about one other thing. There's no point in having vapormages if anyone can pull the same tricks." He shook his free arm loosely before injecting the syringe right below his shoulder. "And if *that* was the best a vapormage could do, well then." He threw the spent syringe aside. "Our execution remains unmatched."

Tobias stepped back to where Kell and Alejandro stood. Sheila stood in front, her sword drawn defensively in front of her. Banner threw off his overcoat to reveal his arms already bulging and turning pale blue.

"Don't look at me like that," Banner said, his face turning blue and his voice simmering to a raspy croak. "I thought you four learned not to show your hand when negotiating. But this isn't a negotiation anymore."

"Bastard's poisoned himself," Tobias muttered in awe.

"This. Is my. World." The words came out as slow growls as the vapor concoction poisoned more of Banner's body, ripping tears in his clothes as his muscles bulged in uncanny, tumorous formations. "Not Lyon's. Not Bathroy's. Not the Guardians'. Mine!"

"You've lost it, Banner!" Sheila shouted.

Banner cackled. His hands, already turning a sickly indigo, twisted into sharp, lanky claws. He raised one in threat, and when Sheila refused to step back, he swung it swiftly at her, lacerating her face. Sheila stumbled. Kell tried to push Banner back with concussive vapor blasts. They didn't expect it to stop him, only to create room for Sheila to recover. Banner took the hits in stride, stepping menacingly towards Kell. He swung at them, but Sheila--now protected by one of Tobias's spells--caught his arm with hers. She moved aggressively to intercept Banner's attacks, protecting the others as they barraged him with spells and throwing knives.

Banner, with a beastly roar, rammed at Sheila, bowling her into the rest of the group. Sheila growled back with fury as she stood. "Kell!" she shouted, holding her claymore out to her side. Kell's energy was faltering, but they had enough left to wrap her blade in flaming vapor. She dove to attack. Kell leaned on Alejandro's shoulder, their legs aching and weak. Tobias would have to handle the defense while they collected themself.

"Kell."

They turned around. Tobias had removed his goggles. His eyes pleaded at Kell.

"Let me fix this," he said.

Kell righted themself as much as they could and nodded. They could hold the defense, just a little longer.

Banner swung a claw past Sheila and pried an opening. He conjured a blast of vapor towards the rest of the group. Alejandro dove forward, intercepting it. The blast slammed him hard to the ground. He screamed in pain and rolled over to find Kell ready to help him back up.

Behind them was Tobias, sprawled out lifelessly on the ground, a cloud of yellow and white vapor settling beside him. It coalesced into a lichen-furred feline beast the size of a man. Chapalu scanned its surroundings quickly before focusing on Banner and howling.

The summon got his attention. Banner swept indifferently at Sheila, pushing her back, and reared up to confront Chapalu. He clawed into its skin as it approached, drawing smoke, but its poise and posture held up. Banner's following swing stalled, his limbs seizing up, as a desperate jagged Bind from Kell reached him.

Chapalu, bleeding vapor, grabbed the off-balance Banner and pushed him to the floor. It pounced on him with revenge in its silver eyes. It pushed on his head, drawing wisps of smoke from Banner that grew and glowed green and purple, as Banner strained in resistance against Chapalu's weight. Chapalu pushed harder, harder, bearing down on Banner's skull, smoke piling around them both, until a loud crack of bone echoed through the throne room, and the air turned quiet and the vapor hung dead.

It took a moment for Kell to process what happened. The room still had a concussed, unbalanced tilt. Their weight fell onto Alejandro. They felt like broken glass, jagged and fractured.

"I've got you, I've got you." Alejandro lowered them to the ground. "You with me?"

They held on weakly to Alejandro. Sheila, bloodied, knelt beside them. A fading Chapalu looked over the scene.

"I'm home," Kell breathed, a bloody sweetness on their tongue.

T he time immediately after confronting Banner is a bit of a blur, and naturally, it only gets worse with time. I do recall Sheila claiming Lyon's tins and Kell retrieving their arm while I struggled to coax Chapalu back into Tobias. It was difficult. I was quite nervous. Toby won't admit it, and even now I struggle to put pen to it, but he had nearly killed himself to bring Chapalu out the way he had. Far too much canopic. A reckless amount.

The lone summon patrolling the castle did raise an alarm as we took our leave, but it was a simple enough matter. From there, we hid. The city was still locked down for days, first out of curfew protocols and then to figure out what had happened. For a while, I was convinced they didn't know. Minister Feng put forth that report claiming Banner had murdered Lyon before succumbing to his own experiment and I assumed we were home free. Strange to have a successful cover-up and not have a hand in it.

Of course, the truth of that became clear a few weeks later. Somewhere before that, Kell had gotten word to their friend Rocko regarding what we'd done, which must've got word to Grey. The Faces leapt into action. Minister Feng--or, rather, the Teal Face--made his moves with the Parliament to smooth out the transfer of power. As much as he could, at any rate. No point in me spilling ink on the Old Town Riots that boiled over in the capital. All I have said is: Feng is a better leader than Lyon by every possible metric, but I will never claim he's perfect.

That was a tenuous time for us, all alert anxiety, so I neglected to write. We were fortunate that Mr. Feng could be persuaded, and that Dr. Kirkaven could be kept quiet. She had to know that Kell was a sahagin if she could provide that prosthetic, and we had to trust that she would keep the fact quiet. I hope we were right to. Nonetheless, Kell recovered quickly, all things considered. They soon spirited away southward, with Lyon's last weapon. Cyprin's tin.

By that time, Tobias and I were in Farolé--it will forever, in my heart, be Farolé--lending our skills to my people. Even with the cessation declared, the summons were difficult to corral. They never spoke, human-shaped though they were, and they looked at everything around them with a murderous confusion in their eyes. I struggled to see the souls that built them, as they behaved so soullessly. All this to say nothing of the shattered ones that had fallen in battle. Those were difficult to reassemble. Too many had dispersed. At least they didn't fight back.

The cities had started pulling themselves out of the rubble, finding their footing and whatever leadership they could elevate. But, of course, then spells were thrown between brothers. I fear my homeland is dead. Lyon murdered her. The best I hope for, watching things fall apart from the outside, is that from her corpse will rise three or four small nations. Each kingdom its own, perhaps, as it once was. Such is the way of things, I suppose, but it hurts all the same. I fear none will be Farolé, that this hatred against Speakers will linger forever. I should count myself lucky, then, that Emery--or President Sleetre, as I believe they're now being styled--has such skill and patience with people. I could be safe under their leadership. Gauven has refused them, naturally. Not that I suspect they care for his back. Which is good. I don't think I could trust anyone who does anymore.

I've heard little of Sheila. Not an animosity, I hope. I think she just has a plan for herself that doesn't need my involvement. I know she's returned to Windglade and is working to rebuild it, and that she carries a certain bitterness regarding that Cory chap we spoke with once. She sounded betrayed. Her nation has been in its own sort of chaos, with President Bathroy stepping down in favor of a dead man, but I understand the election went well enough. Not that I know much of President Kerns. Though I suspect it hardly matters; the Secretaries retain their positions, along with their petty internal squabbles. Little changes in Bessetrae.

Ah, Sao Neso. I'm becoming fond of the place, frankly. Though I have mixed feelings on the people. They're quite a bit less hospitable as of late. I understand the situation they're in, of course. From the final study Toby and I did, a full 12% of the city could never be recovered. A loss like that is hard for any city to suffer, let alone such an isolated place. It's led to discord and inflamed conflicts. They desperately need the aid that Toby and I have pushed Cymona for. Quietly pushed for, of course. The elections are proving contentious enough as it stands.

I didn't see Kell in Sao Neso. From talking with Gail, they haven't been back since their visit to return Cyprin. That visit lasted most of the time I spent in Farolé. They spent the time gathering the information Toby and I needed to heal everyone that we could, and we appreciate it. We thank them for it, I mean. But they left before we arrived, and Gail didn't want to say why. From what I can gather, there's resentment. Kell represents something in Sao Neso. I can't say for sure what, exactly, but clearly they don't want to be what Sao Neso thinks they are. Beyond that topic, though, Gail's a lovely person to talk with. She told me all about Sao Neso's history and the collection in the vault. She didn't know about the sword. I opted not to elaborate. After all, it wasn't there.

For the moment, neither am I. Toby has settled himself in Port Mab, outside of the campus. He's still not allowed back. They don't enforce that. I'll come by when I can. For Raurack. I'm hoping to graduate, as it were. Prove myself a suitable heir to the art. But our last chat had us talking, at length, about our responsibility as true summoners. Truly, that bell can't be unrung. We will be keeping a very close eye on Banner's new leader, to say the least.

But I would like to get back with Kell. It's been too long since I've rendezvoused with our leader. I have heard rumors of a curious figure with a metal arm out in the Zeimatic jungles. Perhaps, after I visit Crystal, I'll head that direction. They deserve a status update.

Oh, who am I kidding. I miss them. Hard not to miss a friend.

— From the journals of Alejandro Quintana

ACKNOWLEDGEMENTS

First and foremost, an eternal thank you to Jason Champion for lending me a hand when I was at my most desperate. I will never be able to thank you enough for taking me in.

This book would not be what it is without the attentive eye and reliable counsel of my good friend Nathan. He has shepherded this story and this world from its middling origins to where it is now. A major thank you as well to Sydnee Thompson for additional copy editing.

Thanks as well to my Sandia Starforgers groupmates: Kevin Mack, Sarah Hipple, and Doug Rowland, along with Jason Lowrey and the rest of the cohort. I look forward to seeing your finished projects, in whatever form they wind up taking. I'm still amused by the coincidences in our work, Kevin.

To my beta and advance readers: K Lucian Jones, Cy Villyard, and Azaliz, and those who wished not to be listed here. Your advice and opinions are deeply appreciated, and I hope I have done them service. If there are disappointing parts of the story, it's a fair guess that someone pointed it out and I didn't act on it.

Major thanks are in order to professors Mark Rayner and John Roche, who each provided advice and encouragement to me as a writer over the years. I've come a long way since college, I hope. I assure you that none of Tobias's foibles are based on you, though I apologize if any of the academia portrayed hits a little too close to home.

Immense thanks for those within the industry who have generously given time, advice, and insight. Namely, major thanks to Mary Robinette Kowal, Marie Parks, Ben Kessler, Paul Stein, Ariana Osbourne, Chyina Powell, and Tim Steele.

A most surprising and indirect thanks to Ronald Kingsley Read for what he has done to the English language. If you know, you know.

Lastly, thank you to all my friends in my day-to-day life. Eric, Robby, Josh, Jeff, Ayden, Erich, Savannah, Eryn, David, and a dozen more people I'm omitting either from poor memory or because I don't know their actual names. Such is the life of the terminally online.

Zoe Landon, shown here locked out of her house, is a software engineer, writer, and musician from Portland, OR. Along with writing fiction, she's given talks at technology conferences such as OSCON, pushing for accessible and mindful technology communication. She also served homemade buffalo wings to an Academy Award winner that one time. She has been adopted by the stray cats of her neighborhood and is content with the arrangement, all things considered.

Find more of her and her work at https://hupfen.com.